$\mathcal{V}$OICES OF THE $\mathcal{S}$OUTH

FLIGHT

OTHER BOOKS BY WALTER WHITE

The Fire in the Flint
Rope and Faggot: A Biography of Judge Lynch
A Rising Wind
A Man Called White

FLIGHT

WALTER WHITE

LOUISIANA STATE UNIVERSITY PRESS
Baton Rouge

Copyright © 1926 by Alfred A. Knopf
LSU Press edition published 1998
All rights reserved
Manufactured in the United States of America

07 06 05 04 03 02 01 00 99 98   5 4 3 2 1

Library of Congress Cataloging-in-Publication Data
White, Walter, Francis, 1893–1955.
    Flight / Walter White.
        p.   cm. — (Voices of the South)
    ISBN 0-8071-2280-7 (alk. paper)
    1. Afro-Americans—Fiction. I. Title. II. Series.
PS3545.H6165F58   1998
813' .52—dc21   97-49988
                                                          CIP

The paper in this book meets the guidelines for permanence and
durability of the Committee on Production Guidelines for Book
Longevity of the Council on Library Resources. ∞

For my daughter
JANE

FLIGHT

CHAPTER I

THE long train rumbled and swayed, whistle blowing intermittently, screeching discordantly, past smoky factory and office buildings, through rows of one-storied, two- or three-room cottages, outside which on hard packed clay earth played here tow-headed white children or there black or brown or yellow ones. It plunged suddenly into cavernous darkness under a bridge, thick acrid smoke pouring into the open windows of the wooden coaches.

"Union Station—Atlanty. All out for Atlanty," bawled a grinning Negro porter as the train rolled into a long, dingy shed with low-hung roof. Eager, laughing Negroes snatched boxes and bundles of varied shapes from the racks over the seats or pulled mates to them from under the seats. Mimi awoke with a start as Jean shook her gently.

"We're there, *petite* Mimi," he told her. Through the throng, peering vainly through the murky air, redolent of stale banana and orange skins and of bodies in need of washing, she made her way to remove the worst of the soot and grime from her face.

"My father'll be here to meet us," Mary told Jean.

Though he disliked Mr. Robertson intensely Jean was happy to receive the news. He felt bewildered, lost, a malady bordering on nausea at the hubbub around him. Methodically he obeyed his wife's commands to gather their bags and parcels. Then with Mimi, refreshed, alert, her weariness dropped from her as she would have discarded a cape, they made their way out of the coach in the van of the surging throng.

[9]

FLIGHT

Incisive Mr. Robertson kissed Mary and Mimi brusquely, shook hands with Jean and hustled them through the waiting-room labeled "For Coloured" to the sidewalk where a horse-drawn surrey was waiting.

"No—No," shouted Mr. Robertson as the driver started down the street. "Go around by Pryor Street and from there down Auburn Avenue." To the Daquins he explained: "If he'd gone that way he'd have carried you through Decatur and Ivy Streets—that's the slum district—saloons and houses——" He paused significantly, looking at Mimi. "Pretty bad," he added. "Lowest kind of Negroes."

But Mimi did not hear him nor even the newsboy who ran alongside the cab shouting: "Extry! All about the Japs licking the Rooshians! All about th' big battle!" Because it was *terra incognita* to her she tried to see everything as eagerly as she had watched the land from the car window in the long ride from New Orleans. Spring was in the air. The cab, to the accompaniment of various cluckings, "gid-daps," "go-long-theres" of the ancient driver, joggled and bounced over the Belgian block pavement. Mimi sniffed the air eagerly, anticipatorily.

The carriage rumbled and jerked through the ghostly confines of shut business houses, turned into Auburn Avenue lined with blowzy boarding-houses, their porches lined with men and women, a loud, staccato, mirthless laugh occasionally floating on the breeze. Soon the scene changed. Black and brown and yellow faces replaced the white, the laughs became more frequent, more rich, more spontaneous. The April evening seemed more filled with the sheer joy of living. To Mimi the sudden change was pleasant, warming, inviting. Jean, sunk dejectedly in the seat beside the driver so that only the top of his black, crumpled felt hat showed above the high seat, was too engrossed in delightfully painful nostalgia for his New Orleans to notice anything. Mary and her father

[10]

FLIGHT

were eagerly discussing the change in the lives of the Daquins, which to them both seemed so altogether admirable and desirable there was no questioning of its wisdom.

"Got to rush right back to Chicago Thursday—election this fall and two or three important deals—had to see you get started off right——" floated in Mr. Robertson's crisp tones to Jean.

"You *were* a darling to come all the way to Atlanta," gushed Mary.

"Nothing at all—nothing at all," declared her father. He pronounced it "nothing a-tall."

"Wanted to see you get introduced in the right circles, too. Gene thinks his Creole crowd's stuck-up and exclusive—these Atlanta Negroes'll show him a trick or two for fair. Got to get in right—or you'll never get in."

Jean, who squirmed every time Mr. Robertson familiarly called him "Gene," found his old hostility to Mr. Robertson, his voice, his ideas, his coarseness, rising higher than ever before. His gratitude to him in the train began to vanish. He wished fervently his father-in-law had remained in Chicago. He hated his high-handed method of interfering in his and Mary's and Mimi's most private affairs.

Money—money—money—how much is it worth?—how much can I make out of it?—these were the first, last and intermediate stages of Mr. Robertson's every thought, every statement, every action. I'll go through with it, thought Jean, but I'll never let my soul be turned into a money-grubber's. The resolution, even though he knew it couldn't possibly be carried out completely in this new world he was entering, nevertheless gave Jean some comfort. . . .

Mrs. Plummer waddled down the hall, pushed open the screen door, and slapped with the corner of her gingham apron at the insects which buzzed inside. "These nasty bugs'll be the death of me yet," she complained to her com-

[11]

panion, Mrs. Sophronisba King, lean, acidulous, suspicious of all humans and their motives save her own. Mrs. King was as curveless as a young sapling as she went around the room giving quick little jabs at the furniture with an oiled cloth, pursuing relentlessly bits of dust which had settled upon the chairs and table and mantelpiece since late afternoon.

"Heard the news about that Lizzie Stone?" she asked Mrs. Plummer. "You ain't?" she demanded incredulously when Mrs. Plummer shamefacedly admitted she had not. The possession of a juicy morsel which had not yet come to her friend's ears caused Mrs. King's skinny frame to swell with prideful importance. "Why, honey, it's all over town!"

"She always seemed to me such a nice, Christian girl—so quiet and respectable——"

"Mis' Plummer, them's the very ones who'll fool you nine times out of ten—they go to church and they's sweet as pie in the daytime—but slipping and sliding into all sorts of devilment."

Mrs. Plummer's ears seemed to stretch out from her head in her eagerness to learn the derelictions of Lizzie Stone. "Tell me what she's done. You know my heart's bad and the doctor told me I couldn't stand much excitement," she pleaded.

"You know Jerry Reed—he's head of the Royal United Order of Heavenly Reapers?"

" 'Cose I do—ain't I a member of the Ladies Auxil'ry?"

"You know, Mis' Plummer, I ain't one of these no-count women who runs around town meddlin' in other folks's business—I stays at home and tends to my own bus'ness."

" 'Cose you don't, Mis' King—ev'rybody knows you don't gossip. But what's Lizzie and Jerry Reed been doing?"

"I'll tell you, Mis' Plummer, though I ain't vouching for

[12]

the truth of it 'cause I wasn't there to see it with my own eyes—but they tell me they saw Lizzie getting in Jerry Reed's automobile down on Auburn Avenue late last Tuesday night —*and he had all the curtains up.*"

"You don't say! A body'd think she'd have mo' sense than to do her dirt so bold like! I always heard that Jerry Reed wouldn't have a girl work for him unless he could get fresh with her. The nerve of her—she was at church last Sunday, struttin' round just as brazen as any fancy woman!"

"Lord, Mis' Plummer, I don't know what's gettin' into these coloured folks—they gettin' mo' like white folks ev'ry day. Comes from workin' in white folks' houses and in these here hotels—seein' all their dirt and thinkin' they got to do the same things white folks does."

"That's the God's truth! And say, Mis' King, did you know these new folks is Cath'lics? Well, they is—their name's 'Day-Quinn' or 'Day-kin' or something Frenchy like that. He's goin' to work down to the Lincoln Mutual Life Insurance Company—that's the company got them swell offices down Auburn Avenue."

"Cath'lics, is they? Any time I hear tell of coloured folks bein' anything 'cept Baptists or Methodists I know some white man's been tamperin' with their religion. That's what Booker T. said once and he sho' did know what he was talkin' 'bout."

"That's the God's truth! Wonder where these folks goin' to church? They tell me down in N'Awleens where there's so many furriners most anybody can go where they please long's they ain't black. But they better not try it in Georgia."

"Is you got a picture, Mis' Plummer, of any coloured folks no matter what kinda religion they got stickin' their heads in that 'Sacred Heart' church out Peachtree Street? White folks talk about Jesus but the only Jesus they thinkin' 'bout's

[13]

got a white skin. An' the only heaven they want's one got
a sign on it ten foot high, 'No Niggers Allowed in Here.' "

"Lord, 'Mis' King, there they come. An' me settin' here
talkin'. I bet them 'taters done boiled to death!"

Mrs. Plummer rocked briskly in the chair wherein she had
rested her weary frame. The needed momentum gained, she
heaved her bulky person to her feet and disappeared in the
general direction of the kitchen as through the open door
Mr. Robertson's hearty voice came: "Well, folks, here we
are!" . . .

Mimi and Jean and Mary climbed down from the surrey
and entered the house. Mrs. Plummer, her potatoes looked
after with incredible speed considering her size, greeted them
as though she were welcoming them into her own home.

"Come right in! Come right in! I know you must be as
tired as all-out-doors. My name's Mrs. Plummer—I live right
down the street and Mr. Robertson got me to sorter fix things
up——" she poured forth.

"Mrs. King! Mrs. King!" she called. Mrs. King hastened
from the kitchen, wiping her mouth on the back of her hand
as she came, scanning the arrivals from head to foot in one
swift, critical—very critical—glance.

"This is Mrs. King," introduced Mrs. Plummer grandly.
"She was nice enough to help too."

Mrs. King nodded in rapid succession to the three, adding
one for Mr. Robertson though she had seen him only an
hour before. He had employed only Mrs. Plummer to clean
up the house and arrange everything but it had not been a
difficult matter to persuade Mrs. King to assist—it gave both
women ample opportunity to examine at their leisure each
piece of furniture and to speculate on its probable cost.

Without taking off her hat, Mme. Daquin (Mrs. Plummer
called her Mrs. Day-queen) rushed from room to room of
the two-storied house. On the first floor there was a living-

room, "the parlour," to the left as one entered the door, back
of that the dining-room and then the kitchen. To the right
were steps leading to the floor above, behind them a small
room to be used instead of the more formal parlour and
dining-room which apparently were opened only when company came. Above stairs were two fairly large bedrooms
above the parlour and dining-room, while a small bathroom,
its woodwork painted a yellowish white, and a third and
smaller bedroom opened on the other side of the narrow
hall.

"This big front room will be mine," decided Mme. Daquin,
half to Mrs. Plummer and Mrs. King, who had accompanied
her on the tour of discovery and appraisement, and half to
herself, "Jean will sleep in the next room, while Mimi gets
the little room off the hall."

"That po' little skinny man downstairs with the funny
moustache don't seem to have much to say in this house,"
whispered Mis' King to her companion. as they followed Mme.
Daquin. " 'Tain't hard to see who wears the pants in this
family."

Like beagles they followed every word, every expression.
Their scanty store of information about the new-comers would
be sufficient, when amplified during their mutual discussions
on the morrow, as foundation of the extensive tales they would
bear to eager ears in the neighbourhood.

Downstairs Mimi sat in the parlour, wearied, but interested
in sizing up her new home. She was perched in a huge chair,
of brilliantly polished oak, the seat and back of plum-
coloured damask. The chandelier was of intricately twisted
bands of metal painted a dull gold which formed weird and
awesome designs on the ceiling in the reflections from the flickering gas lights. Underneath it there sat an oak table with
elaborately, fantastically carved legs, covered with a faded tap-
estry centre-piece. On it rested a fat family album of red

plush, a diamond-shaped mirror in the centre. Near it rested
an odd-shaped instrument that Mimi longed to examine but
which she contemplated from afar for fear of incurring a frown
from Mr. Robertson, who was advising or, rather, ordering
Jean regarding the steps he must take to "get on" in his new
position. The object was of dark polished wood, a long rod
serving as a sort of backbone. At the end was a glass partly
enclosed with a little wooden fence, on the rod below was a
handle. At the other end was a slotted rack. Near this odd
object rested a pile of cards. Gently raising herself by her
elbows pressed against the arms of the chair, Mimi could
see a brightly coloured picture of a mountain scene on the
topmost card. She made a mental resolution to explore this
mystery at the earliest possible time.

". . . And to-morrow morning right after breakfast you'll
go with me to the office, Gene, where I'll introduce you to
Hunter—he's the president of the Lincoln—Watkins, Jones
and the rest of the crowd. They're a live bunch—that is, live
for this town but pretty small potatoes up in Chicago, and
they've got a gold mine insuring all the coloured folks here
in the South. I want you to stick to the job—no monkey
business or I'm through, you hear me?—and you'll make so
much money you'll wonder how you ever managed to stick
in that dead old hole of New Orleans."

Mr. Robertson's words came to Mimi sharply as his voice
rose. He took a fat cigar from his pocket, bit the end from
it and tossed the severed bit through the open window. She
disliked this bossy old man intensely. She looked at Jean,
wondering that he so calmly submitted to the dictatorial attitude of the man who, though his father-in-law, was not many
years his senior. But Jean heard his words only vaguely, if
he heard them at all. He sat beside his wife's father on the
couch that matched the chair on which Mimi perched and
gazed through the window, the thin white curtains opening and

[16]

closing as a faint breeze stirred them. Somewhere outside, a voice, throaty but rich, plaintively sang of his woes and his "blues":

> "I'm jes' as misabul as I can be,
> I'm unhappy even if I am free,
> I'm feelin' down, I'm feelin' blue;
> I wander round, don't know what to do.
> I'm go'na lay mah haid on de railroad line,
> Let de B. & O. come and pacify mah min'."

The voice died away in the distance but the poignant, nostalgic longing of the unseen singer remained. Jean and Mimi, used to the Creole dilution of the Negro songs, sat straining their ears to catch every note of this barbaric, melancholy wail as it died in the distance, a strange thrill filling them. The swiftly moving tragedy of the song, dying off abruptly as though the singer was too full for further words, stirred them both to the exclusion of all else. Again a voice was heard, this time a woman's:

> "These men I love, honey,
> Sho' do make me tiahed,
> These men I love, honey,
> Sho' do make me tiahed.
> They got a han'fulla gimme
> An' a mouth fulla much oblige."

A loud laugh greeted the end of her song.

"Hey dere, Babe, what'cha doin'?" called the first voice, and in response to the reply: "Nothin' much. Come on in!" the two voices mingled in indistinct words, punctuated frequently with laughter, gay, rich and in unison.

"Gene, are you listening to what I'm telling you?" snapped Mr. Robertson, and Jean came back to realities with a start.

"Certainly! Certainly!" Jean hastened to assure him.

Mr. Robertson eyed him suspiciously and then, as the look of apparent interest on Jean's face seemed to satisfy him, he

[17]

continued his instructions. No sooner had be begun again, however, before Jean's mind began to wander once more. He hoped fervently the singers would again begin but the warm night wrapped them in its vast silence.

Mimi welcomed her step-mother, who came briskly down the stairs followed at a respectful distance by her two companions.

"Everything's just lovely and I don't know really how to thank you, papa," she bubbled. "Mimi, you'd better run upstairs and get your face and hands washed. Mrs. Plummer tells me she's fixed supper for us and we don't want it to get cold. Jean, you and papa'd better do the same thing and don't take all night getting back."

Napoleon, Cæsar, Alexander never spoke to common soldiers more brusquely nor with greater assurance that their commands would be obeyed. Nor did it occur to Mimi or Jean to protest—both were too much under the domination of this person who would never be familiar to either of them.

CHAPTER II

DURING the meal Mme. Daquin and her father talked animatedly of the new life of the Daquins, for which the two of them were so largely responsible. But the thoughts which ran through the heads of Jean Daquin and Mimi dealt with the past and especially with the rapid changes which a few weeks had wrought. Though neither of them knew precisely what the other was thinking, their minds were going over the events which had taken place since that morning which had been the beginning of the new order of things. Had some person possessing the powers of wizardry, an adept in the process of thought amalgamation, been present and woven a picture made of the fragments which filled Jean's and Mimi's minds, the product of his labours would have resulted somewhat after this fashion. . . .

It was a sunny morning in New Orleans several weeks past. Jean Daquin tapped gently on the door. No answer came. Again he tapped—tapped—tapped. Again there was silence. Carefully he pushed open the heavy door, which groaned dismally on its ancient hinges. From within there came the rhythmic inhaling of breath of a sound sleeper. Jean tiptoed to the deep casemented window and drew aside the heavy curtains of dusty wine-coloured velvet.

Warm, intoxicating Louisiana sunshine tumbled into the room as though a giant hand had loosed a celestial sluice-gate. With the yellow flood poured the sensuous blend of odours—of wild honeysuckle, of Cherokee rose in full bloom, of hyacinth, of oleander. Jean stood at the window, his arms

[19]

raised clutching the draperies, and took deep draughts of the air heady as old wine. The trees and flowers sparkled in the sunshine, covered with glittering beads of water from the recently ended shower.

His tiny garden enclosed with the crumbling brick wall had never seemed so beautiful. He picked out one by one the flowers he had planted and tended—the oleander-bush by the house, which, a generation before, had quartered the slave house servants. It was in bloom now, the ground beneath it covered over with salver-shaped white petals. There near it was the bed of pansies—Bernard Dieux, sleeping the long sleep in old St. Louis cemetery this year and a half had given him the cuttings. Over to the left was the Cherokee rose in whose shade he had spent many happy hours, reading a part of the time, more often just sitting and dreaming. Many a day he had sat there or in the cool quietness of the decaying servant house, two-storied, of brick laid between heavy posts, *briqueté entre poteaux*. Its walls were slowly crumbling these late years and its bricks were covered with greenish mould but the old house was sturdily standing up, despite its years, against all the furies of rain and sun that beat upon it. There Jean had sat in the rickety chair and sucked into his nostrils the faint fragrance of his orange-trees that grew just inside and along the old wall. He loved to rest his eyes grown weary with the printed page on their blackish green foliage that provided so perfect a background for their tiny fruit—little globules of deep yellow gold. But he loved these best when they were shedding their flowers—"a steam of rich distilled perfumes," Bernard, who was given to quotation of poetry, used to say of the orange-trees.

"Jean! Why don't you come down?" a strident, querulous voice from below stirred him. Jean hastily quitted the win-dow and shuffled over to the huge and elaborately carved bed.

"Mimi! Mimi! Wake up! Your mother's in an awful

humour this morning! Get up quickly before she comes and gets us both!"

The sleeper stirred, turned over and recommenced her steady breathing. The rays of the sunlight touched her hair as her head rolled to one side. In the shadow it had seemed brown. Before Jean's eyes it underwent a miraculous transformation as the tiny rays of light picked out the coppery brilliance that here was auburn, and there shaded off into a deeper reddish colour. It was like spun gold dipped in flaming cochineal. The curls in tangled disarray framed the oval, cream-coloured face. Half full lips were slightly parted, even teeth gleaming from the red frame. Mimi lay stretched on the bed, the bed-clothes pushed towards its foot, her slender body covered only with the thin night-dress. Small soft breasts rose and fell gently, the promise of approaching womanhood revealed in the curves of her rapidly maturing body.

Jean looked at his daughter, his eyes half filled with joy at her warm beauty, half with troubled anxiety. He had seen too much of life to be unaware of what his child's delicate and fragile beauty might bring to her. At times he had almost wished she were less attractive—when he walked with her along the streets he watched with envious, jealous eyes the glances Mimi, though not yet fourteen, drew instinctively from the men, young and old. He was proud of her, of course—many girls of eighteen or nineteen were not half so well formed. Yet, he feared for her and, more often than not, his apprehension swept over and wiped out his joy in her comeliness.

"Holy Mother, keep me alive—not for life alone, sweet as it is for me, but that I may be with her to guide her steps and protect her!" he often prayed as Mimi knelt beside him at mass, innocent of the anxiety bordering on agony which filled the breast of her father.

FLIGHT

"Jean! Must I come up for you?" came again the voice from below, anger sharpening its usual petulance.

"Mimi! Get up, *chérie!* At once, or we'll both be raked over the coals!" Jean pleaded.

Mimi stirred again, opened her eyes, sat up and smiled.

"Here's your coffee—I'm afraid it's cold but drink it quickly and slip on your clothes. Your mother's all out of sorts this morning and we'll both catch it if you keep breakfast waiting much longer."

"Let her fuss, papa. It's too pretty a morning to bother with maman. She'll quarrel anyhow," smiled Mimi as she took the cup of black coffee and stirred it slowly. "Ugh— it's all cold—I don't want it!" she grimaced as she pushed the cup away. "You go down, papa, and I'll be ready in a few minutes."

Jean took the cup but made no motion of leaving.

"Mimi, we're going to move away from New Orleans——"

"Move away? Where? Why? Leave this old house?" the questions tumbled out of her mouth, her eyes now wide-awake with surprise.

"It's your mother—she's had her way at last—we're going to move to a more 'progressive' town where folks get ahead faster——" His words, despite conscious effort to sound matter-of-fact, were tinged with a bit of irony, with a fragment of bitterness and pain. "Your mother——"

"Stop calling her my mother!" Mimi half angrily demanded, all the cheerfulness gone from her voice and face. "She's only a step-mother!"

"All right! All right!" Jean hastily agreed. "I can't tell you all of it now—but I can't stand this nagging any longer. I've got to have peace even if I have to go to the North Pole to get it——"

"Why do you yield so easily to her? Why don't you tell her right out you won't go and she must stop fussing at you

[22]

FLIGHT

all the time? If I were you I certainly wouldn't let her run all over me!" Mimi declared as she slipped out of the bed and began to dress.

"Mimi!" Jean chided; the hurt her words caused were evident in his voice.

"Forgive me, papa. I wouldn't hurt you for anything." Mimi caught him as he started to the door, tray in hand, and kissed him warmly. Even as he forgave her, he was troubled at the moist softness of her lips.

"After breakfast we'll go for a walk down to the Basin. I'll tell you all about it then and a lot of other things I've been planning to tell you for a long time. Don't be long now!" he cautioned as he left the room.

Mimi smiled as she heard his carpet slippers pat-pat-patting down the hall. Poor, gentle, lovable old Jean. He would never learn the combination to the intricately devised safe called Life, Mimi thought for the thousandth time. Fumbling in his aimless way, living in a world of his own filled with ghostly figures of silken clad ladies and velvet garmented gentlemen—Mandevilles, Marignys, de Pontalbas and Gayarres— he would never understand nor master bustle and hurry and pep of the newer years.

She did not consciously think these things as she dressed hurriedly, yet Mimi sensed that Jean was living in a day that had passed and would never return. Though her step-mother irritated her almost to frenzy, Mimi was aware of the fact that Mme. Daquin was better armed for present-day life than either Jean or herself. She who was Mary Robertson of Chicago, American for many generations, was unencumbered with the hoary traditions which kept Jean with his pride of Creole ancestry content with his dreams, caring little whether his house was better furnished than those of his neighbours and friends, worrying not at all and wholly free from envy if his bank balance was more or less than the man's next door.

[23]

FLIGHT

Mimi often wondered what course their lives might have taken had her mother lived. And even as she wondered she knew the answer—Jean and her mother and she would have lived on and on and on in the old house on Dumaine Street until Jean and Margot had died and Mimi had married some Creole whose ideas about life had dovetailed with those of the Daquin family. Growing poorer and poorer year by year, the sleepy cycle of uneventful days would have continued, as untouched by the outside world as the bayous that bordered the rushing, ever changing Mississippi.

Into these quiet backwaters Mary Robertson had swept. Her coming had been like the digging of a channel that linked the sluggish bayou with the pell-mell hurtling stream nearby. Mimi's mother died when she was nine. His beloved Margot gone, Jean had floundered about, terrified by loneliness, panic-stricken when he found himself the sole keeper and guardian and nurse of a perturbingly active child of nine. He felt as though some malevolent power had inveigled him into a boat, rowed him far from shore and then deftly removed the bottom of the craft. He felt himself splashing, treading water, frantically feeling for solid earth beneath his feet and finding none.

Margot with quiet efficiency had guided him, consoled him, upheld him. With gentle self-effacement she had suggested solutions to the problems which arose in his little sick-and-accident insurance company, woefully lacking as it was in modern business methods, but which furnished sufficient revenue to satisfy their simple needs. So cleverly had she managed these hints, he never knew until after her death how she had planted the seed of these ideas in his head, watched them grow until they met the little crises which arose and then flattered his gentle and simple soul by telling him how cleverly *he* had solved the perplexities of the moment.

FLIGHT

Jean had often told Mimi how Mary Robertson had come to New Orleans on a visit at Mardi Gras time two years after Margot had died and just when he had become most lonely and afraid. His grief had dulled his senses so completely that for more than a year after his wife had died Jean had lived in a state that bordered on coma. When he grieved most was at night and then he sought forgetfulness in wine. Night after night he sat down after dinner, a wicker-covered demijohn by the side of his chair. On the table in front of him rested two objects—a faded photograph of Margot in her wedding gown and an ample-proportioned wine-glass of mottled green.

Mimi used to steal into the room in her night-dress and crouch in the shadows back of the door and watch him, fascinated by his varying moods. One thing only was constant—as soon as his glass was emptied Jean reached down, hooked the first two fingers of his right hand in the handle of the gallon container. Steadying it with his thumb, he raised the demijohn up and over with a flip until its bowl rested on his biceps. Pouring his glass full, Jean lowered the jar to the floor again. The process was repeated at regular intervals. In time Jean's head would sink lower and lower until it rested on the table, his arms his only pillow. Mimi would then cover his shoulders with the damask cover from the couch and creep back to her own bed.

Mary Robertson did not herself know why she had been attracted by Jean Daquin. She knew that, in part, she had been drawn by his gentle manner, so different from the blustering, raw, at times tiresome aggressiveness of her own Chicago. Even to herself she sternly denied that this had caused her interest in Jean to grow. Her father had used his earnings as a physician to speculate in real estate. Through shrewd and clever means he had accumulated considerable wealth in

Chicago's fast-growing Negro settlement on the south side, and this wealth had given him great political power among his people.

Mary Robertson had no recollection of a time when she did not hear from morning to night endless discussions of money and of politics. If her father was not talking of the sums he had made or expected to make from this piece of property or through that election, he usually was conjecturing as to the wisdom or folly of associating with this man or that one, of joining one fraternal order or the other one, of doing this thing or the other, all these speculations revolving around the one desideratum—will it pay?

Jean Daquin, improvident, oblivious of material advantage or disadvantage of any act of his, had opened to her eyes a new world filled with romance, with colour, with beauty. This, combined with the stories told her of his grief over Margot, had appealed to her feminine love of the unstable, the exotic, the unusual. Unconsciously she associated with Jean the exciting revelry of Mardi Gras, and found herself in love with him.

Jean, floundering in the abyss of sorrow, was, in his more sober moments, beginning to develop a new fear when he met Mary Robertson—an apprehension regarding Mimi.

"I'm a poor excuse for a father, *chérie*," he told her a score of times a day despite her sincere protestations that he was the best father any girl ever had. "Here I am, drinking every night until I'm beastly drunk and forgetting Margot would want me to brace up for your sake. I'm no good at all— you'd be better off if I were dead, too."

Here he would pause for the denial of his words which Mimi never failed to furnish. He would listen comfortably while she pointed out his virtues as a paterfamilias—and an hour later would be as unconvinced as ever. Mary deter-

[26]

mined she would capture Jean, distaste for her life in Chicago growing daily as she stayed on in New Orleans long after she had originally intended to leave. She was beguiled by the romance and languorous charm of the Creole quarter where she, for the first time, could forget the petty meanness and prejudice she felt as a Negro elsewhere in America. Mary Robertson swiftly but without Jean's realizing it led him to propose to her.

To him, blundering along like a pilotless balloon, blown unresistingly this way or that by every passing breeze, she seemed the embodiment of all the virtues he himself lacked. Energetic, purposeful, dynamic, she supplied a driving force which smoothed out numerous little difficulties which to him had seemed insurmountable. Under her influence he walked with her in the evenings, methodically answering the soft "Good-nights" which floated down to them from shadowed balconies or from doorways, instead of sitting at home drinking his usual half-gallon of double port. His mind clearer from alcohol, he brought some semblance of order to his insurance business, which had suffered greatly during his year of neglect.

He resisted sturdily and successfully her slightly less than tactful suggestions that more modern business methods be installed.

"No, Mary, I don't want a big business—then I'd be only a slave to it—just a creature run this way or that by the machine I've created. I get my living as things are—and I'm satisfied."

She was too wise to pursue the matter further but his adamant resistance did not prevent her from resolving, silently of course, to bide her time until she had the right and the power to have her way. Her intention was not consciously unkind nor meddlesome. He's got a gold mine practically untouched, she thought, and I'll convince him he can make ten times as much as he does. Jean, meanwhile, thought he had ended the discussion for all time.

.   .   .   .   .   :   .   .   .

Mimi, christened "Annette Angela Daquin" but thereafter known only as "Mimi," was eleven when Mary Robertson entered Jean Daquin's life. From the beginning Mimi had felt a barrier within herself arising against the overtures of friendship Mary Robertson made. There was no dislike which Mimi felt. Nor was there affection. Had Mimi analyzed her feelings towards this new and alien creature who had come, whirlwind-like, into their placid lives, she would have found indifference or perhaps passive acceptance of the newcomer as one of the vagaries of fate. This calm acceptance was in no small degree caused by Mimi's realization that this new creature furnished a much needed stimulating influence on Jean. For Mimi was wise beyond her eleven years. So Mimi accepted her without audible protest even when Jean hinted Mary Robertson might come and take Margot's place. . . .

So Jean and Mary were married first by Father André at the little Catholic church Jean had always attended, and then by the Rev. George W. Brown of the Ebenezer Baptist Church, to which denomination Mary belonged.

To the marriage there arose storms of protest from the relatives and friends of both Mary and Jean. He was alternately reviled and pitied for marrying an outsider, one who, though respectable and worthy, yet was not of Creole blood. *"Le pauvre Jean,"* they wailed, "grief and drink have weakened his understanding." From Mary's relatives, her father in particular, there came an outburst that overshadowed the protest of Jean's friends as a tornado outsweeps the gentle breeze of a woman's fan. Mr. Robertson rushed to New Orleans, stormed, denounced, ridiculed, pleaded, but in vain. Mary met his every mood in kind until, wise from his years of political training, he yielded, remained for the Protestant ceremony, refused to attend the Catholic one, and returned to Chicago, where he boasted to his friends of the "high Creole society" into which his Mary had married.

For a year they were happy. Mary was too clever to attempt revolutionary changes in her new *milieu*, even in the home where the to her slipshod methods of management irked her sorely. Towards Mimi she adopted a conciliatory policy, sensing the girl's latent hostility to her who had taken, in physical ways at least, the place so long filled by the adored Margot.

Mary made few friends among the intimates of Jean and Mimi. They with gentle but unmistakable signs let her know that despite her marriage to Jean she yet was and would ever remain an outsider. Time and time again Jean and Mimi received invitations to dinner, to parties which did not include Mary. The mellow old families, militantly proud of their Creole and Negro ancestry, yielded not an inch to that which went on in the world outside. Deadlines there were which they never permitted crossing. One of these was family. Another was colour. Mary offended in both. She was an outsider. And her skin was deep brown, in sharp contrast to the ivory tint of Jean and Mimi.

For the first year of her marriage Mary was oblivious of these things. She was too intelligent not to notice them but they either amused her or were ignored by her as evidences of narrow-mindedness by those who too long had lived in a world apart. She loved gentle, irresponsible Jean with her whole heart, with a woman's inconsistency, though he offended in almost every particular the canons of efficiency and progress which were a part of her very being.

She was content to spend her time at home, learning to cook

dishes new to her and dear to Jean, green trout and perch from the bayous, oysters fresh from the reefs, pompano and snappers and red fish from the Gulf, new and exotic vegetables and fruits, gumbo, Jambalaya, and combinations of all sorts of ingredients, generously spiced and seasoned. She gloried in the quaint old house and its furnishings—tenderly she cared for the old eighteenth-century piano of mahogany inlaid with brass, the Empire work table with ornately carved legs of St. Domingo mahogany that Jean's great-grandfather had brought to Louisiana when he fled from the Insurrection of 1791 in San Domingo.

During the year of their marriage Jean had told her the story of the refugee a score of times. Time and again he related the tale of tempestuous days, of ruin facing the sugar-planters of the Delta, of commerce paralysed, of the cessation for twenty-five years of manufacture of marketable sugar. She had heard of the black Dominican refugees, of the Spaniards, Mendez and Solis, and their plants on the outskirts of New Orleans, one a distillery, the other a refinery for making syrup.

The indigo crop a failure, their efforts to granulate sugar a failure, they were faced with ruin, complete and absolute. Then came Etienne de Boré and several black Dominicans, among them Jean's great-grandfather. Days of anxious experimentation. Days of hope. Days of failure. The day of the final test. The exultant cry, "It granulates!" Prosperity beyond the wildest dream. Four—five—seven years. Five million pounds of sugar marketed in one year by de Boré. Always Jean ended the story: "And that was done, my dear, by *my* great-grandfather—a Negro from San Domingo!" For the first year she succeeded in refraining from the comment that always came to her lips when she heard the story. It was: "And what about you, Jean Daquin, exhibiting some of your great-grandfather's initiative?" And it was a long time before she could get used to pronouncing his name other than as "Gene Da-Kwinn."

In time, however, Mme. Daquin tired even of the elaborately carved old four-posted mahogany beds, so high that one used a step to climb into them. Even the old silver, the garden, lost their fresh charm as she grew used to them. Like new toys they fascinated her for a while and, with her love for Jean, her mild affection for Mimi and her new duties, her mind was kept free from Jean's backwardness and the continued coolness of Jean's friends towards her. But when this newness wore off she began, at first gently and then with increasing vigour, to point out to him the opportunities for gain he was overlooking. At the same time she began to long for the progressiveness and bustle and eager hurrying of her own Chicago.

Jean at the beginning of her first mild reproaches sought gently to argue with her. He tried to convince her of the charm of the old ways, to prove to her that maximum happiness for them would come not with larger resources that created new anxieties but only in the easy-going undisturbed lethargy of his old life.

"What difference does it make if André or Raoul or Emile have finer carriages than we?—have more money in the blank?—does that mean they are happier than we? No—no—chère Marie! Happiness cannot be bought with dollars—look at the Americans north of Canal Street and you'll see I am right. They scramble and fight and scheme to gain a few dollars and when they have them what do they do? They fight and scramble and scheme for more!"

At the outset she let the discussion end there. But soon she began trying to point out that such a philosophy denoted only laziness—even absurdity. Jean, in turn, met her growing irritation with silence accompanied by a satisfied smile such as a parent would bestow on a child's foolish remarks.

[31]

FLIGHT

It seemed to say to her: "Silly woman, you are so much in error, it's useless even to discuss the matter with you—you couldn't understand if you tried."

Had Jean sought the manner which most surely would infuriate Mary, he could have found none so efficacious as this. Slowly at first, then with increasing vigour, she argued, pleaded with him, scorned or ridiculed his easy-going ways. She found him adamant and her irritation rapidly changed to excoriation. Morning, noon and night she nagged him. She wrote her father, who had invested heavily in an industrial insurance company operated by Negroes in Atlanta. His judgment vindicated, Mr. Robertson used his influence, and Jean received a flattering offer to associate himself with the Atlanta company. As a belated wedding present Mr. Robertson offered them a home in Atlanta, furnished and ready for immediate occupancy.

Then the real struggle began. Mary might not have succeeded even though easy-going Jean was becoming almost frantic at her eternal nagging. He yet loved her and she gave him no cause for divorce, even if such a way out of his dilemma had ever occurred to him, that would have been approved by the Catholic Church.

Two things began to make him weaken. The first of these and of slighter influence was that Mary's darkness of skin prevented him from eating at the old restaurants, Antoine's, Delatoire's, Mme. Begue's. He and Margot and Mimi had often gone there in the old days and without trouble though the proprietors and waiters and the regular patrons knew of his Negro blood. He and Mary had gone once or twice until slight but unmistakable hints had been given him that he was welcome but his wife—"We are most sorry but our American guests, on whose continued patronage we are largely dependent, object to *une femme de couleur*."

There were stormy, very stormy scenes. Jean, his white

[32]

hair and waxed moustache and goatee bristling, his face an apoplectic crimson, refused to listen to the profuse apologies, strode, shoulders back, head high in the air, from the places, vowing "never again to darken your doors, sir!" This vow he kept and the old places knew him no more.

Of greater moment, even, were the changes in the Creole quarter. The old families were dying off, poverty was forcing others to sell their homes. One by one the old houses were razed by boisterous, unfeeling house-wreckers and in their places were going up cheap, viciously plain and garishly ornate apartment houses. One by one the old places disappeared. Graceful lines of sloping roofs were replaced by harshly severe brick or wooden eaves, leaded glass dim with years was ruthlessly removed for plain sashes turned out by thousands by unimaginative factory hands, newel posts of carved brass and delicate balustrades of ancient mahogany were thrown away and in their stead came cheap pine ones, all carved alike.

The new houses were filled by new people, as cheap and noisy and brazen as their homes. Tenants of six months thought themselves old residents and, compared to their neighbours, they were. But to Jean and his diminishing acquaintances of an older day, they were noisily vulgar aliens and barbarians. Strident, unpleasant voices rose in ever increasing numbers and volume so that no longer could one enjoy the stroll of an evening through the once quiet streets.

"It can't be worse even in Atlanta," said Jean to Mimi sorrowfully one day. "I can't stand to see the changes any longer—it's too much like watching at the bedside of a dearly loved one who rapidly wastes away from a loathsome disease."

Then did Mimi know they would some day soon leave New Orleans never to return. The prospect at times frightened her—at times, with the venturesomeness of eager youth, she looked forward to new faces, new scenes, new experiences. . . .

"Good morning, Mme. Daquin," was Mimi's greeting to her step-mother as she entered the dining-room and slipped into her place at the table.

"Morning? It's nearer afternoon," acidulously replied Mme. Daquin. Jean winced and looked appealingly at Mimi.

"You're as shiftless and slow as your father," continued Mary. "You know we'll be busy as can be with packing all this junk your father insists we take to Atlanta——"

"Junk?" Mimi inquired with suspicious sweetness.

"That's what I said and that's what I mean. Junk! J-u-n-k! I'm going to get rid of some of this worn-out fantastic stuff and get me some nice fresh oak. Mahogany's too gloomy and funeral-like."

"I suppose you'd like to throw away that bed you sleep in —over two hundred years old and brought from France—and get a nice, shiny brass one?"

"That's exactly what I'm going to do——"

"You'll do nothing——" burst out Mimi, but at a sign from Jean she stopped talking. The meal was finished in silence. Mary, her broad face, deep brown of colour and framed with black hair that curled attractively, set in unrelieved displeasure, grimly ate without speaking until Jean rose to leave the table.

"You'll find on the table in the hall the telegram to Atlanta telling them you'll be there ready for work on the first. Wait until I finish," she demanded when Jean started to speak. "To-day is the sixteenth—that gives us less than two weeks in which to pack and move. Papa writes me he has sent his cheque for the house he's giving us and it's all ready for us to move into——"

[34]

FLIGHT

"But what about this house?" Jean broke in, panic in his voice at the unexpected imminence of quitting his beloved New Orleans for ever.

"I've seen to that, too," Mary answered methodically but, withal, a note in her voice of pride in her own far-sightedness and efficiency. "Laroux, the real-estate man on Canal Street, telephoned me yesterday he's found a buyer—a company that plans to build an apartment house here—and Laroux tells me he'll be ready to close the deal by the end of the week."

"Sell *this* house, papa!" broke in Mimi. "No—no! We can't let them tear *our* house down!"

"Yes, sell *this* house," affirmed Mary before Jean could reply. "I can't for the life of me see why you are so crazy about these draughty, moth-eaten old places. If I had the money I'd tear all of them down, build nice, modern places and make ten—twenty times the money off of them."

Before Jean could speak Mary swept conqueringly from the room. Mimi slipped her hand into Jean's and squeezed it comfortingly, the pair of them too full for speech.

Ignoring the dreaded telegram, Jean and Mimi left the cool shadows of the house for the cheery brightness of sun-swept Dumaine Street. Oblivious of passers-by, answering salutations and the greetings of friends methodically, they walked slowly through the streets, down the Esplanade, on and on until they found themselves at the gates of St. Louis cemetery. Yet in silence they wandered through the confused, close-packed *vieux carré* of the dead, past tombs piled one upon the other, their walls lined with row upon row of ghostly store-houses, "the ovens" like those of a baker-shop, each large enough only to hold a coffin. Crumbling bricks, covered with vines within which scampered in the dazzling, warming sun-light lizards of green or of gold. Here and there the *Ci-git* and the *Ici Repos* and the names, birth and death dates of

[35]

those buried within had been eaten away by countless storms of rain and sunlight until none could tell who had been buried there.

"It's just as well," thought Jean. "If there are those, relative or friend, who yet remain alive, they know which tomb holds their friends. And if there are none left—what difference does it make? Silly curiosity-seekers who ramble through a place like this as they would a penny arcade during Mardi Gras seeking new thrills—what do their wishes count?"

Their reveries were unbroken until they heard a noise behind them. From beyond a pile of "ovens" a silver crucifix flashed in the sunlight, raised high above the tombs. Soon the cortège appeared, winding its slow way through the tortuous maze of irregularly built tombs, the "Chant for the Dead" rolling out on the still air in lugubrious and chilling melody, rising or dropping as the tombs opened or closed in about the procession. Here and there, where the turning of a passage was too narrow to permit the carrying of the casket at its usual height, Jean and Mimi saw it raised high on a level with the crucifix. They stood hand in hand until the chanting died down in the distance.

"Mimi, that's how I feel to-day," said Jean softly. "Leaving New Orleans, the old houses, the old friends—it makes me feel as though it were I in that coffin——"

"Papa, why don't you put your foot down?" burst out Mimi; "tell Mme. Daquin you just won't go—let her go on back to Chicago if she dosen't like it—and you and I stay here and be happy?"

"It's too late now, *petite* Mimi," he answered. "My word's been given—they're tearing down so many of the old houses —my old friends are dying off, one by one——"

"But you're not old! You're only fifty-two, yet you talk as though you were a hundred——"

"Sometimes I feel a hundred—a thousand. Oh, well, I've

made my decision and I'll stick to it. It wasn't about that I wanted to talk with you. It's related to it but—but it isn't easy to talk about——" he broke off.

They walked slowly in silence as she waited for him to speak. An inexpressible tenderness filled her for this gentle old man—he seemed very old to her to-day. The growing surliness and quarrelsomeness of her step-mother, the alien who would never fit into the scheme of things as she and Jean knew it, infuriated her for the pain it was causing her dear Jean. She felt within her a steadily growing bitterness against Mary and her petty shopkeeper attitude, her scorn for traditions so dear to Jean and herself. As she had dressed, the notion of leaving New Orleans (she had never been more than a few miles beyond the city's limits) had appealed to her, offering as it did new experiences, new scenes, new people, naturally attractive to a girl of fourteen. Her mind had dwelt more on the favourable aspects of the change than on the severance of old and dear ties of tradition and friendship, of quitting familiar scenes, with all the instinctive optimism and disregard of consequences of youth.

But now she felt, on seeing Jean's reluctance to go, as though she were in some subtle manner guilty of disloyalty to Jean. Suddenly contrite, her eyes filled with tears and she clung to Jean in passionate repudiation of her joy at leaving. She realized Jean was speaking—had been talking to her for some minutes. ". . . And yet it ought not to be hard for me. Neither Margot nor I have ever consciously sought to keep from you the fact that the Negro blood in you set you aside, here in America, as one apart, though we have tried to shield you as much as we could from the embarrassments that blood can bring you."

"Oh, is that all that was troubling you, papa Jean?" laughed Mimi.

"You can afford to laugh here in Creole New Orleans,"

Jean cautioned. "But away from here it's a different matter. Here in the place we know I want to tell you of some of the stock from which we Daquins come. It's a record we're proud of—we've helped build this Louisiana of ours —much of what we did's been forgotten but it's there, just the same. I'm telling you, for when you run up against hard situations later on in life—and we all do—the knowledge of what's back of you will give you strength and courage."

Mimi said nothing. Jean went on.

"We Daquins trace our history a long ways back—back to the early days of the convent Louis XV founded here in 1727—the Ursalines—to teach the Negro and Indian girls. You know of beloved Madeline Hachard—she who was a postulant in the Ursaline Convent in Rouen—Rouen beloved of Flaubert and Maupassant. Her letters home tell of their perilous voyage to Louisiana in 1728, of shipwreck and shortages of food and water, of sickness and discomfort. Soon after Madeline Hachard—who called herself "Hachard de St. Stanislas" after she took the veil—and the others opened the doors of their convent, there was need of wives for the young men of character and means. Girls of good family were sent to the colony—*les filles a la cassette* they were called. From these matings sprang many of the great families of Louisiana—and to one of them you and I owe our being. From her who nearly two hundred years ago took the long and perilous voyage there comes down to us a path—at times clear and distinct—at times faded and shadowy—from that path innumerable branches shoot like the limbs of that ancient oak over there."

Jean's words had begun to weave a mysterious spell over Mimi. She looked at the tree to which Jean pointed—vaguely disappointed that instead of its leaves she did not see families, faces with laughing eyes and alluring mysteriousness. Jean had never talked to her like this before—she felt a thrill-

[38]

ing pride that he spoke to her as to one of mature years and understanding.

"You've many relatives, Mimi, of whom you can justly be proud—and some of whom the less said, the better. Like two great rivers from the same mother source, plunging, roaring, or gently purling they flow—parallel much of the way, touching at others, then springing apart to seek their way through diverse lands. We of the so-called coloured branch —many of our ancestry of the proud *gens de coleur libre*— we too have had a large share in making Louisiana what it is to-day."

"Tell me about some of them, Jean," demanded Mimi eagerly. "Tell me of the ones of whom you're proud—tell me of those you're not so proud of."

The sun was high in the sky and beating down upon them with vigour before Jean had finished his story. Mimi was too absorbed to notice the heat or to note the passing of the hours. Jean, with the mellowness acquired only through an unhurried life, had great pride in his ability as a *raconteur*—when he fancied he detected a waning interest on Mimi's face as he delved into the more abstract historical part of his tale, he quickly injected anecdotes, dramatic episodes, colourful vignettes. When Mimi seemed wearied of too great stress on the part Negroes had played as soldiers or labourers or if she appeared surfeited with tales of too great virtue and exemplary constructiveness on the part of those who were her forebears, Jean would, almost shyly and imperceptibly, relate a tale of derring do by one who lived at Barataria with that great pirate and freebooter—Jean Lafitte. Mimi felt a delicious tingle titillating her body as Jean told of that other Jean—he of the swart skin, midnight-black hair and eyes, beard shaven clean from the front of his face. She was glad—very glad one of her line had known this intrepid, carefree adventurer who, a marine

Robin Hood, had plundered and smuggled and risked death a thousand times as though he were passing the time of day on the street corner.

She, too, was fascinated by Jean's picture of the coming into being of the Creole.

"The white Louisianian will tell you the Creole is white with ancestry of French or Spanish or West Indian extraction. There may be some of that kind—but I'm not sure—but most Creoles are a little bit of everything and from that very mixture comes the delightful colourfulness which is their greatest charm. To them the cardinal sin is avarice or stinginess. Dalliance at love—too great devotion to the cup —poverty—all these are minor faults to be forgiven and forgotten. We are not a nation of shopkeepers, thank God, even though you and I, Mimi, are about to desert to the enemy."

Many other stories he told her there. He told of that Governor Perier who armed Negroes in 1729 and sent them to fight that fear-inspiring tribe of Indians, the Chonchas, with whom the black slaves were becoming too friendly, and how, with an ease that should have frightened Perier, these blacks wiped out the Indian enemy. Proudly Jean told how this example and others gave impetus to the later freeing of the slaves which had come largely through their own efforts —the revolt of the slaves led by the Chickasaws and Banbaras and other stirring uprisings—gentle, kindly Jean— who would not have crushed an ant—exultantly told of carnage, of slaughter, of death.

He took great pride in telling Mimi of Jeannot, stalwart slave offered freedom by Kerlerec if he would become the public executioner, a job no white man would take. Mimi lived again the agony of Jeannot, now dead some one hundred and fifty years, who in horror and anguish cried out: "What! Cut off the heads of people who have never done me any harm?" She could almost see him pleading, even

[40]

FLIGHT

weeping, to be allowed to remain in bondage rather than become the public killer. No escape possible, the governor was
adamant, he rose and said: "Very well, wait a moment."
Mimi shuddered as Jean told of Jeannot leaving the room,
running to his cabin, seizing a hatchet in his left hand, laying his right hand on a block and chopping it off. She re-
joiced that he, on exhibiting the bloody stump, created such
emotion he was given his freedom anyhow.

Of Negro troops under Andrew Jackson in the famous battle of New Orleans, of the ability and courage of that Major
Jean Daquin, San Domingan, quadroon whose Negro blood
historians later forgot, he told her proudly. But it was
sadly that he pictured the barriers, the Black Codes, the
rising tide of hatred and bitterness that began to rise against
the coloured Creoles and Americans. To Jean in his gentleness and love of peace these stories of dark days during
and after the Civil War were horrible and painful but in
his honesty he told of them while Mimi's breath came quickly
as he unfolded the scenes like sharply etched prints before
her wondering eyes.

"It's afternoon—Mary will be furious," Jean at last exclaimed, almost with dismay.

They hurried to the gates and home.

"All this is behind you, Mimi," Jean ended as they neared
the house. "Remember it—take comfort in it when you're
depressed.—You're a beautiful child—you'll be a more beautiful woman," he added. "You've warm blood in your veins
—the warmth of old, old wine. Here you'd be safe but away
from New Orleans—I don't know—I don't know. I hope all
will be well with us."

CHAPTER III

UNDER the efficient management of Mme. Daquin, it was not long before they became adjusted physically to their new surroundings in Atlanta.

"I wish you'd stop calling me 'Madam Daquin,'" she querulously demanded one day of Mimi. "I don't want people here being reminded constantly we're outsiders or think we're trying to put on airs. Call me 'Mrs. Daquin' or 'mamma,' or, if you insist on being high-toned, call me 'mother.'"

Mimi vigorously protested, to herself and Jean, against either of the latter terms and compromised on "Mrs. Daquin."

Soon after their arrival they received formal calls. These came usually in the afternoon and were more or less elaborate ceremonials. Mrs. Hunter, willowy spouse of the president of the Lincoln Mutual Life Insurance Company, came with her husband the Sunday after they reached Atlanta. She was cordial—very cordial. Mimi wondered why Mrs. Hunter felt it necessary to implant a slightly moist kiss upon her lips, though she permitted herself to be fondled by the effusive one without audible or visible protest. She submitted and that was all.

"What a darling little girl you have, Mrs. Daquin!" she exclaimed. "And what's her name?" On being told she went on: "Mimi? How very cute. Just like a stage name or opera."

"That's where it does come from. *La Bohème.* Do you know the opera?" Mimi assured her.

"No, I can't say I do—no, I don't believe I know *that* one," Mrs. Hunter, somewhat embarrassed, answered. She did not feel altogether sure that Mimi wasn't trying either to poke fun at her or test her learning.

"My real name's Annette Angela Daquin—but no one ever calls me that. They only call me Mimi," innocently replied Mimi.

Yet not sure of herself, Mrs. Hunter felt it necessary that she justify herself before this queer infant.

"We don't get much chance here to see good plays or hear such music as comes this way. The only play I've seen was 'Ben Hur' and Mr. Hunter has never forgiven me for climbing up the back stairs to the peanut gallery at the Grand Opera House where the coloured people sit. That was grand, though, and almost worth the quarrel I had with Mr. Hunter about going."

And Mrs. Hunter beamed at her husband in a benign fashion. Her duty done in commenting on Mimi's cuteness and beauty, Mrs. Hunter turned her attention to Mrs. Daquin and subjects near to housewifely hearts. They wondered if there would be a late spring—"it's been years since it's been so cool in April as it is now," affirmed Mrs. Hunter—they talked of the rising price of cloth and food and shoes—the art of cookery—"you must teach me some of those spicy dishes they tell me you have in New Orleans"—of local social life in Atlanta and how it compared with that in Louisiana.

Mimi listened alternately to the two and to the more restrained conversation of Jean and Mr. Hunter. The latter speculated, somewhat idly, as to the probable chances of Japan's defeating Russia, Mr. Hunter told Jean of business prospects in the fall if cotton sold well. Her attention was caught, momentarily, by Mr. Hunter, who was deploring the general shiftlessness of the younger people in general and his own son in particular.

"I've always maintained that hard work's what boys and girls need. When I was a youngster my daddy put me in the fields at six o'clock in the morning and I stayed there until six or seven o'clock at night. But these young ones coming along nowadays have got funny ideas. Take my own boy, for example. He's pretty nearly seventeen and for the life of me, I can't make him out. Always talking about doing something big but never knows from one day to the other what line he's going to do big things in. I tell Molly," he confided, leaning closer to Jean and lowering his voice, "it's all her fault. She coddles him too much——"

"Now, William, you aren't going into that here," chided his wife, who had overheard him. "Carl's nothing but a child as yet and he and Mildred are all we've got. He'll come round all right."

Back and forth the discussion raged, Mr. Hunter appealing to Jean for confirmation of his contentions, Mrs. Hunter relying on Mrs. Daquin for aid and succour. On only one point could they agree and that was Carl's essential difference from other children. Not until Mrs. Daquin, in her desire to help Mrs. Hunter and thereby gain her favour, introduced the matter of religion did Carl Hunter's name cease being bandied back and forth like a tennis ball between his parents.

Mrs. Hunter, tired of the argument over her son, swooped down upon the new topic with avidity. It was wholly a verbal swoop. It was difficult to imagine one of Mrs. Hunter's proportions and dignity swooping in any other manner.

"I knew there was something I intended asking you and I almost forgot it. What church're you planning to attend?"

"Well—er—that's a problem we haven't met yet," Mrs. Daquin, somewhat flustered, replied. "You see, in Chicago I was a Baptist—and you know the Baptist saying, 'Baptist born and Baptist bred, be a Baptist till I'm dead,'" she somewhat incorrectly quoted. "But my husband and his daughter, they're Catholics——"

FLIGHT

"Oh, indeed!" exclaimed Mrs. Hunter, her eyebrows making a rapid ascent until they seemed to mingle with the hairs that straggled down from beneath her elaborate *coiffure*. Mrs. Hunter's ears were not so keen as Mrs. Plummer's—the news regarding the religious beliefs of the Daquins had not reached her. Now she uttered the exclamation as though Mrs. Daquin had said: "My husband and his daughter have leprosy!" or "They suffer from epileptic fits."

Mrs. Daquin unmistakably caught the implication—she flushed and twisted the handkerchief in her hands and laughed a silly, titterish and mirthless laugh. Mrs. Hunter turned and surveyed Jean and Mimi as though they were specimens of some new flora or fauna of a weird and unfamiliar species. Her inspection lasted but a minute but it was long enough to make Mimi squirm uncomfortably and she felt vaguely as though she had been caught in the act of doing some loathsome and criminal thing.

They did not pursue the subject. Mrs. Hunter rose soon afterwards, her husband following her lead.

"My dear, on Tuesday of next week I'm entertaining my club, the Fleur-de-Lis—Mr. Hunter calls it 'the eating brigade' but that's because he's jealous, we don't let any men attend our affairs except once a year. You must come, for there you'll meet the right people—it's fatal to get mixed up with the wrong crowd," she smilingly warned.

Mrs. Daquin eagerly accepted the invitation, too eagerly Mimi thought. As she bade the Hunters a formal good-bye, she was thinking to herself: "Why can't she accept the attentions of Mrs. Hunter as though she were used to decent society instead of fawning all over herself?"

After the Hunters had left, there was a silence which was unbroken until they sat at supper. Mrs. Daquin several times looked inquiringly at Jean as though she were about to speak but each time desisted. Mimi noticed the words

[45]

shut off as they were about to be said but knew the flood would not be long in coming. She was right.

"What are you and Mimi going to do about attending church, Jean?" began Mrs. Daquin. "There's no coloured Catholic church here—and you saw from Mrs. Hunter's manner that—er—well, we aren't going to get along as well here as we might if——" The abrupt ending of her uncompleted sentence and the eloquent silence which followed it were sufficient.

"You mean you think we should give up our religion to make money and get into 'society'?" queried Jean in astonishment, his last word tinged ever so slightly with irony.

"Well, I don't mean exactly that," his wife answered. "But you can't attend a white Catholic church here and I just thought you might—well, you might refrain from mentioning you're a Catholic, for you can see from the way Mrs. Hunter acted it puts you in a different—er—it makes you different from the others," she ended lamely.

"What if it does make us different?" Jean demanded, almost belligerently. "Coloured people here, from what I've seen, are always talking about 'prejudice' and they're just about as full of prejudice against Catholics, Jews and black Negroes as white people themselves. You can do what you want, Mary, but Mimi and I will stick to our own religion. And I'm sure we can attend some Catholic church here, so that's an end to that."

There was no mistaking the tone. Being a wise woman, Mrs. Daquin dropped the subject. Afterwards, Mimi hugged Jean in the hallway.

"You were gorgeous, papa Jean. That's one time you bearded the lioness. And if you did it oftener—there'd be fewer times you'd have to do it." Jean grinned at her happily, proud of her approval.

CHAPTER IV

"I MEANT to tell you on Sunday," telephoned Mrs. Hunter the latter part of the week, "to bring your lovely little girl with you to my party next Tuesday. Mrs. Adams is bringing her girl, Hilda, and the two of them can play together."

And so it was that Mimi, dressed in her best dress, a pale yellow confection of lawn, set out with Mrs. Daquin for Mrs. Hunter's house and the Fleur-de-Lis Club meeting. Mrs. Daquin, too, dressed carefully and elaborately. She spent an hour arranging her hair in the style of the day, brushed back from the forehead high over a "rat" that made her head appear as though soldiers had thrown up breastworks, carefully smoothed over. From behind this amazing rampart peeped coyly a lacy hat perched perilously on the back of the head. Mrs. Daquin's modified leg-o'-mutton sleeves, her tightly fitting waist with high neck supported by whalebone stays, her long skirt flaring wide and with a train were all of the latest design, as were the half-mittens of black lace from which Mrs. Daquin's fingers, short and round, emerged shyly like little fat sausages. She knew her sex— she would be on inspection and much depended on the first impression. She was determined that that first glance should establish her as one of the elect.

Mrs. Hunter had said "four o'clock sharp." Mrs. Daquin and Mimi therefore arrived at the Hunter domicile, a huge pile of towers and turrets and bulging bay windows adorned at the most unlikely and unlooked-for places with startling

[47]

varieties of woodwork, at twenty minutes of five. Mrs. Daquin knew the value of a dramatic entrance, of the desirability of being just late enough to have permitted everybody else's arrival prior to her own.

She was not wrong. In the warm April afternoon the door and windows were open. As they ascended the steps there floated out to them the hum of well-bred voices, pitched at just the right angle. Mrs. Hunter rushed to greet them—and from the sudden stilling of the animated conversation Mimi knew the talk had been about her step-mother and herself. They were conducted around the large living-room and presented to each of the carefully dressed women who sat in a circle whose circumference was only a little less than that of the room. "Pleased to meet you's" "Happy to form your acquaintance's," "My compliments" and "How do you do's" greeted Mrs. Daquin; "What a pretty little girl's," and "How cute's" were Mimi's portion.

The ordeal ended, Mrs. Daquin subsided into a chair near Mrs. Hunter's standing approximately at the point where they had started on their circumnavigation of the room. The buzzing conversation began again. Mimi listened to the exchange of recipes and ideas, discussions of the best manner in which jams and jellies and rolls should be prepared, gentle arguments as to the relative desirability of this store or that one.

Mimi looked around the room for Hilda Adams but there were no younger people except herself. She began to feel out of place, to wish she were at home with her sewing or at her piano. Knowing there was no escape she began to examine the women around her. She remembered few of their names but that did not worry her. She noticed that none of the women present were darker than a light brown, their complexions varying from that shade to one indistinguishable from white. Just as this fact came to her she caught a snatch of

[48]

conversation from a group near her that linked itself startlingly with her own observation.

A slender, very slender, woman with lips which she pressed
together closely whenever she began or ended a sentence was
talking.

". . . it seems Mrs. Adams has been going to the Grand
Opera House and buying seats in the orchestra, 'passing' for
white, and seeing all the plays that've been coming here.
Well, the other day, as she was going in, some coloured person saw her and went and told the manager. She tried to
bluff it out but it didn't work—they made her get out."

"Serves her right," sweetly commented one of the informa-
tive one's companions, satisfaction in her tone. "Going
where she isn't wanted. She always did think she knew more
than the rest of us. They tell me she and Hilda wash their
own clothes after dark and hang them up in the yard when
nobody can see them—and then get up before daybreak to
take them in—— Oh! how do you do, Mrs. Adams?—I
didn't see you come in. And how sweet you look! That's
a beautiful new dress you've on," she broke off as the subject of their conversation came up.

Mimi wondered how so miraculous a change could come
over the group which now chatted easily and cordially, very
cordially, with her who had been ejected from the local
theatre and who laundered her clothes after nightfall. She
felt a deep warmth within her for this woman who, because
she wanted so avidly the entertainment, the touch with the
world of ideas, the stimulus that came from the plays which
came to Atlanta, and which her race barred her from seeing
respectably, made her run the risk of discovery. And to the
same degree that she felt a yearning to touch, to smile at Mrs.
Adams and thereby let her know that she sympathized with
her, did Mimi detest with a burning intensity the pettiness
and envy of her detractors.

[49]

FLIGHT

So engrossed had she been in Mrs. Adams, Mimi had not seen Hilda, who stood silent just beyond her mother. Mrs. Adams started to move away to another group and the motion brought Mimi face to face with a girl of her own age with wide, placid black eyes. Hilda and Mimi stood looking at each other, each caught and held fast by some power, neither of them knew what nor even that there was such a power holding them. For a minute—an hour—a century they stood there unable either to move or speak. The spell was broken when Hilda smiled shyly and moved toward Mimi. At that instant Mrs. Adams turned to Mimi.

"You must be Mrs. Daquin's little girl. This is my Hilda ——" she began. "Oh, I see you're friends already," she smiled.

"Come on, let's sit over there on the steps and talk," said Hilda simply, taking Mimi's hand.

Through the buzz of conversation, through the games of flinch (these gentle ladies got a delicious sense of near-wickedness from this simple game played with pasteboard cards which were *not* playing-cards), even through the stir created by the announcement that refreshments would be served in the dining-room, Mimi and Hilda sat there and talked. They began with questions of each other, about school, about their childhood, revealing little intimacies that subtly wove between them a gossamer band of friendship, fragile and almost invisible, yet with the strength of piano wire. Nor was this union born of spoken words. Much more came to each of them from the other in the little moments of silence, when by accident hand touched hand or smile met smile. Mimi, through all of her fourteen years, had had no confidante other than her father and, despite deepest bonds between father and daughter, there are some secrets too precious to be told even to a father like Jean. Mimi felt tender affection surge through her for this new-found

[50]

friend. She longed to stroke her hair, to kiss Hilda on the cheek, just under her chin, to pour out devotion lavishly, without stint. And she could tell from Hilda's smile, her tiny gestures of tenderness, that her love was returned, and happiness filled her being. . . .

Mrs. Hunter brought them back to realities.

"Oh, there you are, little chickabiddies," she cooed. "Come along, I've fixed a cute little table for you two where you can be to yourselves and where you won't be bothered by us old folks."

Hilda gave Mimi a fleeting, wry smile at the blundering condescension of the dowager-like hostess.

"Looks just like a battleship trying to be cute," whispered Hilda. Mimi rewarded her with a spontaneous but subdued little laugh as they followed Mrs. Hunter into the dining-room.

As they sat at the table near the huge bay window Hilda told Mimi in whispers about the women who chattered and ate at the large table.

"That skinny one over there," pointing to the woman who had been telling of the ejection of Hilda's mother from the theatre, "is Mrs. Watkins. Her husband's a doctor and he was crazy about mamma but she didn't like him like she did daddy. They say," and here Hilda leaned across the table and whispered, "that Dr. Watkins is still in love with mamma and it makes Mrs. Watkins furious. She doesn't like mamma and the main reason, I think, is because mamma is so much better-looking and knows so much more."

Mimi wriggled ecstatically at this revelation. She felt the delicious sense of being a conspirator, as the repository of a secret told only to one very dear and close.

"That one with the gold tooth who laughs all the time is the wife of a school-teacher—her name's Mrs. Tompkins—she's been to New York twice—but it didn't seem to do her any

[51]

good. She laughs as much as ever and hasn't anything new to talk about except the new clothes she's bought and how she and her husband could go to all the shows in New York and sit in any part of the theatre they wanted to."

Mimi, as discreetly as she could, turned and surveyed her of the gold tooth. She was not very impressed—she expected anyone who had twice been to New York to have some distinguishing mark or characteristic which revealed two journeys to Manhattan. Mimi did not know what form this mark should have taken, she only felt that Mrs. Tompkins should have differed in some way from those who had not journeyed so far.

The cataloguing was interrupted by Hilda, who asked suddenly, and to Mimi with an eagerness which she could not at the time fathom, if Mimi had met Carl Hunter.

"Mamma tells me I'm a silly little goose," proceeded Hilda when Mimi told her she had not met their hostess' son, "but Carl's the most thrilling boy in Atlanta. He's seventeen and not a bit like the other boys around here—they're so—so babyish. But Carl's different and mamma says he doesn't get along any too well with his mother and father—his father wants Carl to study insurance and banking and Carl doesn't want to."

"Does he know you're—that you like him so?" asked Mimi.

"Ooh—no!" gasped Hilda. "But he *is* different——" she ended. . . .

That night Mimi told Jean of the things she had seen and heard during the afternoon. To her piquant recital of the things said and done and to the vivid little pictures, each etched so graphically and clearly Jean could see the women and their mannerisms, he listened eagerly.

"And how did Mary seem to like it?" he asked.

"She was right at home! I heard her tell two or three of them she just adored Atlanta—reminded her of her Chicago

—and so different from that sleepy old New Orleans!" Mimi grimaced. . . .

"I'm happy you've found Hilda," Jean told her. "You need the companionship of young people—when you're as old as I it won't be so easy to find somebody whose ideas fit in with your own."

"How are things going at the office?" asked Mimi, remembering that she in her excitement had almost forgotten him and his affairs.

"About as well as can be expected—better than I thought they would," he answered. "They're a fine bunch—very much in earnest—and I suppose I'll have to admit Mary and her father are right—they do put things over. Mr. Hunter's the best of the lot—and, well, I suppose in time I'll get myself fitted into the groove——" he ended lamely.

"You're whistling in the dark to keep up your courage!" Mimi challenged him. "You're not happy here and you never will be."

"Not entirely so, I am afraid, but—well, I'll be contented after a fashion," Jean smiled bravely. "I miss the old houses, the old ways. I'd give anything almost to walk once more down to the Basin, to sit in St. Louis cemetery—do you remember the gold and green lizards scampering round, in and out of the vines over the graves, that day we walked and talked there, Mimi? I miss the calmness, the placidity, the smell of the water. Here things are rushing, bustling, matter-of-fact. I feel as if some power has pulled me out of a quiet pool where I was lying on my back floating on the water and thrown me head first into a deadly revolving whirlpool.

"And what are they getting out of all this, these minnows who are squirming and fighting each other?" he demanded with the old gesture of questioning she knew so well. "Here are these coloured people with the gifts from God of laugh-

[53]

ter and song and of creative instincts—do you remember that man who sang as he went past the house our first night in Atlanta?—and what are they doing with it? They are aping the white man—becoming a race of money-grubbers with ledgers and money tills for brains and Shylock hearts."

"But, papa Jean, they've got to do it! They're living in a world where they must either make money or else perish."

"No—no—Mimi! You don't understand what I mean. The whole world's gone mad over power and wealth. The strongest man wins, not the most decent or the most intelligent or the best. All the old virtues of comradeship and art and literature and philosophy, in short, all the refinements of life, are being swallowed up in this monster, the Machine, we are creating which is slowly but surely making us mere automatons, dancing like marionettes when the machine pulls the strings and bids us prance. I know you're thinking I sound like a masculine Cassandra—but some day, perhaps long after I'm gone, maybe you'll think back to this day and agree with me."

To Mimi most of this was rather baffling—she was glad that Jean obviously did not expect her to answer. It was true that she had been fascinated by the song they had heard, she loved the colourfulness of the life she saw around her and she had noticed that in her few contacts with white people she had felt a certain chill that she was not aware of when with her own people.

"Her own people." The phrase interested her. In New Orleans she had thought all people were hers—that only individuals mattered. But here there were sharp, unchanging lines which seemed to matter with extraordinary power. This one was white—that one black. Even though the "white" one was swarthy while the "black" one might be as fair as the whitest of the white.

And within the circle of those who were called Negroes she

[54]

found duplications of the lines between the two major groups. She in the few days she had been in Atlanta had heard enough to know there were churches attended in the main only by coloured people who were mulattoes or quadroons, others only by those whose complexions were quite dark. At Mrs. Hunter's the uniform lightness of skin had impressed itself upon her. And when she had sought to make overtures to Mrs. Plummer's girl, Iwilla (Mrs. Plummer had told Mrs. Daquin proudly her daughter had a Biblical name—it was taken from the verse, "I will arise and go unto my Father"), Mrs. Plummer had called her child into the house and Mimi had heard her being scolded: "How many times I got to tell you to leave these yaller children alone? First thing you know, you'll be coming home saying some of them's called you 'black.'"

All this perplexed Mimi. She was too young and inexperienced to know that these people were in large part the victims of a system which made colour and hair texture and race a fetish. Nor did she know how all too frequently opportunity came in a direct ratio to the absence of pigmentation. It was baffling, annoying. And so too were Jean's criticisms of his new environment. Mimi missed the romance of her old home, it is true, but the new scene with all its rawness and lack of beauty intrigued and fascinated her through its vigour and progressiveness. She began to feel a sympathy, at first faint but growing in strength, tinged with pity, for Jean in his unwillingness to adapt himself to newer ways and customs.

Not that she consciously put these into words nor even into tangible thought. She loved Jean too dearly, too wholeheartedly for that, and any criticism of him, real or implied, would have made her miserable for its imputation of disloyalty. No. It was simply that Jean was the follower of an older day, of an age that was passing even in Louisiana, that

[55]

FLIGHT

definitely had passed here in Georgia and to an even greater
degree farther North. . . .

And Jean's efforts to find his place in the new order and to
make that place as comfortable, as little irritating as possible, met with but indifferent success. He found that he could
not with any degree of pleasure nor of comfort join in the
social activities of his business associates. They were too
vigorous, too forthright for his simple taste. He had no
puritanical streaks in his nature but the lusty laughter with
which the men greeted the stories which were current, usually of a ribald and smutty nature, at first surprised him,
then slightly nauseated him. It was the one thing he disliked
in Mr. Hunter, whom he liked better than most of the others.

He could always tell when Mr. Hunter had heard a new one
—for these stories the older man had a particular smile that
at times bordered on a leer, and a manner of portentous and
cryptic winking. The stories themselves did not so much
disgust him—he had indulged frequently in racy wit and re-
partee with his old cronies at home—it was their general
stupidity and their clinging to one theme.

Jean formed more and more the habit of spending his time
at home, despite his wife's constant urging that he go out and
"mingle more with the men and make himself more sociable."
He read indefatigably, sitting in his room, summer and
winter, until the early hours of the morning, or until his wife
forced him to retire. She, on the other hand, berated and
criticized him much less than in those last few months before
he consented to move from New Orleans. Jean quite frankly
and with an equanimity which amazed him realized they had
grown farther apart than ever and were continuing to find
their pleasure in widely diverse fields. Mrs. Daquin, under
Mrs. Hunter's dexterous management, had been extended and
had accepted an invitation to join the Fleur-de-Lis Club.
More and more Mrs. Daquin, to her intense delight, found

[56]

herself accepted into the inner circle of Negro society and she soon was able with entire naturalness to speak pityingly of those who were not of the elect.

She had won, too, her efforts towards religious conformity by Jean and Mimi, though this victory had come from an unexpected ally. She had gone, not unprotestingly, with Jean and Mimi to one of the local Catholic churches. There they had been refused admission in a firm and unmistakable rebuff, amazement having been expressed that they had even dared to think they could attend services there. Jean, grieved, his faith shaken, had gone later to see the priest, protesting against the refusal of admittance, but he had received cold comfort—even his question (that was more a protest than an interrogation) as to whether or not the Virgin Mary blessed or withheld blessing from Catholics whose skins were dark, remained unanswered.

That he might be forced to sit in a segregated section of the church had occurred to Jean. Of late years that custom had grown in popularity even in New Orleans in the churches not attended wholly by Negroes. But that he might be refused even admittance had been a terrific shock from which he never completely recovered. Mrs. Daquin had said nothing, but a faint smile which seemed to Mimi to shout exultantly: "I told you so!" wreathed her face. Mrs. Hunter's gentle hints that "the" church to attend was the Congregational had not fallen on barren ground. It was not long therefore before Sunday morning found her and Mimi and Jean in one of the pews there. . . .

Not many months passed before Mrs. Daquin was as much at home as though she had lived since birth in Atlanta. Mimi, too, was accepted in time, though with reservations. Her affection for Hilda was so apparent there was no mistaking that she esteemed her above all the other girls she met. Both of them had completed their grammar-school careers

[57]

when Mimi came to Atlanta—both entered high school at Atlanta University in the same class that fall. They walked to school together and they walked home together. They confided each to the other their innermost secrets, they aired their grievances against whatever displeased either of them, secure in the knowledge that the other would understand and would be in complete sympathy. There came, of course, little differences, but these soon evaporated in the warm surge of reconciliation.

This very friendship in a manner prevented Mimi's acceptance into the fold of complete conformity. Mrs. Adams was invited to all the parties and she in turn did her share of entertaining. But always there was an air of detachment in her social relations—she seemed merely to be going through the motions of things which did not greatly interest her, if indeed she did not derive a kind of quiet amusement from the frantic efforts to out-entertain each other.

Instead of attempting to serve courses more in number and elaborateness, to decorate her house more gorgeously than the member of the Fleur-de-Lis Club who had entertained the last time, Mrs. Adams served simple but well-prepared "collations," as they were called. The sensing that they were more attractive for their very simplicity did not serve to sweeten the tempers of those who depended on elaborateness. This same simplicity governed all Mrs. Adams' actions whether in social or other relations. It had brought to her the damning reputation of being "stuck-up" and there is none other accusation more certain to gain a measured unpopularity. This reputation, though unfounded in fact as in the case of her mother, had been attached to Hilda and, in turn, to her friend, Mimi.

To about the same degree Mimi's lack of religious conformity militated against her. She felt a certain bitterness against the Catholic Church for its surrender to a race prej-

udice which to her seemed silly, but her animosity towards
that Church was based most largely on the fact that the surrender had hurt Jean. With the fortunate tendency of youth
not to bother itself too greatly about creeds and dogmas,
Mimi might quickly have forgotten or at least put into the
limbo of half-forgotten things most of the religious duties
which to her in New Orleans had seemed so natural—as
natural as eating or sleeping. Though Jean rarely mentioned
it now, Mimi knew he grieved deeply that he could not attend mass—that down deep beneath the calm exterior he
presented to the world and even to his family, Jean felt the
loss keenly of church attendance. And when Mimi saw this
hurt, it caused her frequently to speak of the differences she
noticed between Catholic and Protestant devotees. Usually
these were, quite naturally, more critical of the Protestant, and
this constant reiteration of her own unconformity to local creeds
and beliefs in time caused the phrase "those Catholics" to be
instinctively synonymous with her name and Jean's. . . .

But it was the instinctive cruelty towards and jealousy of
woman to woman which created difficulties for Mimi. Something of the colourfulness of the sapphire and purple and
jade green waters round New Orleans had gone into the making of Mimi. There was in her too something of the grace
of the languorous waves of the Gulf of Mexico as they
lapped the jagged shores of Barataria. In her too was the
luxuriousness of tropic plants bursting into startlingly vivid
and beautiful reds and yellows and greens and blues. Her
reddish hair in the sunlight was a magnet that caught and held
the eye, the mind meanwhile feasting on its brilliant decora-
tiveness.

And in combination with these reminders of tropic warmth
and colour was Mimi's air, piquant, vaguely mysterious and
seductive. Not that she was aware of all this, nor did she
do other than laugh when Hilda compared her to some

other girl, always to the disparagement of the other one. There were other pretty ones—several of them, in fact, more beautiful than Mimi. Yet, none of them possessed the combination which was hers and, not having lived in Atlanta all her life and thus newer to the eye, Mimi without apparent volition drew to her side most of the younger men. And the eyes of even the older ones she drew to her, covered, if the wife of the beholder was at his side, by a studiously casual remark like "That little Daquin girl is certainly a pretty child!" . . .

CHAPTER V

IT was at one of these little parties, the room ringed with fat, chatting mothers whose conversation did not so absorb them that they failed to notice any action, however insignificant, that Mimi met Carl Hunter. Hilda brought him to her with the simple introduction, "Mimi, this is Carl." He, giving her a quick glance that seemed to her to take in not only her physical self but to pry down deep into her innermost thoughts, paused a minute before speaking. When he did speak his greeting was only a cool "Hello." Others passing stopped and the conversation in the little group became general. When she looked again Carl had gone. She did not see him again but on the way home she spoke of him to Hilda.

"I don't think much of your friend, Hilda," she said. "He didn't say anything and he seems to have an awfully good opinion of himself."

"No—no, Mimi, you mustn't say that," Hilda quickly defended him. "That's just his way—you just wait until you know him and you'll think differently."

"Dear, I don't want to hurt your feelings but from what I've seen I'm almost sure I don't want to know him."

"It's too bad he's going away. He told me his father's going to let him go away and work this summer and then enter school up North next fall. Oh, dear! I don't know what I'll do—he thinks I'm nothing but a little girl but he's only seventeen and I'm going on fifteen."

The despair of unrequited love in her voice—and what pangs of love can be more acute, more painful, more deliriously ecstatic than those of youth?—touched Mimi deeply.

"Forgive me, Hilda. I was only joking. I think Carl's real nice and the way his hair falls down over his head is adorable."

Hilda smiled bravely through incipient tears and her smile gave forgiveness. . . .

In the autumn they entered high school together and the long hours they spent together deepened the love they had for each other. Mrs. Daquin was busy with her household affairs, her friends, parties at her own home and at the houses of her friends. They settled down into a calm, routinized existence little touched by events of the outside world. They even were little affected by that other world which lived alongside them in the same city—that realm known as "white." Except in the stores or on the street cars there was but little contact, and, particularly in the latter, they sought to lessen the number of the contacts as far as possible. Here there were these two parallel existences, meeting but seldom, for Jean and his wife and Mimi soon learned that to avoid meeting was to avoid trouble or at least the possibility of trouble.

On one or two occasions they saw how easily disturbances could come. The laws of Georgia provided that in the street cars white people should sit from the front of the car towards the rear and coloured people should start occupying the rearmost seats and as their number increased they should occupy seats towards the front. One afternoon Mrs. Daquin and Mimi were returning from a shopping tour. They sat towards the middle of the car on boarding it but later several coloured people back of them alighted. The conductor, a short man with small eyes and narrow face adorned with red stubble, came to their seat and in an unpleasant, unnecessarily gruff tone demanded:

"Here, you! Move back there where you belong."

Mrs. Daquin stared at him in amazement.

[62]

"Are you speaking to me?" she demanded.

"I ain't talking to nobody else," he replied. "Come on! Don't give me no argument. Get on back there with the rest of the niggers!"

A titter went up from the staring passengers. Mrs. Daquin felt the blood rising in her face and her anger mounting.

"I'll do nothing of the sort. I am going to stay right where I am," she challenged, her voice shaking with anger, though she was trying hard to control it.

"You'll move back there or I'll put you off the car," the conductor shouted, more angry than ever as he felt the realization coming to him that he had stirred up an argument which might not end as easily as he had supposed.

"Come on back, lady," a voice from the rear called. " 'Tain't no use having no argument and he's got the law on his side."

This unasked-for advice only served to make Mrs. Daquin and Mimi, who remained silent but who longed to join the argument, more adamant.

"You want me to stop the car and call a cop?" her tormentor queried belligerently.

"You can do whatever you please—I will not move!" was her answer. . . .

Muttering something about "biggity niggers," the conductor retreated to the rear of the car, defeated.

They left the car at their corner and an obscene remark floated back to them from the discomfited conductor. Jean told Mr. Hunter of the affair and asked advice but that which he received was of slight comfort to them.

"I know just how you feel about it. It makes me mad as blue blazes, too, but what can you do about it? If it had been you or me that conductor would have used physical violence and he'd have been helped by every white man on the car. About the only thing that saved your wife and daughter was that they're women—they can get away with lots more than we can because they are women. No, Daquin, you might as well let the matter drop and forget it. Protest will do no good and you haven't a chance in the courts." . . .

On another occasion one of Jean's associates whose skin was brown but whose wife's was fair, assisted his own wife in boarding a car. A crowd of whites jumped down from the vehicle and pummelled him viciously before his wife could explain that she too was a Negro. . . .

Jean bought for their use a horse and surrey and thereafter they never rode in the cars. He was conscious that this was an ineffective compromise with principle but he was happy in that compromise in that it gave him greater peace of mind.

With such exceptions their lot was not a very difficult one. In the stores Mrs. Daquin was not allowed to try on hats or shoes or dresses before purchasing them and they frequently were forced to wait until whites who had entered after they had were served. But with time they became accustomed to these slights and particularly when they found that with but few exceptions these were accepted by their friends as the expected thing, unpleasant but inevitable. "You can get used to being hung if you're only hung often enough," seemed to be current philosophy, except in the cases of the younger ones. . . .

Beside their regular lives of work and play they found an additional outlet in various affairs at the colleges which were situated in Atlanta. There were occasional musical evenings, now and then some speaker of note came and lectured. There were basball and football games between the teams of the local schools and a few with teams from institutions located in other cities. In the local papers they read of events going on in the outside world, some of them exciting lengthy comment and interest, others less. General rejoicing greeted the victory of Japan over Russia, the nation of smaller men being enthusiastically supported largely because they were a coloured nation. "Teddy" Roosevelt was acclaimed a great friend of the Negro despite the Brownsville affair, though to Jean it seemed much of his popularity among the coloured people in Atlanta was due to the fact that he was a Republican. The San Francisco earthquake elicited a certain degree of interest and sympathy, though, being far away, its maximum reaction usually was summed up in the remark, "Isn't that too bad!"

Twice the world thrilled to stories that men had at last plunged through the frozen wastes of the North and come to the top of the world. And because one of them was discovered to be a liar many, many wiseacres shook their heads portentously and opined that the other one might be lying too. Among the younger men there were frequent discussions of the relative merits of a promising young Negro prizefighter named Johnson recently emerged from Texas who was achieving a considerable reputation with his fists.

One cloud that had appeared first as a tiny speck began to grow with distressing speed during the summer of 1906 and brought deep concern to the more thoughtful ones. By these, certain ominous signs had been seen all through the long hot months of the summer when nerves are frayed and tempers sharpened to razor-blade keenness by the sultry heat. A period of unemployment had caused a marked loafing of whites and Negroes followed by a long series of petty crimes. Saloons and dives and "social clubs" sprang up like mushrooms and throve. A bitter political campaign was waged, its central issue the question of disenfranchisement of Negroes and "Negro domination." A play, "The Clansmen," a distorted picture of Reconstruction filled with venom and hatred, came to Atlanta and stayed during this time of strain, and whipped into fury bitterness between white and black. Some crimes against women were reported, others were not chronicled. A man named Turnadge committed a crime terrible in detail but little was said of it. Turnadge was white. Other white men committed other crimes and the press said little of it. Twelve or more Negroes were charged with rape or attempted rape. Circulation-seeking newspapers brought out "extra" after "extra," screaming in twelve-inch headlines, "THIRD ASSAULT," "FOURTH ASSAULT," "NEGRO ATTEMPTS TO ASSAULT MRS. MARY CHAFIN NEAR SUGAR CREEK BRIDGE," "ANGRY CITIZENS PURSUE BLACK BRUTE." It meant little at the time that later it was to be discovered that all but two of these reports were without foundation in truth.

To most of the citizens he encountered, Jean found, the tenseness meant little. It was considered variously as a bit embarrassing, rather unfortunate, and mostly as the slightly aggravated condition of the usual state of affairs. But to him, unused to the ominous rumbling which terrified him, the situation seemed grave, very grave indeed. In the few contacts he had with white people, on his daily visits to the bank uptown, in his contacts with tradesmen and men and women on the streets, he saw with troubled eyes the glances of suspicion, of hostility, of hatred. Once on entering the bank he stood near the desk of the cashier, who had always had a smile and cheery word for Jean, whom he liked. Now he looked grimly at Jean and demanded, in what was almost a snarl: "What do you want, Daquin?"

"I came to see you about some notes, Mr. Stewart," Jean answered, troubled, "but—I wonder why you've changed—you're usually so pleasant and to-day you're—why, you're——"

"There's reason enough, Daquin. You've read the papers. Why don't you better-class Negroes do something to stop your criminals from attacking our women?"

"We're as bitterly opposed to attacks on women, whether they're white ones or coloured ones, as you are, Mr. Stewart. That is, we're opposed when they really are attacks."

[66]

"What do you mean—when they *are* attacks?" the cashier demanded.

"Just what I say—how many of these attacks reported in the papers are really attacks? They spread the story of an alleged or a reported attack all over the front page—but when they found the woman was mistaken or hysterical from reading all these other wild tales, they stick it in an insignificant item on the inside, if they mention it at all. There's trouble ahead if these inflammatory stories aren't stopped, Mr. Stewart. And it seems to me it's up to men like you who've got sense to stop them—the crowd that makes up the mob isn't going to do any thinking for itself—it never does."

"That isn't the point, Daquin," Stewart asserted. "You Negroes have got to stop these real attacks!"

"There are more ways than one of looking at that," was Jean's troubled rejoinder. "In the first place, nearly every one of these 'attacks' has on investigation been found to be untrue. Yet, your papers are screaming madly every day without much investigating of their stories beforehand that more and more assaults are being committed. A second thing is that it's up to the police and the sheriff's office to catch and put in prison any man suspected or accused of a crime whatever his colour. If one of your race kills somebody or attacks a woman, you don't rush around saying that it's up to the white people to catch him—quite properly you say it's up to the police. And a third thing—there've been several attacks on coloured girls by white men of late but I haven't seen those listed as part of the record of assaults."

"That kind of talk won't get you anywhere, Daquin. You're only fooling yourself and the fact there's a certain degree of truth in what you say only makes it the more dangerous for you to be talking that way—you'd make most of these white people mad because you have done some thinking about the situation."

[67]

Jean interrupted him with a gesture of impatience.

"Mr. Stewart, have you ever tried to look at this thing from our side of the fence?"

"No-o-o. I haven't given much time to it, I reckon," Mr. Stewart answered reflectively, his face indicating a degree of surprise that there was another side which had not occurred to him.

"Well, just let me tell you a little about it then. The son of a friend of mine, a lad of twenty or thereabouts, yesterday morning was coming out of his own father's home, rather hurriedly as he was late for an appoinment. Reaching the street, he remembered he had forgotten a package and he turned to go back when he brushed against someone behind him. As he started to apologize he saw it was a white woman. This woman was telling my wife about it and she said the boy's face became a mask of terror, realizing as he did what would happen if she had screamed. He stood still a minute, too frightened to move, and then he turned and ran for dear life down the street. Now suppose, Mr. Stewart, that woman had been easily frightened—you'd have seen in the papers that same day the report of another 'attack.' "

"Yes—yes—I know it's hard for you, too. But we're sitting on a keg of dynamite and none of us can tell when some fool's liable to set it off. We can only hope for the best," Mr. Stewart ended piously.

Jean did not know that after he had left the bank, having forgotten the business matter which had brought him there, so engrossed had he become in his conversation that a little group of men had gone to the cashier's desk and demanded that Mr. Stewart tell them what Jean had said. This Mr. Stewart did not do—he did not know how Jean's words and thoughts might be taken. . . .

At home Jean found but little more understanding. His wife, busy with her own affairs and having little contact

[68]

other than with her friends and with shopkeepers who carefully concealed their feelings, scoffed at his forebodings.
"You're not used to anything like this and you're too easily
scared," she laughed. "Mrs. Hunter tells me they have lots
of situations here just as delicate and they've all blown over
in time. Same as this one will blow over as soon as the
hot weather ends." Her air of finality in citing Mrs. Hunter
as authority convinced Jean there was little need of pursuing
the subject further in that direction.

Mimi was more sympathetic but she showed by her puzzled
frown she did not comprehend his reasons for worrying.

"White people—and coloured people—you didn't used to
separate people into such definite classes before you left
New Orleans, papa Jean!" she declared, somewhat confused.
"After all, what real difference does it make? A difference
in colour, different hair, different features, but what do those
matter in the long run? Why can't people be just people
and stop all this meanness?"

"That isn't the point right now, Mimi," he explained. "I
suppose it's silly but I'm worried—this thing's mighty serious and it may be you and I and the rest of us may see
some pretty dark scenes. Oh, why did I ever leave New Orleans? I'd never have had all this trouble—at least, it
wouldn't have been so terrifying——"

"It'll blow over," Mimi comforted him.

"Blow over"! There was that phrase of Mrs. Hunter's
again. He was miserable. He saw his old house in Louisiana,
his garden, his flowers. He could almost see his old friends,
Bernard, Pierre, André. He wished he were sitting once more
in the old café on Chartres Street, with his friends spending
long hours in comfortable, soothing conversation, sipping their
glasses of *le petit gouave,* that heart-warming, gently exhilarating concoction from old San Domingo. He could smell
the wild odours of the tropical, luxuriant flowers, the mildly

[69]

FLIGHT

intoxicating smell of the wild orange, the honeysuckle, the
roses, fragrant pines. He could close his eyes and see the
delicate pink and white of the oleanders, could hear the
soft-throated cries of the hucksters, many of them with huge
gold ear-rings and brilliantly coloured dresses, their heads
bound with gay headkerchiefs. *"Belles des figues! Belles
des figues! Pralines, pistache! Pralines, Pacanes!"* they
called. A violent nostalgia assailed him, its accompaniment
a bitter distaste for the harsh scenes of his new home. . . .

Long, tense days crept into anxious nights. Feverishly
busy with the making of money, men and women, white and
black, good citizens and Christians all and in their own minds
true to their own various standards, did nothing. Along
towards the middle of September a few of them began to
be disturbed. Calls were sent out for mass meetings to check
the wave of hatred and passion that rapidly was mounting.
Somnolent, apathetic city officials began to become vaguely
apprehensive. The grand jury was called to meet on the
twenty-fourth. Slowly, terribly slowly, the Gargantuan creature of public opinion began to rub its eyes sleepily and
grumblingly bestir itself. . . .

On a Saturday afternoon when September had crawled its
torrid way two-thirds into October, Mrs. Daquin took her
turn entertaining the Fleur-de-Lis Club. Jean closeted himself in his own room, alternately reading and taking short
cat naps. He did not want to be forced to hear the rumble
of chatter and gossip nor was he unaware of the shortness
of his wife's temper had he blunderingly impeded the smooth
running of the carefully constructed plans for the afternoon's
pleasure. Mimi and Hilda brought him his supper, which
he ate slowly as he gazed into the dusty, sere garden backing
the house next door. The leaves of the corn stalks, the
tomato plants, the cabbages were yellowed and dried, mute
appeals for saving showers.

[70]

FLIGHT

He must have fallen asleep, for it was night when Mimi rushed into the room and shook him until he was awake.

"Come quick, papa Jean! Mrs. Daquin is sick!" she urged.

Jean rushed downstairs. All the women had gone save Mrs. Adams, who had loosened Mrs. Daquin's corsets and clothing.

"I think it's indigestion," was Mrs. Adams' calm reply to Jean's fearful questions. "Hilda's telephoning for the doctor. You and Mimi help me get her upstairs."

Jean was grateful for her cool command of the situation. They got Mrs. Daquin into bed before the doctor came. He came, examined, looked grave, then more cheerful. His orders were terse.

"Keep her quiet—hot applications—give this prescription every two hours—this one every four hours. Afraid all the drug stores round here are closed, so you'll have to go down town—probably to Jacobs'—they stay open late."

Mimi remembered the conversation with Jean as he started to leave the house.

"Wait a minute until I get my hat. I'm going with you," she announced. He protested, told her she should remain at home with Mrs. Daquin.

"Mrs. Adams and Hilda will stay. I've just asked them."

She had returned, hat on, before he could answer. Realizing that further argument would be unavailing, he and Mimi set out for the distant drug store. . . .

A hot Saturday afternoon, traditionally a half-holiday, had brought into town hundreds of country people. Saloons were doing a rushing business, those labelled "For White" and those bearing signs, "For Coloured Only." Late in the afternoon an elderly white woman had gone to a window to close the shutters. A Negro was passing on the sidewalk. Her mind inflamed with the news stories she had read, she screamed. Someone telephoned for the police. Newspapers

[71]

FLIGHT

got wind of the story, rushed "extras" on the street bearing letters five inches high, "ANOTHER WOMAN ASSAULTED." Before the police could reach her house, the woman telephoned it was all a mistake—she had only been hysterical. In the meantime, too late to be stopped, presses had begun to rumble and roar and belch forth flaming sheets of alarm, the ink smearing in its freshness. Others followed, "SECOND ASSAULT," "THIRD ASSAULT," "FOURTH ASSAULT."

At first it was a gentle murmur of hatred. Then it began to swell. Papers were snatched eagerly from panting newsboys. Over the shoulders of each purchaser hung a group, standing on tiptoe to grasp the story of the latest outrage. The grumbling grew. Little flames of violent words shot up. They grew in number. They shot higher. They combined in volume until one great peal of implacable Negrophobia went up like the din of a continuous thunderclap, like a pipe organist treading angrily on his foot-pedals in dissonant roaring. The entire city was as a huge boil, packed tight with putrescence. A pin-prick was applied, the festering, purulent tumour burst open and flung high its venom. Spattering, smearing, befouling matter came down and sprang, like the sown dragon's teeth, into howling, murder-bent mobs. . . .

Jean and Mimi had noted the little knots of angry men gathered on street corners muttering and cursing. They had hurried past these, hoping that they might safely reach the drug store and return home.

"I don't like the looks of these men," said Jean. "They're in a nasty mood and it wouldn't take much to start trouble."

Here and there they noticed a policeman, paunchy, helmeted, swinging night sticks but doing little to disperse the rapidly growing crowds. It was with a deep sigh of relief that Jean reached the drug store. They had to wait nearly an hour

FLIGHT

while the prescriptions were being filled. Leaving the store, they found the embers had burst into flame. A huge man, shirt-sleeved and collarless, his eyes bloodshot and venomous, was perched high on a box haranguing the crowd, which swayed and eddied ,and shouted approval of the speaker's remarks.

Fascinated, Jean and Mimi stood in the doorway and watched the spectacle. "Five Points," the intersection of five heavily travelled streets, was rapidly becoming filled with a milling, motley throng. Other speakers ascended hastily improvised rostrums, the tail end of a delivery wagon, a fire hydrant, the projecting ledge of a show-window. The movement of the crowd became swifter, the blood lust was roused, the killer was eager for the victim. . . .

A Negro was seen walking down Marietta Street, one of the five thoroughfares focusing in Five Points, unaware apparently of the scene he was approaching. Mimi saw him and wanted to shout a warning to him. It would have been fruitless—the roar was too great and her voice would have been as the falling of a single drop of water on the shore while near-by boomed the surf. It would have been almost suicidal—the pack might easily have turned on them. Nevertheless she wanted to cry out to this unknown man to flee. It was too late. One man in the crowd spied him just as Mimi saw him, just as she uttered a little scream of terror. Up went the roar, "There's a nigger now!"

Too late the Negro saw his danger. He turned to flee but before he had gone many yards the pack was upon him. Mimi saw him strike out, dodge, attempt to elude his attackers. It was useless. Down he went and a great bellow of hatred, of passion, of sadistic exultation filled his ears as he died. Mimi covered her eyes with her hands and pressed close to Jean as she saw the flashing jack-knives.

She was never able to tell, even in her own thoughts, what

[73]

happened to her in that terrible moment. To her before that dread day, race had been a relative matter, something that did exist but of which one was not conscious except when it was impressed upon one. The death before her very eyes of that unknown man shook from her all the apathy of the past. There flashed through her mind in letters that seared her brain the words, "I too am a Negro!" . . .

"Come on, Mimi, we've got to get out of this!"

Jean's words made her uncover her face. From near-by Decatur Street, thoroughfare of saloons and dives, of pawn-shops and rooming-houses, of cheap restaurants and tailor shops, there came the crash of breaking glass.

"They're breaking into the pawnshops to get weapons," was Jean's correct conjecture. Here—there—everywhere the howling mobs rushed. Street cars were stopped, Negroes pulled from them, stabbed, kicked, beaten to death. Few shots were fired—the quarters were too close—some member of the mob might get hurt.

A shout went up that made all others seem puny. Out of a side street lurched a carriage drawn by two horses. On the box there half crouched a white man. Taut reins in left hand, in the right he held a long, winding, cruel-looking whip. In the back crouched two frightened Negroes. On and on the carriage swayed and rushed. The driver with one motion lashed the foaming horses, with almost the same sweep he swung backwards and across at the yelling men who sprang at the carriage like starving wolves at a dangling carcass.

Shouts of pain and fury from the lashed, who fell back, huge welts on their faces, mingled with the pounding of the horses' hoofs. Above it all there came a piercing yell from the driver, an obbligato of exultation and challenge welling above the deeper-throated rumble of the crowd. Breathlessly Jean and Mimi followed the carriage as far as they could see it,

[74]

FLIGHT

a prayer in their hearts for the escape of the three. There
came a subtle change in the sounds growing fainter in the distance. A note of bafflement entered the deeper tones. A final
roar of disappointment told them the carriage had escaped
with its human burdens, and happiness filled them.

Clutching Mimi's hand, Jean cautiously sped from doorway
to doorway as the crowd, lessened by those who had gone in
pursuit of the carriage, thinned out. Across the broad expanse
of Marietta Street they scurried. Once they crouched in a
doorway while a crowd sped in pursuit of a crippled Negro
bootblack who hopelessly sought to distance his pursuers. He
fell, the mob atop him. Mimi screamed. A member of the
mob heard her, turned and thrust his face into Jean's. He
snatched off Jean's hat and peered into his face in the dim
light.

In terror, Jean lapsed into French.

"Mon Dieu!" he cried, in dismay.

" 'Scuse me, brother! I thought you were a nigger!"
apologized Jean's tormentor, handing Jean his hat. . . .

On they sped, down Peachtree Street, to Auburn Avenue,
down Auburn Avenue to Pryor Street. There, as they started
to cross, a shout welling into a roar made them draw back
into the shelter of a doorway. Up Pryor Street sped a young,
well-dressed Negro. Inch by inch, foot by foot, yard by yard
he gained on his pursuers. One by one he left them behind
until only one was near him. Here was one who ran as swiftly
as the intended victim. Mimi and Jean saw the Negro glance
over his shoulder. From his pocket they saw him take a
pocket-knife and open it. In so doing he lost a few feet.
As the two racing figures were abreast the hiding-place of
Jean and Mimi, the pursuer lunged forward, clutching at the
shoulders of the Negro to drag him to the earth. Twisting,
turning, the Negro plunged the knife to its hilt in the

[75]

breast of his pursuer, who gasped, groaned and ludicrously sank to the ground. Without pausing, the Negro turned down Auburn Avenue and soon was lost in its shadows. . . .

The mob rushed up, gathered around the victim, peered indecisively down the street where the Negro had fled, discussed and voted against following him as the street led to the Negro section. A cry went up. Another victim had been sighted. Off it sped its death cry again in full volume. Down the street and home scurried Jean and Mimi, weak with fright and the horror of the scenes they had witnessed. . . .

All during Sunday and Monday the three remained at home. Reports came to them of bloody fighting in South Atlanta, of Negroes in despair fighting bravely and successfully to check the mobs, of the coming of troops. The ghastly episode ended, slowly the town returned to its normal state. To Mimi there came whenever she remembered it a chill terror that almost became unconsciousness. In the still hours of the night she would awaken from a sound sleep screaming with terror which turned on awakening into hysterical sobbing until Jean came to her and comforted her. The healing brought alone by time lessened her spasms, but many days passed before she could smile again.

CHAPTER VI

MIMI dated thereafter her consciousness of being coloured from September, nineteen hundred and six. For her the old order had passed, she was now definitely of a race set apart. At times this created within her moods of introspection which veered dangerously near the morbid. At other times it inculcated a deep and passionate scorn of those who were her own and her race's oppressors. She chuckled when she read or heard of or saw their imbecilities, their shortcomings. She looked with scorn on their provincialism, their stupidity, their ignorance. Conversely, she found herself magnifying the virtues, the excellencies of her own people and, at the same time, she tried to explain away through a process of subtle sophistry all their faults.

In time the continuation of these practices began to work a decided and noticeable change in her outlook on life in general. She found herself in time thinking of practically all things, it mattered not what their nature nor how remotely connected with race or colour problems they were, in terms of race or colour. This distorted vision seriously handicapped her but she was unaware of it for it coincided so completely with the viewpoints of her friends. "Poor white trash" became the ultimate of scorn, of contumely, of disparagement. In marked contrast with her former jovial and friendly manner she became almost malicious in little cruelties to tradesmen, to hucksters, to clerks in stores who happened to be white. In these episodes she took acute delight in the fact that her cream-coloured skin, her Gallic name and her French accent gave her immunities she might not have possessed had she been more distinctly Negro.

When first she had come to Atlanta she had been captiously critical of the foibles and petty vices of her new friends. She had recoiled from their bearing of tales, their tearing down of reputations on scanty and imperfect reports of alleged shortcomings. She had hated the obsession of the men on the making of money, the vying of woman with woman in dress, in grandeur of entertainment and of homes. But with the passing of years and particularly after the scenes she had witnessed in the rioting, she began to take these as a matter of course and she found they no longer shocked nor annoyed her. She did not know if she were becoming inured to the new order, if she were succumbing to the new point of view.

Her association with Jean and the lack of contact in her youth with children of her own age had given her a maturity of mind far in advance of her years. She was pained now when she realized that her talks with Jean were becoming more and more infrequent and when they did come they were somewhat less understanding than they had been before. Her sense of loyalty kept her from thinking consciously that Jean was being rapidly left behind by the procession of events, that she who once had seen life eye to eye with him was far beyond him. But though she would not admit it, nevertheless it was true and therein lay the reason why both he and she sought less and less for the old comradeship which had meant so much to both.

Jean, however, saw with clear eye the changes being wrought in Mimi. Her new attitude towards race grieved him though he fully understood the reasons for that change. He knew that a blind race obsession would materially arrest her development and he deplored its rapid growth. He knew that

argument and direct attack would be of little avail—Mimi's
face on that memorable and terrible night had revealed to
him the bitter travail of soul which was going on underneath.
Nor would he have argued against her feeling of hatred
towards the whites with whom she came into infrequent
contact, had he felt that good would have come of it.

He sought instead to counterbalance it through carefully
casual remarks regarding the genuine worth of this man or
that one, to place in Mimi's hands, or where she would surely
come upon them, articles, newspapers, books which would fill
her mind with beauty and truth. Once it was an excellent
translation of the short stories of Balzac. Another time it was
"The Way of All Flesh." Or a Thomas Hardy novel, though
he kept from her "Tess"—that, he felt, was too—well, a little
too advanced for one of Mimi's tender years. He did not
know that before they had left New Orleans Mimi had spent
many hours locked in her own room while she surreptitiously
devoured (almost literally, her nose was so close to the pages)
the tragedy of Tess. Nor did he know she had read every one
of the morocco-bound volumes of Maupassant he had so carefully placed on the topmost shelf. Now Mimi read (or re-
read) the volumes he gave her, she listened to his long talks
and she answered the questions he at the most unlikely moments would ask her about her reading, for she knew it would
have given him pain had she not done so.

And Jean's strategy was not wholly a failure. It gave Mimi
a sense of almost malicious delight when she found in class-
rooms that she was more or less familiar with a sonnet of
Shakespeare, that she knew who Chaucer was, that Tennyson
was something more than the shadowy figure of a man who
had "written poetry or painted pictures or something." Only
with Hilda did she refrain from stressing, ever so gently, the
advantages she possessed in having chosen a father like Jean.

With Hilda she shared the stories that gave her pleasure, with Jean's permission she loaned Hilda books and therein was built another link between them. . . .

To the trumpet-heralded tune of the martial "God of our fathers, whose almighty hand . . . ," Mimi and Hilda, clad in white, filmy dresses identical of material and design with thirty others, marched forth one sunshiny June morning when the new century had reached its eleventh year. In their hands were clutched rolls of paper, each tied with a bow of ribbon. The required tasks for completion of the normal school course had been done, the seal of official approval was bestowed. There were presents and congratulations, parties and sighs of relief that it was all over.

Jean sat in the throng of parents and relatives in the seats reserved for them, his eyes moist as he watched his tiny Mimi pass another milestone between that day when he had anxiously hovered outside Margot's door and womanhood. As the music rolled its sonorous way upward, growing more and more faint as the huge chorus followed the graduates from the chapel, he lived once more the twenty short years that had so miraculously sped by on winged feet.

It was as though it were yesterday he had stood waiting eagerly for some word from Margot's room. As he had heard her agony he had hated this new-comer who was causing his Margot to descend into the shadows. When finally he had been admitted to the room he had rushed to the bed, refusing even to look at the intruder, and had fallen on his knees weeping bitter tears of suffering and relief. He had taken a solemn oath Margot would never go through the ordeal again, an oath which later the doctor had confirmed as necessary—another child would have killed Margot. . . . The years of happiness the three of them had spent together came back to him. The first step, the first word, the first tooth. Long walks wandering through the old winding streets of New Orleans, little

[80]

fat hands clutching his and Margot's fingers. The first days of school. Margot's illness and death. A sharp pain went through him that shook him like a convulsion.

"What's the matter? Sick?" inquired Mrs. Daquin. "No— I'm all right," he whispered, resenting the intrusion into his reverie of her who had come after Margot.

The years of indecision, days followed by lonely nights when he had sought to achieve oblivion in the mottled green wineglass. Mary. The coming to Atlanta. Years of discontent. Years of unhappiness. He was better off, materially, of course. He had made money, it's true, but he wondered if he would have even held his job had it not been backed by Mary's father with his money and his influence. Good Lord, he had been slowly achieving the respectable status of solid citizenry under the combined urging and guidance of Mary and Mr. Robertson. And what was it all worth? Was any of this petty striving and scrambling worth half the things it took out of you?

And Mimi—she had grown away from him, too. There was between them of course the old affection—he never doubted that for a minute. But the little ways that revealed the bond beneath, they were becoming fewer each passing year. Oh, well, she is young, he thought, while I'm old and away behind the new generation. He was proud of her, nevertheless. As she marched from the chapel and passed successively the long, narrow windows, the sun streaming in had made her beautiful hair burst into a wild, exotic, flaming red beauty. It stood out against the blacks and browns of the heads of the other girls like a radiant setting sun in a sky of rain clouds. He was happy she was so pretty—he hoped she'd be married before he joined Margot. He had watched the little ways, the growth of tiny revealments of the warm blood which coursed beneath Mimi's laughing exterior. He was afraid, terribly afraid, of leaving her alone. Alone? Yes, he con-

[81]

cluded, that's exactly what would be the case if anything happened to me. Mary and Mimi would never agree were he not there. . . .

"Come on, Jean," Mary roused him. "It's all over. . . . Oh, how do you do, Mrs. Lewis? Yes, it's sad, in a way, to see our little Mimi become a young woman right before your very eyes. Yes, she did look nice . . . and she's a dear— Mr. Daquin and I adore her.—Oh, thank you so much, Mr. Thompson.—Where's Mrs. Thompson?—There she is! My dear, that was a beautiful gift you sent. I was just thanking your husband for it but I want to thank you both. . . ."

Here, there, everywhere Mrs. Daquin nodded or flung a cheerful, religiously proper phrase. Jean and Mimi owe all this to me, she was thinking. It was I who brought them into a civilized community. . . .

It was that summer that Carl Hunter came home. Mr. Hunter told Jean why.

"That boy's been there at school all these years, spending money and having a good time. I told him if he flunked any more of his studies he would have to come home and work. I guess he thought I was fooling but he'll see whether I am or not. Either he's going to come back here and work or else I'm through with him."

"Aren't you a little hard on the boy?" Jean ventured to inquire. "He's young yet—hasn't found himself—he'll come around in time. . . ."

"Come around?" Mr. Hunter snorted. "He's twenty-three now, and when I was his age I had been working for six years. No, I'm through coddling him and he's got to strike out for himself or go under. . . ."

It was at a picnic late in June that Mimi saw Carl again. She remembered the curt manner in which he had greeted her at the party years before and she found on seeing him again that she still resented the cavalier way in which he had acted.

She determined to treat him with the same coolness and lack of interest. As he spied her and Hilda a three-piece orchestra began to play in the covered pavilion.

"Hello," he casually greeted them both. Mimi stiffened, it was the same word he had used five years before.

"How do you do?" she questioned but in a tone that said plainly she did not expect nor did she want an answer to her inquiry.

Carl grinned.

"My! You're upstagy. Will you dance with me?"

"Thanks, no. You'd better dance with Hilda," was Mimi's answer as she turned away.

Hilda had stood there, saying nothing, but fighting to keep her eyes free from tears. She felt the electrical current that flashed between the two of her friends—heavily charged with antagonism—but Hilda was too wise to let that ill feeling reassure her. His five years' absence had not changed Carl— she knew he cared no more for her now than he did then. And here was Mimi, the only girl with whom she had ever felt completely happy, the girl she loved passionately, catching and holding Carl's interest and attention. Hilda knew Mimi was not doing so deliberately. She knew Mimi too well to believe that. She knew, too, Mimi would rather have done almost anything than hurt her. Despite these reassurances of herself Hilda felt the first bitterness in her heart against her friend, the first twinges of jealousy. Her pride was hurt, it was true, but beneath that and far deeper was the pain caused by the sudden realization that Carl had never been, was not now, and never would be interested in her. She wanted to cry, to dash madly through the woods near-by, to get away from everybody and everything and cry until no more tears would come.

All this raced through her mind at Mimi's words. She smiled bravely.

"No—no. I don't want to dance," she lied cheerfully. "You two go ahead."

She watched them leave trying hard to keep from herself the certainty that her best and dearest friend had created in an instant, with two or three meaningless words, an interest which she had hoped and dreamed she would arouse. It was hard —terribly hard. Consciously, she held Mimi blameless. But underneath it was a bitterness, a feeling almost of nausea, a pain that made her think of the Spartan youth smiling while his abdomen was being gnawed underneath his tunic or shirt or whatever they wore in those days. The figure gave her a bit of cold comfort. She toyed with the idea, turning it over and over in her mind as she went and sat silent with her mother. . . .

Mimi was wholly unaware of the emotions she and Carl had roused in Hilda. She knew of Hilda's carefully shielded affection for him, but she had been so absorbed in her own reactions towards him she had neither noticed the expression on Hilda's face during the brief episode nor had she caught the too elaborately casual way in which Hilda had urged her to dance with Carl. As she walked with him towards the pavilion all her old resentment against him surged through her. She detested his cool and aloof superiority, his calm assumption that she would gladly dance with him. Carl too was silent. His thoughts were of this girl who was Mimi, yet was not the Mimi he had only casually noticed before. Her flaming hair intrigued him, he had always loved that torch-like shade of gold and red. And she had a temper, too. That was fine—he liked folks to show some spirit.

They danced. Mimi loved to dance. She found herself forgetting her resentment, she had to keep reminding herself that she was angry. And Carl did dance well. No stepping awkwardly all over her feet as did most of the other boys. The big bass fiddle moaned. The violin chirped.

FLIGHT

The mandolin pertly strummed. Every few minutes the players joined in the song. From near at hand came the smells of meat being barbecued. With it mingled the fragrancy of pines and the shout of children. It was going to be hard to remain aloof.

The music stopped. Its spell broken, she found her resentment rising. But Carl only stood and grinned happily at her.

"That's the best dance I ever had," he announced.

"How many times and to how many different girls have you said that?" she countered.

"Many, many times and to countless girls! But I meant it each time I said it."

At any rate he didn't protest he had never said such a thing before.

"Shall we sit over there and talk? I'd like to," he asked, simply.

They sat down and watched the crowd. Over near the pavilion sat a little cluster of middle-aged women, heads close together but not so close that they missed anything going on around them.

"The anvil chorus commences," Carl commented, nodding his head at the group. "The old tabbies will now proceed to dissect every soul around here."

"Oh, they mean no real harm. Why bother about them? That's about all they care about," Mimi easily remarked.

"Why? The hit dog yelps. They've begun again on me right where they left off when I went away to school nearly six years ago. I am discovering that I'm an extremely worthless fellow—I smoke cigarettes, I don't see much use in going to church and listening to a lot of platitudes about religion mixed with bum philosophy and worse science—the direct opposite of most of the things I learned in school. I haven't sense enough to listen to it and keep my mouth shut—

[85]

I go around mouthing my own disagreement with a lot of ignorant preachers!"

"Why go to the trouble of expressing your own opinions? Why not ignore the things that annoy you by their falseness? It would be much easier——"

"Ignore them? Lord, I've tried a thousand times and just when I think I've tied my tongue, out pops an objection and I'm in hot water again. My dad's disgusted with me—he says I'm a conceited, useless young fool and I'm more than half-way inclined to believe he's right. He's yanked me out of college 'cause I flunked math and physics again even though I did fairly well in languages and literature and one or two other things. He says I've got to go to work in the insurance business or he's going to wash his hands of me."

"What makes you so restless—makes you kick against the traces all the time?" Mimi found herself taking delight in siding with Mr. Hunter against Carl.

"I don't know," Carl answered, a faint note of bafflement, almost of despair, creeping into his voice. "All my life I've been just what you called me—a kicker. I've tried to conform—but all the time I find myself saying: 'Is *that* so?' when some greybeard starts to lecture me. And most of the things that everybody accepts as axiomatic, as truths never to be questioned, seem to me false and absolutely without value. In college I ran across a passage one day from Spinoza that fits it exactly where he says that 'truths are the falsehoods grown hoary with age.' "

"You're just pessimistic—you'll settle down in time," counselled Mimi, finding herself interested in spite of herself.

Carl picked up her words.

"Pessimistic! Settle down! I've heard those words with variations a thousand times! Why should I settle down? If I'd only work like a slave for ten or fifteen years, make some money, marry some respectable but dull girl who'd have a lot

[86]

of babies and get fat in a few years, and then drop into a rut from which I'd never get out, then I'd meet the approval of all those tabbies over there as a 'fine, upright, Christian young man'!" His last five words were filled with distaste for the respectability the community wished for him.

"I don't want a lot of money," he went on vehemently. "I want to see things and live things and—and——" He peered at Mimi, somewhat doubtfully and hesitantly, then blurted it out as though he expected to be spanked: "write." It was almost a shout of defiance. To Mimi there was much of the childish in his gesture of defiance, but there was also something fine about it. The burden of the conversation of the other boys of her acquaintance usually was: "When I'm making such-and-such a number of dollars" or "When I'm a doctor and have established a big practice." Carl interested her much more than she had believed he would. Indeed, she had not thought about his interesting her. There was something of her own spirit in his defiance of local *mores*, his words made her realize just how deeply she herself had sunk into the rut of conventional standards.

"But why can't you write or do whatever you want to do and at the same time work in your father's insurance business?" she asked sympathetically. "We're living in a material world—money *is* necessary—and you don't have to sell your soul simply to earn a living, do you?"

"The whole thing gives me a pain and I hate it—I hate it!" was his answer. "All I've heard since I've been back is a lot of men telling dirty stories and confessing the loss of their sexual powers by boasting of their amorous adventures. If it isn't that, it's these old women spitting out lies about every woman who isn't present. I've gotten to the place I wince every time I hear something nice about a person—I know it's liable to be only the preface to a whopping big story tearing that same person to pieces."

[87]

"You're exaggerating—you're letting a handful give you an obsession that puts the same stamp on all of them," she protested. "There are lots of women and men who'd fit into neither of the classes you've given."

"I know it—there are lots of folks like Mrs. Adams, for example, and Hilda, but the trouble is they're the kind who attend to their own affairs. It's this other kind that sets the example and they're the ones who do the talkng you've got to listen to. . . . Say, I guess we'd better not sit here too long or they'll begin talking about you."

"Let 'em," retorted Mimi, and she was rewarded by his smile of thanks.

"Nope. You can't afford it. But you're the only person I know I could have talked to like this and who'd have understood. . . ."

Hilda sat beside her mother, silent for a long time. Seldom did her eyes leave Mimi and Carl. Though she could not hear what they were saying, she knew from the absorbed, eager way they were talking they had found some subject of deep mutual interest. To her their blissful ignoring of others was as excruciating as though red-hot irons were being applied to her own flesh. At first she furiously rejected the thought that Mimi was deliberately seeking to attract Carl. As the distant conversation continued she began to toy idly with the notion, turning it over and over in her mind, though it pained her, much as one will constantly probe a sore tooth with one's tongue.

Then she hugged the belief closely to her, firm in the conviction Mimi was maliciously trying to take Carl—her, Hilda's, Carl—away from her. She knew this wasn't true, she hated herself for her distrust of her friend. But back she went each time to that same distrust which bordered dangerously near hatred. It was like meeting a person afflicted with some facial or bodily affliction, a hare-lip or a glass eye, determining not to notice the deformity, yet fascinatedly unable to keep one's gaze from returning to the very thing one determined not to watch.

Hilda was all the more ashamed of her feeling toward Mimi because, so far as Carl knew, there was no reason why Hilda should have any claim upon him. There had never been any word of love between them, he had always been rather fond of her in an off-hand way, had called her, as long as she could remember, "Little Sister." She hated the term not alone because it seemed to her banal but more because of the mild affection it implied, vastly inferior in intensity to her own emotion. Reason, however, plays but small part when one's love is concerned, thought Hilda, and she returned to her brooding. . . .

"It seems to me you're making a mistake," Mimi meanwhile was saying to Carl. "You keep harping on the way the women here gossip—that's no practice peculiar only to Atlanta and the folks you and I know. Women do that everywhere, it seems to me, and I often think men do more gossiping than women. Does it ever occur to you there are a lot of things on the other side of the shield?"

"That's the only reason I came back here," Carl eagerly replied, the look of morbid unrest changing quickly to one of alert cheerfulness. "When I get most pessimistic about our own folks all I need to cheer me up is to look at unhappiness of white people. You ever notice that no matter how hard the luck he may be in, the Negro can laugh and sing and forget all his worries? They call it shiftlessness and laziness but, Lord, when I see the terribly unhappy way these white people live, so busy making money and keeping 'the nigger in his place,' I think we're mighty well off. Say, would you like to go with me sometime to a camp-meeting

[89]

or some of these other places where you'll see the thing that's kept the Negro from being wiped out—this thing they call 'spirit' or 'soul' of the race?"

"I'd love to," answered Mimi as they walked back towards where Hilda was sitting. Hilda was able to manage a smile but Mimi noticed all during the day that she was strangely silent and aloof. The first coolness of consequence during their friendship had come between them. Mimi was at first puzzled and wondered what might have caused it. Then she remembered Hilda's shy admissions of her interest from childhood in Carl. Mimi knew then, or rather she sensed, the reason for Hilda's attitude. Mimi said nothing to her, knowing the unwisdom of mentioning the subject and fearing that the breach might be widened if she spoke of it. And, being human, Hilda's pouting irritated her.

"She's silly," thought Mimi, "getting angry with me simply because Carl and I talked for a few minutes. If that's the kind of friend she is——" Mimi did not complete the thought but she felt vaguely amused and annoyed at Hilda. At the same time she looked forward to talking with Carl again. He was different. . . .

CHAPTER VII

To Mimi there was no more fascinating thing in the life she saw around her than the song, the laughter, the deep religious faith and the spontaneous humanity of the people of whom she was now a part. In New Orleans she had been stirred by the music which had a distinctive Negro note but which had been influenced to a definite extent by French songs that made it a sort of Africanized French. Here she felt much more vividly the rhythmic surge and sweep of the Negro music untouched by other influences—the ecstatic pouring forth of melodies that often were not melodies but a wild and intoxicating thing that made little chills run up and down her spine and filled her eyes with tears. With Carl she came upon new phases of this life in out-of-the-way places which had hitherto been unknown to her. She began to see and understand the deep spirituality which lay back of this people of hers, to comprehend the gifts which had enabled them to withstand oppression which would long since have crushed a weaker race.

The day when a convict gang began to repair the street in front of their home was one Mimi never forgot. She awoke hearing a wild, plaintive, poignantly simple melody so strange she thought herself yet asleep. Drawn by the music, she dressed hastily and hurried to see from whence it came. In the street a strange sight met her eyes. A crowd of Negro convicts, clad in the broad-striped and ill-fitting garb of rough material, huge balls of iron attached to their ankles by heavy chains, were tearing up the street with synchronized strokes of their pickaxes. Up and down the sidewalks strode

[91]

the guards, sawed-off shotguns on their shoulders. One of these was a stalwart fellow with stooped shoulders, unshaven, his mouth stained by the tobacco he constantly chewed. Another was of shorter and stockier build, equally unshaven and tobacco-stained, one eye missing, the empty socket shrunken until it gave his face a curiously unbalanced and evil look.

Up and down the guards strode, keeping ever-watchful eyes upon their charges, who worked and sang, apparently in blissful ignorance of guards or toil or any external thing. Occaionally one would stop for a drink of water brought by a remarkably ragged young Negro who nearly all the time was playing when he was most needed. The thirsty one would dawdle, invent all sorts of ingenious methods of delaying, take as long as he could in assuaging his thirst. If the operation consumed too much time there would come a warning from one of the guards, ominous, threatening, but shaken off as lightly as the water from the proverbial duck.

The convicts were of all shades and sizes and shapes. In the awkward garb they were a ludicrous, ill-assorted lot. Some there were with the shifty, roving eyes of tricksters. Others wore on their faces the hall-mark of the criminal of dangerous type. The faces of a few of these bore livid scars of varying lengths gained by knifings in desperate fights. But to Mimi most of the men were kindly of expression, were obviously those arrested and convicted on petty charges because the city needed them or men like them to work its streets.

There was one item only in which this motley crowd was as one. A stalwart Negro with a ringing barytone led them in the song which had awakened Mimi. On and on he sang, verse after verse of a wildly sweet and simple song, joined in the chorus by the others. Like the beat of a giant metronome there came a grunting "Hunh!" as the shining points of

FLIGHT

the pickaxes were plunged into the red clay. There was little
rhyme and little melody in the song, but rhythmically it was
without flaw.

> "Oh, she ast me—hunh!—in de parlour—hunh!
> An' she cool me—hunh!—wid her fan—hunh!
> An' she whispered—hunh!—to her mammy—hunh!
> 'Mammy, I love dat—hunh!--dark-eyed man—hunh!
> Well, I ast her—hunh!—mammy for her—hunh!
> An' she said she—hunh!—was too young—hunh!
> Lawd, I wish'd I'd—hunh!—never seen her—hunh!
> An' I wish'd she'd—hunh!—never been bawn—hunh!
> Well, I led her—hunh!—to de altar—hunh!
> An' de preacher—hunh!—made us one—hunh!
> An' she swore by—hunh!—God that'd made her—hunh!
> She'd never love—hunh!—another man—hunh! . . ."

Mimi's heart beat faster and faster as she watched and
listened. She sensed that the song carried the toilers far
above their miserable lot. For them the toil and sweat, the
louring guards who shouted staccato commands or flung crisp
oaths when one of the convicts slackened or appeared to
slacken in his labour, did not exist. She began to comprehend the thing Carl had said to her of the "over-soul" the
Negro possessed. . . .

"Look at some of these coloured folks around you," he had
said to her, "most of them poor, having to work like dogs
for a meagre living, deprived of practically every ordinary
outlet in the way of amusement. Are they depressed, morbid,
bitter? Not on your life! They can find amusement where
nobody else can. But look at the white folks who are just
about as bad off financially—they're grouchy and morose,
hating everybody on earth and themselves most of all though
they don't know it."

Mimi could see, though as yet with some difficulty, just what
Carl had meant. She wondered if she were in such a plight
as these convicts if she could have had the courage to sing.

[93]

She was afraid she would not have been that optimistic—she doubted that she could have used song even as an opiate to forget hard circumstance as these men were doing. She marvelled at their toughness of fibre which seemed to be a racial characteristic, which made them able to live in the midst of a highly mechanized civilization, enjoy its undoubted advantages, and yet keep free that individual and racial distinctiveness which did not permit the surrender of individuality to the machine.

In slavery it had kept them from being crushed and exterminated as oppression had done to the Indian. In freedom it had kept them from becoming mere cogs in an elaborately organized machine. Some people called it shiftlessness, laziness, inherent racial inferiority. Mimi herself at times had heard these charges made and frequently she had believed them and had been ashamed of them, especially during the years she had lived in Atlanta and particularly since that terrible night during the riot. The forced growth of her race-conscious attitude had accelerated this shamedness of her people's apparent lack of assimilation by industrialism—now she began to feel glad that this was so.

She wished she could make up her mind just what she would have them be. When she listened to Mr. Hunter and the type of hustling, progressive, acquisitive men which he represented, she doubted seriously the wisdom of the Negro's doing anything other than acquire wealth, forge ahead in business and commerce and manufacture as many of them were doing. But when she talked with Carl or, more strongly, when she heard Negroes sing or laugh, she wondered which road would lead to greater happiness.

On Communion Sundays she went through the same process of ratiocination. The passing of the bread and wine after the sermon, the bread hard and tasteless, the wine in a huge silver cup passed from hand to hand, was followed always by a silent prayer ending with the singing of a Spiritual, "Were You There When They Crucified My Lord?" She never forgot the emotions which the song created within her as plaintive, eerily sweet, stirring verse after verse winged its way through the small church and lost itself among the age-stained rafters. For years afterward the song made her imagine she had pains in her neck and back, for the song was always sung bent forward in prayer. It was with this weariness that she associated the terrifyingly real agony of Jesus which the words evoked. "Were You There When They Nailed Him to the Tree?" "When They Pierced Him in the Side?" "When He Bowed His Head and Died?" "When They Laid Him in the Tomb?"

Verse after verse told with terrible inevitableness the grim story of His agony and sacrifice and to Mimi she lived each time she heard the song the tortures of the Crucified One. Always she longed for them to come to the verses of hope and happiness, when they rolled away the stone, when He rose from the dead. The rising and falling "Oh—oh—oh—oh——" which preceded the wail, "Sometimes it causes me to tremble—tremble—tremble," changed now from dolour and pity and pain to an exultant, happy pæan of exuberant joy in the resurrection. Always Mimi was glad to reach the open air outside—the song did too many things to her down inside. Afterwards she felt as though she had been the victim of some peculiar metempsychosis—that during the minutes of the song her soul had taken flight from her own body to that of some other rarer, more sentient, more delicately strung being of infinite beauty and understanding, to return only when the spell had been broken.

The other spirituals worked spells upon her of varied kinds. Carl took her frequently to out-of-the-way churches, some of them housed in miserably poor, ramshackle edifices, others in more pretentious buildings. In them all she found that

[95]

deep earnestness, that abiding faith and hope and patience which she found herself able more and more to understand. Humble, simple folk most of the worshippers were, with envy and malice and smallness like all other humans, but blessed with that rare gift of lifting themselves emotionally and spiritually far, far above their material lives and selves. She was filled with inarticulate rage when she sensed all too often that the preacher was far inferior to his flock, that he played upon their emotions and fears and hopes only to earn for himself a comfortable livelihood free from too much toil. These leeches, fattening on the sacrifice of washerwomen and other humble ones who worked terrifically hard to earn their small wage, stirred in Mimi and Carl the desire to wreak some sort of vengeance upon them. Their rage usually resulted in avoiding such churches and there were many to which they never went a second time for this reason. Mimi soon was convinced she had found an accurate measuring-rod of worth in Negro preachers—the worse the preacher, the longer the coat he wore.

But they did not confine their visits to churches. Carl took her to parties where usually to the music of a three or four-piece orchestra of strings they danced or watched others dance with a lissom grace and abandon that intoxicated them like old, rare wines. Among all sorts and classes of their own people they rambled, oblivious of the criticism that came to them occasionally. The storm was rising though they did not know it. It broke with disturbing fury when one night Carl suggested they go to what he termed a "honky-tonky" dance. To Mrs. Daquin's rather sharp inquiry regarding her destination, Mimi answered shortly that that was her own affair, and she thought no more of the matter at the time.

The dance was held in a small, poorly lighted and ventilated hall. The floor was so crowded they did not attempt to dance but sat and watched the others as they somewhat noisily but gaily swung and swayed about the floor. Carl acted as guide, interpreter, expositor.

"That's what they call the 'eagle rock,' " as he pointed to a dusky couple whose shoulders swayed in a fascinatingly free, peculiar rhythm. Many years afterwards when Mimi saw blonde chorus girls on Broadway swaying their shoulders and bodies as these two were doing, she remembered always where she had first seen it done. "Those two over there are 'ballin' the jack,' " Carl explained as he pointed in the throng to another couple whose knees were in motion in contrast to the shoulders of the first pair. Here, there, all around the hall he pointed out to the fascinated Mimi the originality of the dancers, moving according to no set form other than their own impulses as stirred by the weird, feet-moving strains of the Negro orchestra.

And the orchestra was doing its share with the same joy as the dancers, as though it too had paid its way in for the pleasure of playing. Carl explained that practically none of its members had ever taken a music lesson, none of them knew anything about the theory of music.

"They've just got instinct and rhythm—and, well, what else do they need?" he ended with a smile.

Mimi had never known that anything like this existed before. Over it all there was a primitive note, a freedom from inhibitions that gave grace and ecstasy to the dancers and the musicians. It exhilarated one and made him forget the stuffiness and dimness of the hall and the sometimes fetid smells which arose as the dance went on. She knew that here was something original—she could not explain it nor could she tell how or why she felt that here was a vital and living thing. She only knew it had a vibrant, warming quality, and that was enough.

"Remember Dunbar's lines?" Carl asked. Without waiting for a reply he recited them softly:

FLIGHT

"Cripple Joe, de ole rheumatic, danced that flo' frum side to middle.
Throwed away his crutch an' hopped it, what's rheumatics 'gainst a
fiddle?
Eldah Thompson got so tickled dat he lak to los' his grace,
Had to take bofe feet an' hold 'em, so's to keep 'em in deir place.
An' de Christuns an' de sinnahs got so mixed up on dat flo',
Dat I don't see how dey's pahted ef de trump had chonced to blow."

She smiled appreciatively at the quotation.

"It does just that to you," she remarked. "I'm seeing better every day just what you mean." . . .

It was not chance that caused Mrs. Plummer and Mrs. King to see Mimi and Carl as they left the hall. Always they took a short cut homewards from prayer meeting which carried them past the two-storied brick building which housed on its top floor the hall.

"Look there, Mis' King!" whispered Mrs. Plummer. "Ain't that that Day-quinn girl with that Carl Hunter coming outa that joint?"

"It's her, sho's you born," Mrs. King assured her. "I told you she'd bear watching. Playing off respectable and going in such places——"

"That's just what I say," eagerly put in Mrs. Plummer, determined that her friend should not get ahead of her in the discovery made by her own sharp eyes. "An' her ma's such a good woman—though they tell me she ain't her own ma, only her step-ma. But you remember I tol' you befo' they come here you couldn't depen' on these here Cath'lics—I'm a good Methodist and I ain't got much use for Baptists but they're regular Christians, anyhow——" Mrs. Plummer shook with quick breaths, the combined result of her eagerness and the speed at which Mrs. King was hurrying down the street so that she could keep the couple ahead within sight.

"That girl's headed straight for trouble—carrying on like that!" Mrs. King affirmed. "Hurry up, can't you? I want to see where they're going *now!*"

[98]

FLIGHT

"Ain't I hurryin' as fast's I can?" Mrs. Plummer grumbled. "And ain't I as anxious as you to follow 'em? Oh! They've gone in her house," she complained, a note that closely approximated disappointment in her tone. The chagrin was deepened a minute later when she saw Carl leave and turn down the street towards his own home. . . .

It was Hilda who first told Mimi of the talk that was being spread about her and Carl. Mrs. Daquin had heard it, too, and had spoken to Jean about it, demanding that he forbid Mimi from seeing Carl again. This Jean had hesitated about doing. He trusted Mimi implicitly and he was fond of Carl. He had liked him ever since the day on which Mr. Hunter had confided in Jean his disappointment at Carl's failure to show a keener interest in the insurance business.

With Hilda it had been different. When the story put into circulation by the Mesdames Plummer and King had first come to her, she had undergone a variety of emotions. First was indignation against those who dared say anything against Mimi. She resented, too, any disparagement of Carl for whom her affection, unexpressed though it yet remained, had grown instead of decreased since he had begun to show so deep an interest in Mimi.

And, being human, she found herself just a little bit glad this had come to them. She had two reasons for this feeling, the first of them being summed up in the words, "It serves them right!" Had Hilda cared less for Mimi and Carl, her momentary elation on hearing that they were being talked about would have been far slighter, if indeed she had felt the emotion at all. The very intensity of her passionate love for them both made her capable of greater cruelty, a vindictiveness that bordered on gloating over their descent into disfavour. A second reason for her fleeting satisfaction was wrapped in the possibility that through some means, she knew not what, there might come a break in the friendship between Carl and Mimi.

[99]

Then she would, if the fates were kind, gain the interest and perhaps later the deeper affection for herself which she was sure Carl was lavishing on Mimi. Who can tell? she reflected; stranger things than that have happened.

As soon as this emotion became a conscious one, Hilda furiously rejected it as treachery of the basest kind to her friends. Filled with remorse, she rushed to see Mimi, fearing a return of the unworthy feeling. Her task there was made less easy by the somewhat cool manner in which Mimi greeted her. A very decided chilliness had entered into their hitherto warm relations which they both very distinctly dated from that day of the picnic early in the summer. Hilda through an essential honesty that governed all she did or thought found herself unable to act towards Mimi with the old cordiality and, to save both of them embarrassment, had stayed away from Mimi as much as she could. Mimi noticed this change and wondered what had caused it. Vaguely she felt it was due to her own friendship with Carl but she could not see why this should affect Hilda—it was only a friendship and nothing more. She had become vexed with Hilda and hurt that Hilda by her actions had shown there was a certain distrust of Mimi's loyalty. Thus the breach had widened and the intense pride of the two had kept each from making any advance that might have closed it.

The two girls faced each other, praying for an opening while they talked of little and unimportant things which served, rather ineffectually, as a mask for their real feelings. Ineffectually, for both knew the other was eager for some chance phrase, some little thing, which might put them at ease. Five—ten—fifteen minutes passed. They still talked of inconsequentialities. The air was becoming more tense. They each longed, ached desperately, for some way out of the difficult situation between them. Hilda began to wish she had

not come, to think of excuses for leaving, her mission un-
fulfilled.

It was Mimi who in desperation and uneasiness broke the
spell.

"You've been acting queerly all summer, Hilda," she challenged. "Why have you acted so?" She hated herself for
the awkward way in which she had spoken, the almost bel-
ligerent note in her voice when she had intended to speak with
utmost casualness.

"Why?" Hilda echoed. "Don't you know why?"

"No—I can't see—— Has it anything to do with Carl?"
she blurted out, knowing, as she spoke, it had wholly to do
with Carl.

Hilda flushed and twisted her hands. Now that it was out,
she felt a sense of nakedness, of being stripped bare and forced
to walk through crowded streets, as she had often dreamed—
a dream that always awoke her with fright. Even to her
mother, close as she was to her, and to Mimi she had never
dared reveal the extent of her love for Carl. A natural shyness and a fear of being made or thought ridiculous had
forced her to keep her real feeling to herself. Now that Mimi
had put it into words, she wished fervently she had kept to
her former secretiveness. Not knowing the extent to which
Carl's and Mimi's friendship had developed, she felt she had
laid herself open to ridicule. Her perturbation was answer
enough for Mimi.

"But why have you acted as you have?" she pursued the
inquiry. "You of all people ought to know there's nothing
between Carl and me——"

Hilda silenced her with a raising of her hand.

"Tell me—truthfully—Mimi—is that true?"

Her tone was so earnest, so appealing and fraught with
apprehension, Mimi was startled.

[101]

"Of course I am telling you the truth," she answered, irritation creeping into her voice despite her efforts to keep it out. "Don't be silly, Hilda. And you might at least have trusted me."

"I have trusted you—I have trusted you, Mimi, and I've hated myself for ever doubting you, but you know how I've always liked Carl——" she ended miserably.

Mimi's heart filled with pity and her eyes with tears. She clasped Hilda in her arms and Hilda clung to her passionately, pleading through her tears for forgiveness. All the misunderstanding was wiped away and they smiled happily through their tears. It was some time before Hilda could tell her the thing which had brought her. She felt great relief when Mimi merely laughed at the slanderous tales which were going the rounds.

"Oh, I'm not paying any attention to these gossipy old women around here. Why should I? If I had done anything of which I felt ashamed, it might worry me, but why worry one's head over something that doesn't exist? Life's too short for that." . . .

CHAPTER VIII

MIMI went to her room after Hilda had gone, and lay across the bed for a long time in deep thought. Hilda was a silly little goose for her anxiety, she thought, but she must care a great deal more about Carl than she, Mimi, had ever dreamed of. She determined to see Carl, tell him as much as was necessary about Hilda's affection for him, and then refuse to see or go out with Carl herself. It was little enough for her to do for Hilda who had been so loyal a friend. And it would be a service, too, for Hilda's shyness would prevent her from ever indicating to Carl that she cared for him. She herself would hate to break off the companionship with Carl which had come to mean so much to them both and from which she had derived so much. His alert mind appealed to her, the reading he had done and the eager, lovable way in which he rushed to share with her anything he had come across in his reading which he thought would interest her, his keen interest in things other than those right under his nose, his quick and unforetellable changes of mood, at one minute happy and carefree and an excellent companion, at another changing abruptly to a serious-minded, at times morose and dissatisfied individual. With a woman's love for the unusual, the unstable, the unforeseen, she was attracted by these various moods. She had grown tired of most of the other boys of her acquaintance, for she could tell in advance, almost to the exact words, what each of them would say under any given circumstance. She had never had this feeling with Carl and he seemed to be possessed of an unending and never uninteresting variety of humours, most of them of mercurial state.

FLIGHT

But with all these varied characteristics there was among them nothing which even remotely resembled a tendency to become mushily sentimental. Here, too, he was different from the others. Mimi had learned on several unpleasant occasions the proneness of the youth she knew to wax tender often when there was not the slightest provocation or encouragement. Their friendship had never been marred in this fashion and that was the reason, Mimi was certain, it had grown so beautifully and naturally. It had been a frank, eager companionship based on mutual interests and mutual understanding.

No, it would not be easy to give up this friendship, but she owed it to Hilda, who, in her way and as one of her own sex, had been equally if not a better friend than Carl. Certainly their companionship had been of longer duration and therefore made greater demands upon the parties to it. She was glad now there had been no word of love nor even any thought of love between her and Carl. He had never entered her mind in this guise and she could soon forget him.

But could she? The thought made her pause in the smooth course of her reasoning. Now that Hilda had brought the fact tangibly to her consciousness, was it true that her feeling towards Carl was so wholly Platonic? She began to have her doubts. It wouldn't be so easy to give him up as she at first so glibly promised herself and Hilda. Who would there be who could take his place—who could interest her as Carl had done? Knowing the futility of attempting to answer a question when there was in her own mind no question existing, nevertheless she went slowly, painstakingly through the list of all the young men she knew. One by one she discarded them until she came to the point she knew she would reach—only Carl remained.

Rousing herself from the lethargy into which the circle of thought had plunged her, she went back to her original determination to end the companionship at once. She felt like a squirrel who had been madly racing in one of the barbarous, treadmill cages, rushing, but always remaining at the same point. She would give Carl to Hilda—she smiled irrelevantly at the conceit of physically handing over to another one who outweighed her by many pounds—and end the stupid misunderstandings at one time. She smiled again at the gratification of those who had been gossiping about her and Carl—they would smugly congratulate themselves that they had caused her to break off her friendship with him, little knowing how far from the truth they were. Well, let them smile, she concluded.

Mimi went down to supper filled with a warming sense of having done something noble, sacrificial. It pleased her to have this feeling, she almost felt for herself a little of the pity of martyrdom. It was this mood which enabled her to answer Mrs. Daquin's elaborately casual bringing up of the scandal.

"Oh, by the way, Mimi, I've been hearing something about you and Carl Hunter that doesn't sound so nice——" Mrs. Daquin began.

Mimi smiled easily at her, even encouragingly, and went on eating.

This attitude was not at all what Mrs. Daquin had expected. She had looked for tears, violent storms, protestations. In truth, she had feared what might come and her fear had kept her from mentioning for several days the stories she had heard. She had laid her plans for a gentle, casual opening and had steeled herself for an outburst. Mimi's placidity made her feel uncertain, rather foolish.

"Yes?" Mimi inquired sweetly, too sweetly Mrs. Daquin thought, when the opening was not followed up. "Just what did you hear?"

Mrs. Daquin looked appealingly at Jean but he to all out-

ward signs was intently examining the plate of salad before
him. No help obviously to be expected from that quarter,
Mrs. Daquin braced herself and proceeded.

"They're saying you and Carl were seen coming out of a
disreputable dance hall one night last week——"

"It's true. What of it?" broke in Mimi.

"What of it? What of it?" Mrs. Daquin's second interrogation was almost a thin scream. "Jean, do you hear what
your daughter is saying? She brazenly admits she and that
Hunter boy went to a disreputable, vile place and then she
asks: 'What of it?'"

Mrs. Daquin's anger was fast mastering her, despite her
previously determined plan to retain mastery of the situation
through calmness and scorn. Mimi's willing admission of
her guilt, as Mrs. Daquin considered it, had taken some of the
wind out of her sails. Or, better, instead of a strong head
wind Mrs. Daquin's craft had been suddenly assailed by a
veering wind from port. Like an inexperienced sailor she
sought to bring her helm around and steer her boat into waters where there was less danger of squalls.

Jean looked up from his plate and stared hard but in not
unfriendly fashion at Mimi. He answered his wife's question without looking at her.

"Yes, Mary, I heard her. What about it, Mimi?"

"Carl did take me to the dance, papa. I wanted to see
some of these new dances, hear the music, see a side of life
among coloured people I had never seen before. We went
there, we stayed awhile, and then Carl brought me home.
Do you see anything wrong in that, papa Jean?" Mimi ended
calmly.

Before Jean could reply his wife burst in upon the conversation, able no longer to restrain her anger.

"Wrong in it? Mimi, haven't you any sense of decency
at all? Even if you didn't do anything but what you said,

[106]

think of what the neighbours will say! Think of what——"

"I told my father, Mrs. Daquin, what took place, and I'm not in the habit of lying to him," Mimi with cold fury, her eyes flaming with suppressed anger, said. "Furthermore, I resent your words 'even if you didn't do anything but what you said.'"

The two women glared at each other across the table. But Mrs. Daquin's anger was beyond the heeding of the danger signs in Mimi's eyes.

"Young woman, you can't——"

"Mary, keep quiet!" Jean half rose from the table, his hands pressed against it with such force all the blood had fled from his knuckles. "Mimi has told me what happened and that's enough."

Jean's voice held a note which even Mary in her anger could not help but respect and fear.

"But, Jean dear," she pleaded, her tone changing miraculously. "I'm only thinking of our good name——"

"Damn your good name!" the unfamiliar Jean snapped. "I'm sick and tired of your petty bickering with these little folks you're so mad about—these busybodies so worried keeping track of other people and meddling into their affairs. As for this present matter, I want it stopped right here. Whether Mimi acted right or not, she's told us what's happened and that's enough of it. Do you hear me?"

It was a long speech for Jean and it was not often that he permitted himself to become so angry. He did not know it but it gave him the opportunity of expressing his opinion of these aliens, so different to those of his own New Orleans whom he missed more and more. And his nostalgia was none the less potent and painful because he knew that even had he remained in New Orleans he would not have been happy. Just as when a man dies, his good traits or those good traits given him by popular belief are magnified after his death and

FLIGHT

his faults are minimized until they disappear altogether, so
Jean remembered as the years passed only the beauties of New
Orleans and he forgot the changes which had been so largely
instrumental in persuading him to move to Atlanta.

But, though calmed, the fire of Mrs. Daquin's wrath, hotly
burning because she feared any scandal might jeopardize her
own social position, was too great to be quenched even by
Jean's outburst.

"All I've got to say then, Jean, if that's all the thanks I
get for trying to keep our name clean, is that Mimi had better
not see Carl Hunter again, even if he's the son of my best
friend."

Jean was about to speak again angrily, when Mimi stopped
him.

"Neither of you need worry about that—Carl and I won't
see each other again."

Both Jean and his wife looked inquiringly at Mimi and
waited for an explanation but none was forthcoming. But
Mrs. Daquin concluded at this unexpected acquiescence that
there was more to the incident than appeared on the surface.
She privately concluded that Mimi had effectually hood-
winked Jean and that it was fear and guilt which made Mimi
so readily consent to the breaking off of the friendship with
Carl. . . .

Her interview with Carl was not so easy as Mimi had supposed it would be. He came readily enough when she sent
for him. He supposed she wanted to discuss with him the
talk which had come to his ears, too. A look of amazement
came over his face as she quietly told him of her resolve,
followed by an expression that was almost dismay when she
guardedly told him of Hilda's affection for him.

"She likes you, Carl," Mimi ended, "and she's been thinking all summer that I, her best friend, have been trying to
vamp you away from her. She knows now, though, there's

[108]

nothing between us. So for her sake and since this talk's been started, we'd better see less of each other." She added, almost as an afterthought: "I do hate, though, the satisfaction we'll give these old tabbies."

"But, Mimi," Carl protested, his face eloquent of the pain within, "Hilda's an awfully nice kid and I'm fond of her—just as I'm fond of my own sister, Mildred. And I'd like to know who saw us at that dance so I could take one good punch at them!" he added with bitterness.

"It wouldn't do any good—they'd be sure then we'd done something terrible," she counselled.

"Just now, Mimi, you said there's nothing between us. I haven't thought of you that way, Mimi, but—but——" he stammered, trying to take her hand.

"Don't be silly, Carl," Mimi laughed, moving away from him. She felt a sense of guilt, of disloyalty to Hilda that she had phrased it so crudely. As Carl repeated her words she was ashamed of them—they sounded almost as though she had uttered them in the hope of a denial from Carl. "We've had a good time together and I've learned a lot and I'm grateful. You've given me a faith in my own people that I have never had before. Before I came to Atlanta I never thought much about 'white people' or 'coloured people.' I just thought of people as people. And then came that terrible night of the riot. After that I hated all white people and began to think every Negro was perfect even though my common sense told me I was foolish. Now I begin to see the good and the bad, in white people and coloured people—and that's something."

But Carl heard none of the things she was saying. He sat with his face in his hands, his shoulders drooping dejectedly. He raised his head as she finished speaking. Mimi was touched with the look of pain upon it.

"Mimi," he pleaded, "let's forget all this silly talk and

let things go on like they were before. I was wrong in taking you to that hall—it wasn't wrong in itself but wrong in the eyes of these people here—so I shouldn't have let you go. You're the only person here I care about seeing. Oh, Mimi, don't let's break off here. I'm a weak and foolish creature and the only thing that's held me up has been you."

Desperately, despairingly, he pleaded, but Mimi, though she felt herself weakening, steeled herself against the almost overwhelming impulse to take Carl's head into her lap and hold it to her breast as she would a child's. The confident, rebellious man had become a child and the mother instinct, strong within her, almost overpowered her. She found herself swept by a flaming, consuming affection for Carl. Had he remained assertive, sure of himself, she would have mastered it easily. But his self-revilement, his dependency upon her touched her deeply. Love had come to her and now she must put it from her. Loyalty to Hilda and the promise she had made to her demanded it.

"No, Carl," she firmly reiterated her resolution. . . .

CHAPTER IX

THE blazing suns of August and September cooled into the golden haze of Indian summer but its beauties brought little happiness to three young people of Atlanta. Hilda had listened with tearful gratitude to Mimi's recital of her talk with Carl. Hopefully she had waited for some sign of interest, some word, some gesture from Carl, but day followed day and she yet was looking in vain. Languidly she prepared for the opening of school when she would begin her career as teacher, the customary interlude between student days and marriage for the girls to whom custom forbade pursuit of any other calling. Hilda passed through various periods of hope, of despair, of rage against herself, against Mimi, against Carl. At times she consoled herself that all affairs of this sort took time, that she need but wait and then her own excellencies would become so apparent, Carl would see how desirable it would be for him to follow up the opening she had made through Mimi's intercession.

At other times she reviled herself as a hoyden, a brazen creature, a person without shame. Her talk with Mimi assumed gigantic proportions as a stripping bare of all her inner self, shamelessly flaunting her affection for a boy not worth the sacrifice. She castigated herself with all the cruelty of some zealot, crazed by religious fervour, who subjects himself to all manner of barbarities. Tartarus itself nor the Spanish inquisition contained such instruments of torture as those with which unrequited love can flagellate its victims, Hilda learned, and her unhappiness was not lessened by her lack of one in whom she could confide. She

[111]

dared not risk further pain even from her mother, who might not understand, she thought, and whose lightest word would be as salt to a raw, quivering wound if she should speak lightly or with uncomplete understanding. Hilda's conviction that her procedure had been wrong and very unwise, certain to drive Carl further from her than achieve any other end, only added to her unwillingness to confide even in her mother.

She thought several times of talking again with Mimi but each time, upon reflection, she rejected this procedure. As time passed with no sign from Carl other than he seemed to avoid her now almost obviously, she began to harbour a new suspicion of Mimi—she wondered if Mimi had said to Carl exactly what she had told Hilda she had said.

She made for herself greater unhappiness by conjecturing phrases or sentences (or implications in phrases or sentences) that Mimi might have used in talking with him. Especially did such thoughts race through her mind after she had turned out the light at night and crept into her bed. Like a child frightened by ghosts and goblins and weird figments of the disordered brain, she shrank in terror from her own thoughts. She saw herself being laughed at by Carl and Mimi, being ridiculed as a brainless, silly little fool.

Daylight always brought relief from these tortures and regret for having entertained such thoughts. She would then rush as soon as she could to Mimi and try by unexplained little tendernesses to atone for her distrust. Mimi was often puzzled by these outbursts and she wondered what caused them. She was too wise, however, to ask directly—she waited for some voluntary word from Hilda, which Hilda, in her shyness and because she was so thoroughly ashamed of her suspicions, never vouchsafed.

Nor was Mimi so free from her own worries that she could expend much thought on the problems of others. After her dismissal, Carl had resolutely avoided her, his pride too great to permit him to risk a second rebuff at her hands. Three times she had seen him approaching her on Auburn Avenue. Twice he had turned into a side street. Once he had entered a grocery store where she was certain he had no reason for going other than to avoid her. With a woman's perversity of mind, she was annoyed that he should so explicitly obey her command that their friendship be kept on a mere disinterested plane. Mimi had never before been touched by the flaming torch of love nor even of affection despite her volatile and tender nature. The self-imposed abstention from companionship with Carl which had formed, she now discovered, so large a part of her thoughts, was resulting in the steady growth of an interest that before the rupture had been largely an impersonal one. As he continued to avoid her, Mimi determined to tell Carl how foolish she thought him to carry out her quixotic request too literally. Many days passed, though, between the making of the resolution and its execution.

Then one Sunday morning she saw him enter with his mother and sister and father the pew they always occupied near the front of the church. With all the eager impulsiveness of youth in love or youth imagining itself in love, Mimi felt a delightfully pleasant sensation in watching the back of Carl's head, in being near him. She wanted to put in place the rebellious lock of hair which sprang in disarray from the top of Carl's head like the feather from an Indian's head-dress. She wanted eagerly to talk with him again as they used to, she wanted to ramble from subject to subject in that comradely way which she missed now that the talks had been ended. The gossip which had partly led to that abrupt severance of their companionship had died down, though Mimi knew from experience that rumour, apparently dead and forgotten, was many-lived and any misstep of the future could and would resurrect all previous reports. She knew they could arise again and always did, springing into life with new vigour like that mythical being whose name she could never remember who, thrown to earth, received new strength by contact with it, and entered the struggle again invigorated and more powerful than before.

To regain the friendship she had lost, however, she was willing to risk the wagging of tongues. She stood with bowed head watching Carl with irreverently slitted eyes as the services neared their close. "The Grace of our Lord and Saviour, Jesus Christ, the love of God the Father . . . now and for evermore, Amen!" droned the minister, his head tilted back, closed eyes raised to the low-hung ceiling.

The human impulse to talk, to move, to be saying or doing something, anything rather than endure introspection however slight, found gushing release as soon as the minister finished. Cloaks and wraps half donned as the benediction was being pronounced were adjusted and feminine hats given the final pat of arrangement, while little eddies of gusts of greeting and conversation flew back and forth. Comments, most of them admiring, were made on the sermon; inquiries, most of them perfunctory, regarding the health of those absent and those present; remarks on the weather, all the petty chit-chat which serves as the mucilage that holds together everyday social relations.

Mimi manœuvred her way from the pew into the aisle, timing it so exactly that she reached the end of the seat just as the Hunters were passing up the aisle. She greeted them inclusively but her eyes were on Carl. He sought to avoid her but as his parents passed on he was left standing face to face with Mimi. She smiled easily, he somewhat embarrassedly.

"I haven't seen you lately—that is, only at a distance," she said. "I saw you enter Wright's grocery rather hastily one day, though," she added maliciously.

Carl flushed and seemed anxious to escape.

"Why should you see me?" he demanded, half angrily.

"You practically told me to stay away from you just because of some silly old fools gossiping——"

"You know that isn't the truth," she corrected him. "But I didn't mean for you to avoid me as though I had some sort of contagious disease."

Carl's aggressiveness vanished, a tortured, hurt look in his eyes.

"It's best things go along this way, Mimi," he pleaded. "If we can't be the kind of friends we were, it's wisest I stay away from you altogether."

His earnestness, for some reason she could not explain, created within her a vague uneasiness. He went on hurriedly before she could speak, his voice lowered to prevent those near overhearing.

"I've done a lot of thinking during the last few weeks and I think you were right in breaking off our friendship. No, I don't mean on account of Hilda—I wish I did care for her, it would make things easier. But I don't and that's all there is to it. I was happy with you, Mimi, because you made me content to go along and try to satisfy Dad by working. But now I see I was just fooling myself—I never will be an insurance man——"

"But, Carl, you've no right——" Mimi interrupted him.

"Right? What do I care about right? And who's to say what is right for me and what isn't? I'm no fool—I know pretty well what I'm doing and I know I'm a pretty rotten sort—you'll know what I mean by that before long—as soon as the anvil chorus starts on me again."

"Why don't you come to see us any more, Carl? You know papa and I'll always welcome you." Neither of them noticed that Mrs. Daquin had not been included.

"No—I've caused enough talk about you already," he answered cryptically as he lost himself in the crowd. . . .

[115]

FLIGHT

For many days Mimi thought of the talk she had had with Carl. Naturally his mysterious statements of the talk he was certain to create piqued her interest. As discreetly as she could, she sought to find out what he referred to but with no success until Mrs. Hunter called at the Daquin home a week or two later and asked to speak to Mimi, *alone*. Mrs. Daquin, bursting with curiosity, regretfully complied with the suggestion that she absent herself.

As soon as the door closed, Mrs. Hunter explained her mission. She prefaced her story with a disconcerting question.

"Mimi," she demanded, her eyes fixed on Mimi's face, "do you love my Carl?"

"Oh, Mrs. Hunter, why do you ask me such a question?" Mimi, startled, parried the query. She was amazed—she had never asked herself so directly the question Carl's mother had flung at her.

"Don't be frightened or worried—I was so in hopes you did care for him. His father and I are terribly worried about him —he has always been a restless, queer sort of a child but as long as you and he were friendly he seemed satisfied. Oh, yes, I know the silly talk that was going around," she put in as Mimi started to speak, "but nobody who counted ever believed that rot."

"That wasn't the reason we did what we did, Mrs. Hunter," Mimi quickly broke in. "It was on account of Hilda——"

"Hilda? What did she have to do with it?"

Mimi told her the story while Mrs. Hunter showed on her face the amazement she felt.

"Silly little fool!" she pontifically announced when Mimi had finished.

"She isn't a silly little fool and she's far too good a girl for Carl or any other boy I've seen around here!" Mimi hotly declared, her anger flaming high at the disparagement of her friend. It never occurred to her that she had applied the same term to Hilda or at least terms suspiciously similar in meaning.

"Oh, don't misunderstand me, dearie," Mrs. Hunter hastened to cover her hasty statement. "Mind you, I didn't mean she wasn't good enough for my Carl but that she didn't show very good judgment. But that isn't what I came to talk about. It's this. Carl, since you and he stopped seeing each other, has taken to staying out nights with all sorts of people and three times this week he's come home drunk. He's in such a nasty temper I've been afraid to say anything to him and I know there'll be a terrible scene when his father finds out about his carryings-on."

"I'm sorry to hear Carl's acting this way, Mrs. Hunter, but what have I got to do with it?" Mimi, puzzled, asked.

"I was wondering if you'd let him see you occasionally—and —and I thought maybe you cared enough to be willing to do that and see if he would stop. Oh, Mimi, he's my boy and I want you to help me to save him from himself."

Mimi did not know what to say. She felt sorry, terribly sorry, for Mrs. Hunter—knowing her, she knew the ordeal through which the older woman was going, imperiously proud as she was, in abasing herself before a younger woman, an outsider, and confessing her weakness, her impotence in saving her own son. On the other hand there was her promise to Hilda. True, Carl had said twice he did not care and would never care for Hilda, but that made her own promise none the less binding. She felt impatience with Carl coming over her. She was not puritanical by nature but Carl's rapid succumbing to temptation vexed her, he was destroying the ideal she had created in her mind of which he was the embodiment.

Her indecisiveness was due more than to any other cause to her own lack of understanding of the full importance of Mrs. Hunter's words. This was not because of stupidity, it was because of Mimi's amazing innocence of life. She had never fully realized why there should have been so much talk regarding the visit she and Carl had paid to the dance hall. The people she saw there she knew were not of her class nor were they of the kind she ever encountered. Margot and Jean had closely guarded Mimi from all influences which they felt might contaminate her mind. They had seen to it that her playmates were from families which observed indentically the same customs and beliefs as did the Daquins. At school Mimi had heard phrases which would have shocked her had she understood their import but, knowing nothing of what they meant, she had given them no particular thought.

The same circumstance had existed during the years in Atlanta, where it was considered highly immoral to mention even the most rudimentary facts about oneself. Mimi had asked questions but these had been more or less skilfully evaded. She had asked only once about certain amazingly distressing things she noticed in her body and the answer to that query, implying as it did that she had said something she should not have mentioned, had sealed her lips. But in her own mind she had wondered at and been distressed by these things, by periods of intense depression when the most minor incident made her cry or laugh. Thus Mrs. Hunter's dark suggestions regarding Carl's deviations meant little to her and she wondered that his own mother and father could be so lacking in control over him that she had to appeal to her to help save him.

"I asked Carl at church two weeks ago," she began, Mrs. Hunter meanwhile waiting anxiously for Mimi's decision, "why he never came to see us any more and he told me he didn't want to."

"Oh, please, Mimi," the mother pleaded, begging almost piteously for her boy, "ask him again and again until he does come. You can save him—if you will."

FLIGHT

"I've asked him once and if he doesn't want to come to see me then I won't ask him again," Mimi said firmly.

Mrs. Hunter rose, her eyes wet with tears. She jabbed them jerkily with a tiny square of linen, ludicrously small for one of her bulk, Mimi thought irrelevantly even as she pitied the older woman's plight. . . .

Mrs. Daquin sought skilfully to pry from Mimi the reason for Mrs. Hunter's visit but Mimi evaded her questions and went to her own room. Her resentment against Carl increased. It was so silly of him to act as he was doing. Mrs. Hunter was an old frump, it was true, but she was a decent old sort after all. Mimi wondered just what he had been doing. Getting drunk was pretty bad for a young man who was yet in most respects a boy. Mimi remembered Jean and his demijohn of double port-wine after Margot died and before Mary Robertson came to New Orleans. Her loyalty to Jean and the contact with intoxication having removed some of its terrors made her maintain stoutly that getting drunk wasn't the worst sin in the world. She wondered what sort of people Mrs. Hunter was referring to when she spoke of Carl's new associates. There had been a note in Mrs. Hunter's voice when she said it that brought little chills of apprehension to Mimi. Suppose Carl were killed by these shadowy and horrible creatures. Mimi felt an iciness gripping her that took her breath from her. The very indefiniteness of the danger that threatened Carl made it all the more terrifying and horrific. . . .

CHAPTER X

IT was not long before Mimi knew in greater detail the reasons for Mrs. Hunter's apprehension. Like a great orchestra beginning *pianissimo* upon a symphony, the tongues started clacking in soft and cryptic whisperings. Carl, with reckless disregard of the conventions, made no attempt to conceal his derelictions, his wandering from the ultra-strict codes which governed his family and the set in which it moved. He gave the prying eyes and clattering tongues an abundance of fuel, his flaunting of local standards serving much as the upward sweep of a conductor's baton would draw forth a great swelling tone from his players. Carl was seen no more at church despite several acrimonious discussions on the subject with his father. Twice he was seen at a moving-picture show with a girl who was *déclassée*—years before, her name had been linked in somewhat opprobrious fashion with that of a married man of the town. It was true no proof had been produced of any wrongdoing on their part and, as was the usual custom in such affairs, the man's connexion with the embryonic scandal had been long since forgotten. With the passage of years the blot on her name had grown through the very indefiniteness of the original rumour. For years she had been considered by the good Christians of the town almost as though her offence had been that of being "a fancy woman."

Carl had known the girl for many years, as long, in fact, as he could remember. When Mimi had refused to see him, he had by chance met and talked with the girl one day and she had interested him. Even when he said to her one day: "Why haven't we been friendly all these years?" she had made no defence of her reputation nor had she complained of the years of ostracism she had undergone. Had she done either of these, Carl's interest in her would probably have died instantly. Knowing in a hazy sort of way of her story, he was attracted by her calm acceptance of it, and he found himself more and more drawn to her. Neither of them thought of their friendship save as friendship. But it would have been a feat of no mean proportions to convince those who saw them together that there was nothing questionable about their relationship. Her halting suggestion to Carl that he might bring unpleasant comment upon himself if he were seen too frequently with her had angered him—he resolved to go with her wherever and whenever he chose.

This affair, together with the known fact that Carl was drinking rather heavily, was all that was needed to consign him to the outermost circles. His family's standing saved him from complete condemnation, though at the same time it brought more criticism upon him. He knew that had he come from a less respected family little would have been said regarding his derelictions. But the fact of his dissipation, which he took little pains to conceal, only furnished the groundwork for the reputation that grew with startling speed. Bandied about over tea-cups and back fences, across pews and shop-counters, through telephone and letter, a character of infinitely intricate pattern was woven around him.

All this meant little to Carl, however. He knew now that his feeling towards Mimi was not the disinterested, impersonal affair he had thought it. Women were queer, he concluded. At times they can be as ruthless and as without scruples as pirates or highwaymen and then turn right around and permit far-fetched and ultra-chivalrous and foolish little consciences to destroy happiness for themselves and for others. He knew Mimi did not love him but he could not understand why she had insisted, all because she felt she owed some vague sort of duty to Hilda, that they sacrifice all the happiness there had been for them in their companionship.

And while Carl was rambling through the misty and unhappy realm of his thoughts, Mimi was treading much the same path. She heard the stories of his dissipation—her friends saw to it that she should hear them with all current elaborations. These, instead of having the intended effect of driving the wedge between her and Carl deeper, appealed to her vanity—she rather enjoyed the romantic glow which filled her on realizing that a man was throwing his life away for love of her. She found, too, that Carl occupied an increasing part in her thoughts. At night she lay awake for hours, seeing his face, hearing his voice. The separation which she herself imposed began to act as a boomerang upon her emotions—instead of holding herself in check, as she had never experienced any difficulty in doing when she was seeing Carl regularly, she now found that she could no longer keep him from her thoughts. With rapidly growing intensity these moods came upon her until the mention of Carl's name caused a queerly delightful sensation within her. . . .

Mrs. Adams took her turn entertaining the Fleur-de-Lis in October. Jean objected strenuously to going but Mrs. Daquin insisted.

"It's only once a year husbands are allowed to attend and it's little enough to ask you to go just this once. Besides, Mrs. Adams will feel badly if you don't go," she had pleaded, successfully.

After they had gone Mimi sat on the porch enjoying the crisp, chilly air. Tiring, she was entering the house when she saw a familiar figure enter and pass through the circle of light cast by the corner street-lamp. She waited until the shadowy form was passing the gate. It turned and looked up at the darkened house as it passed and she was happy that it did so.

FLIGHT

"Carl," she called softly.

The figure stopped studdenly.

"Won't you come in awhile?" she urged.

Carl stood indecisively at the gate, then opened it and entered. As he greeted her a mantle of constraint like a pall fell upon them both.

"Come inside—it's rather chilly out here," she remarked.

He followed her into the parlour and sat silent while she adjusted the shades and switched on the light.

"Well, you're back again even if I did have to shanghai you," she laughed. The forced pleasantry and the laugh both fell rather flat, she felt.

"Why did you make me come in?" he demanded, sullenly.

"Make you come in?" she laughed again.

"Don't try to be coy, Mimi, or evade my question," Carl almost angrily charged. "You told me to stay away from you——"

She evaded the challenge.

"I've been hearing a lot of talk about you lately," she sought to change the subject.

"What of it? And what's the use of discussing it? These people here would talk about Jesus Christ himself."

Mimi watched him closely. Here was a newer and more bitter mood than any in which she had hithertoo seen him. And he looked badly, too. His face was haggard. Under his eyes were dark circles, and the eyes themselves were sunken, reddened. Deep lines were in his face. He looked distrait, miserable. As she watched, his face became softer and he sank it in his hands. In muffled tones he began to speak again.

"Mimi, I'm a weak, vicious creature and no good to myself or anybody else. I used to fuss a lot about these people around here who talk about other people's affairs—I still talk about them and hate them. But, after all, they're right—I'm everything vile and low they've said I am—"

[123]

"You mustn't talk that way, Carl. You're nothing of the sort."

She tried to comfort him but he stopped her with a gesture of mingled impatience and denial. His abjectness stirred her deeply. She felt again the wave of tenderness coming over her that she had experienced the last time she had talked with him in this very room, the time she had sent him away. She was a little frightened—her emotion was deeper, more moving than before. His unhappiness had subtly transferred itself to her and she found herself filled with an almost overwhelming desire to touch him, to hold him near her.

Carl raised his head and looked searchingly at her. His gaze disturbed her, moved her, made her uncomfortable. She remembered the day she first met him, the inclusive way in which he had surveyed her and the resentment his look had stirred in her. There was no resentment now. Instead there was a fear he might see way down beneath and know how she had missed him, how she had longed for him.

"Mimi, there's one thing I want to tell you now that I'm here. I feel like a dog in telling you—I have no business even thinking it. But I want you to know—no matter what stories you hear—that—that—I love you!" His tone was half defiant, half tender, as he nervously flung the last three words at her.

Mimi sat silent, her eyes in her lap. With Carl's declaration a great peace came upon her. Doubt, fear, uncertainty left her.

"And I love you, too, Carl," she said, simply.

With a bound he crossed the room and sat beside her.

"You—love—me—too?" he asked, amazement, doubt that he had heard aright in his voice.

Mimi, her eyes filled with tears of happiness, could only nod.

"Oh, Mimi darling," Carl half sobbed, and pillowed his face on her breast while she pressed him close to her, holding

[124]

him with all the tenderness that had been pent up within her, holding him as though he would fly away never to return if she relaxed for an instant the tightness of her grasp. . . .

It seemed years later when Carl left.

"Mimi, I wonder if we have done right?" he asked as he stood at the door, his voice worried, uncertain.

Mimi only smiled as she kissed him. . . .

She had been asleep for a long time when Jean and his wife returned.

After she had undressed and turned out the light she lay in bed and thought of Carl. Life was funny, she mused. People came into one's life, flickered like the figures in a movie thrown on an imperfect screen and passed out of one's consciousness leaving no memories of importance behind them. Most people were like that but every so often there came those, always few in number, who stayed and, by staying, created all sorts of difficult and unpleasant or pleasant complications. She wondered why nearly everybody she knew or had read about made simple little problems into tremendous ones and harried themselves with things which, seen later, were of such slight worth. Conscience? Right? Honour? Justice? Truth? What were all these except little shibboleths which man had created in his own mind like little gods and before which he prostrated himself in abject grovelling? Truth? She remembered the thing Carl had once quoted to her from Spinoza—truth is made up of the lies grown hoary with age.

But after all there must be something in these things men had lived by and for which they had died. She wondered what it all could be. Were they worth all the agony and bloodshed and sacrifice they had brought?

Here I am, she mused, a woman, a Negro. Life for me if I were white would be hard enough, but it's going to be doubly so when I have race problems added to my own difficulties as a woman. She toyed idly with the notion as to what her lot would have been if she had been born white—if she were to cross over the line and forget the Negro blood in her body. The idea was not attractive. In New Orleans the women who attracted her most and whom she admired above all others were not white—at least, they were not Anglo-Saxon. They all lived in the Creole quarter and Jean had pointed out many of them who had Negro blood, some of them knowing it and others in ignorance of it. She had not needed Jean's telling her to pick them out—there was something tangible yet intangible about them which indicated it to the observant eye—a warmth, a delicate humanness, an attractiveness which did not belong to the women who lived north of Canal Street.

And here in Atlanta she had watched them, noting the subtle differences even in those like herself whose skins were fair. No wonder that in New Orleans in the old days, as she had read in the books of French travellers, the men often deserted the balls where their wives and daughters were, and slipped away to those more resplendent ones where quadroon women held sway. Mimi remembered a comparison one of them had made between these who had Negro blood with the American women —"frank, warm-hearted . . . with manners more interesting than the Americans . . . the roundness and beauty of shape in the women also contrasting with the straightness and angularity of American figures."

She had asked Jean, in her innocence, to tell her about these balls but for some reason she could not explain he had evaded her question and seemed to be somewhat embarrassed by it. No, she concluded, with all its faults and petty unpleasant features, she would rather remain with her own people. They got, apparently, so much more out of the life they lived with all its barriers than those who had more but seemed infinitely less happy with it.

Her thoughts, she realized, revolved always in a circle of

[126]

which the exact centre was Carl. She wondered why he and she had not ended their worries sooner by acceptance of the love which had come to them. It had all been so futile, so childish, and Mimi, with the reluctance of youth to think of itself as youthful, felt rather ashamed that they had acted in such callow and infantile manner. Now that she had stopped fighting against the love for Carl which she realized had been in her heart all the time, her fretful and worried air left her. She lay in her narrow bed and smiled tenderly as she felt again his lips from which his kisses at first had fallen upon hers like gentle, soft blows. She stirred happily as she felt once more the rough possessiveness to which his lips had changed—she was not conscious of hurt until now when she realized her own lips were swollen slightly where he had pressed her close to him, while she had yielded happily. She was wondering where it would all end as she fell asleep. . . .

It seemed to her she had hardly closed her eyes when she was rudely awakened. Mrs. Daquin was shaking her roughly, a dressing-gown thrown hastily over her night-dress.

"Mimi, come quickly!" she was calling. "Something's happened to your father."

"What's the matter? Have you called the doctor?" asked Mimi as she hurried down the hall after Mrs. Daquin. Mimi was now thoroughly awake, a strange fear in her heart.

"Yes, he's on the way here," the older woman whispered as they entered Jean's bedroom.

Jean was lying on the bed stretched at full length. His breath came with difficulty and his face was covered with a cold, clammy perspiration. Mimi with a little cry of distress and fear, quickly checked, flung herself on her knees beside the bed. She tried to feel Jean's pulse but could find no trace. She pressed her head against Jean's breast, trying to hear or feel his heart beating. An icy terror came over her when she could feel no throbbing. Jean groaned heavily as though in

[127]

great pain. Mimi was happy to hear it—at least, that was a sign that Jean was not dead.

The doctor found her there beside the bed while Mrs. Daquin stood at the foot, weeping and wringing her hands, all her efficiency and forthrighteousness fled in the face of this phenomenon. He gently led them from the room.

For hours, it seemed, they waited there. Once the door opened hastily and they heard the doctor, who had rushed past them without speaking, telephone another physician, speaking ominously of strychnine and nitroglycerine.

As he re-entered the sick-room he muttered in answer to Mimi's question something about Jean's heart. "He's a sick man —a very sick man," floated back to the two women as he closed the door. . . .

Morning found them waiting. For the first time Mimi felt close to Mrs. Daquin. Unconsciously they had clung together, brought close by the spectre which hovered over them. Mrs. Daquin brought a wrap and put it around Mimi and Mimi smiled her thanks. It seemed quite a natural thing that Mrs. Daquin should let her arm remain around the girl's shoulders when she had placed the wrap there. Mimi snuggled near her and in her embrace Mimi felt a security from the dreadful thing in the room where Jean lay.

The door opened and the two doctors, haggard from their work, anxiety and loss of sleep, emerged, closed the door softly behind them. Dr. Adams led them to the lower floor before speaking.

"Mr. Daquin has had a very serious attack. Heart trouble. Brought on by acute indigestion. We've given him a double injection of strychnine and nitroglycerine to speed up his heart action. At first I couldn't get any heart action even with my stethoscope. Thought he was gone. He's resting now. Keep him quiet. I'll be back in an hour or so."

FLIGHT

Mimi felt, as Dr. Adams uttered his crisp, staccato sentences, as though she were a condemned criminal standing before a judge, hearing a terrible sentence pronounced upon her. Jean —her Jean—gentle, uncomplaining, always kind—dangerously ill. It didn't seem possible.

"I'll tell Mrs. Adams and Hilda to come over and do what they can to help you," Dr. Adams promised as he left the house. . . .

The news of Jean's illness spread rapidly. Before Mimi and Mrs. Daquin could finish dressing they began to come with offers of help. Mrs. Adams and Hilda were the first. Hilda and Mimi held each other close, all differences melted away by the sadness which had come to Mimi. For a long time now Hilda had known from Carl's attitude that her hopes were of no avail. She had freely unburdened her woes at last to her mother and in the telling of them and the ready sympathy which she received from Mrs. Adams had found the peace of resignation. She knew through some psychic means that Carl loved Mimi and her new-found calm enabled her to feel thoroughly happy for their sakes. . . .

All day they came. Mimi never knew there could be so much solicitude, so much genuine kindness. One came and prepared a meal, another tidied the house, another volunteered to do errands. Mimi felt ashamed of her dislike for some of them in the past. Affliction had shown her the real worth which lay beneath the petty malice, the ignominious bickerings and jealousies which to her had seemed the outstanding characteristics of many of these folks.

Jean slept the greater part of the day. Late in the afternoon Dr. Adams gave him another stimulant. Mimi had begun to show the strain through which she had been and he urged her to go for a walk. Returning, she found Mrs. Daquin waiting for her in the hall.

"Your father's been asking for you. Dr. Adams said it
[129]

would be all right for you to go in and see him but he must not be excited."

He smiled as she entered the darkened room.

"I'm sorry I've caused you so much trouble," he apologized as Mimi kissed him tenderly. As she bent over him she noticed for the first time how white his hair had become. His moustache and goatee, too, without their daily brushing and waxing, looked less magnificent than they had always seemed. Jean's eyes were sunken, his face lined with the suffering he had been through. An ineffable pity filled her, she wished eagerly even as she knew it was futile that she could take his place.

"Do you remember that day in the St. Louis cemetery just before we came here?" Jean was asking.

"Do I remember it? I'll never forget it," she assured him.

"It seems a long, long time ago."

A reminiscent, far-away look came into Jean's eyes and he lay there, his thin hands resting on his chest, for several minutes without speaking. Mimi waited. At last he stirred, smiling again at her, this time apologetically.

"We were happy there, weren't we, Mimi? I've never been satisfied here. Too much rushing about, no time for living—real living. And you and I—we haven't had the time here for the long walks we used to take when we were home. No—no—I'm not blaming you," he assured her as she started to speak. "We've both been too busy——"

But Mimi felt a sting in the words. She knew there was none intended, it was her own conscience that lashed her. She wished fervently she had not been so selfish, that she had thought more of Jean. She knew now he had never been happy in Atlanta. His leisurely, reflective nature made him unhappy, he was wholly out of place anywhere save in some easy-going place like his beloved Louisiana.

"I suppose it's been for the best, though. Young people

like you haven't much patience for the old ways and customs
—you, too, would in time have become unhappy there. But
I didn't intend to ramble off like that. It's about you I
wanted to talk. . . . You've grown into a beautiful woman,
Mimi," he declared, proudly. "Every day you look more
like Margot did when I first knew her. And you've ways like
hers—only you've more spirit, more fire. . . ."

Again he lay silent and Mimi, knowing instinctively he was
living again his days with Margot, hardly dared breathe lest
she break the spell. The room grew dark but neither of
them noticed it. From outside came the soft cries of children at play far away, the bumping of a short, fat street car
as it meandered down Auburn Avenue, the shrill voice of a
woman calling her child to supper.

"I'm worried, Mimi—not afraid—just worried. I've had
these heart attacks before but I said nothing about them because I didn't want to worry you and Mary—but this one last
night was the worst one yet."

She sought to comfort him, telling him little falsehoods
about the allegedly minor importance which Dr. Adams had
attached to the attack. It'll pass over and he'll be none the
worse for it, were the words she put in the physician's
mouth.

"Did he say that really?" Jean asked anxiously, yet hopefully.

She assured him that those were the exact words. Jean
leaned back on his pillow, a more peaceful look on his face
which removed some of the shame she was feeling on account
of the lie. She would have lied a thousand times cheerfully
if they served to make him more content.

"He didn't seem so optimistic when he was talking to me,"
Jean mused. "I suppose he was trying to scare me so I
would stay in bed."

"Of course that was what he intended. Doctors assume

patients will do just about half what they are told to do, so they are told to do twice what they need to do," she encouraged him.

"I'm tired, Mimi—so tired. I think I'll take a little nap now," he said after a pause. "I wanted to talk to you because I didn't know how serious this attack might be—tell you to remember, whatever happened, you're a Daquin, but now I've heard what the doctor said, that can wait. You're a beautiful girl, Mimi, almost too beautiful. But you'll come through all right—just make up your own mind what's the right thing to do, pay no attention to what other people say, and then do what you think is right."

Automatically she thought of Carl.

"Last night, after you and Mrs. Daquin left, Carl came by the house and I called him in," she told Jean. "He was very unhappy—I never saw him so downcast. We talked awhile—then—then—oh, Jean, he told me he loved me—and it made me mighty happy——"

"Carl's a good boy, Mimi. A little too flighty—a little weak, too, I'm afraid—but he'll come around all right, I think. They don't understand him and they're always rubbing his fur the wrong way but—Carl's got the right stuff in him."

Jean lapsed again into one of his retrospective moods. His eyes slowly closed and soon he fell asleep. Mimi kissed him gently, lowered the shade to keep the light from the street lamp from disturbing him, and stole softly from the room. . . .

CHAPTER XI

A<small>T</small> midnight Dr. Adams made his last call for the day. "He's resting easily now and I think he'll sleep through the night. Call me if you need me. And you'd better get a little sleep yourself or I'll have two patients," he advised Mimi as he left.

His words brought realization to Mimi that she was tired. She sent Mrs. Daquin to bed, telling her she would lock up the house and see that everything was attended to. She then tiptoed into Jean's room and found him breathing gently, his face, with a smile upon it, turned towards the door.

When he called at seven the next morning Dr. Adams said that Jean had been dead about three hours. Mimi found on his face the same smile that had been there when she had seen him last. Mrs. Daquin came into the room weeping but for Mimi there were no tears. Death had come too suddenly upon her, its swift snatching away of her Jean had rendered her incapable of thought, of every emotion. She knelt by the bed, her head resting beside Jean's, stunned, inarticulate. Dr. Adams tried to pull her away, telling her it would be better for her if she did not stay too long there.

"No, Doctor, I'm happier here. I've just a few more hours with Jean now. Leave me here alone, won't you?"

He led the weeping Mrs. Daquin from the room and Mimi was alone with Jean. Jean dead? She couldn't believe it was true. She touched his hand, stiffened, cold. It terrified her. How many times she might have held it, warm, pulsating, responsive.

[133]

FLIGHT

No—she had been too busy with her own petty affairs, her own insignificant worries, to think of him—longing for his quiet old home, unhappy in an environment and among people he did not understand and whose ways were not his. She had known in an indefinite sort of way that Jean was not happy, that he and Mary grew farther and farther apart each year, each month, each day. A spasm of remorse swept through Mimi—remorse that held her in an icy, terrifying grip—when she realized now how she might have been of comfort, of consolation, to Jean, and instead had chased merrily after her own whims and fancies, giving little thought to him. She knew now that these later years must have been terribly lonely ones for him. She felt she would cheerfully have given ten years of her life to have him back for one year, for one month, even for one day. Then she would show him the quality of her love for him. Holy Mother, why did one see these things only when it was too late?

She was glad they had had their talk yesterday afternoon. It had been like old times, she and Jean had been so happy together. Even in his own illness his thoughts had been of her —he had wanted to live not for his own sake but only for hers. "You'll come through all right," he had said. She wondered if she would. Without Jean's physical presence she speculated what her relations with Mrs. Daquin would be. In his quiet way Jean had had a very real control over his wife. Mimi sensed now as she had never done before that despite his gentleness, which sometimes seemed to be almost weakness, his apparent softness had had great strength behind it—strength enough to hold in check Mrs. Daquin's aggressiveness and domineering attitude. Jean had not spoken sharply often but when he had his wife listened and obeyed. He had never had to speak twice.

Why don't I cry, she wondered, like all women do and most men when death comes? She was conscious of a slight feeling of guilt because of her dry eyes. She wondered if she was showing proper respect. She looked at Jean's peaceful face. Her own face was set in hard, tight lines, her teeth were clamped until the muscles of her jaws ached, but no tears came. Jean dead? No—no—no—it couldn't be true. . . .

They found her there, dry-eyed, when the undertaker came to prepare Jean for burial. She was calm until the dingy wicker basket, sagging with the weight of its load, was being carried through the door. She was thinking of that day Jean had referred to yesterday—that day in the St. Louis cemetery when the funeral procession passed near them. Jean had said he felt just as though his own body were in the casket. She knew now what he had meant—her own body was there in that straw container.

"Be careful!" she cried as one of the men let the basket strike against the door. A sharp physical pain shot through her body, followed by nausea as the men righted the slipping basket. Then all went dark for her. Without a sound she sank to the floor, unconscious. . . .

When she awoke she was in bed. Hilda sat near and smiled at her when she opened her eyes.

"Papa says you must keep quiet, absolutely. Mama is seeing after things and Mr. Hunter is taking care of all the arrangements for the funeral——"

The ominous, horrifying word brought a little cry of anguish from Mimi. Hilda's eyes filled with tears at her ineptness.

"Ask your mother if she'll try and get some candles. And see if she can get a priest for the funeral. Jean would be happiest if he was buried that way," begged Mimi.

When Hilda had hurried away to execute her wishes, Mimi tried to get up but found herself too weak. She was glad to sink back into the soft pillows. Yes, Jean would be happiest if he had a Catholic burial. He hadn't been to mass for years now but he had never allowed the narrowness and prejudice of priests who after all were human and with human fear and cowardice and prejudice to destroy his faith. Reverently, Mimi made the sign of the cross. . . .

The morning passed before she had strength enough to rise. She talked over with Mrs. Daquin, Mrs. Adams and Mr. Hunter plans for the funeral. Jean's sister in New York whom Mimi had never seen had been telegraphed and had wired she was leaving for Atlanta at once. They decided the services were to be held on Friday. Mrs. Daquin thought it best to have a Protestant service but Mimi was obdurate, immovable. This was the last thing she could do for Jean and she was determined that it should be done, if possible.

Late in the afternoon, in the lull of visitors who were called home by household duties, Carl came. To both it seemed impossible that less than twenty-four hours before they had been so happy together in that very room.

"There's no use of my saying I'm sorry, Mimi. You know it—I loved your father better than anybody except you. He seemed to understand me—I—I——" His sudden rush of feeling made it impossible for him to speak. His eyes filled with tears as he touched Mimi's hand, gently and but for a second.

"Yes, Carl, I know . . ." she whispered. . . .

By Thursday evening Mimi felt she could no longer stand the torture of greeting people, answering the same questions over and over again, performing the many additional tasks the death had brought. Mrs. Daquin seemed actually to be enjoying after a fashion the new importance which Jean's death had brought to her as his widow. Not that she let it

[136]

show on her face. She saw to it her eyes bore the appearance of much weeping and her general air was that of a Christian martyr about to be thrown to the lions. To Mimi she seemed to have donned the atmosphere of the sorely tried and heavily bereaved with full attention to the effectiveness of details, wearing the rôle as an accomplished actress would. Mimi found all her old antagonism rising again—Jean's life, she reflected bitterly, would have been much happier had his wife expended some of that energy now used in simulated grief towards happiness for Jean when alive.

There was but one place where Mimi felt at peace, and that sitting beside Jean's casket. To-morrow morning Jean's sister, Mrs. Rogers of New York, would arrive. To-morrow afternoon the funeral. Mimi crept quietly into the parlour. The room was unlighted save for the illumination from the flickering candles. Through the partly opened windows floated a warm breeze of an unusually balmy late October evening. The lace curtains swayed lazily back and forth as though bidding a languid farewell to the body in the casket just beyond their reach. In the dimness they seemed to Mimi like long slender fingers seeking vainly to caress the sides of the box which held all that remained of Jean.

The house was nearly deserted. One by one they had gone away. Mimi, wearied by the incessant stream, felt a great eagerness to find the peace she could get nowhere else save near Jean. It annoyed her to find she was not alone. Mrs. Plummer and Mrs. King sat near the window conversing in lowered voices. Mimi ignored them, drew a chair close to the casket and sat there gazing at Jean's face. On it was unmistakable peace—she almost wished that she were there beside him. The extent of her loss was creeping upon her. Without Jean she felt lost, terrified, afraid. To whom could she turn? Mrs. Daquin? Obviously, no. Mrs. Hunter? Hilda? Hilda's mother? Carl? Each of them had his

[137]

FLIGHT

good points but none of them were so all-inclusive, so gentle, so understanding, so unselfish. Nor even was she herself, she realized. For here I am thinking only of myself—had I done less of that when Jean was alive, I would have made his life and my own far happier.

"... her eyes ain't even red ... if she was so crazy about him as she pretended to be, she'd . . ."

Mimi suddenly became conscious of the sibilant whispers which came to her from the two women by the window. Lost in the grief bottled up within her like turbulent waters held by a great dam, she had been oblivious of comments during the days since Jean had died. Even to the undoubtedly sympathetic ones she had replied methodically, listlessly, giving little thought to the words, words, words. Now as the sinister, malevolent whisperings came to her, the inevitable reaction to the apathy she had felt flamed into being. She rose from her chair, bitter hatred welling up for the evil-tongued old women. But even as she opened her mouth to speak, an overwhelming sense of the futility of it all came over her, a sense of inappropriateness, the lack of respect for Jean if she were to engage here in what would be but little more than a fishwives' quarrel. She checked the hot, bitter words that pressed for utterance and rushed from the room.

In the security of her own room she lay on the bed and envied the peace on Jean's face. Again and again the picture melted into the face of Carl as he had left the house the night Jean died. She wondered if this fantastic trick of her mind were not sacrilege, if it were not in some manner disloyalty to Jean. Yet, one was living, the other gone, and she felt a comforting sense that Jean would not think her disloyal. She wondered what course her new relations with Carl would take. Now that Hilda was removed from the problem . . . ? Weighing, pondering, wondering, she lightly slept. They'll surely be gone now, she thought, as she on awaking descended

[138]

to the parlour once more, drawn back to Jean as iron filings are attracted by a powerful magnet,

The chairs by the window were empty and Mimi was glad. She sat again by the casket and peace again came to her. How long she sat there she did not know, lost as she was in her own rambling, chaotic musings. Again there came to her a feeling she was not alone. The whispering rose once more, this time from the shadows on the other side of the casket. She sought to put them out of her mind, to lose herself again in her own thoughts. After all, she thought, they are trying to show their respect for Jean and their willingness to be of service. It is thoughtful of them to come over here and sit up. From the kitchen came the sound of voices and the aroma of coffee. Maybe they'll leave soon if only to get something to eat.

They did not leave. Though she made every effort to close her ears and mind to the words which floated jerkily to her, Mimi found her resentment rising again. Mrs. Plummer and Mrs. King discussed the probable price of the casket, the furniture. They speculated as to what the widow and daughter would do now, in what sort of financial circumstances the deceased had left them. Mimi heard Carl's name linked with her own—followed by an appreciative chuckle from Mrs. King in response to some remark made by her companion which Mimi could not hear. It was obvious the women had not seen or heard Mimi re-enter the room, for the frankness of their comment indicated their assumption they were alone. On and on they roamed, by innuendo and by unqualified assertion destroying, maligning, tearing to pieces. . . .

A cold, blind fury seized Mimi. She jumped to her feet. The women gasped as Mimi's bloodless face framing flashing eyes filled with fury rose at the head of the casket, the light from the tall candles giving it a terrifying, ghostlike appearance.

"You two get out!" Mimi demanded. "You might have had enough respect for my father here to have silenced your filthy, lying tongues! Get out! Get out! Get out!"

Her voice at first was but little more than a sharp whisper. As her anger mastered her it rose until her words carried to the hall beyond. Mrs. Plummer and Mrs. King, thoroughly frightened, hastily edged around the room towards the door, keeping as great distance as was possible between them and Mimi, who slowly circled her body so that her eyes remained upon them. The two gossips hurried through the little knot which had gathered at the door, drawn there by the commotion. As the door shut behind them Mimi sank into her chair and wept as Mrs. Adams came in and put her arms about her. . . .

Down the street hurried two indignant, surprised women. Mrs. Plummer speculated plaintively in an aggrieved tone as she panted her way homeward.

"I wonder what was the matter with her," she asked her companion. "We didn't say nothing to make her r'ar and tear like that—and over her dead father's body at that! Some folks sho' is funny!"

"Mis' Plummer," her companion declared portentously," it's the truth that hurts! You remember the old sayin's, 'The hit dog yelps!' and 'Where there's smoke there's fire!' Guess we weren't so far wrong at that. . . . Guess that gal will bear watchin'." . . .

Early the next morning Mrs. Rogers came. As she entered the house Mimi rushed to meet her. Her aunt took her in her arms, murmuring gentle words of consolation to Mimi, who felt instantly the presence of a friend and ally. Mrs. Rogers was of medium height, younger than Jean but so like her brother that Jean seemed only a replica to which white, close-cropped hair, a moustache and a little beard had been added.

"Poor, dear Mimi," she whispered, her eyes wet. She pressed Mimi to her in a warm outpouring of real affection, affection which sprang into existence unreservedly, binding them together in a flash of understanding and love. . . .

Mimi and her aunt talked a long time together just before Mrs. Rogers returned to New York two days after the funeral.

"What are your plans, Mimi? What are you going to do?"

"I don't know, Aunt Sophie—this thing has come on me so suddenly I'm all upset. I suppose I'll stay on here as long as I can get along with Mrs. Daquin——"

"Why did Jean marry her? She's not our sort at all—an estimable woman, I suppose, but—well, she just isn't the sort —not Margot's type at all."

Mimi told her the circumstances of the marriage, of the years of misunderstanding which had followed the union.

"Just like Jean to do a thing like that," his sister observed when Mimi had finished. "Why stay on here with her? Won't you go back to New York with me?"

"Oh, Aunt Sophie, I'd love to—but I can't leave Atlanta right now——"

"What's his name?" Mrs. Rogers demanded with what to Mimi seemed uncanny shrewdness.

"Carl Hunter," she answered frankly, her face reddening. "You see, he needs me." And she told the story simply, fully, knowing that her aunt would understand. When she finished, Mrs. Rogers smiled sympathetically.

"I see—I see. But if ever things get unpleasant here, send me a wire and come on to New York. I've been pretty lonely since Henry died and I've always wanted a daughter. I'd try to make you happy and I don't think there's overmuch happiness here for you with Jean's widow. And up North

[141]

you'd have a much better chance than here where all you can do is to teach school or get married. The last isn't bad if you get the right man—but, don't hurry—a girl with your looks and brains can go a long way if she only keeps her head. . . .

CHAPTER XII

SHE would not have believed that so soon after Jean's death she could find herself settling back into a routined life. At first there had been the long, empty days and the longer nights when the house seemed a vast, empty place from which the spirit or thing or whatever it might be called which had made it different from other places had fled. But Mrs. Daquin had removed most of the things which too vividly brought back memories of Jean.

"There's no use of keeping things that only make you sad," she had said. "I get the creeps every time I go to see Mrs. Simpkins—those dried flowers from her husband's funeral hanging in the frame in her parlour. There'll be nothing like that around here—a dead person's dead and you can't bring him back, no matter how much you loved him."

At first Mimi had objected strenuously to Mrs. Daquin's seemingly ruthless disposal of all the things which to her were so intimately associated with Jean. They had, however, brought little furniture from New Orleans, only Jean's books and a few odds and ends. These latter Mimi removed to her own room and then she willingly consented to whatever changes her step-mother desired. A new parlour set was purchased as soon after the funeral as was decently possible. New wall-paper appeared in the long dark hall and in Mrs. Daquin's bedroom. Out, too, went the bedroom furniture of mottled walnut. A brass bed with frolicsome curves and angles of shiny metal contrasting with the cloudy dullness of the heavier portions took its place. The imperfect set of plain white china with the narrow border of gold and blue was stored in the attic. In its stead appeared china of awe-inspiring combinations of bluebirds kissing on the wing, many cupolaed pagodas, sampans rowed by fat-bellied Chinamen, and trees of a design never produced even by a profligate Nature. Mimi took only a perfunctory interest in these changes other than vouchsafing a listless "They're pretty," when pressed for comment by Mrs. Daquin.

Mimi at times was amazed at her ready acceptance of the uneventful life. She was grateful that she had apparently been wrong in her estimation of her step-mother. Mrs. Daquin seemed changed, chastened by Jean's death. She had really loved her husband in her own fashion even when she had been most irritated by what to her seemed his lack of intelligence in grasping opportunities for advancement or gain. Now that he was dead, she found herself regarding him not in the light of the later years but more as she had during their short courtship and the first year of their marriage. This mood was sustained by the very evident advantages which she found coming to her as a recently bereaved widow. She knew that in time this too would pass. In time Jean would be but a faint memory to most of those with whom she associated.

It was not conscious dishonesty nor was she a deliberate *poseuse* when she accepted the little attentions, the deference which they bestowed on her. Mrs. Daquin found herself for the first time a personage in her own right. All her youth she had lived under the dominating influence of her father, and even after her marriage to so retiring a person as Jean, she found that her handicap in being a woman in a conventional society was very great. Her father had not attended the funeral but he had wired and written her repeatedly urging her to return to Chicago. This she resolved not to do—at least not unless circumstances compelled such a step—for she was enjoying too greatly for immediate surrender her new importance.

The mood thus engendered worked to Mimi's advantage though she did not fully understand the reasons for that good fortune. Mrs. Daquin was kindly in her manner, far more so than she had ever been before. When after a few weeks they began to be seen on the streets, Mimi was always to be seen with her step-mother, both clad in the depressingly sombre blacks of sorrow which custom demanded. Mimi's oval, cream-coloured face topped by its aureole of reddish gold peeped out with startling beauty from the black bonnet tied under her chin with strings of the same colour. Mrs. Daquin did not fare so well in her melancholy raiment, her brown skin and hair offering not so marked a contrast as in Mimi's case. She suffered the loss of comeliness cheerfully, however, for its added advantages in sympathetic attention.

Careless as usual of material things, they found Jean had not made a will. Mr. Hunter had volunteered to relieve them of the burdens of settling the estate and his report had shown that not much had been left. Jean had not secured the full value of his property in New Orleans and the cash he had secured had been invested largely in purchasing stock in the Lincoln Mutual Insurance Company. This would in time prove a sound investment, but at present there was little return from it. The deeds to the house given them by Mr. Robertson had been made out in Mrs. Daquin's name. Mr. Robertson volunteered to contribute a definite sum each month to their support when he saw that his daughter had no intentions of returning to Chicago as he wished. Mimi, trained to do no work which would bring her appreciable income or which she could have accepted without lowering their social status, found herself faced with the Hobson's choice of teaching school or enduring the loss of many little comforts and even a few necessities which before had seemed to her so natural she had never given thought to their source. She did not grumble but began at once to prepare for the examination as a school-teacher in the spring. In fact, she was glad to find a definite thing on which to concentrate—it served as an opiate when Jean's loss seemed too great to bear. . . .

Into this new life Carl came with much larger importance than Mimi had supposed was possible. In time Mrs. Daquin, who had never been able to find out from Mimi the purpose of Mrs. Hunter's mysterious call but who had linked it up after a fashion with Carl and Mimi, offered no objection to Carl's visits to the house. This lack of hostility changed in time to actual welcome due to the increased cordiality of Mrs. Hunter towards Mrs. Daquin which the latter sensed was in large measure because of his visits. This welcome was strengthened by Carl's evident reformation. No longer was he seen with questionable companions. He had not been seen under the influence of liquor since he had begun again to visit Mimi, and every Sunday now he was to be seen with his parents and sister at church.

The old comradeship, deepened and enriched in a subtle but unmistakable way, was returning. Memory of that night during which so much had taken place, their reunion, Jean's death and all the rest, had kept them from the torridity of feeling which had swept over them then. Instead there was a comforting sense of unity which ripened and deepened through the unspoken avowals of their love that flashed between them whenever they met.

This feeling was always deepest as they walked out in the evening. During the latter part of September and the early part of October there had been many crisply cold nights. Dying October and budding November brought that year balmy nights and pleasant days that were reminiscent of late summer. Through the darkened streets they strolled arm in arm. Here and there were street lamps which shed little light more than to a radius of fifteen or twenty feet. Back in tidy little yards sat squat little houses or imposing two-storied ones with an occasional light peeping from them in friendly manner. Up above, a moon, slender and graceful like a fragile, spreading horseshoe of coruscation, or full-bodied and vigorous in its yellowish brilliance. Mimi always liked the new moon best— it stirred her by its slender grace. But Carl preferred the full ones—"no wonder the Greeks and Romans gave a 'corona' as a badge of victory—those old boys were poets, and real ones— they saw that there could be no greater beauty and splendour than in an award resembling that band of light up yonder."

It was not long before they were accepted as "going together." With the ready forgiveness accorded a man who has transgressed against local codes of conduct, Carl's derelictions of the past were forgotten, or, if not forgotten, thrust into that indefinite realm of things not to be mentioned again save in most intimate conversations. It was assumed that, now Jean was dead, Mimi would soon be marrying, and the assumption more or less naturally followed that she would marry Carl.

Between them, however, there was no thought of to-morrow nor, for some inexplicable reason, did there come to their ears the now friendly discussions regarding what they would do which were going on. They floated along happily on the stream of their new-found contentment, as oblivious of the future as two bits of wood held together by a string on the bosom of some placid pond. On rainy nights or evenings when Mimi did not feel like walking or going to a moving-picture show, they sat at home, Carl talking or reading some bit of verse, or some story he had come across, while Mimi sat and sewed or just sat. Carl's restlessness had almost left

[147]

him, he seemed more contented, he now actually took a deeper interest in the work his father wanted him to do. More and more there entered his conversations his plans, his hopes, his eagerness to please his father. Mimi learned that even under his former discontent there was a deep respect and a sort of affection that Carl had for his father. She saw that the older man's will worked with great effect upon that of his son—too much so, she feared. . . .

Early in November she found that this was even more true than she had suspected. One morning she was awakened by a dream. In it she saw Jean again, standing beside her bed, his eyes sad, his finger pointing accusingly at her. No word came from his lips, but his face had on it an expression she had never seen in life, one that made her shrink from it into the warm, comforting embrace of the bed-clothes. She lay awake and then fell again into troubled slumber.

When she awoke she felt a violent nausea and a dizziness that made her glad to lie down again. She called Mrs. Daquin, who listened to her recital of her ailments and then gave her some medicine, advising her to remain in bed. Later Mrs. Daquin brought her breakfast and sat with her as she toyed with it, eating little. It's nice of her to do this, thought Mimi. She's getting more lovable every day.

As she still felt badly in the afternoon, Mimi went at her step-mother's suggestion to see Dr. Adams. A few questions, an examination, and then Dr. Adams looked gravely at Mimi.

"You're going to have a baby, Mimi," he told her.

Mimi gasped, echoing his words. A great happiness filled her, happiness mingled with a sweeping flame of love for Carl. A baby! Hers and Carl's! Her face shone with a great light, the light of contentment and love. There was no feeling of shame nor could she clearly understand why Dr. Adams' face should remain so grave and worried. On that

[148]

eventful night she and Carl had been caught up and swept on by a great tide of passion, an emotion overwhelming, beautiful, sacred. She had given of herself freely, without thought of consequences and without any sense of shame. To her it had been a magnificent, a pure and holy giving. Her smile puzzled Dr. Adams.

"Mimi, I'm afraid you don't realize how serious a thing this is. Do you know what'll happen to you and your reputation? And who's the man?"

She told him simply and freely. Still her manner was a source of wonder to him. Ordinarily such a message would have brought forth tears, protestations of innocence, pleas for help. Mimi did none of these.

His face was set in grim lines as she told of Carl.

"The scoundrel! We'll make him marry you and save your name from being dragged in the mud."

"No—no, Doctor, you don't understand. We've done nothing wrong, and if we have I'm as much to blame as Carl. Please don't say anything about this until I see him. . . ."

She telephoned Carl, who came over to her house at once. She greeted him happily, the light of love yet shining in her face.

"Carl," she cried as soon as he entered, "I'm going to have a baby!"

"You're what?"

"I'm going to have a baby—Dr. Adams told me so this afternoon—I'm so happy," she ended, a puzzled tone creeping into her voice.

"Did he ask you who was the father?"

"Yes, of course he did."

"Who did you tell him?"

"Why, you, of course."

He turned on her roughly.

"You little fool, what did you want to do that for?"

She gazed at him in dismay. She had expected a happiness equal to her own. Instead Carl glared at her as though he wanted to spring at her throat. With his anger was mingled fear—humiliation—she knew not what emotions passed rapidly over his countenance.

"Don't you tell anybody else," he demanded. "And to-morrow I'll take you to a doctor who'll fix you up——"

"Fix me up?"

"Yes—fix you up! Don't you understand?"

Realization of what he meant came slowly to her. A bitterness filled her, bitterness that knew no end, bitterness worse than any she had ever known before. This, then, was the Carl she had loved, a shrivelling coward. What a fool she had been to have believed that to him their love was the beautiful thing which it had been to her.

"My dad'll kill me for this—he'll drive me away like a dog . . ." Carl was saying hoarsely.

He straightened up, fear leaving him.

"No—no—Mimi. We'll go straight to mother and she'll help us. We'll go away and get married—pretend we eloped."

He sought to put his arms around her. In his gesture there was a new note of possessiveness, his indecisiveness of the minutes before now gone.

She shrank from his touch. Her head went high and in her eyes was a look that frightened him.

"We'll do nothing of the kind!" she cried. "I was a fool —you are right. I thought you were fine—clean—different from the others. You're not. You're just the same weak, vile sort that you were always hating and denouncing."

"That's all right, Mimi," he sought to quiet her. "You're all unstrung now. We'll get married and give the kid a clean name——"

Mimi looked at him and in that glance was something that silenced him.

"Unstrung? Give the baby a clean name? After what you just suggested? You'll do nothing of the sort! I'm going to have this baby, do you hear me? I'm going to have him and he's going to be *all mine*. I guess he can get along lots easier with just a bad name than he can with a cowardly father——"

"Mimi, you don't know what you're saying!" Carl, now thoroughly alarmed, pleaded. "We've got to get married!"

"Got to? Well, we haven't got to and we won't! I'll get along somehow, don't you worry, but all the love I had for you has turned to black hate! This baby'll be mine—all mine!"

She rushed from the room, leaving him standing there. . . .

Safe in her room, she let the tears she had fought so hard to check in the parlour below flow without hindrance. As from a distance, she heard the front door slam and she breathed more easily, knowing Carl was no longer in the house.

She wondered why she had acted as she had, knowing as she did the full reason. Bitterness filled her as she went again and again over the scene just ended. Faith, deep, unlimited, had been killed. A bitter laugh mingled with her tears. She saw Carl now for the insincere *poseur* that he was —him whom she had thought decent and clean. For the first time there came over her a sense of shame—a feeling of guilt. She wondered how Mrs. Daquin would take it. Mimi determined resolutely that if there were a scene or recriminations of any sort she would leave and never return.

From below came the sound of Mrs. Daquin's voice, calling her. Mimi dried her tears away and went down. Mr. and Mrs. Hunter sat in the parlour. Behind them stood Carl, his head down. Mrs. Hunter rose and attempted to take Mimi in her arms. Mimi evaded her.

"You poor, dear child!" Mrs. Hunter consoled her.

"Thank you, Mrs. Hunter, but I don't need any pity—it's your son who needs it more," Mimi told her. Her voice was hard, flat, cold.

Mrs. Hunter was not to be deterred.

"But you and Carl must get married right away and save your name. When the baby's nearly here, you two can go off on a long trip. Oh, dear, I'm so terribly upset—I almost feel like I'm the guilty one, pleading with you to save him——"

Back and forth the discussion raged. Mr. Hunter urged. His wife pleaded. Mrs. Daquin stormed. But Mimi remained firm. . . .

After they had gone Mrs. Daquin took her turn.

"You silly little fool. You're crazy. You're going to get these crazy notions out of your head and marry Carl. I never in all my life heard of so silly a thing as this idea of yours. What if Carl is a weak and worthless scamp? Any kind of a man for a husband is better than none when a girl's in your fix. . . ."

On and on she went, denouncing, pleading, scorning, appealing.

Mimi listened to the Niagara of words but they served only to make her more determined to do as she had declared she would. Jean's words came to her—the advice he had given her long ago as they were about to leave New Orleans— "decide in your own mind the wisest, the best thing to be done, and then do it." As she looked at the four faces she wondered what Jean would say if he were here now. Even as Mrs. Daquin stormed, Mimi knew there was much right in what she said. She would be condemned, her name derided. She knew she could not remain in Atlanta. Even if she could,

[152]

the looks of disdain, the insults, would be unbearable. They had done that for years to the girl Carl had been going to see and they had had no definite proof on her of wrong-doing.

She wondered what she could do. Where could she go? She had no training by which she could earn a living. And she certainly would not go to any city where she was liable to meet anybody who knew her. She thought of Aunt Sophie and her invitation to come and live with her in New York. No, she couldn't accept that invitation now. Aunt Sophie would be just like these people here, would hate her for her misdeed. Suppose she did marry Carl. His parents would see that they wanted nothing. But always there would be in their minds, she was sure, the thought that she had come to them under a cloud—that she had done something dis-graceful and by that means had married into their family. Mimi felt sure in time they too would hate her as much as she now hated Carl. No, her mind was made up. Whatever she might have to suffer, it was better that she keep her own soul free. That would certainly not be true if she married Carl now.

Wearily she faced her step-mother and spoke. The words came slowly, painstakingly, as though she were explaining a complex matter to a rather stupid child.

"Yes, I know all that you say is true. I am foolish. I am bringing on myself a terrible responsibility. But I can't marry Carl—not now. He wanted me to go to a doctor—to fix me up—those were his very words. I hate him—and if I live to be a thousand years old I'll hate him more every day I live. Don't you worry—I'll go away—I don't know where, but anyway you won't be bothered with me any more. But I won't marry Carl. My mind's made up and I won't change it. . . ."

A few weeks later Mimi boarded a train for Philadelphia.

She could give no reason why she chose that city to which to go. The nearest she could explain her choice was that Philadelphia was large, she knew no one there and she was sure she could lose herself in its vastness. Mr. Hunter offered her money but she took only that which was due her through his purchase of half, her half, of the stock Jean had owned. Mrs. Daquin pleaded with her to the hour of departure to marry Carl, but Mimi's determination grew stronger with her pleading. As the train wound its way through the maze of tracks and puffed its way northward through the bare red hills of Georgia, she gazed from the car-window with the feeling that she had definitely closed the pages of the first book of her life. She stared at the darkening landscape long after the lights in the car were turned on, and wondered what was written on the pages of that second book whose cover she now was lifting. . . .

CHAPTER XIII

MONTH by month the time rolled slowly by for Mimi. She slept late in the morning, went out for walks in the afternoon or to a moving-picture show, retired early every evening. On Sundays she stole unobtrusively into the Catholic church near where she lived, varying this occasionally with attendance at the Methodist church to which the elderly couple with which she boarded belonged. They were simple, kindly people who made a comfortable living from a small catering business which kept them away from home a great deal. Mimi thus had the house to herself a large part of the time, for which she was grateful, as it relieved her of the strain of meeting and talking to people and answering embarrassing questions.

The old couple frequently speculated to themselves who and what she might be. To the woman's indirect and friendly questions Mimi gave evasive answers which seemed to satisfy the simple and uninquisitive nature of the elderly woman. To her neighbours she said that Mimi was a young widow grieving for her dead husband, which explanation, in view of the mourning garments Mimi yet wore for Jean, was accepted in good faith. Mimi often wept at the expressions, either by word or unobtrusive actions, of sympathy which came to her from the elderly couple and their friends. And often, too, guilt assailed her, for she felt she was accepting these ministrations under false colours. There were moments when she felt she could not accept them any longer, that she must tell them the true story. Always before taking such a step, however, she restrained her impulses. She knew no one else in Philadelphia who would take her in, she was paying for her room and excellent food a ridiculously low sum, and her little store of money which had seemed so large when Mr. Hunter had given it to her, was shrinking with dismaying speed.

When the long, dreary, slushy days of winter had given way to the invigorating and friendly warmth of an early spring, she spent most of her days sitting in the park. Used to the tropical heat of New Orleans, the biting winds and driving snows of the North made her miserable and depressed, though her years in Atlanta had inured her to a degree against the cold. But she did not like cold weather, and the coming of the days when she could see the delicate green of the sprouting grass and budding trees made her very happy.

She would take with her to the park a book or more often a newspaper but she seldom read. She was content to sit and watch children at play or gaze at friendly squirrels who so ludicrously sat rapidly revolving a nut disentombed from earthy caches in their little forepaws as they bit into its hard shell.

Even the sinking of a huge vessel like the *Titanic* after collision with an iceberg off the Canadian coast with great loss of life could not stir her. Nor could the hectic days of an election year stir her from her apathy. A former school-teacher from New Jersey, a prominent member of Congress, a twice-defeated candidate for the Presidency, a fat, jovial and weak President, and a vigorous ex-President were scrambling madly for nominations, but so far as Mimi was concerned, they might just as well have been struggling for the rulership of an obscure island in the South Seas.

As the time of her ordeal approached she achieved a calmness of which she had never believed herself capable. Her hatred, her contempt for Carl had passed and in its stead had come a complete lack of feeling towards him. She saw him now in perspective more and more clearly as the weak individ-

[156]

FLIGHT

ual he had proved himself to be. She wondered why she had
not seen it sooner, why traits of his which now were revealed
all too clearly had been invisible to her. His indecisiveness,
his succumbing to indifference and easy vices when they had
first parted on Hilda's account, should have been a clear warning to her. She did not object to his drinking or other derelictions on moral grounds. As a matter of fact Carl's association with the girl who was *déclassée* had not seemed to her
as a thing to be condemned. Towards the girl Mimi had had
a very kindly and sympathetic feeling and she had had no
word of condemnation or scorn for her. Mimi now realized
that she should have seen in these little strayings from which
she had saved Carl at such a cost to herself the true measure
of Carl's character. But even as she saw now what might
and should have been, she knew that at the time she had been
so blinded by her love for Carl she could never have realized the full importance of the things then under her very
eyes.

Her sense of contentment had its roots in a deep spiritual
awareness which gave her great comfort. She seldom
thought now of the condemnation she was doubtless receiving
in Atlanta. Instead she was happy, very happy she had acted
as she had. She and the baby would get along somehow and
they would be very happy together. Lacking respect, de-
spising Carl, she would never have been happy with him,
and her religion would not have allowed her to divorce him.
What though her money was disappearing so rapidly? By
economy she would surely have enough to last her through her
confinement and permit her to spend a few weeks in the
country until she was strong again. Then she could easily
get a job and she and the baby would be happy together.

She loved the restless stirring within her body, she was
happy at the signs of creation. It was a sensation at times
beautiful, at other times she was overwhelmed with the mar-

[157]

vellousness of it all. She experienced little surges of exultant joy that within herself she too had spiritual reserves which kept her soul free and intact despite what the world might say. Gone was the sense of being a depraved, a disgraced, a low creature which had assailed her those last few days in Atlanta. She was free! Free! Free!

Round and round she twisted the wide gold band on her left hand. This she was ashamed of after a fashion. Mrs. Manning, with whom she lived, had glanced significantly one day at her left hand as she sought gently to induce Mimi to talk. To avoid suspicion Mimi had gone to a pawnshop on South Street into whose windows she often glanced as she passed, fascinated by the clusters of knives and revolvers and boxing-gloves and baseball-mitts. Subconsciously a small sign had impressed itself upon her memory. It read:

LARGE ASSORTMENT OF WEDDING RINGS FOR SALE CHEAP

She knew that the bearded Jew who sold her the ring guessed her secret, her guilt had made her so nervous. She had taken the first one that fitted her finger, paid him to his joy and amazement the first price he had named, and hurried from the shop. It was a cheap and awkward-looking affair but it was an orthodox wedding ring. Whenever she glanced at it or felt it on her finger a wave of guilt, a depressing sense of her dishonesty, swept over her, but she kept it on whenever she emerged from her room, for it saved her embarrassing questions and kept down talk. . . .

One question occupied her more than any other. What her future and that of the child might be did not worry her half so much as did the sex of this stranger from another world who soon would be with her. She wanted it to be a girl on some days, more often she eagerly wished for a boy. Marriage for herself was now obviously out of the question—a

[158]

FLIGHT

boy would be less trouble and there would be fewer people to demand of him the story of his parentage than would be the case with a girl. Day after day this speculation went on endlessly, and she always came back to the exact spot in her reasoning from which she had begun. . . .

It was a boy. A hot night in early July saw his entry into the world after two days and two nights of pain which tore Mimi's body with its burning shafts of agony. When it was all over she lay in her narrow cot in the maternity ward of the public hospital and passed her hand lovingly over the tiny, shapeless mass of red flesh. There had never been any question in her mind regarding the name she should give him . . . Jean, of course. For his sake she had cheerfully lied in answering the usual form questions. . . . She had hoped to take at least a private room. But she had spent her money faster than she had realized and the private room would have made the weeks in the country impossible. . . .

She was glad afterwards she had put up with the lack of privacy and the other inconveniences of the public ward. Mr. Manning had arranged for her to stay with a friend of theirs in New Jersey and there Mimi was so contented, so happy, in the little cottage near Camden, she wished she could have remained there always. She loved to give Jean his bath, to feed him, to shower on him little attentions and superfluous affections. His clutching hands dug into her flesh as he nursed and the exquisite pain of it sent deliriously exhilarating tingles throughout her body. And she talked to him as though he were old enough to understand, whenever she was certain no one could overhear her.

"You're mine, baby Jean, all mine. . . . No other person owns any part of you. . . . I'll work for you, sacrifice everything for you . . . and we'll be happy, so happy, together. . . . You'll never know the agony your mother went

[159]

through. . . . I'll give everything gladly to save you and keep you free. . . ."

All too soon she was forced to return to Philadelphia. Up to this time Mimi had refused to permit herself to worry over the problem of earning a living for herself and little Jean. She told the Mannings frankly of her financial condition. They so readily showed their willingness to help her, it brought tears of gratitude that could not be checked. Her regular hours during the long months when she was awaiting Jean's arrival, the willingness she had always shown to help with any task around the house, her regular church attendance, had all combined to endear her to the elderly couple who had no children of their own.

"Don't you worry one little bit, honey," Mrs. Manning told her. "You'll never have to worry about rent or food—so long's we've got anything to eat and a roof over our heads you've them too."

They sat in the dining-room until long after midnight the evening Mimi returned from the country, devising ways and means of Mimi's earning in some way enough to supply the needs of herself and *"Petit* Jean," as she called the baby, to differentiate him from the Jean who had gone. Mr. Manning scratched his white head and pursed his lips as he gazed at the ceiling.

"You say you haven't been taught a trade—you're too good for housework—hm—let me see—let me see-e-e," he spoke half to himself, half to the two women. Mimi volunteered the information that she could sew rather well. "You can? Why'n't you tell me that before? Why, that settles it all! I'll speak to some of my customers and get you plenty of work doing sewing by the day." A smile, beautiful in its radiant joy at solution of the vexing problem, wreathed his face.

"But what about the baby?" his wife inquired. Mr. Man-

ning's face fell, wiped as clean of its elation as a blackboard
when a damp cloth is passed over it. "I'll tell you what we
can do," Mrs. Manning went on. "Days when I'm away we
can put him in a day nursery."

Mimi was not allowed to begin her new life for some time,
however. On one pretext after another her day of beginning
work was deferred by the Mannings. The most frequent excuse was that most of the people who needed the services of
a seamstress had gone away for the summer. Though Mimi
had now been in Philadelphia more than eight months she
knew little of the city. Her life before the baby was born
had been so limited a one she had seldom been farther from
home than a few blocks. The hugeness of the city, its teeming streets, the roar of traffic, the hurrying throngs, each
person in it set on his own affairs to the exclusion of everything and everybody else, frightened her. When she ventured
out alone she always had the feeling as though some huge hand
had picked her up and thrown her into a raging torrent. And
always she regained the haven of home with a prayer of thanksgiving in her heart that she had not been killed in the bustle
by one of the wagons or trucks that rushed down upon one with
such terrifying speed. Used to the somnolence of New Orleans
and the lesser traffic of Atlanta, she often wondered why she
had ever chosen Philadelphia as her city of refuge—"City of
Brotherly Love" was certainly an anachronism to a stranger
like herself.

She was happy with the Mannings but her inaction worried
her. Except for a few dollars she was now completely without funds. She had had to buy a number of things for the
baby but even though she had made most of his clothes herself, cloth and thread and buttons cost. She did not tell the
Mannings of her worries, for they invariably sought to dismiss
them from her mind. But she had overheard snatches of
their conversation when they did not know she was near—in

the small house a secret conversation was most difficult—and she had noticed little economies they practised, and not because of parsimony. The two were getting old, there were fewer and fewer calls every year now for their services. Younger and more progressive people were gobbling the bulk of the catering jobs. Their older customers they yet retained, but some of these were dying off and others entertained less, for they too were getting old. Their sons and daughters who now had their own homes went to the established firms where newer and fresher and more bizarre effects could be obtained than those of the old order furnished by the Mannings.

Having always been thrifty, the Mannings had saved some money, but they knew and Mimi knew that they would need all of this in the years to come when even the little work they now did would be gone and they would be too old to do any work at all. Mimi was miserable when she thought of this and she seemed to herself to be a leech feeding off the bodies of these two who had been so generous to her, a stranger.

And this guilty feeling was added to when she thought, as she frequently did, that she had eaten of their bread under false colours. Mrs. Manning might as well have applied hot irons to Mimi's flesh unwittingly as to mention Mimi's "late husband." Never was there any malice or inquisitiveness in her voice, and that lack of suspicion hurt Mimi a thousand times more than accusations and recriminations.

"If your poor husband had only lived to see the baby!" or "Does the boy take after you or your husband?" she would say gently, and her innocent words would make Mimi feel like a distillation of all the Judas Iscariots, the Benedict Arnolds, the Tartuffes, the Pharisees and all the other deceivers and hypocrites of history. Now that she had regained her strength, her inaction annoyed her, the very food she ate at times almost choked her because after all it was charity and more, charity granted through deceit and lies. Time and time again she determined to blurt out the truth to the Mannings whatever the result might be, but each time she decided to put off her confession until she was earning enough money to provide for the baby at least if the Mannings should turn against her. She justified this in her own mind by assuring herself that had she been alone she would have told them her story long since whatever the consequences might have been. But when she saw *"Petit* Jean" cooing and kicking in the old-fashioned crib which Mr. Manning had brought down from the attic where it had lain for many years (they had had one child who was born dead), Mimi felt she could not in common sense risk the possibility of the baby's suffering.

Her qualms of conscience were solved for her in an unexpected manner. Early in November the first sleet and snow of the year came down upon the city. Mr. Manning was returning home after a shopping tour, a heavy basket on his arm. Nearing the house, he slipped and fell. The doctor set the broken hip and announced that he would be confined to his bed for many weeks. Mimi stayed as long as she felt she was needed, she did not want Mrs. Manning to feel she would desert her when her services were needed. But she located a boarding-place, arranged for *Petit* Jean to stay by day at a nursery, and secured work sewing by the day through scanning the want ads and inquiry through the Mannings and one of their friends. The elderly couple objected to her going but they were not adroit enough in concealing their feelings to keep from her a note of relief. . . .

Month after month of the drab life rolled by. At her new home Mimi realized now how kind the Mannings had really been to her. Not that her new landlady was unkind. She too was good in her way, but lacking in understanding, in sympathy. Because her income was uncertain and she knew there would be days when she would have no work, Mimi had taken a place where she could obtain lodging at the lowest figure possible and at the same time secure respectability. Early in the morning she rose, gave Jean his bath and dressed him, prepared his breakfast and her own, took him to the nursery and went to her work. Returning in the evening, she brought him home, prepared him for bed, got her dinner and soon afterwards retired. This regular schedule was broken only by the all-too-frequent days when she had no work. The one bright spot in the week was Sunday, when she kept Jean with her and took him for short walks. She gave up attendance at church, for she was envious of anything which took her away from Jean.

Of social life or recreation there was none for her. She could not afford to spend money for even moving-picture shows. She occasionally visited the Mannings, telling them glowing accounts of the ease with which she was meeting her new life, telling these little falsehoods so convincingly that they in their innocence believed her. Mr. Manning was slowly getting better but his age was against him, his bones did not knit as rapidly as they had hoped. Always they asked Mimi when she would return to them. But she could tell with no great difficulty from their voices and the worried look on their faces that things were not moving so well with them and that their invitations, while sincere, would, if accepted, have multiplied burdens already heavy. She assured them she was having no difficulties whatever, and even brought little gifts of flowers or fruit to them which meant the sacrifice of food often for herself.

She made no calls nor had she any other intimates than these. Her trials and difficulties had given a depth to Mimi's expression which, instead of making her less attractive, had added a richness to what had been a childish, flowerlike beauty. Almost automatically she drew to her the gaze of

[164]

men whom she passed on the street and she knew what these looks meant. She hurried along with downcast eyes to escape them, frightened by their boldness. She felt safe, for she seldom ventured forth after nightfall, but even in the daytime these unmistakable glances caused a nausea to well up within her. In the episode with Carl, Mimi had given herself freely and with no sense of shame or guilt but she had loved him when that had taken place. But these unsolicited attentions caused a revulsion within her which swept through her like a physical illness.

One of her best-paying customers for whom she sewed regularly every Thursday lived in Germantown. Often the work was so great she did not leave until very late but she was glad of this, for she was paid generously for her overtime and received her dinner, which meant an additional saving. One Thursday afternoon as she came down the stairs from the room where she always worked she met the husband of her employer.

"Hello," he greeted her, "and who are you?"

She told him. After answering various questions regarding the length of time she had worked there and listening to his surprised comment that he had not seen her during all that time, he let her pass. But the following Thursday he was there again, this time earlier than before. He came into the room where she was hurrying through her work.

"Tell me about yourself," he demanded, pleasantly, too pleasantly Mimi thought.

"There's little to tell. I work for my living."

"Your husband's dead, then?" he remarked, looking at her black dress. Mimi yet wore mourning, partly because she could afford no new clothes. She began to gather her work to avoid his questions.

"You don't mean to tell me you're coloured?" he pursued,

[165]

incredulously. "My wife told me about having a coloured girl sewing for her but I never expected to see anybody looking like *you!*"

"I am coloured," Mimi assured him firmly as she tried to leave the room.

"Wait a minute—wait a minute," he hastened to add. "I don't mean any harm. I was born in the South and I always liked Negroes."

"That's very kind of you—but I've got to hurry home," Mimi nervously answered as she sought to leave the room. He stood in front of her, his hands clasped behind his back, and the smile on his face made her think instinctively of a fat, sleepy-eyed and sleek cat teasing a mouse before devouring it.

"Those pretty little hands of yours are too delicate for hard work—and I never saw such lovely hair—do you know, I always was peculiarly susceptible to yellow hair——"

He drawled the words in what doubtless seemed to him to be an effective manner. He almost purred them. Mimi did not know whether to laugh or cry. She had seen scenes like this in the movies, and the cheap melodrama of such episodes had invariably made her want to snicker at their absurdity. But here was the thing she had laughed at in mild amusement happening to her, and it wasn't all play, she knew, nor was she unaware of the very real danger behind his smooth and would-be seductive manner. At first she had been frightened, now she had to put forth a very real effort to keep from smiling. He felt the change in her manner and mistakenly thought it to be progress on his part.

"You don't have to work so hard if you don't want to," he suggested, his words becoming bolder not so much in the actual phrases he used as in their increased suggestiveness. "I have no objection to coloured girls—in fact, I really prefer them——"

FLIGHT

"That's really very nice of you—very generous indeed," Mimi observed, her amusement now rapidly conquering her apprehension.

"Oh, no, not at all—not at all!" he protested, thinking her serious. "Even when I lived in the South I had none of the usual prejudice."

"How very remarkable!" cooed Mimi. Her voice had in it the velvety smoothness of swan's-down.

To himself he thought, this is easier than I expected, as he advanced possessively towards her.

"How soon am I going to see you?" he queried softly.

"Don't be silly!" Mimi calmly advised him. "In the first place you are fat. In the second, you are old and bald. In the third, you are white. Fourth, you are vain and stupid and ignorant and repulsive. Don't think I'm falling back on the sentimental melodramatics of the 'poor working girl.' I'm not—I let you run along just to set the stage for telling you my opinion of you."

Her voice was as dispassionate as that of a schoolgirl monotonously listing the products from Brazil. There were no heroics, no tears, but only a relentless cataloguing of the physical and mental defects of the would-be Casanova. He gasped.

"You little fool—you ought to feel proud that I, a white man, would even want you—a nigger!"

Her face flamed at the despised word but she kept her temper.

"I'm not surprised at your thinking that. I suppose even that such a notion is natural—you've made your own ideas about your own attractiveness and irresistibility and you've told yourself so often you're invincible you believe it yourselves. Seducers of servant-girls! A noble accomplishment!"

Infuriated at her impassivity and her ridicule, so markedly a contrast to what he had assumed was complacence, he

[167]

sought to seize her. She eluded him with the same coolness and remarked as she left the room: "It doesn't really seem wise, does it, to create a scene in your own home where your wife is within hearing distance?"

A faint, mocking laugh trailed back to him as he stood there after she had gone. . . .

CHAPTER XIV

MIMI was not greatly surprised when she received a
message that she would no longer be expected on
Thursdays at the Germantown home. At first it
amused her. Had she resorted to tears or pleading for release or any of the usual methods of damsels in defence of
their virtue, she reflected, the curt note of dismissal would
not have been sent. Man is a peculiar creature. So long as
by implication or any other means he is allowed to imagine
himself the superior being, whether that superiority came
through brute strength or intellect or wealth or any other
means, he is manageable and easily gulled. But when he is
made ridiculous and the little bubble of his conceit is pricked
by a woman's obvious contempt, he becomes a vengeful and
ridiculous person.

Mimi was sustained by her elation at the ease with which
she had escaped an unpleasant and possibly dangerous situation. She was glad she had retained her poise. She felt
angry only when she remembered the nasty way in which he
had implied and later definitely stated that in his opinion she
should have been happy, being coloured, to have attracted his
notice. For the first time she saw the reasons for Jean's apprehension in those talks which seemed to have taken place so
many years ago. Life for any woman who was unprotected
and who sought to live up to certain ideals was hard. But
when that woman was coloured she was more than ever at
the mercy of those who were her constant pursuers. She
found her old race-consciousness surging up again. Bitter-

ness against the husband of her former employer welled in her not so much because he had assumed she would be amenable to his suggestions but more because he had so readily assumed that she, being coloured, would offer no objections whatever.

But when her joy in her victory and her bitterness at the vanquished had passed, she found that the revenue lost in this manner was seriously affecting her. She found other jobs but none of them were as regular nor did they pay as well. Every dollar counted, every fraction of a dollar earned or expended made a difference. Once or twice she had been a few days late in paying the rent for the small room in which she and *Petit* Jean lived. The lessened cordiality with which her landlady greeted her pleas for more time for payment made this an ordeal she avoided even when it meant, as it frequently did, the forgoing of meals for herself.

Petit Jean thrived and grew, singularly free from the maladies of childhood. With what to Mimi seemed amazing speed, his monthly birthdays sped by and accumulated—the fifth, the sixth, the seventh, the eighth. As long as he was well and clothed and fed, Mimi's own difficulties seemed of little more than passing moment. Nothing greatly matters, she comforted herself, when seen in perspective—it is only when a thing is happening that it frightens and pains one. She found a new strength coming to her out of the problems and perplexities she was meeting. It was, she found, like looking into a mirror. When one did look the image was there and if one was sick or unhappy it gave back a reflection of that condition or mood. But as soon as one removed himself from a place in front of the looking-glass the image was gone. She consoled herself with this convenient philosophy and found in it a courage of which she would not have believed herself capable.

But inevitably there came to her periods of depression.

FLIGHT

Most frequently these occurred when she thought of Jean's future. Suppose her own health failed. She could not go on indefinitely this way, common sense told her, going without food, improperly clothed, saving nothing. Her rather ample wardrobe which she had brought from Atlanta was nearly threadbare and she just could not afford to spend money on adornment for herself. Little garments for Jean, talcums, soaps, and the infinite variety of essentials which an infant required for his comfort took all she could earn and more.

It seldom occurred to her she could have asked and received aid from the Hunters, Mrs. Daquin or her Aunt Sophie. The idea at times of greatest need came fleetingly to her, hazily, but she resolutely put it from her mind before it could find lodgment there. Whatever else might come to her, she would never yield to such temptations, at least she would never permit herself to beg from her step-mother or Carl's parents. To do so would have been surrender of the principle for which she had so bravely fought—the determination to keep her own soul free. However adroitly worded, a plea to them would have been admission of defeat, of her failure to make good the lofty words of determination she had spoken. She knew they did not understand the motives which had driven her on. In truth, she sometimes wondered if she herself knew them. But when she held Jean in her arms, when his toothless smile greeted her on her calling for him at the nursery, when his warm flesh rested against her side in bed, she was happy to a degree which she knew would never have been possible had she accepted the easier way out of her difficulties. No, despite all, she knew, her course had been the only one she could have taken in the face of Carl's abject failure to measure up to the high qualities with which she had in fancy endowed him.

One extravagance, a pitifully small one, she permitted herself. In the late spring she passed an old second-hand book shop on a side street. She lingered at the weather-beaten old table outside the shop, fingering, examining, peeping into the battered and worn books displayed there. Volume after volume she looked into but most of them were dull and prosy stuff which bored her. She lingered so long the proprietor came to the door and stood there looking everywhere except at her, with too great casualness, Mimi reflected with a smile. It amused her to watch him with equal lack of obviousness, knowing that his suspiciousness led him to remain there. She named him "Old Scrooge," for he looked at though he had stepped from Dickens' pages with his fringe of dusty grey hair, his square, steel-rimmed spectacles, his baggy and nondescript clothing.

The game interested her and she lingered, idly fingering book after book. Her delay was repaid when a dingy, much-handled volume seemed to spring from the table, bringing with it a strange thrill. Jean had had a copy of this same book. So had Carl. Both of them had with elaborate indirection kept it from her and, with natural curiosity, she had always been eager to know why. And, with equal naturalness, she had made a solemn vow to read it from cover to cover when she could put her hands upon a copy. It was "Leaves of Grass." She opened it eagerly. Her eyes fell on the yellowed page. They read:

O ME! O LIFE!

O Me! O Life! of the questions of these recurring,
Of the endless trains of the faithless, of cities fill'd with the foolish,
Of myself for ever reproaching myself (for who more foolish than I, and who more faithless?),
Of eyes that vainly crave the light, of the objects mean, of the struggle ever renew'd,
Of the poor results of all, of the plodding and sordid crowds I see around me,

Of the empty and useless years of the rest, with the rest me inter-
twined,
The question, O me! so sad, recurring—What good amid these,
O me, O life?

Answer

That you are here—that life exists and identify,
That the powerful play goes on, and you may contribute a verse.

The old man, the shop, the passers-by, everything was blotted
out by the words, powerful, true, so applicable to her own
case. "That the powerful play goes on, and *I* may contribute a verse," she repeated softly, consciously changing the pro-
noun. She paid the man for the book, cheerfully giving up
the food which the book would cost, and hurried home with it.

When she had put Jean to bed she sat and read over and
over again the words. "Foolish and faithless." "For who
more foolish than I, and who more faithless?" She had
been foolish, to the dead Jean she had been faithless. To
herself, but a wild happiness filled her that in the hour of
difficulty, at the time when she had been forced to make the
biggest decision of her life, she may have been foolish but not
faithless. She fell asleep whispering: "That the powerful
play goes on, and *I, Mimi Daquin,* may contribute a verse."

The words gave her a comforting sense of direction. She
had been blindly wandering, groping, striving towards a goal
that had never been clear, indeed she had never even vaguely
visualized any destination other than the struggle to do those
things which seemed to her to be right. Even for this indefinite rightness or wrongness she had no tangible definition—
she sought only by instinct or conscience or some other indefinable guide the path to truth and beauty and happiness. . . .

This new consciousness gave her faith and courage at a
time when she needed these things more than she had ever

[173]

needed them before. Summer came with the usual migration of the few regular customers she had to the seashore or the mountains. Mimi no longer called on the Mannings, for she could no longer conceal even from their unsuspecting eyes the extent of her distress. She saved the small fee at the day nursery, for it was seldom now that she had to be away from home. Her rent was several weeks overdue and the relations between Mimi and her landlady had reached an actually strained point.

"Stuck-up niggers think they can sponge off of common ones—humph! I'll show her she can't make no footmat out of me!" she overheard her landlady saying to her husband one evening. "An' I ain't never been satisfied she's respectable—if that baby's got a daddy he must have had some relatives she could get money from. I'm tired of foolin' with her and if she don't pay me by Sad'dy I'm goin' to put her and her baby right out there in the street!"

Sick at heart, hungry, discouraged, Mimi slowly struggled up the stairs to her room. Even *Petit* Jean's coos of welcome could not cheer her up. She lay on the bed beside him and wept.

And as though she had not already enough to bear, she found new trouble awaiting her that dwarfed all that had gone before, when she returned to the house the following evening after another day of fruitless search for work. Mrs. Williams, her landlady, had volunteered to care for Jean while she was out, despite her words of the night before. When the rickety screen door banged behind her, Mimi heard Mrs. Williams calling from the rear of the house. On an old davenport lay Jean, vomiting wretchedly. Intermittently he screamed, writhing in the paroxysmal pain which recurred every few minutes. On his face was a ghastly pallor and he seemed in a state of complete collapse.

Mimi rushed to the cot and fell on her knees beside Jean

as she flung anxious questions at the perspiring, frightened woman above her.

"Yes'm, I called a doctor—my doctor—and he said it wasn't nothing but cramps. He gave your baby some castor oil, but soon as the doctor left he began throwin' up and yellin' mo' than ever." . . .

Mimi, frightened as she was, remained calm.

"While I take him up to my room, will you get Dr. Newton?" she asked. She knew him by sight, having seen him at church often when she had gone there with the Mannings. His name came instantly to her, for she had been told many times of his eminence among the coloured physicians of Philadelphia. He came at once, trim, alert, intelligent. His brown face was a mask as he asked questions and examined Jean. Long brown fingers probed the baby's abdomen, methodically, confidently he measured pulse and temperature. Coolly he recited the symptoms as he found them:

". . . vomiting, at first contents of stomach, then bilious . . . collapse . . . pallor . . . feeble pulse . . . temperature normal . . . abdomen relaxed . . . increasing prostration . . . rising temperature . . . tumour, sausage-shaped, curving . . ." He turned to Mimi. "What's been done for him?" Mimi told him of the doctor called by Mrs. Williams, of the administration of castor oil.

"He said somepin about 'fectious diarrhœa," Mrs. Williams added, her fright now gone with the coming of Dr. Newton.

"Gave him castor oil?" Dr. Newton asked, incredulously. "The blithering fool!"

Mimi and Mrs. Williams showed their dismay at his words.

"Thank goodness he's probably vomited it all up by now." His words were punctuated by Jean's pathetic screams.

"Mrs. Daquin, your baby's got a bad case of intussusception—folding back of a part of the intestine over another part," he added as she showed her lack of comprehension of

[175]

the longer word. "Or, to make it simpler, it's acute intestinal obstruction. The only chance of saving him is through an operation—and it'll have to be done without an hour's delay."

Mimi sank her head into her hands. Had she just heard the death sentence pronounced on her, she would have felt not half as terrified as the thought of her *Petit* Jean going under the knife. She felt sick, disheartened, beaten. She raised a haggard face, her hair dishevelled, to the doctor.

"Isn't there anything else than operating?" she pleaded.

"Nothing," he told her. "And even then the chances are somewhat less than one in ten. This sounds hard and brutally frank—but it's best you know the truth," he added kindly, deep pity in his voice for her distress.

"Then operate," she declared, firmly, all panic gone from her face and voice. . . .

They drove rapidly to the coloured hospital where Dr. Newton was to operate on Jean. Mimi held his tiny form close to her, stifling its screams in the softness of her breast. On her face was fear, despair, agony without hope. She was haunted by the spectre of death, she saw before her *Petit* Jean lifeless, never again to coo and smile and welcome her with soft little cries. Not until now did she realize how much he meant to her. She felt guilty of a great crime, of putting food into her own body when it might have averted this horrible thing. Even Dr. Newton's assurance in answer to her timid questioning that physicians did not know the cause of the malady other than that it was due to the thinness of the intestinal walls of an infant, that most frequently it occurred in apparently perfectly healthy and well-cared-for children, her feeling of guilt did not leave her. Jean's eyes were closed. He seemed to be in a deep stupor from which he roused only when another spasm of pain came over him.

[176]

FLIGHT

Mimi kissed him feverishly, madly, as the nurse took him gently from her. . . .

Up and down the hall she paced oblivious of everything save the tragic scene being enacted on the other side of the closed door. The odour of the anæsthetic stifled her, choked her, made her want to cry out in suffocation. The feeble little cries and groans as Jean slowly passed into unconsciousness made her frantic. She wanted to burst open the door, snatch him from the cruel knives, take him and the two of them plunge to simultaneous death in the waters of the river near-by. The immaculate nurses who passed rapidly infuriated her, they seemed so calm, so callous. She wanted to seize them and shake them until their teeth rattled, screaming: "Don't you realize that my Jean—*mon pauvre Petit Jean*—is being cut to pieces in there!" . . . She wanted to do all these things but she did none of them. She paced frantically back and forth, back and forth, for hours, days, centuries, past the closed door. . . .

"Operation's a success—he's resting easily—won't know until a day or two. . . ." The words came to her as from a great distance. "You'd better go home—there's no good you can do here—it'll be half an hour or so before he comes out from under the anæsthetic . . . and then he'll probably sleep. . . ."

"Mother of God! Save him! Save him!"

It had been a long time since a prayer had passed Mimi's lips. But now she prayed—prayed with the fervour of Luther, of Savonarola, of St. John, of all the martyrs, yea, with a fervour greater than all of these, the plea of a mother for her child. . . .

All night she alternately tossed in her narrow bed or sat by the window looking into the darkness outside. Above, a

[177]

pale moon was sheathed in dusky blue swirls of clouds, so delicate and wispy they looked like graceful twistings of chiffon,
but this beauty she did not see. From near at hand the fast-
dying noises of the city came to her, the hum imperceptibly
fading away as the crowds thinned out, but she heard none
of these. Any minute Jean might be dying, she thought with
a shiver. And then she would hurry down the stairs to telephone the hospital. Always she received the same answer,
he's resting easily.

Though she tried to keep the thought from her mind, she
knew she had come to the parting of the ways. I wonder I
ever thought I could go through with it, she reflected. For
my own sake I don't care. But I'm not making enough money
to keep us and I won't be able to save anything at this rate
for the future—for *Petit* Jean's future, she amended. Rent
due Mrs. Williams, the surgeon's fee, bills for the hospital.
She cudgelled her brains for some way of making money. The
Hunters? No! Mrs. Daquin? A thousand times no! The
man in Germantown? A bitter smile came over her face.
It wouldn't be wise for him to make such an offer now.

The thought brought her to herself with a shock. Defiantly she answered her own question—I'd do even that if it
would save Jean! She had reached the stage of desperation.
The long months of anxious toil and uncertainty, of worry
and undernourishment, had gathered their toll. Now that
Jean's life hung in the balance, she felt that there were no
means to which she would not go. But all the possible
sources of help she could think of would serve only to help
her out of her present dilemma and would offer no lasting
solution. Only one thing was certain—it was not only impossible to go on as she had during the last few months but
she was seriously jeopardizing Jean and his future. She did
not know but that she might have a serious accident or be-

come dangerously ill, perhaps die. What then would happen to him if he should live? She had sacrificed so much for him already, she would under no circumstances want him to go to the Hunters or to her step-mother, even if either of them would take him.

She wrestled with her problem but morning found her no nearer its solution. As soon as daylight came she dressed and went to the hospital. Jean had come out from under the anæsthetic. He greeted her with a faint smile, infinitely pathetic in its unconscious bravery. She sank to her knees gazing into his face as though he had died and had come to life again before her very eyes. And as she looked deep into his brown eyes and pallid face she offered a prayer of thanksgiving to the Virgin for life for Jean. . . .

Dr. Newton found her there.

"Well, he pulled through all right and, barring set-backs or complications, he'll be well before long," he cheerfully told her.

After they left the room Mimi told Dr. Newton frankly of her financial position. It galled her to be forced to confess her poverty but she could see no other way out of it and she was unwilling to do other than be truthful about it.

"Oh, that's all right," he assured her. "We doctors are used to waiting for our money. And the Mannings have told me about you—I'm not worried. Pay me when you can—no, I'll tell you what. Operations like the one I did on your baby are mighty rare. I've been practising medicine for fourteen years now and it's the first one I've ever seen outside of a clinic. You pay the hospital bills and I'll just dismiss the bill. The case is so remarkable a one that I'll gladly let the fee go——"

She protested vigorously against his proposal. She was grateful, so grateful the tears stood in her eyes. But, fol-

FLIGHT

lowing so closely upon her confession of poverty, it smacked
too much of charity, and she would not, she could not permit
that.

"Well, have it your own way," he finally agreed. "But
don't hurry."

She was touched by his kindness. He hurried away. When
he was gone a dozen phrases of thanks came to her mind,
vexing her that she had been too stunned by his generosity to
think of them before he had gone. . . .

As if Fate felt ashamed of the blows it had dealt her,
there came to Mimi several profitable jobs during the four
weeks Jean was in the hospital. One of these lasted more
than a week, the making of the trousseau of a girl who belonged to one of the old Philadelphia coloured families.
She never knew that she had been recommended by Dr. Newton, but the money she earned enabled her to pay not only
the hospital bill but to settle a part of the debt she owed Mrs.
Williams. Now that Jean was out of danger and well on the
road to recovery, Mimi worked with a song in her heart and
happiness in the belief that her darkest days were past.
And when he was returned from the hospital she bought little
things for his amusement, toys, games, dainty bits of the
foods he was allowed to eat. She was envious of everything
which separated her from him even for a short time, she be-
grudged the hours they spent in sleep, for they robbed her,
she felt, of so many moments of conscious knowledge of and
contact with him.

The acuteness of her desire to be with Jean was rooted
not alone in the to her more than miraculous escape he had
had. It was, too, in the decision she had reached through
that illness and the inevitability of execution of that decision pained her beyond measure. Mimi had faced during
her dark hours when Jean's life hung in the balance the
practical situation before her. Ruthlessly she had cut away

[180]

all the entangling meshes created by her love for Jean and
had considered as dispassionately as she could the question as
to what course would be for his greatest good. She found
she could not approach the Hunters or her stepmother and
she would rather have died herself than to have surrendered
Jean to either of them. Those contingencies therefore were
definitely out of the question.

So too was the possibility of her attempting to carry on the
struggle she had now been making for more than a year. If
only I could get some money saved and secure a steady income,
perhaps start a small dressmaking establishment of my own, I
could see my way clear. But these possibilities seemed to her
much more remote than the probability of her jumping safely
to the moon. Another thing was certain. There was little
chance of her making any great progress in Philadelphia.
New York to her seemed the only field in which any marked
advance could be made, but here again there were the same
problems if not greater ones.

Mimi found a certain grim amusement in remembering
the tenuous plans she had so confidently builded and which
now had tumbled about her. Realizing her own weakness for
the first time, comprehending that she could not make the
fight alone, she wrote tentatively of her distress to her Aunt
Sophie. The second day after her letter was posted there
came an answer—a warmingly cordial letter—scolding Mimi
because she had not called upon her aunt for aid long before,
offering Mimi whatever aid she needed. From the envelope
there fell a cheque of generous size. And the letter ended:

"Alone you will have little trouble, especially if you come to New
York. But with the baby it will be harder—you would have to be
away all day—and people, even here, do talk. I know just how you
feel about it, but why don't you put Jean in a home until you can
get on your feet? I don't urge this—I merely suggest it. Do what
you think is wisest and best."

FLIGHT

Finally a decision had been made, the only possible way out, and she wept many bitter tears before she would let herself even consider this solution. Always, however, she had come back to it—the suggestion of Aunt Sophie—the one stable thing in a sea of uncertainties. She would put Jean in a children's home, work as hard as mortal could toil, save her money until she had accumulated enough to assure herself and him freedom from their more immediate wants, and then get him again when she had gained her objective.

And here she was confronted with another problem. She was unwilling to put him in a Negro orphanage, for their all-too-slender resources made it problematical if he would receive the care and attention he needed. She would rather struggle along in her present hopeless way than have him neglected. Nor would she want to place him in a white orphanage as a Negro child—she knew the insults and slights he would be forced to suffer. The only recourse left to her and the one she decided upon was to place him in a Catholic orphanage and say nothing about his Negro blood. This had been done, she knew, even with children not nearly so fair as Jean. His French name would be an additional safeguard to him and further assurance he would be given all the advantages available.

She had had some qualms of conscience about this procedure. She had wondered if she were doing the right thing, if she were not placing Jean at such a disadvantage in the event his coloured blood were discovered that it would be greater than if his race were told of at the beginning. But she soon dismissed these fears from her mind. In the first place, it would be only for a short time, and in the second, he had so little coloured blood there was really little question that could be raised. Overshadowing both of these was the mood of desperation in which her ill fortune had forced her. Just as in the hours of that night when Jean was lying at the hos-

[182]

FLIGHT

pital she had been willing to go to any length to save him, so now she was willing to take any step, legal or illegal, to secure for him as much security and comfort as was possible. It was the relentless, the ruthless, the uncompromising logic of a mother fighting for its own, and obstacles of whatever size were bowled over in eagerness to gain that end. . . .

She had decided on a home in Baltimore, for she felt that there where so many Catholics lived there would be greater advantages for the unfortunate children of that faith. The bleak November day when she carried Jean there was no more cold and dreary than Mimi's heart. *Petit* Jean seemed to feel the impending separation. He clung to Mimi, showering little affections upon her that tore her heart with pain. Her eyes filled with tears, she rushed from the place as though it were plague-stricken to take the train to New York. She had written her Aunt Sophie telling her plans and she had received a letter, short, but warm and sincere. Her aunt had approved her plans and urged her to come to New York and live with her while she was working out a solution to her problems. Mimi had accepted gratefully, glad of the haven to which she could go.

CHAPTER XV

JUST as she had had the feeling on leaving Atlanta that she had closed the pages of a volume in the story of her life, so now did Mimi sense intuitively that the second book was being shut, never to be opened again. Through the fading light of a dreary, cold day the train sped across the desolate Jersey meadows. Just dipping below the horizon, a frigid sun gave a sickly brilliance but no warmth. Mimi shivered. The dreariness of the landscape was relieved only by the lank chimneys of factories belching turgescent billows of smoke. From these dingy buildings poured streams of men as dingy as the factories from which they were emerging. Dinner-pails in hand, they plodded wearily across the waste places in knots of twos and threes, home to slatternly, waspish wives.

Into the murky darkness of Newark the train rumbled, paused momentarily, and then went its way into the gathering darkness. Lights began to twinkle in the dusty windows of the factories and the nondescript homes along the tracks. Into Manhattan Transfer and out again, past a fertilizer factory that filled the car with the fetid odours of offal, and the train plunged into the roaring, alarming bowels of the earth beneath the Hudson River. Mimi knew of the tunnel and was prepared for it but the shock coming so suddenly following the dismal screeching of the whistle blowing for the tunnel frightened her. Midway where there is an opening going up from the tunnel to the air above she felt relieved that the ordeal was over but again the train rushed on into darkness after the flash of grey. Her ears pounded. She pressed the

[134]

heels of her hands against them to relieve the roaring in them. She was glad when at last the electric engine pulled its way into the maze of winding tracks on the New York side. . . .

Bewildered by the hugeness of the Pennsylvania Station, made timid by the rushing throngs all seemingly with some definite destination the reaching of which in the shortest possible time was apparently of vast importance, Mimi with protest yielded her shabby bag to the porter and followed him up the narrow stairs. She peered upwards at the faces which scanned the incoming passengers through iron fences which made her think of prisoners or animals eager to escape. She was gripped with fear—no Aunt Sophie was to be seen, but that fear was changed to happiness when she was inundated with affectionate greeting by her aunt.

"You poor dear, I ought to be angry with you for not coming to me sooner, but I'm so glad to see you I just can't be," her aunt welcomed her.

Threading her way deftly through the crowd, she led Mimi, her eyes distended at the bewildering massiveness of the building, down into the earth again. Ashamed of her greenness, Mimi shrank from the roaring monster that leapt upon them from the yawning blackness of a cavern made blacker by dim lights but faintly discernible in the cavern. With a horrible grinding of brakes the creature came to a stop and Mimi found herself shoved into it. Station after station they passed and once more they came to the street, this time in a setting more familiar to her, yet strange, and her bewilderment was decreased but little.

For here was a new life, teeming, exotic, individual. Hurrying along the streets, coming out of restaurants, standing in doorways and on street corners were groups of Negroes, well dressed, jubilant, cheerful. Here and there hurried coloured men in twos and threes, clad in smartly fitting dinner

FLIGHT

jackets, snow-white bosoms peeping from heavy overcoats, musical instruments, violins, saxophones, mandolins in cases clutched in their hands. They hastened into the subway kiosk Mimi and her aunt had just quitted and were swallowed up. From near by there came to them the bewitching odours of frying corn and chicken, of pig's-feet. They came from a stand where a middle-aged coloured woman was serving her wares to passers-by.

"That's 'Pig-Foot Mary'—she's making lots of money at that little stand and she's saving it, too," Mrs. Rogers informed Mimi.

She was thrilled by the new scene. Gone was the morbid, morose, worried air of the people she had encountered at the other end of the subway. Here there was spontaneous laughter, shrewd observations which brought loud and free laughter from listeners. There was an exhilarating sense here that these people knew the secret of enjoying life. Black and brown and yellow faces flitted by, some carefree, some careworn. Mimi sensed again the essential rhythm, the oneness of these variegated colours and moods. It was all vivid, colourful, of a pattern distinctive and apart, and she warmed to the friendliness of it all. . . .

Behind them stood two flashily dressed coloured men as they took it all in. The voice of one worried, the other conciliatory.

"Say, Sam, I sent the fifty dollars and my application to Jim Washington like you told me to," the worried voice complained, "and I ain't heard nothing a-tall from him or the Idlehour Social Club either."

"Ain't you heard you was blackballed?" the other inquired with a markedly incredulous air.

"No, I ain't. I wonder who could've blackballed me," he speculated, the worry in his tones increasing. "There's Pudd'n' Jones—he's a friend of mine and he wouldn't do that

[186]

to me. And there's Babe Carter and Spider and Bill Johnson—they're friends of mine and they wouldn't blackball me,
I know. Say, was there many black balls in that box?" he
inquired, hopefully.

"You've seen a bowl of Russian caviare, ain't you?" his
friend asked.

"Yeh—but what's that got to do with them blackballing
me?"

"Well, boy, just this—that box when they voted on your
name looked just like a bowl of caviare." . . .

"Come along, Mimi, we can't stand here all night—dinner's
ready at home," urged Mrs. Rogers. Mimi could have stood
there for hours. The colourful scenes fascinated her, made
her want to stay there and watch the comedies, the tragedies,
the shifting panorama of life as it flowed, now swiftly, now
slowly, by. Down Lenox Avenue they walked. Harlem,
which first had been Dutch "Haarlem," then Irish, afterwards
Jewish and German, was in the flood-tide of transition to a
Negro city within a city. From the doorway of a former
private dwelling in a side street near bustling Lenox Avenue
came a resonant flooding swell of music. High above the rest
sounded a heavy barytone, chopping off of the words like little
sausages, setting the beat like a metronome for the other singers.

> "What a friend we have in Jesus,
> All our sins and griefs to bear."

Verse after verse poured forth, mingling with the clatter and
roar of the crowds outside. Mimi and her aunt paused unwittingly outside. The song had ceased. The barytone voice
of the preacher was lifted in prayer, his words punctuated by
fervent "Amens!" and "Hallelujahs!" and "Praise Gods!"

"We are vile, sinful creatures, O Lord, strayed from the
path You tol' us to follow. (Ain't it the Gospel!) Reach

FLIGHT

down from Thy heaven with a sword of flaming fire and wipe
from the face of the earth these hell-holes of vice that're sending the souls of our boys and girls to damnation! (Yes,
Lord, reach down!—Amen!) Wipe out, Jesus, the dance
halls and theatres, the gamblers and the drunkards, the
wolves in sheep's clothes who're workin' 'gainst Thy cause.
. . . Purify us, Lord! Save us! Save us! . . ."

The preacher's voice swayed and rumbled, excoriating the
sinners, pleading for redemption of their souls, damning to
everlasting hell-fire those who were unrepentant. The unseen voice was talking to a God who was no mystery to him,
a very real and ever present and potent Deity. Down the
street his words followed them as they went home. . . .

Mimi looked back on her days of suffering and poverty almost as though it had been a terrible dream. Her aunt deluged
her with kindness, delicately drew from her the story of her
unsuccessful struggle in Philadelphia against odds that proved
too great for her. The one link with that nightmare of pain
and worry and anxiety was her aching need of *Petit* Jean.
Night after night she cried herself to sleep. Night after night
she awoke when all the rest of the household was asleep, feeling him near her, his warm flesh nestled against her side.
She could feel his tiny lips against her own, his hands clutching at her breast, his laugh sounding in her ears. Only the
thought that some day soon she would be able to have him
with her again comforted her, only the realization that she
could not possibly make her way as fast towards that goal
if he were with her restrained her from going back to Baltimore and taking him from the home.

Her Aunt Sophie was, she found, gifted with a fund of hard
common sense but with it she possessed a warmth of feeling
that made Mimi know the older woman understood all her
difficulties without the necessity of putting into words her

various moods. Mr. Rogers had held for a number of years before his death a responsible position in a bank down town. He had left his widow some money and a few shares of stock in various corporations that brought her a steady, but small, income. By practice of rigid economy Mrs. Rogers could have lived in fairly comfortable circumstances but she was unwilling to do this. She had married young and was of a more progressive nature than her brother, although she understood Jean as well as had Margot. After her husband's death Mrs. Rogers had taken a course in manicuring, massaging and the treatment of the hair and scalp. She then had opened a small "beauty parlour," from which she derived a small income after all expenses were paid. Best of all, it kept her busy, and that was of greater importance to her than the money she earned. With a widowed sister of her husband she kept a small flat near Lenox Avenue, and it was to this she welcomed Mimi. . . .

The morning after her arrival Mimi had a long talk with her aunt.

"You've had a hard time, Mimi," the older woman said. "You've made what people call a serious mistake—it's not for me to judge you nor am I going to. If you did, you've paid for it—and you've done a mighty brave thing, to my way of thinking, in sticking it out as you have. Your problem now as I see it is to forget the past and decide what you're going to do with your future. You're young yet—just twenty-one, aren't you?—you're much better-looking than the average. The best part of your life's ahead of you. The question you've got to decide is what you're going to do with it— make it fruitful and full and happy? Or let the past swallow you up?"

She paused while Mimi sat in thought.

"Jean—and his future count much more than mine, Aunt Sophie."

"Yes, I know how you feel. What I'm going to say may sound mighty hard and unfeeling but you know I don't feel that way. With Jean you'll be so handicapped you'll settle into a rut out of which you'll probably never emerge. He's well fed, he's sheltered, he's clothed, he's being trained, educated. He hasn't your care and training, I know, but working all day, you wouldn't be able to give him much attention if he were with you. . . . In Philadelphia you by some miracle were able to avoid meddling inquiry about Jean's parentage. Here you wouldn't be so successful, I know. There are gossips everywhere—and in every race. So my advice is to let Jean stay there a few years, run down to see him whenever you can afford it, and get to the place where you can have Jean with you again. And—who knows?—perhaps the right man——"

"No, no, Aunt Sophie. That's all done for now. I'm through with men——"

Mrs. Rogers smiled.

"You say that now. But wait awhile. Youth and especially youth like yours can work wonders. Standards are changing—New York isn't New Orleans or Atlanta—the man who may come may have sense enough to see what's back of your—well, your so-called misfortune. Men are simple creatures after all though we women make of them in our own minds an insoluble riddle."

Wise in the ways of the world, tolerant and understanding of human foibles and weaknesses, Mrs. Rogers smiled reminiscently.

"I've seen lots of things in my time, Mimi, and I've learned a lot of things, too. There are some people whose notion of getting along in the world is to butt their brains out against the walls that come up in front of them. Others go to the other extreme and dodge every obstacle, taking the easiest way out. Maybe they're both right—but I doubt it. The

[190]

best way is to hold on to your ideals, yield only when you have to, but keep that thing we call our 'soul' intact, no matter what we go up against."

She toyed with the handle of her coffee-cup ruminatively.

"Take men, for example. Mr. Rogers and I had our times of disagreement, every married couple does. Much as I loved him, there were times when he irritated me so I could almost cheerfully have choked him. But I learned soon how to handle him—and when all's said and done, all men are alike—they differ in little ways but, by and large, they're the same. One of the things I learned was this—never, never argue with a man. On the other hand, don't fall into agreement too easily with his opinions. If you always insist you're right—even if you are and you know it—he'll think you stubborn and mulish and you stir up all sorts of stubbornness in him. And if you always agree with him he'll think you're soft and weak and silly. But if you express an opinion different from what you're sure is right and then—not too easily—let him convince you of the error of your reasoning—then, my dear, he'll be putty in your hands!"

"But suppose he should have the same opinion as your wrong one—what then?" Mimi inquired, interested in spite of herself in the philosophy her aunt was unfolding.

"Then exercise a woman's right—the privilege of changing her mind. But you won't have to do that often—man likes to prove his self-assumed masculine superiority too much to realize how you're handling him."

"That sounds dangerously like opportunism—er—it might even be called deceit," Mimi laughed.

"Yes, I suppose it can," Mrs. Rogers frankly admitted. "But life's like that—you can go tilting at windmills and getting knocked over for your pains or you can adapt yourself to the things you find around you. After all, the important thing is to work out for one's own guidance the philosophy

in keeping with one's ideas and ideals and then extract from
life all the happiness one can without destroying what's more
important than everything else—one's inner self. When that's
gone, then you can have every material thing there is—and
you'll know misery such as even you have never experienced or
ever will know. . . ."

The new life she was ushered into through Aunt Sophie
seemed by comparison with her experiences since she left
Atlanta almost idyllic to Mimi. Through her aunt's influence,
she secured work sewing, the only thing she could do by
which she could earn money. But for this she had a certain
gift. She loved the feel of silks and satins and chiffons; the
finer the fabric, the more she liked to handle it and make it into
alluring garments. All day she worked and in the evenings
she either stayed at home and made dresses and other garments for herself to replace the worn things she had brought
to New York, or with her aunt she walked through the streets
of Harlem or rode on the bus down Fifth Avenue. Occasionally this schedule was varied by a visit to the theatre, which
Mimi loved. A new world was opening to her and in it she
found greater happiness than she had believed she would ever
know again. These unfolded before her eyes a gloriously
fascinating scene and she sometimes felt as though a giant
scroll were being unwound for her own amusement and interest. This joy was added to by the modest yet steady progress
she was making towards reclaiming Jean. Each week she
added to the little sum in the bank. At times she seemed to
be making tragically little headway, at times she was delighted
at the speed with which the dollars accumulated.

Most interesting to her was the transition she saw going on
around her in Harlem. Gradually yet surely there was being
builded a Negro city here in northern Manhattan. For hours
she would sit silent, listening with a strange eagerness to the

stories her aunt told her of her own people in New York. She insisted that Mrs. Rogers take her to the sections where Negroes had lived in years past; they wandered through Broome and Spring Streets, where Negroes had lived before the Civil War, through Sullivan and Bleecker Streets and Minetta Lane in Greenwich Village, now settled thickly with Italians, among them little groups of coloured people who had never lived anywhere else.

But neither of these settlements nor the former habitats in the Twenties and Thirties interested her nearly so much as the section which Negroes had but lately quitted for Harlem. She made her aunt tell her of the Maceo and Marshall's and other rendezvous of Negro and white musicians and writers and bohemians. She asked many questions about Williams and Walker, about Aida Overton, Jim Europe, Buddy Gilmore who served as model for trap drummers in all the orchestras, Ernest Hogan, Cole and Johnson, and many others of the stars of the stage. Mrs. Rogers had lived near the Marshall and had known everybody who was worth knowing. She told Mimi of the brilliant Sunday nights when they used to dine to the music of a Negro orchestra at Marshall's, when one was always sure of finding interesting companions and acquaintances. She told of this orchestra, the members of which played and sang and danced and established the vogue out of which sprang the modern cabaret. Mimi wished fervidly she had been a part of this brilliant scene, might have known in the flesh these of whom she had heard so often even in New Orleans.

She was new enough to this growth to enable her to see how it formed itself and gradually spread over a greater territory. It seemed that every month saw the opening up to coloured tenants and buyers of new blocks. A group of white property-owners became alarmed and formed a holding company to buy all property occupied by Negro tenants and eject them. This step was promptly met by a countermove on the part of an intelligent coloured real-estate dealer who formed a Negro realty company to purchase for coloured tenants apartment houses of the best class. Then came panic among the whites, who deserted houses long before there was any invasion of their neighbourhoods by coloured tenants. Prices dropped and Negroes reaped the benefit by buying at these figures. The district spread with increasing rapidity and the new city was definitely in the making. . . .

Mimi kept track of these changes through the interesting circle of friends which frequented her Aunt Sophie's house. There were types she had not known before—business men who had a broad vision of the city that was to be, men who were eager, of course, to make money but who made personal gain secondary to the deep love of race and pride in the advances of that race toward a more secure foothold than was theirs in most parts of the country. There were the wives of these men, some of them of small minds fixed on nothing but dress and gossip and petty, unimportant social affairs, but others of them intelligent and valuable aids to their husbands. Some of the women were in business for themselves like Mrs. Rogers and they were no less shrewd and far-seeing than the men, in a number of cases more so. It was through these and their conversations, to which was added her own deductions and observations, that she saw the thing which interested her develop. This live, pulsating, vigorous movement fascinated her, for it gave her interests which kept her mind alert, and free from too great concentration on her own problems.

So too, in addition to Aunt Sophie's friends, who soon became her friends as well, she and her aunt found great joy in modest excursions down town to the theatres and greater happiness in music. They purchased the cheapest seats available and climbed the innumerable stairs at the Metropolitan or at Carnegie Hall to hear a favourite opera or singer. To

Mimi these were as drugs or liquor to addicts—they swept her up, up above her narrow, difficult existence to a world where cares and sorrows and toils did not exist, where there was an ecstatic abandon to the intoxicating music that thrilled her so. She would have enjoyed the music under any circumstances but it gave her greater happiness because she knew she could not afford even these inexpensive and harmless debauches. It was her aunt who urged her to take them, who frequently paid for the tickets, telling Mimi they had been given to her because of Mimi's insistence upon bearing an equal share of all costs of their journeys. On this point they often had good-natured quarrels—Mimi had a violent hatred of sponging, of feeling under obligations to any person, even to one so near as her aunt. She knew her aunt had obligations she must meet, rental of her apartment and shop, the current expenses at both places, the care of her sister-in-law, a chronic invalid who seldom left her room and who played as little a part in the household as the decrepit chair in the closet on which old newspapers were piled. She was unwilling to add further to her aunt's burdens and insisted upon paying for her room and board as though she had been merely a boarder. . . .

Another spring came and went, this time a happier one than Mimi had known for several years, merged imperceptibly into summer, when the only variations she permitted to her regular routine of work were trips to Coney Island with her aunt and some of their friends or rides down town and back of an evening on the Fifth Avenue buses. Mimi had decided that she could never make the progress which was so necessary if she continued only to do plain sewing. She always had a knack for devising new and unusual designs, many of them impractical but all of them touched with a distinctiveness that separated them from other clothes. She began in the fall a course in designing at a trade school, taking the course in the evenings. Despite the uneventfulness of her life and the steadiness of her application to the uninspiring routine, her health improved, colour returned to her cheeks, and her face lost its worried, haggard look. For Mimi was sustained by the goal towards which she was pushing—all else seemed trivial and unimportant beside the reaching of the day when she could bring *Petit* Jean to her again.

CHAPTER XVI

MIMI forgot the days of her misery. The years spent in Atlanta became hazy and unreal in the eager happiness of her new life. Again she had the feeling that the things which had distressed her so had never really happened—that they were either the phantasmagoria of a nightmare or the sorrows of an existence she had lived prior to this life. Her step-mother she rarely thought of, she had returned to Chicago and there had married again. The Hunters she equally had removed from her thoughts. When she did think of them or of Carl they seemed unreal, like apparitions of an indistinctly remembered dream. She had completely recovered from even her hatred of and contempt for Carl. In the light of her life since she had left Atlanta, she saw him now even more clearly as the weak individual he was. She was amused now when she remembered how devotedly, how passionately she had loved him during those short months. "I *was* a silly little fool then," she laughed amusedly at herself when she did remember. The entire episode seemed to her now a rather cheap and worthless thing. The only comfort she could extract from it was the satisfaction that she had not succumbed to a dishonest compromise.

Even her years in Philadelphia began to fade into the land of half-remembered, half-forgotten things. She occasionally corresponded with the Mannings but as the months sped by she found her interest lessening even in this contact with the old couple who had been so kind to her. The one link to both of these episodes in her life, for she now looked upon them only as episodes, was *Petit* Jean, and he served as a link

FLIGHT

and as the centre of all her hopes for the future. Under the
skilful guidance of her aunt she had thrown off her moroseness
and spells of despondency and was working indefatigably
towards securing all the things which would bring happiness
to her and Jean.

Back of her lay disappointment and sadness, ahead of her
lay only hope. It was in this mood that she went with her
aunt one Friday evening to a dance at Manhattan Casino.
They had been invited to join a box party in which were included several younger people, three or four young men and
three girls beside Mimi, in addition to Mrs. Rogers and two
older persons. For the dance Mimi had made for herself a
party dress of pale green charmeuse—green with the greenness of young leaves in springtime—a green that was indefin-
ably between jade and Eau-de-Nil.

"You look like a rosebud—a marvellously golden flower
springing out of its leafy greenness," Tom Henderson whispered to her as they danced together.

The not very subtle compliment pleased Mimi. She was
happy, too, she was capable of pleasure from such a source—
she had thought herself impervious to polite remarks of this
sort—she fancied she had put all this behind her for ever.
She was glad that this was not so—after all, she yet was
young. And he had seemed so sincere when he had said it.

All the evening she danced, danced with a lightness and
ease that brought young men in droves to the box when she
rested there between dances. Her feet seemed endowed with
wings, for she moved over the floor without conscious effort.
And the music! She had heard of Ford Dabney, had been
told of the way in which his orchestra could play. But she
had never dreamed that any human beings could entice from
inanimate objects such intoxicating, inspiriting music. Once,
and once only, was she able to sit in the box and watch the
dancers.

FLIGHT

"It's a pretty sight," her aunt said to her.

"Pretty? That isn't the word for it!" she enthusiastically declared.

It was a waltz. Faces of all colours, peeping from gowns of all shades ranging from delicate pinks and blues and lavenders to gorgeously passionate reds. There were faces of a mahogany brownness which shaded into the blackness of crisply curled hair. There were some of a blackness that shone like rich bits of velvet. There were others whose skins seemed as though made of expertly tanned leather with the creaminess of old vellum, topped by shining hair, blacker than "a thousand midnights, down in a cypress swamp." And there were those with ivory-white complexions, rare old ivory that time had mellowed with gentle touch. To Mimi the most alluring of all were the women who were neither dark nor light, as many of them were, but those of that indefinable blend of brown and red, giving a richness that was reminiscent of the Creoles of her own New Orleans.

"Look at that girl over there, Aunt Sophie—the one with that marvellous black hair and that brownish red skin—the Spanish-looking one with the dress of corn-flower blue. There is my ideal of beauty—no sallow, colourless type but the warmth of a thousand Caribbean suns is in her face."

Mrs. Rogers laughed easily.

"No—you're right, there is no colourlessness there—but those you see who are so fair they can pass can get ahead lots faster than those with lots of colour. Do you see that girl who looks like white—the one with the black dress covered with *passementeries?* She works down town in one of the most exclusive shops in New York. She's a forewoman and makes more money than three-fourths of the men in Harlem."

"What's she doing up here?" Mimi asked. "Isn't she afraid she'll be seen or that some coloured person will go down and tell she's a Negro?"

[199]

FLIGHT

"Nobody's told on her yet—and when she's through with her work she comes back to Harlem. She's got mighty little use for white people—hates them—she was born in Georgia and her brother was lynched when he beat up a white man in a quarrel."

"Who's the fellow over there—the one with the black hair who looks like a Japanese?" Mimi queried, now thoroughly interested. She scanned the flaming chequer-board of colour, picking out the ones who interested her.

"Where is he? Oh, that's Tod James—he's assistant cashier of a bank down in the financial district. He's married white but ever so often the call of Harlem is too great and he bobs up here again. He's had an amazing career—born in Texas, was mixed up in two or three revolutions in Mexico and South America, has travelled all over the world, made and lost three or four fortunes, and now has settled down to a comfortable, placid existence in Wall Street."

"Does his wife know he's coloured?"

"That's she dancing down there with the slender brown chap—looks like she knows what he is. And she was born in Tennessee but had sense enough not to stay there."

"And who's the flashily dressed fellow standing there looking on?"

"I don't know his name but he runs a club where they have entertainers and music for dancing—they call them cabarets. You'll find all sorts of people here—it's a pay dance and anybody who's got the price can get in. There are women who are being kept and men who live the same way, doctors and lawyers, and about every class in the world represented here."

Mimi felt a thrill of adventure run through her. Perhaps she had brushed against some of these fearful characters and it made her tingle with adventure.

[200]

"Goodness, haven't they any lines they draw?" she wanted to know.

"Strictest in the world—you've noticed you've been asked to dance only by folks you know and who move with our set."

Mimi laughed.

"I don't know about that. See that nice-looking chap over there in that box? I've never seen him before and he asked me if I wanted to dance with him."

Mrs. Rogers peered in the direction of Mimi's nod.

"No, you haven't seen him," she told Mimi grimly, when she had located him. "He's probably one of the most notorious gamblers in New York—has never been known to do a lick of work. I told you you'd see all sorts of people here, didn't I?"

The music began again and there was a wild rush to the dance floor. Mimi sat and watched the kaleidoscopic scene, brilliant, colourful, fascinating. New York is the only place on earth where such a crowd could be got together, she mused. Like one body the crowd on the huge, densely packed floor swayed and moved with an easy grace, laughing, carefree, exuberant. There was a natural spontaneity to the movement, a rhythmic unity that gave Mimi the impression that the dancers had been rehearsed with great pains by an expert *maître de danse*. They moved with graceful animation, with a decorous but fascinating abandon. Her aunt was speaking.

"It's lucky for the Negro he was given the ability to forget—there are at least a dozen people down there I've recognized who probably don't know where they'll get money enough to pay their rent. Yet there's not a soul having a better time than they. He can work all day methodically and steadily as long as he knows there will be opportunities to forget harsh and unpleasant things." . . .

[201]

FLIGHT

Mimi did not see Mrs. Plummer as she descended the stairs when the music began for the next dance. That estimable person had come that afternoon to New York and she now was receiving her first glimpse of New York life. She wore a brilliant purple confection of velvet, adorned with extraordinary little flowers of an indescribable and unknown species and shape. She seized the arm of her cousin, with whom she was staying, and though in the noise there was no need of caution, she whispered:

"Who is that girl with the green dress and red hair—I mean what name does she go by here?"

"That's Miss Daquin—she's Mrs. Rogers' niece and she's very popular—some of the women don't like her but that's because she's better-looking than most of them. Men like her because she pays no attention to them——"

Mrs. Plummer snorted.

"Miss Daquin! So that's how she's getting by, is it?"

She was in her element. New York did not terrify her any more by its hugeness and strangeness. The eyes of her friend picked out Mimi's form as it appeared and disappeared through the dancing forms. Mrs. Plummer was giving a complete, more than complete, account of Mimi and her life.

"These society coloured folks make me tired," Mrs. Plummer was saying. "They look down on us ordinary folks but they're carrying on their deviltry just as much as any of us. And they do some of the craziest things! That girl was carrying on round Atlanta with this Hunter boy and when they found out she was going to have a baby she just went crazy—said she didn't want to marry the boy! Can you imagine anybody doing such a fool thing?" she demanded rhetorically.

"I always did think there was something funny about her," her vis-à-vis answered satisfactorily. "You can't fool me—I can spot 'em a mile off. What became of the baby?"

FLIGHT

"The Lord only knows! I heard tell she had it and I don't know whether it lived or not. Must not of if you say you ain't never heard about it. Some funny things happen in this world——" . . .

On and on the thread was unspun. In the years since Mimi had left Atlanta, the stories about her, with the facile growth that age always brings, had gained almost the proportions of a myth. Never had any girl taken so absurd a position as she. Always they had been only too glad to marry even when they had lived with their husbands but a short time. Not understanding, gossip had assumed there was more to the story than appeared on the surface, and various inventive minds speculated as to the untold part.

Rumour had scoffed at the notion Mimi had refused to marry Carl even though he and his parents were willing. That was too improbable, too far-fetched. The Hunters had volunteered no information and tongues had run wild. Some had it that the father of the child was uncertain—every man under seventy years of age who had ever been on the most casual terms of friendship with Mimi was discussed as the possible father. Others were firmly convinced Mimi had trapped Carl with an eye on the wealth which his father was credited with possessing. Those of this persuasion were convinced she had been bought off or frightened by the Hunters.

Forgotten except by a few, Hilda and her mother among them, were the derelictions popular report had credited to or charged against Carl. Mimi had fled, therefore she was the guilty one. "The wicked fleeth when no man pursueth," the wise ones said. The scandal was a juicy morsel that served its purpose well over many back fences and at innumerable parties, at church and on front porches. Only Hilda and Mrs. Adams championed the cause of Mimi, but soon, because their views were well known, the subject was not mentioned to them. Scandal thrives only when it is retailed to those with open ears and credulous minds. . . .

Mrs. Plummer's friend was well capable of holding her own in the dissemination of interesting news. Mimi alone would have been a target almost too small for the guns of the talkative ones. But as the niece of Mrs. Rogers, in business, well known, and with enemies gained through the frank comment and eyes with which Mimi's aunt saw readily through pretence and sham, Mrs. Rogers herself could be hurt through the mud plastered on her niece. Mimi found herself being avoided at church, on the street, at the few affairs which she attended. At first she paid no attention to them but in time they were too obvious to be ignored. She had not seen Mrs. Plummer during the two weeks that she had visited in New York. The first intimation Mimi had of the talk which was going on was given her in a weekly publication, *The Blabber*.

Modelled upon *Town Topics*, it devoted its pages to not too cryptic references, almost invariably scandalous ones, to persons of prominence. Its editors had been handled roughly several times, the paper had been sued frequently, but seldom were any copies left on Harlem newsstands more than a few hours after it appeared on Thursday mornings.

Mimi read the reference to herself three times before she could realize that once again she was confronted with suspicion.

"All Harlem is agog," the paragraph ran, "with some hitherto hidden chapters in the life of one of our most attractive and popular young women. She and the relative with whom she lives have been seen often at the smartest affairs and the breath of scandal which has been stirred will undoubtedly prove a nine days' sensation. Innocence, according to all who know the young lady of French extraction, has been her most

FLIGHT

evident characteristic. But it seems there has been a coloured gentleman in the firewood. Harlem is asking what the charming miss has done with the baby. Something should really be done about the doors of family closets—they will pop open at the most inopportune moments and permit glimpses of unsuspected and embarrassing skeletons. . . ."

"What's the use, Aunt Sophie, of trying to be decent? I don't see the need of trying—I might as well give up the struggle and admit I'm beaten," she despairingly told Mrs. Rogers.

"Don't be silly, Mimi. They've talked about everybody. It'll all blow over in time."

"No—you're just trying to console me. People forget decent things—they never forget a thing like this."

"There's something in that, but the people you really care about will have sense enough to see this in a broad light. And those who don't see it and give you credit for trying to atone for your mistake don't count—you'll be better off without their friendship."

They sat at dinner and Mimi could almost hear the tumbling down of the walls she had so confidently been building. For the first time she felt sick at heart, crushed, without hope. She could withstand poverty, physical pain. But the averted glances of those who had been her friends, the ostentatious turning of heads when she passed on the street those with whom she had been on terms of intimate acquaintanceship, the sudden death of conversations at her approach which told her more plainly than if the information had been shouted through a megaphone that they had been talking of her, the boldness in the eyes of some of the men where there had been only respect before, all these and a thousand other little cruelties were the things which hurt. Hurt her painfully, more painfully than mere physical pain. She envied her aunt's calmness, her philosophical acceptance of people's habits, whether these hab-

[205]

its were good or bad. She tried to keep her mind on the comforting flow of words with which Mrs. Rogers was seeking to bolster her courage.

"People have gossiped from the beginning of time and I suppose they'll keep right on until Gabriel blows his trump. I don't know why it is but there's one thing that's always true —they tear you to pieces not for what you've done but for getting caught. Take some of the biggest men in America—men who everybody knows have stolen railroads and banks but who've never been caught at it—why, they're popular idols. There are lots of magazines with big circulations that fill their pages with stories of how these giants have gained wealth and fame by 'honesty, hard work, sticking to the job.' That's bunk! Do you remember the story of one of these 'self-made' men who was telling a college class that his secret of success was 'pluck! pluck! pluck!' and the irreverent boy who asked the pompous one who he had plucked? That's the true story of a lot of these people who haven't been caught with their hands in the other fellow's pockets."

Mimi smiled a wan smile. This was interesting, perhaps, but it didn't help her much. Mrs. Rogers went on.

"And coloured people are no better than anybody else. The motive is the same everywhere in the world and with all races and sexes and classes. If you aren't of any importance they don't gossip about you because nobody's interested. But they've got to have something humiliating, something that'll bear down a person's reputation, something malicious and spiteful. It's got to be about somebody who's got something to lose, it'll have to be something that'll stick, something that'll be dangerous but not too dangerous for the person who's gossiping. And above everything else it's got to be spread with a high and lofty manner—the biggest spreader of tales I ever knew always started her most vile story the same way. She'd say: 'I stay at home attending to my own business and I

[206]

FLIGHT

don't meddle in other people's affairs, but have you heard that——' and then she proceeds to give you a long account of what some person has done, all of it told in a tone of Christian forbearance and pity and tacit regret."

"That's a very interesting and logical analysis but it doesn't offer much comfort. It's just like a doctor explaining why your leg broke when you're lying in a hospital bed."

"You're depressed and worried—there's no need giving in to what these people say. Just face it and it will all blow over. And I'll stick with you always, Mimi."

Mrs. Rogers watched Mimi, more worried over the girl's troubles than she would admit even to herself. In a few months Mimi had become a part and a very important part of the household. Younger people came and she had always preferred associating with young people. "It keeps me young, too," she would say when the subject was mentioned. The house would be unbearable if Mimi went away or did anything desperate. She feared this though she laughed at her fears. But the set look on Mimi's face, the despondency which was greater now than when Mimi had first come to New York after putting *Petit* Jean in the orphanage, the utter dejection so evident in Mimi's face and body, made her definitely apprehensive.

"You're a darling, Aunt Sophie, but I just can't stick it out. I can stand a lot of things—I've had to—but what's happened here will just keep on happening every place I go. I've tried to go straight—God knows I have. But these meddling people won't let me have any peace. Do you remember that night at the dance you pointed out a girl to me who was working down town, passing for white?"

Mrs. Rogers admitted she had, but wondered what that had to do with Mimi.

"Just this," was the answer she received. "I never thought I'd want to leave my own people. I wouldn't leave them now

[207]

but they've driven me away—driven me to the point where I've either got to drop out of sight where I won't be hounded again or else I'll do something terrible. If that girl can pass I think I can too. My name is French, I speak French—at least well enough to fool anybody who isn't French—I can sew, and they'll never think me anything else but French. I'll see you, of course, but I'm leaving Harlem, leaving coloured people for good. I'll live my own life, make more money than I can here, I'll be able sooner to have Jean with me, and —well, there's no other way out. . . ."

CHAPTER XVII

A GAIN Mimi had the feeling she was closing a book in her life and opening a new one. Just like a novel by Rolland, she thought. Or, better, her life to her was like one of those Harlem apartments of seemingly interminable length, with no hall and with each room opening into the next one. Railroad flats, she had heard them called. She felt she was always opening the door of another room, passing through it, then opening and closing behind her, never to be reopened, the door of the next cubicle. Those years of childhood in New Orleans had been the first one, happy and carefree years when she was more content than ever afterwards. The next had been Atlanta, then Philadelphia, then Harlem. Four separate lives, and here was a new one opening before her. She wondered how many more through which she must pass before the final exit. Sometimes now she wished she could skip all the rest and make that last step, wherever it might lead. In her moments of greatest depression she thought of suicide but these morbid thoughts did not remain with her long. *Petit* Jean and thoughts of his future would have driven them away even if she had not felt a deep aversion to death by her own hand.

From a newspaper advertisement she was able to secure a small room with a private family, living in the lower Nineties, respectable but commonplace. In the matter of linear feet and rods and miles she was not far distant from Harlem but in other ways she might as well have been halfway round the world from the scenes she had once known. Here the towering apartment houses, most of them five or six stories in height and of cream brick and with terra-cotta or stone trimmings, housed countless numbers of families, belching them forth from seven to nine in the morning as small business men and stenographers and manicurists and clerks dashed madly for the nearest subway or elevated station. At the little newsstands they would snatch, according to tastes, copies of the *World* or *Times*, though, more than any other purveyor of the news, they bought issues of "the paper for people who think." Sleek and well fed, powdered and rouged and lipsticked with expert hand, they were swallowed up by the yawning and insatiable pits and were whirled to down-town jobs by the rushing, roaring subways.

Later in the day swarms of children poured forth from the same apartments, in winter bound schoolward, in summer to the nearest park or the street, chaperoned by quarrelsome mothers or older sisters. Yet later came elaborately coiffured and gowned young women, invariably pretty, who toiled not nor spun. Evening came and the Gargantuan beehives reversed the process and swallowed again the hordes they had spewed forth in the morning hours. Phonographs blared raucously, voices were raised in babels of song or quarrelling or loud laughter. Midnight, and the din died down. Sleep, engulfing and obliterating as a candle-snuffer, brought peace, broken only when a late and noisy party was quieted momentarily by sleepy, irritated voices shouting: "Hey, cut out the noise down there!"

It was in one of these huge rabbit warrens that Mimi found shelter. The house she lived in looked down upon most of the others in the block—it boasted in the entrance hallway rows of dusty but imposing palms, set in tubs painted a bilious green, and between these tropic relics stood uncomfortable-looking chairs of imitation needlepoint. No one seemed aware of the purpose of these chairs, which always reminded Mimi of the photographs she had seen of the electric chair at

FLIGHT

Sing Sing, for not even the oldest inhabitant of the house, who
had been living there now for a year and a half, had ever seen
anyone sitting in them. But they added class, tone, éclat.
And they likewise added a few dollars to the rent of each apartment in the house so adorned.

She had not wanted to leave Harlem. Mrs. Rogers had argued, pleaded, almost wept. At times Mimi had been on the
point of weakening, had almost thought seriously of trying to
stick it out. Each time that she had almost convinced herself
that this was the wisest and only course, some new evidence
of the ordeal would come to her and make her vow anew that
she would not attempt to live it down. Years before she had
heard a story which Booker Washington had told in which
he likened Negroes to a basket of crabs—when one of them
had with great energy climbed almost to the top of the basket and freedom, the others less progressive than he would
reach up with their claws and pull him back to their own level.
This had seemed to her then merely an effective story coined
for oratorical purposes, but now its applicability was forced
upon her with painful truth.

Though she had to a considerable degree recovered from
the intense consciousness of race which her experiences in the
riot at Atlanta had engendered in her, yet Mimi, despite the
shortcomings which she saw in her own people, had a loyalty
to and an affection for them that was almost an obsession. She
never spoke of this feeling, for she felt that to those who understood, explanations were unnecessary, while to those who
needed an explanation, whatever she might say would have been
obscure and difficult of understanding. In other words, to her
it was as useless for her to attempt the depiction of her loyalty
as it would be for a man to maintain loudly and persistently the
faithfulness of his wife. She had always felt an instinctive
distrust of those Negroes who boasted of their loyalty and devotion to their race. It had seemed to her that if such faithful-

[211]

ness were genuine and unselfish it needed restatement no more than did the affirmation by a woman that she was respectable.

Thus her passing from the race seemed to Mimi persecution greater than any white people had ever visited upon coloured people—the very intolerance of her own people had driven her from them. And in the deception she would have to practise as one ostensibly white, she felt she was doing a mean and dishonourable thing. She would do so, she determined, for there was no other course open to her. But in her new life she missed the spontaneity, the ready laughter, the naturalness of her own. She saw morose, worried faces. Here there was little of that softness of speech to which she was accustomed. Here there was an obsession with material things that crowded out the naturalness that made life for her tolerable. I've made my bed now, she reflected, and there's nothing for me to do except lie in it. . . .

She did not experience the difficulty in securing employment that she had feared. There had been vague rumblings of discord and war in Europe, but all that seemed very far away, too distant ever to affect America. The mad rush that ushered in Easter and spring, the return like homing pigeons of the wealthy from Palm Beach, the momentary pause in New York before taking wing again for Europe or the mountains or the sea-shore, taxed to the limit the shops of the modistes and milliners, the makers of boots and gowns and habiliments of a thousand kinds for those vaguely classed as "society."

Deft fingers flew, the needles of sewing-machines flashed in and out like pelting raindrops of silver in a summer shower. Yards and bolts and tons of filmy silks and *crêpes de Chine* and organdie turned overnight into dainty dresses. A long, nastily cold winter was gasping its last long breath and little wisps of softer breezes fanned the cheeks of the scurrying throngs, telling them spring was near.

FLIGHT

The unforeseen demand for new and more clothes brought with it the need of workers. Mimi, having set her face on the new life she had chosen, determined she would start at the smartest places in seeking employment and work gradually downwards until she had gained what she wished. She knew the names and addresses of the most exclusive modistes, the shops where gowns and frocks were purveyed to the smartest-dressed women of New York and Oshkosh and Sioux City. To her surprised delight she was successful at the first place to which she applied—at Francine's—known wherever the best women's clothes were known.

Francine's name was greeted with that tone of respectful homage granted only to the names of Paquin and Lucile and Worth and Bendel and Jean Patou and Frances. At Francine's one entered into an atmosphere where milady's attire, the choice of material and model, the selection of millinery, was raised to the plane of a religious ceremony. Soft-voiced priestesses respectfully assisted in the rites, making suggestions in tones which were not too respectful nor yet too haughty. Purchasers of models from Francine, even though they had bought there for many years, were never allowed to forget through subtle yet unmistakable means that they were after a fashion being shown especial favour when they were permitted to enter Francine's door.

Madame Francine herself was the high priestess of the temple of feminine adornment. Only the most favoured customers saw her or were served by her after their first visit. If that customer were of great distinction either through family connexions or wealth, she might be allowed the honour of Madame's personal service. But if she were of less than the topmost bough of society or if the wealth she represented was expressed in less than seven figures, then she never saw Madame Francine after her initial entrance into the temple.

For Madame Francine knew the value of a stage setting

FLIGHT

much better than most of the theatrical producers whose lights flashed nightly a few blocks westward. She knew that the place for her temple was then to be only in the upper 30's or lower 40's, just a step from the Avenue. She knew the supreme importance of keeping from the transaction of bartering every least suggestion of buying and selling. She knew the necessity of proper first impressions upon the purchaser, and of maintaining that impression.

One entered her place after a magnificently apparelled doorman had opened one's carriage or motor-car door. Inside, one found oneself in what in reality was a salon, free of course from every tiniest suspicion of vulgarity, of trade. The carpet was of black and grey, the woodwork of a grey in which there was the faintest suggestion of tan, the draperies were of grey and mulberry. The shaded lights from the wall sconces and ceiling gave no harsh glare, the illumination furnished being only just enough to combine the needed air of respect for the wonders beyond and above and the light necessary for the rites of conversation in lowered tones. Chairs and couches of delicate build matched or purposely contrasted with the colours in rug and draperies. Soft-voiced, slim and perfectly gowned priestesses glided noiselessly forward to greet one and inquire one's wants as though being welcomed into the home of the priestess—welcomed, perhaps, not by the mistress of the home, but by a poorer relation of the mistress who lived there. On an onyx table there was perhaps a hat perched upon a stand. Or in a softly lighted built-in case there rested a rarely exquisite and beautiful purse. Or a bottle, richly carved, of perfume. Or a bit of gold or silver filigree, of amber and lapis from a dim little shop on the Ponte Vecchio. Or a miraculously carved comb for milady's *coiffure*. In solitary splendour it reposed—its grandeur not a whit less than that accorded a string of matchless pearls in one of the temples devoted to jewels in the Avenue near-by.

[214]

FLIGHT

And when the visitor had made her wants known she was conducted, if her need was of gowns or tailored suits or hats, up the winding marble stairway to the miniature theatre on the floor above. She was aided in the ascent by the balustrade of metal covered with mull velvet.

Madame Francine's sense of the appropriate and impressive setting rose to its heights in the room she entered at the top of these stairs. Here the rugs were of grey, the woodwork and walls and draperies blending unobtrusively in the colours of the show-room below. On a marble mantel to the left stood in solemn dignity a marvellously fashioned clock, so beautifully made, one felt it almost a profanation that it should measure unimportant things like minutes and hours. To each side of it there stood a delicately carved candlestick of shiny brass, their brightness matching the framework of the long table with marble top on which rested sketch-books of designs and models. The tiny stage fitted with footlights and drops, its flooring of squares of black and white marble, glowed with impressive and anticipatory dignity. Daintily clad and perfumed and manicured ladies lolled at ease upon divans or in straight-backed chairs, according to tastes and sizes, while mannequins pirouetted and posed and paraded around and across the stage. Every detail had been minutely scrutinized, every bit of unobtrusive allure had been utilized to induce the dawdling audience to the point of conviction and purchase. Instinctively one lowered one's voice—the temple must not be profaned. One bought, too, for few were strong enough to resist the feeling that all this had been designed and executed solely for one's own private delectation, and certainly one could not be guilty of base ingratitude through failure to render homage by ordering one or more of the creations displayed. . . .

But all this magnificence was terra incognita to Mimi for many, many months after she had begun work as a finisher at Francine's. There were four other floors occupied by work-rooms and tailoring-rooms and lunch-room. There was the basement used as an office and stockroom and shipping-room. In the upper stories the finishers and drapers and drapers' assistants and fitters and clerks and stenographers and tailors moved and had their being. These were never seen by customers, nor were the first two floors ever seen by any employees save the sales persons, except when viewed in hasty peeps after hours. These workers entered through rear or side doors, ascended to their work tables by rear elevators, saw nothing of the pageant enacted daily in the same building.

Timidly Mimi told the imposing and business-like fitter her qualifications as a wielder of the needle and thimble. In these less dignified purlieus there was no need of lowered voices, and the rush of work in the pre-Easter season had shortened tempers and sharpened tongues. Mimi would have fled madly from the scene had not she so eagerly wanted work, and work at Francine's. Timidly, yet desperately, she emphasized her ability and experience. She clinched her claim to fitness by her training at the Manhattan Trade School, though the diffidence with which she advanced this argument would have defeated its purpose had not there been need of a finisher at Francine's and a very pressing need on that particular day when Mimi made her application.

Deftly, quickly, she did the work assigned her. From eight-thirty each week-day morning until five-thirty she plied her needle, head bent low at the table given her in the long work-room on the fourth floor. She seldom spoke to any of the other thirty girls except when addressed directly, but she stole many a furtive glance at them, envying their pert assurance, their complete lack of awe at their surroundings save when the eyes of the fitter or a very rare visit from Francine herself hushed their whispered chatter. "Talking and work don't go together—one or the other will be neglected and al-

FLIGHT

ways it will be the work that suffers," the fitter had told Mimi
on her first day. The other girls obeyed this injunction—to
have done otherwise would have brought reproof and in time
dismissal. But no sooner did the fitter leave the room than
they gushed forth a torrent of whispered comments, of subdued
snickering. And even when the coldly efficient fitter was with
them but her eyes not upon them, they found ways of com-
munication to relieve the tedium of silence.

Because her wages were small as a finisher and because her
need of work was great, Mimi obeyed implicitly the instructions given her. She made few friends, and even these few
were kept at a distance. Only one girl progressed beyond the
barrier Mimi imposed. Sylvia Smith was the name she gave
Mimi, and their tables adjoined.

"How do you like Old Faithful?" Sylvia inquired as she
led Mimi to the lunch-room where the girls were provided with
tea or coffee at noon while they ate the lunches they had
brought.

"Old Faithful?" Mimi, puzzled, inquired.

"Yeah—the fitter we got," Sylvia mumbled as she bit deep
into a sandwich.

"Oh—she's very nice."

"You don't know her, kid. She's a pain—just wait until you
do something wrong—you'll want to jump down her throat
when she bawls you out with all the other girls grinning at you
behind her back."

"I hope then I'll never make any mistakes," Mimi murmured.

"Don't worry, kiddo. You'll make 'em. And the best way
to handle Old Faithful is to keep your mouth shut and let her
gab on until she runs out of breath. The one we had before
she came was a coloured girl—she knew her stuff and we didn't
try no monkey business with her, either. But she treated us
like we were human——"

[217]

"A coloured girl?" Mimi asked, alarm creeping into her voice.

"Yeah. Say, where you from?"

"New York, now. New Orleans was where I was born."

"Oh—I thought you talked like you was from the South. Well, up here being coloured don't count as much as it does down your way——"

Mimi hastened to disclaim the imputation in Sylvia's voice.

"That's all right, dearie. I wasn't accusing you of prejudice."

"No—no, I'm not prejudiced," was Mimi's reply. She felt a sense of guilt at her duplicity, but at the same time Sylvia's words gave her assurance that the task of passing would not be as difficult as she had feared.

"Race prejudice is a lot of bunk," Sylvia was philosophizing. "Take me, for instance. I went to Manhattan Trade, too. My real name's Bernstein—but you can't get by in some of these places if they think you're a Jew. So my name here is 'Smith.' I'm starting at the bottom just like you, to learn the tricks of the trade, but some day I'm going to have my own business. You see, my mother's French and I took after her, so I can pass for French even if I don't speak any of that lingo. So I know what prejudice means, dearie. Some of the girls tried to get nasty when they put Miss Lawrence over us— Miss Lawrence was the coloured woman—but I liked her and she soon had 'em under her thumb, believe me."

As Sylvia chattered on, Mimi felt an urge to tell her new friend that she too was sailing under false colours, but she feared to reveal this fact so early in their acquaintance. Caution urged her to remain silent though she felt she could trust Sylvia implicitly despite the fact she had seen her for the first time a few hours before. She liked Sylvia. She was slangy. She was coarse, after a fashion. But it took no very keen eye to see that beneath these externals she was made of fine stuff.

Ambitious, too. Just like a Jew, Mimi thought, and though she meant nothing derogatory, she was ashamed she had used a phrase so often spoken in dispraise of Sylvia's race. Yes, she was going to like Sylvia.

"Say, Mimi—you're French, too, aren't you?—let's have lunch together every day. I don't have anything to do with the rest of the girls—all they think about is clothes and lovers—but I like you."

"And I like you, too, Sylvia," Mimi shyly answered, stirred by the prompt offer of friendship.

"That's O.K., then. We'll be real pals. And any time you want to know anything, just call on me.

"Tell me, Sylvia, what became of Miss Lawrence—the coloured woman who was a fitter? Is she still working for Francine?"

"Nope—some of the girls objected to her and raised such a row she left. She's got a place of her own in Harlem—she's married now and Francine don't know it but a lot of these swells go all the way up there to get Miss Lawrence to do their clothes. Francine would throw a fit or two if she found it out." . . .

Mimi liked her work. She started at fifteen dollars a week but before many months had passed her pay was increased. The hours were not as long as they seemed and she learned to like Sylvia more and more as each day brought forth some new sign of the determination and keen intelligence that lay back of Sylvia's rather slangy and disrespectful manner. With Mimi there was none of the subtle antagonisms Sylvia felt towards the other girls. This hostility was born of Sylvia's contempt for their greater polish and worldly cleverness, their air of distinction with which they aped the manners of the patrons of Francine's whom they watched when the girls walked on the Avenue during the lunch hour. Sylvia would never have admitted it, but there was, too, envy in her heart of these among whom she felt like the proverbial ugly duckling. Mimi saw without difficulty the motives which inspired Sylvia's distrust and dislike, but she never hinted even that she understood. Sylvia would have been hurt, pained terribly, had she felt Mimi ascribed her emotions to such sources. But whatever their source, they served as a driving power of tremendous strength in Sylvia's life. She often told Mimi her plans and dreams, at first shyly, then freely.

"I was born way down on the East Side—father and mother came here from France when they had only one child. I was the third and there were four after me—no chance down there at all. So I made up my mind I was going to get somewhere and I pulled out of that hole and here I am. I had to sew on men's clothes that mother brought home from the factory—started sewing when I was eight years old. I didn't get much education, and living down there, I soon lost what little I had, got to talking rough and using slang—oh, you needn't try to save my feelings—I know I'm rough as a dockhand. But I'm going to night school—and some day I'm going to be somebody."

Sylvia's face, dark and in moments of intense feeling strong with the mark of Israel upon it, lighted up as she looked down the years and saw herself sitting as Francine now did in a delicately beautiful "studio" of her own, while all around her bustled employees of Madame Sylvia.

"Take Francine, for instance. She says she is French, but you and I are lots more French than she is—every time she opens her mouth and spills some French words, you can hear Killarney all through it. And if she can get away with it—well, I can put it over, too."

Under Sylvia's direction Mimi began to see new worlds in New York she had never thought of penetrating. At first to occupy her mind, later because the pursuit of knowledge was

an intriguing and comforting thing, she began to spend her
evenings at night school. She finished her course in designing,
she studied French, soon regaining her old-time proficiency in
the tongue which had once been more native to her than English, she took courses in English literature and economics and
psychology. With Sylvia she attended lectures at the Rand
School and at Cooper Union. Most of the theories advanced
there seemed to her visionary and impractical—the burning
intensity of most of the students and hearers frightened and repelled her. Like alchemists of old searching, probing, seeking
diligently for the mysterious and elusive secret by which baser
metals could be changed into gold, so many of these seemed
intent on finding some panacea which could be applied willy-
nilly to all problems, economic, social, political, and in a
flash solve them all. Though she kept her thoughts to herself,
nevertheless the test tube in which she tried all these solutions
and solvers was in their reactions towards Mimi's own people
—her own, even though she had deserted them. Do they include consideration of the Negro as a human being just like
themselves when they talk glibly of the "comrades" and "the
brotherhood of man"? was the question she found herself constantly asking.

It was at the very beginning of Mimi's work at Francine's
that a t Austrian archduke was assassinated at Sarajevo. Aus-
tria, Serbia, Germany, France, Great Britain, Belgium, Japan
—or e by one they tumbled into the whirlpool of slaughter and
blood and bullets. Headlines screamed and front pages were
filled with stories of Belgium invaded, of the Marne and Lou-
vain. Francine apparently was untouched except there was
more work to be done now that Paris and its energies were
turned to the making of guns instead of gowns. Mimi was
deeply moved by the stories of scores, hundreds, thousands of
deaths, but in time she scanned the headlines as she hurried
home in the evenings on the subway with the calm acceptance

of these horrors which long familiarity brings. Sometimes she remembered the phrase they had used in Atlanta when coloured people were subjected to indignities and injustice—"You can get used to being hung if you're only hung often enough." Or, at other times, she accepted the stories of slaughter with a fatalistic, a not altogether hopeless philosophy which might be summed up in the words: "Oh, well, it's white people killing white people—the more they kill, the better the chance for coloured peoples." But most of the time she thought of these things not at all, but centred her attentions on her work, her studies, the slow accumulation of enough money to bring *Petit Jean* to her.

CHAPTER XVIII

THERE was little variation to the life Mimi led. She paid occasional visits to her Aunt Sophie or Mrs. Rogers came down town for a hasty luncheon or a leisurely dinner with her. She told her aunt glowingly of the progress she was making, gave her vivid little pictures of her life at Francine's, of the girls with whom she worked. Once or twice a year, she went to Baltimore and spent a few days with Jean. These visits cheered, saddened and comforted her. She treasured each minute spent with him, watching with eager eyes the rapid growth of the infant into a sturdy, intelligent child. He had Mimi's reddish hair and her brown eyes. His mouth was sensitive like Carl's but the chin was that of his maternal grandfather. The authorities gave excellent reports of him though they hinted broadly that Jean was—well, inclined strongly towards mischief. Mimi's passionate sadness on leaving him was tempered always with the assurance he was being cared for as well as could be hoped for in such surroundings and she always returned to New York filled with determination to work twice—three times as hard as ever until she could bring Jean back with her and care for him properly. She was reaching the point where she could take care of his immediate wants from her earnings. But she knew it was best she let him remain there until she could more nearly assure that he could be taken care of even if she herself should get sick or die.

Of social relations she had none. Sylvia invited her frequently to go to Coney Island, to the movies, to dances, but these Mimi always declined. She liked Sylvia very much as an individual but she was always afraid she would not like the young men and women of Sylvia's set. Having been all her life unsuccessful at dissembling or pretence, Mimi was certain Sylvia would detect any dislike of Sylvia's friends and she did not want this possible breach between them.

But this was not the deeper reason for Mimi's refusal nor was even she aware of the cause of her abstention from all relations other than those of her work and school. As a girl Mimi had had a fragile, flower-like beauty. The hardships she had undergone—the agonies of flesh and spirit—had not coarsened or embittered her. Instead they had given her an air of hard brilliancy like the glistening surface of porcelain, beautiful, alluring but chilling to the touch—and as impenetrable. Men instinctively turned and looked at her again as they passed her on the street. She was, of course, not unaware of these attentions nor did they altogether displease her. But her experiences with men, the disastrous one with Carl, the unpleasant ones in Germantown and New York, had made her frankly sceptical of men and their motives. She was frankly repelled by the contacts she had had with men and she had definitely vowed that she would concentrate on her work and Jean's future to the exclusion of everything else. She was strengthened in this vow by the realization that she would never be able to give up Jean and that his existence with the necessity of explanation of his existence would mean almost inevitably the rupture of any friendship other than a most casual one which she might form.

So year after year Mimi went ploddingly along the way she had laid out for herself. One by one girls left Francine's employ, some to get married, some to work elsewhere, some because they were discharged. Yet others, usually very pretty ones who had served as mannequins or in other ways had come in contact with men who had accompanied customers to Francine's, left mysteriously. Some of these paid visits later at Francine's as customers themselves or visited the workrooms clad in expensive furs and gowns, wearing beautiful jewels. Sylvia too left in time to open a shop in upper Broadway, somewhere in the Nineties. "I'll start in the K.W. neighbour- hood—there's more money there when you're beginning," she told Mimi. "I wish you'd come along as I begged you and go in partnership with me." But Mimi preferred to stay on at Francine's where she was sure of putting aside each week money for Jean.

The years of the war rolled by. In time khaki-clad Ameri- cans marched up Fifth Avenue and were whisked mysteriously away. The war became a grim, horrible reality and its influ- ence was felt in time even in the quietude of Francine's. Mimi worked on uncomplainingly, steadily, intelligently. She loved to handle the delicate fabrics, especially those of brilliant col- ours. To her the filmy stuffs were embodiments of a land far, far away from harsh realities. When no one was looking she would run through her fingers a fragile bit of silk or chiffon, smoky blue or icy green, as a miser would his gold. Most of all she loved the passionate reds, the vivid blues, the more pro- nounced shades. In a world of indefinite gropings they were to her positive, real things instead of the vaporous and lighter shades. She often laughed at her foolish dreams interwoven with these fabrics—the little glamorous stories she made up for her own amusement to relieve the tedium of endless rows of threads and bastings. Yet, they gave her comfort and she continued to dream. . . .

Her skill and her inventiveness in time penetrated even to that sacred, dread room on the third floor where Madame Francine herself sat in stately splendour when she was at the shop. Mimi had been at work there for nearly a year when she had been made a draper's assistant. Her time had stretched into a year and a half when she had become a draper. Soon after America had entered the war, when wives whose husbands had become enormously rich overnight began to hear for the first time that it was "the thing to do" to have Lucile or Frances or Bendel or Francine make their clothes for them, Mimi had become a fitter with some thirty girls under her. She had purchased a few Liberty Bonds. Some more money she had put into certain stocks which gave promise of yielding comfortable returns. In time she hoped to put some money into real estate where she could be sure Jean would be provided for, whatever happened to her.

More often now did she come into direct contact with the customers. Of them all, there was none so hard to satisfy as the queenly querulous Mrs. Bennett, wife of him whose name was synonymous with wealth and social position. Because Mrs. Bennett was so hard to please, Madame Francine had asked Mimi always to attend to that grand dame's wishes. When one day no design submitted to Mrs. Bennett was satisfactory, Mimi asked her to leave the matter in her hands.

". . . Yes—yes. I'll do it, for I'll scream if I have to worry over getting a simple evening gown a minute longer. Besides, I'm late already to a luncheon engagement. But remember, Miss Daquin, this is a very, very important occasion and my gown must be perfect. If it isn't—well——" and Mrs. Bennett's voice trailed off into a silence many times as expressive as any spoken words might have been.

The result of Mimi's labours, a creation of green charmeuse and silvery ornaments, made Mrs. Bennett beyond all doubt the most strikingly gowned woman at the dinner to the British nobleman who spoke approvingly of her beauty many times to her during that memorable evening. And Mrs. Bennett enjoyed no less the poorly concealed envious looks which came from her friends as the Englishman hovered near her. Nor did Mrs. Bennett fail to tell Francine how pleased she was with Mimi's creation nor to recommend Mimi to all her friends. And Francine began to watch Mimi and her work as she her-

[226]

FLIGHT

self found that the years she had given in building her establishment were beginning to take their toll. . . .

A cold and nasty November day, with icily grey clouds and nipping breezes, brought a summons to Mimi from Madame Francine herself. One year had passed since the war had ended. New York and Paris again were busying themselves with the making of fine raiment—almost forgotten already were the days of terror and sorrow.

She was perturbed by the summons though common sense told her that the great Francine herself never condescended to perform so vulgar an act as that of discharging an employee. Yet, Mimi feared with the unreasoning fear of the unknown, the unfortellable, the indefinite. Hastily she went over in her mind the events of the past few months. The mistakes she had made had not seemed to her so terrible at the time. Had she offended some customer of wealth, of power? She could think of none who might have complained. Suppose, she reflected wretchedly, I should be discharged just when I am beginning to get on my feet, to see clear sailing ahead? But that's silly, she sought to comfort herself, I've done nothing so terrible that I need get scared like a baby in the dark. All this ran through her head as she made her way to Madame Francine's office.

"You've been with me how many years?" the imposing creature asked Mimi.

"Six years—next spring."

"I hear you've made a number of interesting new designs since you've been a fitter?"

"I don't know how much they are worth—but I have done one or two things——" Mimi answered, somewhat embarrassed. This was reassuring. At any rate, whatever came out of the interview, she wasn't to lose her job, not immediately, anyhow.

"Ah—modest, eh? Well, I like that in you—swelled heads

[227]

don't go very far with me. Oh, excuse me! Sit down, won't you?"

Mimi sat. The request was more a demand. She poised on the edge of the blue and gold chair as though she was not at all sure it would sustain her weight. Must learn something about furniture, she resolved. This room's Louis XIV, I think, she thought to herself, as she gazed around the room with quick glances while waiting for Madame Francine to continue.

"How'd you like to go with me to Paris next month to get new styles?"

Mimi came back to the subject at hand with a start. She gasped.

"Go with you to France?" she echoed.

"*Certainement!*" came the answer as Madame Francine remembered her French. "You speak French, don't you? And you've a keen eye. And you can use your own head—your imagination. I'm not so young as I once was. It's a real bother for me to chase around as I must—going to the shops, the races, the theatres and the opera, the smart hotels and restaurants, everywhere I can pick up ideas. You see, my dear, I always carry an artist with me who's got a mind like the sensitive, so sensitive plate of a camera—he sees a gown or a hat and he never forgets a single detail until he has sketched it on paper."

"I see," murmured Mimi, though she didn't see at all. Her mind was too filled with the prospect of going to Paris. But she must have made her reply sound interested and intelligent enough, for Francine went on.

"Only the department stores and wholesalers buy models—we only absorb ideas and then develop them ourselves. That's why we can ask and get two hundred dollars and up for a gown while the department stores sell theirs for seventy-five." In her voice there was a tinge, faint but unmistakable, of scorn when she spoke of "wholesalers" and "department stores." So

might have Marie Antoinette's ladies-in-waiting have spoken
of the common people. Or so might one of the war million-
aires have spoken of one of his victims. Or an Englishman of
anyone not an Englishman.

"We'll sail the last week in December and we'll be in Paris
six weeks. I make two trips a year—June and December.
I'll introduce you over there and if you make good, I'll let you
go over for me at least once a year alone. . . ."

On and on she talked, of models and *commissionaires*, of going into some of the Paris shops as a potential purchaser to
see all the models, remembering the best of them minutely
for later reproduction or amplification. Usually the latter, for
representatives of other New York establishments use the same
tactics. She told of other tricks of the trade while Mimi devoted half of her mind to absorbing the flow of words and the
other half to a study of Madame Francine.

This was the first time she had ever had time to gaze upon
this magnificent, awe-inspiring creature so close at hand.
Mimi, with her usual irreverence for the majestic, before which
most others bowed the knee abjectly, could not refrain from
the inward comment that Madame Francine, if subjected to a
psychological test, would assay about forty per cent sheer
bluff, thirty per cent knowledge of her business, and thirty per
cent sound common sense. She was tall, slender, simply clad
in a close-fitting gown of grey. A string of amber beads and
a touch of colour at the wrists accentuated the greyness of the
dress and made its simple dignity all the more impressive.
Her skin was of a milky whiteness, her eyes large and brown
and placid, her hair of a rich brown beginning to fleck with
grey. Exquisite, exuding elegance that made many of her customers of better birth feel at times awkward and boorish.

Only the nervous little jerks of her fingers revealed that her
calm air was an acquired one, indicated the abundance of
nervous energy beneath that calm which had enabled Madame

Francine, who had been born Margaret O'Donnell, to reach the heights she had attained. But the Madame Francine who sat opposite Mimi had travelled a long way from the Irish immigrant girl who had looked with startled eyes upon the expanse of New York bay as she clutched feverishly the hand of her squat and unimaginative father. She *must* be fifty if she's a day, Mimi reflected. No, that can't be so. She's been in business for over thirty years—she must be sixty. Anyway, the old girl's certainly taken care of herself, Mimi decided, as she gave polite and reassuring answers to the questions which occasionally interrupted the even flow of Madame Francine's narrative. . . .

"In the meantime, you'll give up your workroom and spend most of your time with me. There are a lot of little points about the business you need to learn—I need a pair of strong, young shoulders on which to rest a part of my burdens"— here Madame Francine gave a gentle upward motion of her shoulders that would have convinced even a Parisian of her Gallicism—"and from all I can see, you're the best one here to share these burdens with me." . . .

For six weeks while the shops above them rushed through young mountains of work, making creations of all sorts for the Palm Beach migration of the socially and financially elect, Mimi and Madame Francine spent several hours together each day in the sheltered quietness of Madame Francine's private office—"my studio" she called it. Mimi saw and met and heard about women and men whose names she had seen in society columns and in the smartest magazines but whom she had never seen in the flesh. She heard of the idiosyncrasies, the foibles, and the predilections of each of them. She learned the things each liked to hear. More important, she memorized the things they did not like to hear. She listened to lengthy accounts of the business routine until her head swam and she felt sure she could never by any means digest a tenth of it.

And there were other things she learned too—phases of the business which she had never suspected before, marooned as she had been in the workrooms. Had she gossiped more with the girls, she reflected, she would have known these things sooner. She learned the names of the men customers whose wives and whose mistresses both purchased their gowns at Francine's. And she was properly impressed with the necessity of never—*never*—permitting any mix-ups in the delivery of gowns or hats. She learned the necessary precautions in advising the book-keepers about the bills for these goods—which bill was to be sent to the man's home and which to his office, marked "Personal."

Too, she was admitted to the secret of the victimizing of these men both by their wives and their mistresses. She heard Madame Francine explain suavely how many of the wives, permitted unlimited charge accounts at as many shops as they chose, were given little cash by their husbands. Madame Francine answered Mimi's guileless question why husbands with money to give did not give it to their wives with a knowing little laugh. "Wives with too much money to spend might—with interesting young men around—well, they might forget they're wives." Mimi listened with amazement as Madame Francine told her how the wives—and the mistresses—frequently came and bought gowns costing three hundred dollars for which a bill was sent to the man for four hundred.

"And what becomes of the extra hundred?" Mimi asked.

"We give that in cash to the customer, little innocent! . . , What will happen if we don't? They'll go to another shop and we'll have lost a customer."

Despite all she had undergone, Mimi realized that she knew pitifully little about the ways of the world. Duplicity, deceit,

lying, dishonesty, all around her and she had never even suspected it. I am a silly little innocent, she mused. In a flash
Whitman's lines came back to her:

"Of the endless trains of the faithless, of cities fill'd with the foolish,
Of myself for ever reproaching myself (for who more foolish than I,
and who more faithless?) . . ."

She was faithless and foolish. If she weren't she'd drop the
whole thing and get herself a job scrubbing floors, washing
dishes, anything rather than be a willing part of this sort of
trickery. But even as she scourged herself and despised herself for her weakness, she knew she wouldn't scrub floors or
wash dishes. There's Jean to think of, was her dominant
thought. But she resolved she'd get out of the whole business
and work at home when she had earned and saved the money
she must have. Miss Lawrence had done it and some of her
customers had followed her all the way to Negro Harlem.
She could do it too—perhaps open a shop of her own as Sylvia had done.

She was glad she had done nothing so foolish when a few
days after Christmas she stood on deck and watched the ser-
rated sky-line of New York, clad mistily in a blanket of snow
that fell like a great celestial curtain, drop silently in the distance. The thrill and mystery of departure no longer of interest to her, Madame Francine had already gone to her state-
room, while Percival Edwards, the sketch artist, had fallen an
easy victim to sea-sickness before the hawsers had been cast
off and the huge ship had nosed its way from its slip. The
long, dark pier with its distinctive odour of things nautical,
the crowds of passengers and of others who had come to bid
them a snowy and chilly farewell, the trim officers of the lux-
urious vessel that seemed so immense Mimi felt an immediate
sense of security replacing her fear of the sea, all these excited and delighted Mimi. Only in short trips of a few hours
on the Gulf of Mexico before they had left New Orleans had

FLIGHT

Mimi ever before been on a ship. Those little boats of her childhood could have been stored away and forgotten in the hold of this huge boat, she reflected, as the shore became fainter and fainter in the greyish white curtain of snowflakes. She drew her shoulders deeper into the collar of her fur coat until there was but a thin slit of creamy flesh visible between the collar and the tight-fitting little toque that covered her head. This *is* life, she thought comfortably. A big liner, Paris, the boulevards, the shops, the theatres, the opera, the restaurants, all the life of *la plus belle ville du monde*—the phrase came to her from the text-book she had used but a short time before. . . .

Even Madame Francine's at times crotchety querulousness and Percival Edward's effeminacy could not ruffle her spirits in Paris—it was all too marvellous, too intoxicatingly beautiful, that she was at last in the one place she had always dreamed of visiting. The torn and unkempt streets could not destroy her happiness—*c'est la guerre*," she heard on every side, but for her there was no destroyed beauty—she saw beyond the disorder and envisioned the city as it was before shells and neglect had ruffled its beauty. She loved the reviving splendour and gaiety of fashionable life, loved it so well that Madame Francine was forced several times to remind her not too gently that she was in Paris for work and not as a lady of leisure. These reminders brought her back to herself for a time but soon her thoughts were again far from sketching frocks or absorbing ideas. All too soon for her the six weeks one by one began and ended, one after the other. She did not want to return to America. She wanted to stay for ever in Paris. She would do it, she promised herself, with the recklessness of those infatuated with the charm of a place when leaving it. She would bring Jean to France, educate him there, and blot from her memory and his all the dark days in their own

FLIGHT

America. This dream remained with her for a long time after they returned to New York. . . .

"My dear, I'm an old woman now and I can't make the trips I used to," Madame Francine told Mimi after they had made their second trip to Paris. "It's nice of you to deny my age," she smiled at Mimi's eager protestations that she was not old. "But it's true, nevertheless, and I've got to shift even more of the burdens on you. Do you think you could go without me to Paris next time?"

With a woman's eye for such signs, Mimi had noticed the telltale wrinkles in Madame Francine's chin which, despite massages and all the other means she had used to retain her youth, had become each year more evident until now when she held her head at a certain angle they reminded Mimi of the neck of a plucked hen. Under Madame Francine's eyes hung revealing pouches that of mornings were dark and wrinkled. Francine had had a desperate struggle to establish and maintain her position—the competition had been cruelly keen, any lessening of her efforts would have meant the swift relegation of the business she had built to a place in the rear of the procession. This strain was now telling on her. She was weary. She no longer was able to drive herself and those under her at high speed. Only the will to make Francine's *the* place where smart New York came for its clothes remained. She would always keep a supervisory eye on the shop. But she was glad she had Mimi. Under her direction the pace would be maintained, Francine's name would not die out, Francine's gowns would yet be known as the last word in feminine circles.

Closely she had watched Mimi and she had been satisfied. She had given the younger woman many useful hints and her delight had known no bounds when these hints had been taken, elaborated, overhauled and embellished in

[234]

such fashion the books had shown a decided increase in business transacted. Francine was forced to admit, though her confessions were rueful ones and kept to herself, that Mimi's tactful handling of several wealthy customers who had been wont to buy the bulk of their wares at other modistes' had resulted in the transfer of practically all their business to her own place. And there were, she noted, a number of women with wealth and little else, who under no circumstances would permit any other individual to advise with them on colours and fabrics and designs save Mimi. Madame Francine was content—Mimi would do. Some day, who knows but Mimi will be able to take her own place and she could with satisfied mind retire for the long rest and the leisurely life she had always promised herself?

CHAPTER XIX

THE success she was achieving made Mimi happy, as was to be expected. The dark days in Atlanta, since Jean had died, the pitiful and defeat-crowned struggle in Philadelphia, the abortive effort in Harlem to pull herself from the mire, and her flight away from her own people seemed now fantastic and unreal. At times they were to her almost as though she had read of them in a novel—one of those stories of a "poor working-girl beset by temptation and sin," a story for backstairs consumption. At other times she shuddered when she realized all that she had been through, wondered how she had ever had the courage, the will-power to keep her head above the lashing, foaming waters instead of sinking restfully beneath them without struggle. Naturally, she was happy when Francine's virtual surrender of the shop to her had been more than a promotion—it had been an accolade of victory.

But, as is the way of the world, that victory brought with it many things which were not so pleasant to think about. It had now been six years since she had left her Aunt Sophie. Those years had been filled to the brim, packed tight with work all day at a table in the shop, with evenings filled with school work and lectures varied only occasionally by a visit to the theatre or a concert, with dreary, lonely meals and solitary rooms where she had felt as though she were lodged in a cell. Of naturally strong and normal desires common to her sex and to humanity, she had had many bitter struggles with herself. There had been times when she wondered what use, what value there was to the unremitting routine to which she had con-

[236]

FLIGHT

demned herself. She had been tempted—sorely tempted—to yield to the "one hour of glorious strife"—to find relief in some folly, some wild breaking of the bands which bound her with terrific solidity. Time and time again she had gone almost to the edge of the abyss and gazed fascinatedly down into the alluring depths below. But each time she had withdrawn in terror, her breath coming in little gasps of fear, every nerve rigid. Only her experiences which had brought to her such misery saved her, they and *Petit* Jean. She feared the possibility of letting herself be hurt again. Better anything than that, she whispered often to herself when alone in her room at night. And after each temptation she plunged with doubled zeal into her work, seeking to find an opiate there which would absorb the restless urge within her body.

When even work could not dull the ceaseless desires she felt, she would often walk at night through to her unknown and queer sections of the city, peering into doorways, watching the ways of the varied peoples that make of New York a world within itself, packed with races representative of every nook of the world. She rambled through districts where no word except Spanish was heard, ate in tiny restaurants where the faces were all long and brown and where the food was spiced with condiments whose name she did not know but which she was certain had come all the way from Spain. As she ate she listened to soft-throated guitars and love-burdened songs sung with the rich amorousness of a nation of love-makers. She walked past rows of red-brick houses with trellised balconies and beautiful Moorish oriels, past houses reminiscent of the Alhambra, through streets that made it impossible for her to believe she yet was in New York.

Through streets where naught but gaily clad Gipsies with brightly coloured dresses and midnight-black hair, with sparkling yet mysterious eyes and gold necklaces and bracelets, were seen. She loved the touches of colour they gave to rows

[237]

of dilapidated and abandoned stores through the hanging of vivid strips of Turkish gauzes and calicoes across the dusty windows, the thronging of the streets of love-making young girls and boys, of surprisingly agile old women and stalwart men with fierce and terrifyingly strange faces. Or perhaps she wandered on the lower East Side through streets packed from curb to curb with Jews, arguing, strolling slowly of an evening under the garish lights from stores selling jewellery and clothing and food and amusement. Sometimes she ate in a restaurant on Houston Street where she could obtain white caviare and strange, exotic dishes served nowhere else, while the proprietor, who had come to America from Roumania, played the cymbalom, accompanied by a pathetic old blind man. She found down here a new standard of appraisal of these people, who, if for no other reason than that they, like her own race, had known bitter persecution, appealed to her with colour and romance and kindred emotions. She was often repelled by the bustling, noisy, aggressive younger generation, for ever concerned with profits and losses. But the older generation, the women of the calm eyes and heavy wigs, the men with magnificent beards and extraordinarily well-formed features, appealed to her more than almost any other type she had ever seen.

Through the Italian section she wandered along sidewalks littered with fruit and vegetable stands, listening to voices singing to guitar accompaniment songs of Venice and Genoa and Naples. Diminutive Sicilians slithered past her in the shadows, huge Calabrians swaggered, haughty and handsome men and women from Milan and Tuscania occasionally strode proudly by. But most of all she loved the lightness and gaiety of the streets where the French lived, to listen to their gay love-making and the delicately beautiful songs which flowed forth as naturally as did the speech which she understood and loved. She sat in cafés and lazily watched men and women playing bezique at the small tables as they sipped greenish drinks from tall glasses. Shamelessly she eavesdropped on conversations regarding the merits of Anatole France as a writer whose work would live, whether the poetry of Mallarmé or Villon were to be esteemed as highly as some would have it, whether there was any city in the world, past or present or future, which had, has or might have the charm of Paris, whether there had ever been an artist who ranked with Yvette Guilbert. All, all these Mimi loved, not alone because in these varied scenes she could forget her own perplexities, but because they were lovable and exotic and charming in themselves. . . .

Her rise to the position where she was second in command of the rapidly expanding business brought other problems to Mimi no less serious than her own wishes and desires. At Francine's she had been known as Miss Daquin from the beginning. This had not mattered a great deal, now that she was the virtual head of the establishment. She had long since moved to her own apartment near Gramercy Park but embarrassing explanations would have been necessary had she brought Jean to her. Those could have been met in time but again she worried over the decision as to what would be best for him.

She had partially solved that problem by removing him from the orphanage and placing him with a family in Westchester County where she could see him frequently and where she could direct the training he should receive in the kindly French family with whom he lived. She chose this plan, for she knew that her long hours at the shop, the multiple duties of evenings, and her three months each year in Paris would effectively prevent her from giving Jean the guidance and care that a boy of twelve needed. She ruthlessly put aside her own wishes, plucking them out as though they were malignant growths which health demanded should be uncom-

[239]

promisingly destroyed. She sought only to consider the things which would be of greatest good to him. The change from Baltimore to Westchester County made her happier but yet there was the ceaseless longing to have him near—aching and unappeasable yearning for him that could not be stilled. . . .

She saw Mrs. Rogers several times a year but her aunt was the only coloured person now a part of her life. There had been a number of coloured girls who at one time or the other applied for work under her when she was a fitter. These she had put to the same tests that she gave to the others—if they measured up to them, they were employed—if not, they were refused. At first when such applications had come she had been fearful—had debated whether or not she could take the risk of employing one who might have known or seen her when she lived in Harlem and who might start talking. She had often heard, without giving much thought to the matter, that usually when coloured persons went white, in order to prove their whiteness, they were more anti-Negro than anybody else. When she was faced with the problem herself she understood more fully what lay back of that feeling—she was not altogether free from it herself. But she had employed them and there had been none who had told that she was coloured, though one of them had, on leaving Francine's, privately told Mimi she knew who Mimi was.

In the early years after she had left Harlem she had on numerous occasions met former acquaintances of hers on the street. Sometimes she had bowed and spoken a few words—sometimes she had passed rapidly by and hated herself for doing so for days afterwards. Six years and more had apparently wiped all trace of her former days from the slates of Harlem, the ever-changing population either too busy or too uninterested to continue their concern with her and her affairs.

FLIGHT

Though she denied it to herself, sometimes with a trace of bitterness that her own people had forced her to live a life of duplicity and deceit, nevertheless she felt frequently a yearning for contact with her own people, for whom she had the same passionate love of the days following the riot in Atlanta despite all she had suffered at their hands.

She was lonely, for despite her success she had no intimates, none she could call friend, though she might have had them had she chosen. She missed the warm colourfulness of life among her own, she had never been able to shake off the chill she felt even when her present-day associates sought to be most cordial. And she resented bitterly the airs of superiority they assumed. Frequently when she heard contemptuous remarks about "niggers," "coons," "darkies," from those who showed by their words their complete ignorance of Negroes, she felt like reminding them that to her there were two ways of achieving and maintaining superiority: one, by being superior; the other, by keeping somebody else inferior. And she felt no better that her life made her keep silent when these attacks were made. Once or twice she had sought to disprove the contention of some obviously biased person. Her face had flamed and she had relapsed into a silence that galled her when she had been met by the curt statement that in itself was a challenge: "Oh, you're a 'nigger-lover'—and from the South too!" . . .

Steadily she kept to the course she had set despite these and other distractions. Madame Francine's visits to the new shop in Fifty-seventh Street became more and more infrequent, now that she spent most of her time in her home at Mount Vernon and her winters in Florida. Mimi was now actually the mistress of the place and she occupied the room which would have been Madame Francine's, though there was always a desk ready for her when she chose to come in and consult with Mimi on matters of importance. . . .

FLIGHT

Mrs. Horace Crosby, late of Chicago, where her Rotary Club husband had manipulated certain markets in grain, very much to the advantage of the Crosby exchequer, waddled puffingly, her succession of chins joggling with jelly-like quiverings above her ample breast, across the narrow pavement of the Rue de la Paix to her waiting motor-car. Her rotund, much bepowdered and berouged face broke into a cherubic smile that spread like ripples on a placid pond when a stone is dropped into it, as she saw a trim, reddish-haired young woman approaching. She turned and effectively blocked the passage of the young woman, making non-recognition even less possible by extending her fat arms adorned with numerous bracelets and her fingers much bedecked with diamonds.

"Well, now, if this ain't lovely—to run across you like this in Paris, Miss Daquin! You must get right in and come to the hotel for luncheon with me. I just must show you some of the lovely things I've bought—real antiques and pictures and lots of pretty things—but Horace says I'm a fool to spend so much money on these 'Frog' things—tells me they sting me every time I go in a place——"

Mimi tried to plead a multiplicity of engagements, but to no avail. Mrs. Crosby as a poor woman had had a knack of making people do what she wanted them to do. Now that her aggressiveness was backed by wealth far greater than she had ever dreamed as a girl the world possessed, she could be evaded now only by one's abrupt taking to one's heels. Mimi made a wry face as she entered the lavender car adorned by the huge Crosby monogram in gilt. Resistance was useless, she realized, and Mrs. Crosby did buy a lot of things from Francine. Though her gowns always looked as though they had been purchased on Fourteenth Street in New York, somewhere east of the Avenue.

"My dear, I bought the cutest, sweetest little statue yesterday—the darlingest little Cupids with bows and arrows you ever saw. Horace tells me the only place I can put it is in the garage—we've got so much stuff now, the house is running over. But I don't care—it's a dear—and it must be good, for it cost me twelve thousand francs! And I bought it from the artist himself—oh, Miss Daquin, you should have seen him. Big dark eyes and long hair and the sweetest velvet jacket—he looked just like a Sicilian bandit, though I've never seen one, but I just know they look like that. He made me feel all creepy inside—say, I'll take you down to meet him—he's such a dear I know you'll fall in love with him right off——"

"Thanks—you're very kind but I just can't possibly make it this afternoon," Mimi hastily interrupted her. "Ought really to be at work now but just couldn't resist the temptation of having luncheon with you," she added as she saw the childish pout of disappointment which flitted instantly over Mrs. Crosby's face when she met opposition to any wish of hers.

"Well, some other day then—but you *must* see him!" Mrs. Crosby smiled, mollified by Mimi's insincere compliment.

Mimi sank into the soft cushions and watched the shops and passers-by along the boulevard, her mind only half given to Mrs. Crosby's chatter. It wasn't so difficult to get along with this spoiled old woman, she decided. She runs on and on and apparently doesn't expect answers even to her direct questions. By the time they reached the hotel Mimi had become as used to the incessant chatter as she had to the steady hum of the motor.

To say that Mrs. Crosby, with Mimi in her wake, swept through the lobby of the hotel, would in a measure be an inaccurate statement of that massive lady's progress. Her movement from one spot to another was to the irreverent-minded and to those crass souls who either did not know or, knowing, were unintelligent enough not to be properly impressed by Mrs. Crosby's notion of what constituted the grand manner, might be properly described as an astounding combination of waddling, rolling, wheezing, limping and shuffling. Sometimes she seemed like a huge wave of flesh rising and sinking, rising and sinking, until she subsided upon the shore of her objective. At other times Mimi thought of her as one of the puffing, noisy tugboats in the East River—that is, if one of these boats were painted a brilliant pink or blue. Mrs. Crosby was wholly unaware of the disrespectful allusions or comparisons her friends made behind her back. But even those who saw beneath the ludicrous exterior down to the simple soul beneath could not refrain from amusement at the spectacle she presented. Even her closest friends dared not hint that she was other than the impressive, jovial, lovable creature she fancied herself to be.

Luncheon ordered, of truffles and soup and sweets and "just a teeny-weeny little chop—no, garsong, you'd better bring me two chops, because I'm starved," Mrs. Crosby began presenting for Mimi's approval the things she had gathered through the modern Aladdin's lamp represented by her husband's chequebook. Statuettes and "genuine" laces, oils, and drawings, usually of tender scenes of lovers strolling through sylvan bowers or kissing each other awkwardly under impossible-looking trees, odds and ends of all sorts of trinkets designed by masters of inutility and banality, boxes and closets and trunks disgorged an endless display of loot. Ninety per cent of the stuff is junk, Mimi concluded. Had she been asked by Mrs. Crosby to advise her before she had bought them, Mimi was certain she would have done everything in her power to have prevented their purchase. There was no need nor did Mrs. Crosby want criticism now, only exclamations of praise and appreciation of the beauty and value of the oddly assorted variety of things which littered every available object in the room by the time luncheon was ready. So Mimi murmured politely: "How sweet!" or "How very charming!" and tried as hard as she could to make her voice sound sincere.

FLIGHT

Luncheon finished, Mimi began taking surreptitious peeps at her wrist watch as she waited for some lull in the Niagara of words which poured from the Crosby mouth. She thought she saw her chance when the telephone rang.

"Answer it, won't you, Miss Daquin, for me? That's a dear! These silly little French phones annoy me so—why don't they show some initiative and put in telephones like we have in America?"

"There's a man named Forrester calling," Mimi told her when she had answered the telephone.

"Oh, Jimmy Forrester! Tell them to send him right up! No—no, dear, you can't run away now. Jimmy is the cutest and sweetest boy—even though he does laugh at me and some of my ways. He swears he doesn't but some of the things he says sometimes sound suspiciously like he's chaffing—that's a nice word, isn't it? I picked it up in London last week— . . . Oh, dear! you really must go? I do wish you'd take the afternoon off and come along to help me buy a few little things I need. . . ."

But Mimi already had put her hat on and was half-way to the door, with elaborate indefiniteness promising to look in on Mrs. Crosby again "the very first time I can steal a minute or two." Privately she was vowing to have no minutes free for her rotund hostess as long as she was in Paris. These promises and Mrs. Crosby's reiteration of her demands that Mimi spend all her spare time with her took a longer time than Mimi knew. She wanted to get away but her hostess had launched into a life history of Jimmy Forrester and resignedly Mimi listened.

" . . . He comes of a very good family in New York—they haven't much money but they've got position—Jimmie's connected with a big brokerage house in New York that handles a lot of Mr. Crosby's business—Jimmie does practically all of Horace's buying and selling of stocks or bonds—frightfully smart, Jimmy is, and bright as a steel trap—Jimmie's just like he's my own son. . . ."

"Hello, Jimmie dear—I want you to meet a friend of mine who's been trying her hardest to slip away before you came. Miss Daquin, this is Jimmie Forrester. You two ought to know each other real well"; and Mrs. Crosby beamed with maternal benedictions upon them.

Jimmie Forrester—James H. Forrester was the name engraved on his stationery—bowed and scanned Mimi from head to foot as he bowed. He was tall and slender, brown hair greying at his temples, his face lean and tanned. His face in repose, was indistinguishable from thousands of carefully groomed and tolerably handsome young men to be seen any afternoon on Fifth Avenue or in the fashionable streets near Piccadilly.

But when he smiled Jimmie Forrester became an individual. He had a trick of opening wide his eyes, and Mimi saw that they did not match. One of them was brownish while the other veered more towards hazel, giving him an exotic air which interested her mildly. And his smile revealed oddly crooked teeth, disarranged in a way that brought distinction to an otherwise uninteresting and commonplace mouth, a distinction, she decided, which modern dentistry would have destroyed had the teeth been straightened. All this she noticed in the hasty glance she gave him as they uttered the usual set phrases accompanying an introduction.

"Awfully sorry my coming ran you away—didn't know I was such an ogre," he apologized as Mrs. Crosby hurriedly gathered the more intimate garments she had brought forth for Mimi's inspection.

"You didn't run me—I should have been gone long since——"

"The Holy Behemoth's been talking you deaf, dumb and blind," he whispered with a nod in the general direction of Mrs. Crosby, who was humming a music-hall air she had heard the night before. Or, rather she hummed with a peculiar dissonance the tune she thought she had heard.

"Not so bad—she has her good points. I wish I could have saved her the job of buying a lot of the things she's been showing me."

"Don't flatter yourself—neither wind nor wave nor howling storm can stop her from dumping Horace's money all over the place. There's a glitter that springs to the eyes of shopkeepers all over Europe whenever Eulalia appears on the scene—they hustle to drag out all the junk they think they've been stuck with and unload it on her, telling her it's genuine Rodin or Millet or whatever springs to their minds at the moment. Even Horace, who has twisted the tail of Wall Street dozens of times, is powerless before Eulalia—she's irresistible when she sets out to do a thing—— Gosh, here she comes!"

Some undefinable bond had sprung into being between them. By the time Mrs. Crosby had puffed her way around the room once or twice bearing armfuls of clothing into the bedroom beyond, they felt they had known each other much longer than the few minutes they had stood there.

"Let me take you wherever you're going," he asked her but she declined and hurried away. But when she reached her hotel in the Rue DuPhot that evening she found there had been three telephone calls from Mrs. Crosby. As she turned away from the desk determined to change her dress and slip away for a quiet meal alone, the telephone rang again and she heard the girl say: "Yes, Mam'selle Daquin has just come—I'll connect you at once!" Fearing it might be Mrs. Crosby, Mimi went to the telephone and found her fears well-grounded. Even through the machine one got a distinct sense of gushing good will, of sweetness and light.

"My dear, I was so afraid I'd never get you—we're having dinner to-night—just a little comfy party of us—and you must come—I won't take 'no' for an answer. All the shops are

[247]

closed now and you can't work all the time, it's not good for any of us—'all work and no play,' you remember. . . ." Mrs. Crosby's voice was laden with little unexpected thrills and flute-like runs that she fancied were quite cute and fascinating. She never got out of practice, for she generously bestowed the silveriness of her tones on male and female alike, even on the servants, who could not as easily flee from them. Mimi knew she would go even as she felt herself a spineless sycophant as she agreed. Hardly had she washed her face before the car was announced. She got some small satisfaction from seeing the new respect on the faces of the hotel attendants as they looked with awe upon the lavender Rolls-Royce with its shining silver trimmings and silken upholstery.

She knew Forrester would be in the car, having sensed that he had been responsible for the dinner invitation. As they were whirled through the Boulevard Madeleine and down the Rue Royal to Maxim's she listened to Mrs. Crosby's cooing exclamations of pleasure that she had accepted, while she watched the rounded broadness of Mr. Crosby's back and the straight lines of Forrester's in the seats in front of them.

"Jimmie went quite mad about you this afternoon," Mrs. Crosby whispered as she sought to maintain her perilous balance while the car slithered around corners and came to an abrupt stop. "Raved about you, my dear—said you were the most beautiful woman he'd ever seen. You should be proud —there have been loads of women who've run their fool heads off after him and he never even looked at them."

Mimi was not at all certain that Forrester had said all this, nor even that he had been the hard-hearted, stern woman-dodger Mrs. Crosby tried to make of him. But she did notice that he managed to bring his chair as close to hers as he could and that he took advantage of every occasion, which were not few, to say meaningless little things in a confidential tone, when Mrs. Crosby became interested with little squeals, as some acquaintance was spied in another part of the dining-room. His manner was entirely open but the way in which he said these things seemed to imply that they had a bond of understanding between them, a bond secret and very precious. This disturbed Mimi in a way she could not explain even to herself. Jimmie Forrester interested her, there was something intangible about him that made her afraid of herself. Once he leaned over as Mrs. Crosby was excitedly pointing out a friend who had just entered. "You are more beautiful now than you were even this afternoon!" he whispered. The remark was not brilliant nor was it one she had not heard before. But it made queer little tingles chase each other through her, she felt herself blushing as though she were a girl of sixteen.

"Don't be silly," she admonished herself. "You'd be a pretty fool to let yourself get interested. It's hopeless. It can't lead anywhere but to bitterness and disappointment. Keep your head! Keep your head!"

She gave herself this sage advice and found herself promptly disregarding it. She was glad when the dinner was over and she escaped, pleading headache and weariness. Safe in her room, she tried to shake Jimmie Forrester's mismated eyes and crooked teeth from her mind. She failed. She was afraid—terribly afraid. She knew it was folly, suicide, madness. But the vision persisted. For years she had in an indefinite way been lonely, had wanted the companionship of some man who would be to her the summation of the ideals she cherished as the most desirable. These spells had come infrequently, only with great rareness breaking through the vitreous shell with which her experiences had encased her. But they had been after all easy to shake off, for there had been no one man but instead an ideal of her own construction which had never taken form in the flesh. Now that she had met Jimmie Forrester, she vaguely realized that she was not as immune as she had fancied herself. She fell asleep, worried.

[249]

CHAPTER XX

A WEEK's work was crowded into two days. As she sat on deck after breakfast the first morning out, Mimi felt a sense of security which made her comfortable for the first time since she had sat next to Jimmie Forrester at dinner. I'll put these silly, childish notions out of my head, she resolved, and get back down to earth again. And after a few relentless pluckings of thoughts and fancies from her head she secured forgetfulness in reading. She swept through Carl Van Vechten's "Peter Whiffle," read the story of pathetic George F. Babbitt, walked the deck when she got tired, and then resumed her reading. She threw aside Edna St. Vincent Millay's poems —they were too poignantly reminiscent of love and its disappointments, she wasn't in a mood now for such revelations. And she was glad when the crags of Manhattan rose out of nothingness, for here was her familiar world where sanity could be found in hard work again. . . .

New York was sweltering in the terrific heat of early summer. Mimi, back in Manhattan one week, gave up the attempt to work and set forth to find relief somewhere in the greenness of Central Park.

"You ran away!" a familiar voice accused her as she stepped from Francine's door into the street.

"Oh—I thought I left you in Paris!" she parried, laughing nervously at the unexpected appearance of Jimmie Forrester.

"You did—but I'm here now. Shall we eat dinner at the Plaza? Or Pierre's? Or the Brevoort?"

"At none of them. I'm busy this evening."

"You're not!" he challenged her. "And even if you were, you surely wouldn't deny me after I've come all the way from Paris to see you?"

After all, she decided, there's no use in running away. I'll face it now and get it over with. And then I'll not see him again.

"Why did you leave so suddenly without giving me—us—a chance to see you again?" he demanded not unkindly when they had given their order.

"I finished my work and decided I was tired of Paris and wanted to get home."

He said nothing but in his eyes she read his thoughts—she had not succeeded in deceiving him. The consciousness he knew her fear gave him an advantage that made her uncomfortable.

"Tell me about Mrs. Crosby. 'The dear old Behemoth,' you called her, I believe," she sought to divert him.

"She's still buying junk—and Horace is howling louder than ever. They'll have to charter a ship to get the stuff home. Tell me, did I do anything that offended you?"

"Why do you ask me such a foolish question?"

"You ran away," he answered simply.

"No, you didn't do anything to offend me. And I didn't run away. I just came home when my work was done."

"I asked at the hotel and they said you had engaged your room through the fifteenth. And the Behemoth took me to Paquin's and Beer's and Worth's and Drecoll's and they all said you told them you'd had a cable calling you back to the States. And the steamship people told us you'd turned in passage on the *Aquitania* and made them squeeze you on the *Mauretania.* What was the cable that brought you back?" he demanded.

"You took a lovely method of enjoying a vacation in Paris, didn't you?" she laughed, masking the perturbation she was

FLIGHT

feeling that he had gone to all that trouble to find out why she
had gone. "Chasing around to modistes and steamship offices
instead of enjoying Paris——"

"Mimi, don't you know why I did it?" he pleaded. Neither
of them noticed that he had called her by her first name.

"No, I don't," she prevaricated and then was immediately
sorry, not because she had told an untruth but because he
might consider it as an invitation to tell her why he had followed her. That was exactly what he did.

"Don't think me foolish, silly, childish. Perhaps I'm all
three and if I am I don't care. I've always laughed at the
notion of 'love at first sight' but I won't do it again——"

"Don't be foolish. You have seen me twice. You know
nothing whatever about me other than that I work for my living at Francine's. I might be an adventuress——"

"Please don't," he pleaded. "Be serious. Let me finish."

"No, I can't let you go on. There are very good reasons
why there can never be anything between us—and I shan't
see you again," she said firmly, as she rose from the table.
"It's best we let this drop right here—and oh, Jimmie, it
must end now." Her voice, which had begun so bravely and
positively, faltered. At the end it was almost a sob. She left
him there and was gone before he could follow her. . . .

Three times the next day she picked up the receiver of the
telephone on her desk and hung it up again when she heard his
voice. As she started to leave the building for the day, she
saw him waiting outside just in time to dart back into the
building and go out by the back door. He wrote her but his
letters were unanswered. Once she saw him crossing perilously Fifth Avenue, dodging taxicabs and buses by a hair's-
breadth while their drivers cursed and shouted at him fluently
but a near-by shop gave her friendly refuge.

She prayed he would become disheartened, angry with her.

And even as she prayed, a malevolent spirit within her was battling with her prayer and making her hope fervently he would not forget. She knew that if she saw him she would not be able to check the seeds of love which she found had taken root miraculously and sprouted alarmingly. She did not call it "love"—"silly infatuation which will pass away" was her name for it. She debated the wisdom of her course, wondered what would happen if she surrendered to the impulse to yield to this feeling towards him which came to her after she had switched off the night-lamp beside her bed and lay there between the cool sheets and listened to the street noises that came faintly up to her. She shielded the keen sensitiveness to each tiny impact of experience and of thought from heavy blows by trying to keep the heart of reality away from her. For reality frightened her while it fascinated her, made her long to creep away from it and find refuge in some realm of forgetfulness where she would be safe. Warring relentlessly and ruthlessly against that timidity was her common sense, which had been so largely increased by the experiences she had encountered.

Suppose I should marry him? I'd live in constant terror all my life, fearing that he would find out about Jean, about my race. The latter did not seem so important, but could she give up Jean for ever? She knew she couldn't. Fanciful plans sprang to her mind and as quickly were rejected. She thought of telling him Jean was a nephew, the child of some mythical and deceased sister or brother. No, she couldn't do that—she couldn't live a lie like that. She thought of leaving him with the family in County. They had learned to love him as their own child and had looked alarmed when she had mentioned that some day she would take him with her. She could establish a trust fund with all the money she possessed and insure at least reasonable comfort for him. No, that was impossible—she could never give him up that way.

Night after night she rolled and tossed and came no nearer a solution than before. Her eyes now had dark circles under them, she could not eat, she was nervous and irritable even to the customers. The knowledge that this state of affairs could not go on did not add to her comfort. And Jimmie Forrester would not be denied. He brought his mother to the shop to buy gowns but Mimi would not see them, sending word that she was frightfully busy and terribly sorry. . . .

Autumn and the rush season were upon her and she still wrestled with the riddle which seemed wellnigh insoluble to her. Mimi's face had lost much of its colour, deep lines spread fan-like from the corners of her haggard eyes, from her body had gone much of its roundness. To her dismay she found that the more she struggled against the love which she feared, the more securely did it fasten its tentacles upon her. With her now was a stifling, strangling sensation as though she were held in the rib-cracking embrace of a boa constrictor who was crushing her in a room filled with acrid smoke. The passage of days and weeks and months had neither lessened her own distress, blissful in a measure though it was, nor had Jimmie Forrester's zeal shown any sign of abatement. He resorted to telegrams, flowers, books. He used the mails to send proud but pleading letters asking her to permit him only to see her, to walk with her in the park, to go to the theatre or dinner. "Undoubtedly I've made myself a silly ass in your eyes," he wrote her, "pursuing you, bombarding you, besieging you. My common sense tells me I should have taken refuge in pride and shown you that I can become angry enough never to see you again. I've even gone as far as to construct in my own mind little dramatic scenes when I loftily told you, after you had seen the devotion I offer you and had returned it in kind, that it was too late—your coldness has killed my love. And, like one of the old-style villains in a cheap melodrama, I have gloated as I saw you humble while I stood cold and impassive. Oh, yes, Mimi, I've gone through all this and more—more than ever a boy of sixteen in love for the first time has suffered.

"Yet I find that despite all I do to pluck you and the memory of you out of my heart I love you more devotedly every day that passes. Take pity, Mimi, just let me talk with you— see you, sit beside you and hear your voice. I know now there's nothing you can do which can kill my love. I cannot understand why you act as you do—surely you do not hate me completely. If you won't let me see you, won't you write me just one little note and tell me why you have acted as you have?"

That night Mimi read the letter over and over again. She knew what it had cost him to write it—to make such confessions of his inability to stop loving her despite all she had done to kill that love. For a long time she sat by the window and gazed out into the quiet street below. The roar of the East Side elevated trains came faintly to her like the gentle rumbles of far-off thunder. One by one the little groups of children playing near at hand dispersed with shrill shouts of parting until the morrow. A slightly chilling breeze from the East River swayed the yellowish silk curtains lazily. Ever and again it bustled through the windows in little gusts that swept in and were gone. She heard leaves of paper on the table behind her blowing to the floor but she made no move to pick them up. Life for her was like that, she thought. Little gusts came and swept her out of life just as she was beginning to find her way about in the new spot where she had been placed. They took her and tossed her about, this way and that, dropping her willy-nilly into some new place, some new situation in which she had to begin all over again the process of adjusting herself.

There was no pity for herself in Mimi's reflections. She had been flung this way and that, buffeted by winds that often threatened to capsize the tiny boat which was her life. But with it all her lot had not been as hard as it might have been. There had been compensation—Jean and *Petit* Jean, her work, the love of people, human beings she had studied at first to take herself out of herself, and later because she found in them interest and joy in that interest. But all the things hitherto now seemed easy, for through them all she had kept her soul free. Now she was threatened with inundation, the great rising of a wave that rose up—up—up and, bursting into a million silver bubbles, took shape again and formed the face of Jimmie Forrester. That face haunted her with its pleading, its suffering, eloquent of the struggle which he too was making.

From below voices came to her. She recognized one of them as that of Mrs. Mahoney, the wife of the janitor, out for a breath of air before going to bed.

"And I says to him, says I," Mrs. Mahoney was declaring in tones redolent of shamrocks and St. Patricks and harps, "you can't get nowhere by dodging the truth. If you got a hard job in front of you, the only thing to do is to jump at it and clean it up. . . ."

Mrs. Mahoney was probably speaking of housework but her words filtered through the fog of thoughts which enveloped Mimi. "You can't get nowhere by dodging the truth!" The only thing to do is to jump at it and clean it up! She had been dodging the truth and shrinking from doing the very thing which she had known from the beginning she must do. There could be no happiness either for her or Jimmie if there was deceit or concealment of facts which he should know. She determined to tell him everything. If he was repelled by these facts, as she felt sure he would be, then the telling would end this strain for both of them and they could pass quietly out of each other's lives.

FLIGHT

Fearing that if she waited until morning her mind might be changed, she rose from the window and hurried, head held high and all her indecision and haggard fears fled, to the telephone. Her lips were set in a grim line, pressed so tightly together they made a thin red gash across her chalky-white bloodless face. Perversely, her mind flew back to that other crisis—when she waited outside the door which closed her from the operating-room in which *Petit* Jean was being put to sleep, perhaps never to waken again. Then, nerves raw and tingling, she had hovered dangerously near the brink of a collapse in the consciousness that flesh of her flesh was about to die. Now she felt the same quivering nerves stabbing her with fiery daggers as she knew that a thing, close and beautiful and precious, closer to her even than flesh, was even at the moment in danger of destruction, yes, was almost sure to wither up and pass into oblivion. She took the telephone in her hand, for some minutes holding down the receiver with the forefinger of her right hand, even then fearing to take the step which she feared but which she knew must be taken. . . .

Jimmie was at home. Incredulously he spoke to her, hardly daring to believe that it really was she. Come over, Jimmie, I want to talk with you—to tell you some things you must know, she whispered hoarsely. As she sat on the side of her bed after hanging up the receiver, she stared vacantly ahead of her, wondering, wondering. . . .

Hardly had she had time to dash a bit of powder on her face and arrange her hair before he rang the bell. She was shocked when she saw him, the first time in several weeks. His face was drawn and there were telltale hollows in his cheeks, and his eyes were far back in his head.

"Mimi, tell me, have you decided? You need not answer now about marrying me—if you don't want to answer—but

[257]

won't you let me try to show you how I love you?" he pleaded. "I've suffered agonies, Mimi darling—sometimes I believed I was almost crazy——"

"No—no, Jimmie, you mustn't say such things to me—I didn't ask you to come over for that——" Mimi sought to stop him.

"Then why—why did you ask me?" His voice was low-pitched, little more than a whisper, but there was in it a huskiness that showed the strain he was undergoing. Mimi felt sick at heart as she saw the changes that had taken place in him. He was no longer the laughing, debonair, assured individual he had been that day they met in Paris. His eyes burned with a blazing intensity from the deep sockets in which they were sunk, his hands twitched as he alternately closed and opened them, he kept his lips pressed tightly together, and his words came short and crisp from the emotion that lay behind them. Mimi felt her resolution to tell him all slipping away into thin air. She did not want to hurt him further, though she knew that for his own good and hers she must tell him now. She braced herself as though she were about to plunge into an icy bath in January.

"I'll tell you why I sent for you," she began. "I did run away from you in Paris. And I've been running from you here in New York because I knew it was the only way I saw of keeping from hurting you——"

"Hurting *me?*" he asked, puzzled.

"Yes, hurting you! Don't you remember that night just after you came back from Paris and I left you so abruptly at dinner?" He nodded. "I told you then there was no use of your seeing me, that there could never be anything between us. That's why I've deliberately done everything I could to make you angry at me, tired of me, so exasperated you would go your way and I mine——"

[258]

FLIGHT

"But, Mimi, don't you love me? Look at me! Tell me you don't love me, and I'll not say another word!"

He seized her by the arms and turned her around so that they faced each other. She looked directly at him.

"That's just the trouble, Jimmie, I do love you—love you as I've never loved before—love you as I know I'll never love again. That's just the reason you and I must have this talk and then end our friendship——" Her eyes filled slowly with tears as she pulled her arms free. He looked dazed, puzzled, distrait, and let her go.

"You love me? Therefore we've got to end everything here? Tell me, Mimi, what is back of all this?"

Mimi dashed the tears from her eyes with the back of her hand, her handkerchief gone and she too upset to look for it. Determination replaced the expression of pain.

"Here is what is back of it! I told you that you didn't know anything about me or my life——" she began.

"But I do. Mrs. Crosby has given me your whole history—she went to Francine for what she herself didn't know already."

"But neither Mrs. Crosby nor Francine knows anything about me before I went to Francine's eight years ago to work. And there's a lot in my life back of that—I'm going to tell you the whole story and then you'll see why——"

Jimmie shook off his lethargy, his air of supplication.

"Mimi, you'll do nothing of the sort," he said firmly. "I know you—and that's enough for me. Whatever it is you're worried about, I know you well enough to know that the things you're trying to magnify into an insurmountable barrier between us were done through no fault of yours. You're too fine, too decent——"

"No—no, Jimmie," she cried, "you must let me finish——"

"There'll be no finishing. You and I both will be much happier if we just let that drop—dropped for all time. If

[259]

you told me and we married, you'd feel all the rest of your
life that I was holding against you what you want to tell me
now. Or that you'd been mighty foolish in worrying about it
at all. And your trying to tell me just proves what I said
about your being fine and decent—if you'd been less than that,
you'd never have let it worry you at all. There's never been
the slightest thing against you—you can bet your life Mrs.
Crosby would have found it—and she thinks you are the most
marvellous person she's ever met!"

"But, Jimmie——" Mimi made one last, despairing effort
to stop him.

"But nothing, Mimi. There's just one thing that counts now,
nothing else in the world matters. I love you and you love
me—oh, darling, I do love you so!" he almost cried softly as
he took her in his arms and prevented utterance of any other
words from her lips with his own. . . .

They were married on Thanksgiving Day—"those old Puri-
tans who started this custom never knew what wise birds they
were!" Jimmie gaily remarked when they came out of the
church into the crisp November sunlight. The Crosbys gave a
most elaborate wedding breakfast for them in their Park Avenue
apartment—even in her happiness Mimi felt she was in a fantastic curio shop. Just a few friends, Mrs. Crosby had said
when she asked the privilege of furnishing the bridal breakfast.
There sat down some sixty guests and the supply of Veuve
Clicquot and Pommery Sec seemed inexhaustible.

"I've got a cunning little surprise for you, Mimi," Mrs.
Crosby coyly whispered. "I know you'll like it, for you told
me you did. You and dear Jimmie run into the library and
look at it all by your own little selves." They did look. It
was the marble monstrosity of Cupids and bows and arrows
Mrs. Crosby had bought in Paris from the romantic-looking
sculptor with "the big, dark eyes and long hair and the sweetest

FLIGHT

velvet jacket." But Mr. Crosby, gruff and kindly and intensely practical, gave them a cheque—"You youngsters'll know what you want better'n an old man like me—get what you want with it."

Madame Francine wept throughout the ceremony and her tears were because she loved Mimi and not—well, not very much because she did not know what she would do now that Mimi was going to leave the shop. Mimi had wanted to keep on working but Jimmie had been adamant. "You've worked long enough already—now you're going to play!" he had declared, and there was no changing his mind. Jimmie's mother was there, white-haired and kindly and self-effacing, but she had kissed Mimi tenderly and said: "My dear, you're the only woman I've ever seen who's good enough for my Jimmie!" Jimmie became mildly tipsy from the imbibing of many glasses of champagne drunk as toasts, and the breakfast was yet in progress, that is, the liquid portion of it, when Mimi, more lovely than ever in a coral green gown with a hat to match which Madame Francine herself had designed, slipped away with Jimmie at three in the afternoon.

CHAPTER XXI

THE Forrester house sat on the north side of Washington Square. Its high-ceiled walls and hand-carved woodwork, its air of mellowed age were all redolent of days when coaches-and-fours rolling easily through the Square sent flocks of broad-winged pigeons fluttering to safety on the huge, clumsy arch which took its name from the Square. Mimi loved the old-fashioned house—it spoke to her in tender tones of the days of splendour it had seen. Jimmie had wanted to dispose of most of the furnishings and furniture but she had restrained him. A new piece or two added to the comfort of the house, new draperies and wall-paper restored the freshness, and they settled down to a comfortable, happy existence together.

Mimi luxuriated in the unaccustomed idleness, in the realization that she had to do nothing she did not want to do. For the first time she realized how long and how hard she had been working. She saw now how steady had been the grind of the past eight years at Francine's—she had loved it, but now that she saw it in perspective, it made her shudder to see how much of a machine she had become. It had needed the revivifying touch of love to make of her a human being again instead of a coldly inanimate object but little more human than one of the sewing-machines she so often had manipulated. So for months she did little but live the life of the affluent idle, sewing a bit or reading a bit more. She did nothing that could be called work other than supervising the work of her two maids or deciding with the cook what items of food should make up the evening dinner.

FLIGHT

In the mornings, *négligé*-clad, she poured Jimmie's coffee and commented with more or less interest on the things he read to her, between mouthfuls, from the morning paper. She rather wished he wouldn't read to her, for it spoiled in a measure her own reading of the paper after he had gone. He liked to tell her what had happened, usually prefaced by the exclamation, "Oh, look here! Here's a pretty how-to-do! Listen!" And dutifully she would hear him read how Harry Thaw was about to gain his freedom at last or how Babe Ruth had hit another home run, or learned that another woman had shot a man who had betrayed her. Such items together with the market pages ended Jimmie's interest in the sheet, for he shunned all news from Washington or Europe as he would have dodged the plague—"I leave such heavy stuff to the spectacled birds who like it!"

Jimmie dutifully kissed and sent to the office, Mimi did what household duties she wanted to do, went shopping or to a matinée, and then waited for Jimmie's homecoming and dinner. In the evening they went to the theatre or to a supper club or cabaret or, occasionally, they dined at the Crosbys' or with other friends or in turn entertained at dinner. Her placid existence was so restful, so different from the stormy life which had been hers that Mimi wished it could be for ever the same simple one. When Jimmie had swept aside her attempts to tell him why she could not marry him, Mimi had resolutely set her will towards securing some of that happiness which had eluded her. Grimly she resolved that she would be happy, she would forget all that had gone before and by devoting her every energy towards making Jimmie content, she would achieve contentment for herself too. There were two or three times during the first year they were married that she fancied she saw a quizzical, indecisive look in Jimmie's eyes, but some jovial remark had always followed, proving he had not been thinking, as she had suspected and feared, of the things she had wanted to tell him which he had stopped. He loved her with a devotion that made her the centre of all his thoughts, and he was never happier than when she showed her pleasure in some little way in which he had sought to please her. "Not only are you the most beautiful but you're the most appreciative and most wonderful wife a man ever had," he would tell her, and his voice would always indicate beyond any doubt the sincerity that lay beneath his not very subtle compliments. . . .

They had been married a little more than a year. Mimi glanced idly through the mail beside her plate at breakfast as Jimmie performed his usual rite of picking juicy morsels from the *World*.

" 'New Prohibition Shake-up Threatened'—humph! the boot-leggers must have started that—they'll shoot prices way up to the sky for liquor now—reminds me, Mimi, how's my stock? The gin must be getting kinda low—I'll telephone McCarthy to-day. . . . Say, here's a rich bit—about a Jew selling robes to the Ku Klux Klan. By the way, Mimi, have you seen my Shriner's pin laying around anywhere? I must've left it in my grey suit when I sent it to the cleaners last week. Tele-phone them and see if I did, won't you? . . . Here's one from Georgia. Man asks native how much corn he expects to raise this year and the native answers: 'Oh, 'bout a hundred gal-lons.' Say, that's rich, don't you think so? . . . They're talk-ing about passing a law out in Iowa to keep schools from us-ing text-books that mention fermentation—say it's against the prohibition laws. . . . And here's a story where a crowd of women down in Louisiana tarred and feathered another woman and run her out of town. Kinda rough on the gal but she must've been pretty rotten. And over in Texas they lynched another nigger. They're really cleaning things up. This Klan's stirring up things all over—little rough, maybe—but

[264]

these kikes and Catholics and niggers got to be kept under control. . . ."

Mimi listened only half-heartedly to Jimmie's selection of the news which interested him—in fact, did not hear him. She interrupted him as he paused.

"Here's a note from Mrs. Crosby—wants us to come to dinner Friday night—they're having a few people in to meet some Chinaman—Wu Hseh-Chuan."

"That's the bird Horace met when he was in China—official or something Horace had to deal with to get some concession he wanted. Guess we'll have to go."

"You go along, Jimmie, and let me stay at home, won't you?" Mimi asked. "I'm fed up on dinners and parties—you see the same people and hear the same things and drink the same liquors at all of them."

"But Horace and the Holy Behemoth, Eulalia, will get sore if you don't show up, Pet."

"They'll get over it. I really am sick of the same old routine, there's never anything new and it all seems so futile, wasting so much time——"

"That comes from reading these stories by fellows like Dreiser and Sinclair Lewis—I told you they'd make you unhappy. That's why I leave those birds alone—they're always picking flaws in the best civilization the world's ever seen——"

"Bathtubs and radio and big business, eh?" Mimi murmured softly, perhaps a shade too softly.

"Yes—bathtubs—and radio and all the other things you sneer at—but just the same you'd be darned unhappy and uncomfortable if you didn't have these same benefits this civilization's brought you," snapped Jimmie testily.

"Oh, well, if you're going to get angry about it, I'll go. Only, please don't raise your voice so—remember the maid is probably listening," Mimi tried to calm him as he rose from the table.

"Who's shouting?" Jimmie demanded. "And what if I do? This is my house, isn't it, and haven't I got a right to shout in my own house, if I want to?"

He kissed her almost angrily on the cheek. She raised her head, lips half parted, and looked at him, her eyes smiling. He kissed her again on her lips and their warm touch made him contrite, ashamed of his anger.

"Forgive me, Mimi dear—I shouldn't have spoken so hastily. But you know it's good business for us to keep on good terms with the Crosbys—she's a nut and he's cranky as the devil but I do make a lot of money out of him."

When Jimmie had again begged forgiveness for his outburst and had left for his office, Mimi sat in the sunny breakfast room for a long time. She hadn't intended that Jimmie should consider her jocular remark about bathtubs and radios to sound like a sneer. But since he had taken it that way, she wondered what mischievous imp had impelled her to say just those words. Their utterance had loosed within her a nebulous, embryonic discontent that at times worried her, at others made her furiously angry with herself. For more than a year she had been supremely content with the security of the love there was between them, had snuggled deep into the haven she had reached after years of buffeting and struggle and bitter disappointment. In the hectic, glamorous days that preceeded their marriage and during the ecstatic happiness of the months after that event, Jimmie had been to her a composite of generosity and decency and comradeship. She had never deluded herself that he was handsome—not even by a generous stretch of loving imagination could he be termed other than fairly good-looking. But that did not matter. She had long since learned to distrust men who were too obviously good-looking, they always knew it though she blamed her own sex for that, far more than she blamed the men themselves.

Her mind, she was now finding with some concomitant discomfort, had been active too long to content itself with the calm placidity of being a housewife. Jimmie was more set than ever that she should remain at home. Since they were married his brokerage business had prospered amazingly and he lavished clothes and jewellery and other luxuries upon her. "I'm just like a Jew," he laughed one day when he brought her an especially handsome pair of ear-rings, an ornate blending of diamonds and rubies, "dressing up my wife to show that business is good." So far as she could trace it definitely, her discontent was born one night at a gay party after the theatre at one of the very smart and very expensive night clubs. Tired of dancing, she sat and watched the dancers. Grimly they went about the task of acquiring pleasure, their faces set in hard, nervous lines as they executed or attempted to execute quick, jerky, ungraceful and intricate new steps. They are working at pleasure and happiness just as though it were a trade, she concluded. "They dance," she told Jimmie when he had come back to the table puffing and blowing after dancing with Mrs. Shepherd, a young and rather pretty divorcee, "as though they were saying: 'This night is costing me a couple of hundred dollars and I *will* get two hundred dollars' worth of fun out of it!'" Jimmie had looked at her queerly but had said nothing.

After that night she watched the faces in the street, in the theatre, wherever she happened to be. There was always that strained, unhappy expression on the countenances of these people who, like scurrying insects, rushed madly here and there, each as though upon his efforts depended the future of civilization and life and everything else. Like cogs in a machine, she said of them one day, and thereafter she always thought of

[267]

them as cogs. Here they have created a machine of which they are intensely proud and of which they think they are the masters. Instead, ironically enough, the machine has mastered them and they must do its bidding.

From that point she began to inquire more deeply into the manifestations which lay so abundantly at hand. At first she studied these things largely to furnish occupation, perhaps a certain bit of diversion, to her own mind, hoping thereby to fill it so full there would be no room for the vague discontent which was beginning to gnaw her. Out of the chaotic writhings of her growing restlessness she sought and vaguely began to see the dim path which would lead, she thought, to a broader view of the scene of which she was a part. Here and there she heard the voice of one crying out against the monotony, the tastelessness, the vulgarity, the rule by the mob, the lowering faces everywhere. She tried to talk once or twice with Jimmie when they sat at home on the occasional evenings they were not scheduled to dine or dance. She desisted when he laughed at her worries and jocularly remarked: "You cannot serve Rolls-Royce and Mammon!" He repeated the phrase with a satisfied smile, adding: "Not so bad, eh?" Thereafter, she never ventured to mention her thoughts to him again.

One night they invited a young professor, Henry Meekins, to dine with them. He had just returned from a lengthy visit to China and had had the extraordinary good sense to go to the Orient without very many preconceived notions regarding unquestioned perfectness of everything Western and particularly all things American. At dinner he ventured to express the opinion that China, though unblessed with modern plumbing, was more interesting, more filled with beauty and romance, than New York, which he found to be clean and with excellent plumbing but dull and blatant and ugly. Mimi, remembering the first quarrel she and Jimmie had had, and on

[268]

this same point, looked somewhat doubtfully at Jimmie. But he was silently eating.

"Take one of the workmen in Ford's factory," Meekins was saying. "He stands or sits at a bench for eight hours a day doing one small job, tightening a bolt or inserting a plug over and over again, thousands of times a day. He knows nothing and cares less what part that bolt or that screw plays in the finished car—it's a dulling, deadening thing which saps every bit of individualism from him. But a Chinese coolie who hasn't one-tenth or one-hundredth the advantages of the Ford workman, is still a craftsman and not a mere tender of a dehumanizing machine."

Jimmie grunted contemptuously but Meekins was so absorbed in his subject he did not notice the unmistakable comment.

"And they're on to us, too," he cheerfully went on. "Before the war we had them fooled—they believed everything we did or said was right because we said it, we who have built up this great industrial machine. But the war opened their eyes. They see us now for what we are—an army waving banners of Christianity but with guns in our hands, the folds of the banner hiding traders and industrialists who see that missionaries are sent where there are rich resources to be found."

Jimmie could restrain himself no longer, he had to put this visionary young whipper-snapper in his place.

"But look what we do for them—we clean up their filthy towns for them, teach them how to live like decent human beings, and bring them a real religion instead of the pagan, heathenish doctrines they've got!"

"Granted that we teach them sanitation, build them roads and railway lines," Meekins cheerfully agreed. "But do we teach them or, better, prove to them that our religion is better than theirs? As I said, before the war we had them fooled—they saw the advances we had made and there was

reasonable ground for attributing that advance to our religion.
But what did they see during the war? They saw white nations murdering white nations with all the hellish devices—I
beg your pardon, Mrs. Forrester—that industrialism could de-
vise. They began then to wake up and ask themselves: 'What
is this Christianity they've been forcing down our throats at
the point of a gun?' Now they're realizing that we ourselves
don't know what Christianity is—we're divided up into different
faiths—and each one of those faiths is divided in turn into a
thousand different denominations, Baptists and Methodists and
Episcopalians and Holy Rollers, modernists and fundamental-
ists who spend most of their time arguing over what they believe and what the other fellow does not believe. Yet we go to
the so-called heathens with guns in our hands and say, virtu-
ally: 'Take our creeds and our civilization! Don't ask us to
prove they're superior—*we* know they are and if you dare
question or refuse them we'll shoot!' "

"I suppose next you'll be saying there's nothing good in the
white man's civilization—that we all ought to start living in
straw huts and growing rice and nice, fat mice for our food?"
Jimmie challenged him, almost surlily.

But Meekins, young, eager, enthusiastic, was thoroughly
aroused. His eyes shone behind his horn-rimmed spectacles
and his blonde hair rose belligerently above his flushed fair
face.

"No, I don't mean anything of the kind," he said, leaning towards Jimmie. "Our civilization has undoubted advantages—
we have developed the sciences and we have developed machin-
ery and invention to a point the world's never reached before.
Our gods are steam and electricity and steel—we have com-
bated plagues and disease, we have greater material comfort,
we can travel farther and faster than ever before. But when
that's granted——"

"Seems to me," Jimmie interrupted triumphantly, "you've granted about everything that's worth considering."

"No—no, Mr. Forrester, I haven't though. We've developed the printing-press and the telephone and telegraph and the radio, but what has been the result? We've made it possible to spread faster and more easily bigotry and hatred and intolerance and give more power to the mob, whether represented by the crowd that beats up a crowd of Jews or Germans or Russians or Negroes or whether it's represented by nations fighting each other for spoils in some part of the world. And we call ourselves free men, boast of it. Such a notion is silly—we are all of us petty little creatures who are slaves to the newspaper and the radio, to politicians and mouthy preachers, to our employers and the movies, to the telephone and every other regimented idea or thing."

"But you forget our art, our literature, all the other things we've created beside the machine you hate so," Jimmie, now thoroughly aroused and interested in spite of himself, challenged.

"Our art? Our literature? As if other civilizations didn't have art and literature, ethics and philosophies of life and codes of conduct many of them much better than anything we, busy as we are with material things, have created. Through luck and abundant natural resources we've become immensely wealthy—not through any particular effort on our part yet we pat ourselves on the back and think we're God's elect."

Meekins was happy in finding an opponent who gave him opportunity to show the discovery he had made, even though the thing he had discovered had been in existence several thousands of years. Mimi had sat without speaking, glad to see Jimmie aroused from his habitual complacency, glad to hear Meekins confirm and make more concrete some of her own vague dissatisfaction.

FLIGHT

"It seems to me you've both left out the worst thing of all in our civilization," she remarked. They turned to her, apologetically. They had been so absorbed in the contest of opinions, they had almost forgotten her.

"All the things you've mentioned as faults of this civilization of ours aren't so terrible in themselves. In time we might see them and take steps to rectify them. But the terrible thing to me is that though we've developed machines for giving us comfort we've devised at the same time machines for destruction in war, and that will wipe us all out and leave our civilization just an empty, deserted thing for them to discover a few thousand years from now—just like we're digging up Tutankhamen's tomb now——"

"I was reading a book by a man named Stoddard the other day——" Jimmie interrupted her, but Meekins snorted him into silence.

"Stoddard—a professional Cassandra—taking fake biology and distorted history—milking gullible buyers of books for fat royalties!" Meekins half-shouted, forgetting social amenities in his anger. Jimmie flushed a deep brick-red and relapsed into a moody silence. "But Mrs. Forrester's right," Meekins went on. "They are tearing down all they've built and they're creating new instruments of destruction that'll wipe out faster than industrialism can produce."

"There was a story in the *Times* last week," Mimi interjected, glad to find support for her statement, though she loyally resented Meekins' abrupt discourtesy towards Jimmie, "telling of the invention of a new electric ray so powerful it can wipe out every living thing, even to blades of grass, within a radius of twenty miles. A man presses a little button—zip!—and everything's dead. Soon they'll make it fifty miles, then a hundred, then a thousand——"

"Oh, come on," Jimmie pleaded. "It's too nice a night to be so doleful—let's go to a cabaret." . . .

[272]

FLIGHT

To Mimi's surprise Meekins proved an excellent dancer and a jovial companion, even Jimmie laughing with reluctance at his witticisms. When they returned home and were preparing for bed, she commented on Meekins' joviality. "Humph! About as funny as a baby breaking its leg," was Jimmie's comment. Mimi knew he was thinking of the way in which Meekins had stuck to his contentions, which, she was aware from experience, had not been altogether pleasing to Jimmie. All of us hate to hear unpleasant truths, she thought forgivingly. "He's just the sort of damn fool who'd shout 'Three cheers for the Ku Klux Klan!' at a Knights of Columbus picnic!" was Jimmie's final verdict as he turned out the light and climbed into bed. . . .

CHAPTER XXII

MIMI and Jimmie dutifully made their way to the Crosby home. As their car worked its way up the Avenue through the throngs of Jewish clothing workers that poured from the cross streets south of Madison Square, Jimmie recited, with an airy wave of his hand at the homegoing toilers:

"How odd
Of God
To choose
The Jews."

He looked at Mimi, expecting the hoped-for smile at his cleverness, but she continued to gaze at the throngs of work-deadened, stoop-shouldered men and women, the chattering groups of younger people dressed in brave but unsuccessful imitations of their sisters who were strolling the same avenue a mile or two northward. She watched the swirling eddies of humans, swept this way and that from curb to building line, rushing to subway kiosk or surface car, going homeward to close-packed apartments to sleep until time to begin another day of work. Mimi did not breathe freely until the car had swept on past the Waldorf and east to Park Avenue. But the sad, weary faces remained with her.

They were not surprised to find that Mrs. Crosby had run true to form when she had written: "We're having only a few people to meet Wu Hseh-Chuan." As was her custom, the word "few" meant the same thing as a "crowd" to most people. And Mimi, with a smile at Jimmie, noticed that Mrs. Crosby had shown her usual lack of tact in selecting her guests. It was a heterogeneous assemblage—"she must have written the names of every person she ever met, put them in a hat, and then pulled out the first forty," was Jimmie's whispered comment. Mimi saw seven or eight of Mr. Crosby's business associates whom Mimi had met. There were two elderly couples, dressed properly, but obviously ill at ease and uncomfortable, who Mimi learned were relatives from Iowa of Mrs. Crosby.

At the other extreme from these unsophisticated folks were several representatives of the stage, at the moment "at leisure." Mimi had heard from Jimmie of Mr. Crosby's recently acquired interest in the theatre. Jimmie had told the story with much archness and numerous elaborately meaningful winks—"Horace hints he may put some money into a show or two, said a man 'ought to have other interests besides his business.' I'd like to know what her name is and what she looks like," Jimmie had ended his story. Between the guests from Iowa and those from Broadway ranged representatives of various groups such as can be gathered only in a city like New York. And off in one corner, surveying with wise, calm and inscrutable eyes the throng of vivaciously chatting individuals, stood the man Mimi rightly guessed to be the guest of honour, listening to Horace Crosby, who was talking with unusual volubleness.

"So glad you came, Mimi dear," Mrs. Crosby came up and whispered, patting Mimi's arm quickly. "I told Horace he oughtn't expect me to entertain this Chinaman—Chinks always give me the creeps—but he would have me do it. Said it'd mean money to him—it's about some big deal he's trying to put over. I did the best I could—even went down to an employment agency on Madison Avenue and hired special Japanese waiters to serve the dinner—wanted to make him feel right at home. But I've had all sorts of trouble to-day trying to keep Maggie from hitting one of the Japs with a skillet. . . ."

FLIGHT

Mimi smiled sympathetically at the fat, nervous old woman. She smiled briefly and pityingly when Mrs. Crosby had ambled off to greet some incoming guests. Japanese waiters to make a Chinese feel at home, she amusedly thought. Poor old dear, she does mean well. The phrase brought back to her mind the washerwoman they had had years ago in Atlanta, whose most damning verdict ran: "He means well but he do so po'." That was Mrs. Crosby, the Holy Behemoth, all over.

"Mimi, my dear, those orchids look, compared to their wearer, like scrub cabbages!" a voice said softly as she stood waiting for Jimmie to finish talking with a friend. Without turning, she knew it was Bert Bellamy.

"That sounds nice—even if it is a bit silly," she smiled. Bellamy smiled in return. He was used to such receptions from Mimi of his phrases, which ordinarily gained at least gratitude from others to whom he made them. Bellamy was short and rotund, his face cherubic and ruddy like that of a healthy child. Always faultlessly dressed, one somehow felt that he kept at his bachelor apartments a barber, a tailor, a manicurist and a haberdasher, all constantly busy. Bellamy, Senior, had made untold amounts through the stockyards he owned in Chicago and Kansas City, but Bellamy, Junior, shuddered when some uncouth person tactlessly brought up the subject of the origin of the Bellamy millions.

He ostensibly was a writer, but beyond certain vague and delightfully cryptic hints that some day his *major opus* would make the world sit up and take notice, no one could definitely tell what he did beyond assiduous application to his beloved avocation of being a bon-vivant, a Chesterfieldian and immaculate man of the world. Once he had confided to Mimi that he was "the modern Mr. Pepys" but he had mentioned that self-bestowed title no more when she had, with gentle mockery, assured him that if the possession of all the latest gossip was the

[276]

most valuable asset towards that rôle, then he was undoubtedly
the man for it.

For Bert Bellamy went everywhere, knew everybody and, to
him most fascinating, he knew everything about everybody.
He had with admirably masked intentions sought to suggest
to Mimi that he would enjoy taking her to dine some evening
when Jimmie made infrequent business trips. When Mimi,
seeing his hidden meaning, had only laughed gently and told
him she did not make a practice of dining out when her husband was away, he had recognized at once that his efforts
there were futile ones. So he had returned her laugh, called
her a "little mid-Victorian," and let the subject drop, never
to be brought up again. Thereafter they had been friends of
a sort. For he was amusing and often relieved the boredom
of stupid dinners and parties by his scandalous dissection of
the lives of the others present.

"Tell me, Bert, who *are* all these people?" she asked him.

"The Holy Behemoth alone knows—and I doubt if she knows
them all! She's certainly outdone herself to-night!" he exclaimed as they stood looking over the crowd.

"There's Miss Gloria Russell acting literary—no, not that
one—the girl in the pink dress with the teeth sticking out like a
circular awning over a window. She reads the *Times Book
Review* every Sunday—and if you haven't read the books yourself, you'll believe she's read every book that's ever been published. My, how that gal can quote Dante and Homer and
Housman—she must have a bookshelf of Bartletts! She's
hoping some man will seduce her but she's had no luck
yet——"

Mimi laughed.

"Why so bitter? She rebuff you, Bert?" she inquired,
mockingly.

"Lord, no! I'm no saint but I *have* got taste. . . . There's

FLIGHT

old Mrs. Crane that Bob Carroll married for her money, looking miserable as usual when Bob talks to that Scott flapper—
if he doesn't watch out he'll be out of a home and back at
work again. The old lady's nobody's fool—but, gosh, what'd
she expect when she went cradle-snatching?"

"Mr. Pepys, who's the stunning-looking girl dressed in red
who's just come in?" Mimi inquired. The Carroll-Scott affair
was of long standing and she knew all about it. Bert *is* for-
getful, she thought, he's made the same statement about Mrs.
Carroll a dozen times. And the girl who had just entered was
a beauty.

"Whew!" Bert exclaimed when he saw the girl Mimi asked
about. "Fat Horace has got more nerve than I thought. She
is the reason Horace developed so suddenly a keen interest in
the dram-mer. Peach, isn't she?" he asked admiringly, as the
new-comer sauntered gracefully across the room and greeted
Mrs. Crosby. "Her name's Dolores d'Aubigny—though I've
heard she was christened Mary Mason. She's going to be in
the Broadway Futilities next season—and you know what that
means."

Mimi looked at Bert Bellamy inquiringly but he was watching the girl, who apparently was remaining near Mrs. Crosby
much longer than was absolutely necessary. Mimi looked at
Mr. Crosby, who had stopped talking to his guest. She fancied there was a shrewd appraisal of the relative merits of his
wife, fat and ungainly and too heavily rouged and powdered,
and of her who called herself Dolores d'Aubigny, slim and
graceful and beautiful. As she looked, the girl with marked
casualness glanced briefly at Horace and then slowly walked
away from Mrs. Crosby. A flood of pity for the bungling,
ludicrous old woman welled in Mimi's heart. But the object
of her pity was wholly unaware of the little drama being enacted of which she was one of the principals.

[278]

"... and she'll cost Horace a pretty penny before she's
through with him," Bert was saying to her.

"What did you mean just now when you said she was going to be in the Futilities—that I knew what that meant? I'm
probably frightfully dense and way behind the times but I
don't keep up with the latest news like you, Bert."

"I thought everybody knew that Thorne won't allow a girl
in his show unless she's got a gentleman friend who's loaded
with money," he told her, incredulous that she could be so
lacking in information. "That's because these boys will buy
boxes for opening night and come back to see the show all
during its run. If he's got real money, maybe he can be
loosened up enough to finance a separate show, starring, of
course, the girl he's interested in. Mimi dear, you really must
brush up on these things—you don't want people going around
saying: 'She's pretty but so naïve!' Get yourself a teacher—
as a matter of fact, I might be able to squeeze you into
my private class," Bert ended, with a chuckle that agitated his
rotund little body like a red rubber ball that's been bounced
on the floor, Mimi thought. "Thank goodness, there's dinner.
I hope Horace trots out some of that *Moet et Chandon*—I
could drink a gallon," Bert added cheerfully as dinner was
announced.

At Mimi's right sat a banker from a town in Iowa the name
of which she had never heard who talked, when he did cease
momentarily giving his attention to his food, of mortgages and
balances and the "Follies" which he had attended the night
before. "And just to think that 'Lalie Hoskins'd marry a
man with all the money Crosby's got. Why, I used to pull
her hair in school—she sat right in front of me," he volunteered
admiringly when Mimi did not join in his enthusiastic praises
of the current number of the "Follies."

"So you know Mrs. Crosby well, then?" Mimi asked, not

so much to gain further information as to keep the fast-dying conversation going.

"Know her? I should say I do! Why, she and I used to be sweethearts when we was little—I used to carry her books home from school."

Mimi regretted at once her unwise question, for her companion went at great length into the course of the childhood love affair he had had with the to him resplendent woman who sat at the head of the long table. Oh, well, she concluded philosophically, as the story went on and on, he doesn't expect comments from me, so I won't have to listen. She looked about her and examined the queerly assorted lot, ignoring Bert Bellamy's grin of amusement as he nodded towards the gentleman from Iowa who was regaling Mimi with his childhood reminiscences.

Dinner finished, the guests spoke briefly to the guest of honour and most of them left as soon as they decently could. Mimi sensed the bewilderment of the Chinese (she wasn't sure whether the most proper word for him was "the Chinese" or "the Chinaman"). His calm dignity interested her—beside the uneasy and garrulous, the sophisticated and unsophisticated, the smartly and the not so smartly dressed group in the room, he seemed to her to possess the wisdom and the dignity of a bronze Buddha. She went over to him and sat down beside him.

"I was talking last night to a young professor who's spent some time in your country, Mr. Chuan" (she wished she had asked beforehand what the proper form of his name was), "and he was telling us you of the East are beginning to look on Western civilization with considerable less enchantment than you used to."

He looked at her fleetingly but sharply and with acute inquiry. Mimi met his eyes frankly and he seemed satisfied with what he saw in them.

FLIGHT

"There is a change taking place in China—all over the world, in fact," he assented in precise Oxford English. "Gandhi in India, we in the Far East, in Africa, in Turkey, in the whole Near East—there is a stirring going on. But it isn't against what you call your 'Western civilization' nor is it primarily against white people as white people—it's a healthy movement of people who for centuries have been asleep—it's a rising, given form by the late war, of peoples who have been exploited."

"But isn't that the same thing?" Mimi inquired. "These peoples are rising because they have been exploited—and who has done the exploiting but the white nations? I seem to remember a story of a Chinese who told a white man the Chinese could never attain to the marvellous civilization of the white man because, as he put it, 'I can't shoot straight enough.' "

He looked at her again sharply as he smiled.

"We Orientals are accused of being inscrutable—impossible to understand, mysterious. But to us you of the West are just as difficult to comprehend. For example, you spend millions of dollars every year on missions in our country, you send us hundreds of missionaries to win us from our religion to yours. Do you wonder we think you inscrutable when we see unbelief spreading throughout your Christian nations, see you quarrelling and bickering among yourselves over creed and dogma, not apparently understanding just what you do believe? It seems to us that a doctor who is dying of a disease for which he has the cure does not go out and try to force a man passing in the street to take the medicine he himself needs. And you preach to us of your Jesus whose life was built on meekness and love, yet you use guns and warships to force us to accept your religion. And you have just fought a war among yourselves that was more terrible than any non-Christian nations have ever known. And yet you call us of the East inscrutable?" and he raised his eyebrows almost imperceptibly in a gesture of bewilderment.

"I don't blame you for wondering what the sense of it all is—particularly of our religious inconsistencies," she told him. "I was once a devout Catholic but I'm not any more. Such religion as I have is to seek truth but I know now I shall never find it—I can only keep on seeking."

"The search for truth in life and life in truth is, after all, the perfect religion, for in seeking truth we attain that which we can never find in formal creeds," was his answer. "We of the East have been—we are interested in Christianity not as a religion so much as the religion of the nations which have developed science and power. But now we are seeing that the very power you have created may master you and destroy you and us. Do you remember the statement of the Japanese statesman who said to the Westerner: 'As long as we produced only men of letters, men of knowledge, and artists, you treated us as barbarians. Now that we have learned to kill, you call us civilized'?"

"What is your notion," she asked him, tremendously moved by the clear-sighted wisdom of this quiet little man, "of the outcome of all this? Where will it end? From your distance can you see whether we of the West are headed towards greater wisdom or destruction?"

"Who can tell? The great nation or people or civilization is not that one which has the greatest brute strength but the one which can serve mankind best. The machine has been created —and it in turn is mastering its creators. I have been in your country many times and I feel that only your Negroes have successfully resisted mechanization—they yet can laugh and they yet can enjoy the benefits of the machine without being crushed by it. . . ."

As they drove homeward Jimmie, somewhat irritably, asked her: "What were you and that Chink talking about so long?"

FLIGHT

"He was telling me about his country. It was very interesting, too," she answered him. Remembering his reception of the night before of Meekins' opinions, she knew it was unwise to tell him all that she and this wise little yellow man had discussed. But long after she was in her bed she lay awake, looking out across the deserted expanse of the Square. Her discontent was taking form. She felt a new confidence filling her as she realized that perhaps there was some valid basis for the vague unrest which had been troubling her. As she hovered in that indefinite land between sleep and wakefulness, she mumbled to herself: "I don't know what I can do about it all, I'm sure, but there's emptiness, emptiness, everywhere——" From the room beyond there came the steady, rhythmic sound of Jimmie snoring. . . .

CHAPTER XXIII

WASHINGTON SQUARE lay in restful beauty beneath its glittering blanket of snow. Here and there were rounded mounds, hillocks of whiteness whose framework were iron benches that had held countless pairs of lovers in the gentle warmth of spring or the torrid breathlessness of summer. The commonplace, ugly fences had been transformed miraculously into graceful lines of ethereal, ghostlike, shimmering whiteness. The harsh lines of the Arch had been rounded and softened until it seemed like a huge cake of frosted icing baked for some Gargantuan wedding feast. Across the Square loomed the church Stanford White had designed, the cross above the mass of yellow brick purified by its coating of white.

In the little patches of earth enclosed by the fences, gusts of wind were taking the new-fallen snow, swirling it in graceful spirals that danced and pirouetted with such sinuous loveliness that beside them Pavlowa would have seemed a clumsy, heavy-footed rustic doing a barn dance. Here and there scurried along a figure, head bent before the icy wind, or a lumbering Fifth Avenue bus with its green sides visible in spots free from the encrustations of snow. The verdant hue of the buses or the blackness of clothing only accentuated the whiteness around the moving figures. As if awed by the phenomenon of the transformation, old but ever new, all sound was muffled, an encircling blanket of stillness gripped and held all things, animate and inanimate, in its soft grip.

For hours Mimi sat and looked out upon the Square, long hours after Jimmie had ploughed his way down the steps and disappeared in the distance as he forged his way through the snow to the subway. Why, she asked herself—and in presenting the question to herself she placed it before some greater power, some wiser and more far-seeing One beyond the confines of her own mind and spirit—why was I given this restless spirit, this ceaseless inability to be content with what life has brought me? Why cannot I be like other women, able to content myself with whatever comes, refusing to let the tiny mice of search for the unattainable gnaw at my restless heart? She thought of the times when she might have avoided all this seeking, seeking, seeking, by calm and unquestioning acceptance of life as she had encountered it, yielding principles and ideals which conflicted with the ways and customs and accepted standards of the world as she found them. She might have married Carl. She might have yielded to marriage or support without marriage when other men had offered it—acceptance of any one of a number of men whom she did not love and never would have loved but who could have given her ease and comfort and freedom from financial worry. She might have given away or abandoned *Petit* Jean and dropped for all time memory of his entry in the world. Instead here she was wanting him, longing for him more passionately than she had ever wanted him before.

Jimmie had wanted children—had begged her to give him a son, preferably, but if not a son, a daughter. There had been a time when she might have wanted to give him what he wanted. But she had not had the courage to tell him that the granting of his wish did not rest with her. When the time had gone by with no prospect of an heir she had spoken to Jimmie of a boy quite close to her which he had assumed was the child of a relative. He had urged her to bring him to their home but she had not done so. This simple solution had at first pleased her, as an easy solution, but she had been unwilling to adopt it. It would have seemed like deceit practised upon

[285]

Jimmie and though she had acted with the ruthless courage born alone of mother love when *Petit* Jean's welfare required it, she could not bring herself to take this step now that she was able to care for him and to assure him every comfort he needed.

As she sat by the window she thought of the dinner the night before. The calm dignity, the far-sighted wisdom of the Chinese had stood out in bold relief against the background of the tawdry, shallow people around him. She thought of the concept which had always sprung to her mind when she had heard the word Chinese or Chinaman—it always had been of a slant-eyed Oriental shuffling across a laundry floor or a bestial, treacherous villain upon the stage or moving-picture screen. But even allowing for the contrast between that stereotyped concept and the man she had met at the Crosbys', Hseh-Chuan had towered far above the other guests, she decided. It wasn't fair to compare him, who must be an exception even in his own country, with poor pathetic Mrs. Crosby nor even with Bert Bellamy, product of the sophistication of his age. She remembered a phrase she had read in an essay by James Branch Cabell—"Man is, they say, the only animal that has reason; and so he must have also, if he is to stay sane, diversion to prevent his using it." Cynical, scoffing, it was true, but after all was that not the premise upon which life nowadays seemed to be conducted? And were not the Eulalia Crosbys and the Bert Bellamys and the Jimmie Forresters, yes, the Mimi Forresters too, restlessly, blindly, neurotically, unceasingly seeking diversions to prevent the use of that thing they called their intellect?

Again she came back to the figure of countless millions of worried and insignificant little people obeying blindly the implacable bidding of a huge, insatiable machine. Horace Crosby seeking release and forgetfulness in an empty, sordid affair with a woman, beautiful though she was, like Dolores d'Aubigny. Bert Bellamy drugging himself with the opiate of inquisitive prying into the affairs of the prominent and the near-prominent. Eulalie Crosby gaining the sobriquet, so appropriate, of the Holy Behemoth, by her restless rushing about in ponderous worry over trivial things. Jimmie with his lodges and clubs and booster organizations where he could bathe himself in the aura of importance, however brief or illusory. Restless crowds plying themselves with sex or drink or drugs or silly diversions to forget the implacable demands of the forces that drove them on, trying hard to ignore those forces or to hypnotize themselves into believing there are no such powers. The weakest, and often the strongest, realizing the futility of it all, finding peace through a swift snuffing out of life itself.

They have thrown overboard, she reflected, all the spiritual anchorages which gave them security in the past and made them strong. Religion had failed them, for they had made of religion an outer form useful only when it served their own selfish purposes.

Men, as always, prayed to a God of their own creation, a Divinity which only mirrored the petty minds of its worshippers. This man, avid of wealth and power, prayed devoutly and absent-mindedly to his conception of God, a being of unlimited wealth, plastered with diamonds, fat, vulgar and, through his wealth, able to dictate the lives of countless millions of creatures scattered throughout a boundless universe.

Another man prayed to a God of vengeance, a God who had wisely taken counsel of man and decreed that this race or that one should be crowned as the chosen people. Blindly by obsessions of superiority, unbelievable cruelties were prayed over and asked of God by these molelike creatures who fancied their own infinitesimal wisdom superior to that of any other beings, human or devine. One thing and another they asked for, Gods of varying stature were sought and found, in no wise differing

[287]

from the reflection that the humans caught from their bedroom mirrors. Above all, they demonstrated through their prayers that they believed only in themselves and they were unable to accomplish the miracles they sought.

Morality meant merely the observance, usually in the breach, of certain man-made rules and regulations. It seemed to her there was a far greater amount of immorality practised by certain married couples she knew between whom all love had died than in relationships which she could easily imagine but which conventions would condemn with ferocious bitterness. The mouthings of stupid and sensational preachers who ranted and shouted that the solution of all the ills of the world and of mankind could be cured by blind acceptance of outworn theological doctrines that had served their day and then rightly died, sickened her and made her more intolerant than ever of creed and dogma. She did not at all know what she would have desired but she did know that these empty-pated figures were of infinitely more harm than good. They to her seemed parallel figures to the absurd members of bodies like the Ku Klux Klan. She hazily remembered a passage in Thayer's "Cavour" which fitted these groups. She searched the shelves until she found the book she wanted, and read:

"Moribund institutions, whether lay or religious, usually press their most virulent claims. . . . A singular parallel can be drawn between the Papal Party in Italy and the Slave Party in the United States during the sixth decade of the 19th Century. When new ideals began to undermine the civilization from which they had risen, both the Papacy and the Slavocracy adopted a policy of no compromise. Both arrogantly proposed to extend their dominion at the very time when this doom was at hand."

It seemed to her that this was sound—that what had been true in the '60's was doubtless true sixty years later. War had become the great objective of all peoples of the Western world, their religion had become the religion of brute strength instead

[288]

of the doctrines of peace and decent treatment of all others. Arrogant, intolerant, impervious to new ideas unless they be ideas for greater destructiveness in time of war.

Her gloomy thoughts made her shiver though the bitter cold outside was fully overcome by the roaring fire in the wide fireplace. I am becoming moody again, she decided, seeing things and imagining all sorts of horrible things. But she could not shake off her feeling, for her mind had seen too clearly the things which lay back of her own discontent and the restlessness of the life around her.

As she left the window and moved towards the fire, the telephone sent tiny shivers of sound through the quietness of the house. It was Jimmie.

"Terribly sorry, dear, but Horace and I've got to go to Chicago on the Century this afternoon. Throw a few things in a bag like a good girl and give it to the boy I'm sending up. Bert Bellamy happened to be in the office and I asked him to take you to the theatre to-night—hope that's all right with you. If it isn't, you can tell him you've got a headache or something. Sorry, got to rush along now—got loads of work before I leave. Take care of yourself—I'll be back in three or four days. . . ."

He was gone before she had a chance to say much. She was annoyed that he without consulting her had delegated Bert to go to the theatre in his place. She was rather glad, however, to have the house to herself for a few days. Jimmie was a dear but he was frightfully boisterous and uncouth and boring at times. And he annoyed her with his smug little prejudices. He didn't like Jews or Japanese or Italians or any other group that wasn't his own. She remembered his patronizing sneer at the Jews the night before as they drove to the Crosbys'. There were certain classes of Jews she preferred not coming into contact with just as there were classes of Negroes and classes of white people she very much sought

[289]

FLIGHT

to avoid. I'm probably a snobbish creature myself, she admitted, but at least it seems to me that the only people on earth who are not afraid of intellect are the Jews. . . .

Wearied with her gloomy mental peregrinations and her perfervid seeking into the causes of her own restlessness, she ate an early luncheon and, wrapping herself warmly in her furs, set off with free swinging strides up the Avenue, exulting in the sweeping, stinging wind which rushed down the canyon formed by the towering buildings. As she hurried along, little circles of carmine took shape in her cheeks from the lash of the wind, growing redder and redder until it almost matched the bits of hair which peeped from underneath the close-fitting toque of vivid green. I do wish, she thought as she abandoned her thoughts of the morning in the joy of the battle with the stinging wind, I had been so constituted that I did not feel things so much, that I did not have the capacity for suffering as I do. But then, I wouldn't be able to enjoy things so much, so I suppose it all balances up in the end. . . .

For two and a half hours Mimi and Bert sat through a show in which slightly aged jokes and chorus girls suffering from the same malady sought to keep alive a tenuous plot. Bert started humming an improvised verse to an old tune which sounded like "Just another good show gone wrong," until a purposeful-looking woman in front of them turned and glared at him through an imposing pair of lorgnettes. Whereupon he subsided into abashed silence. But not for long, for he soon was whispering to Mimi that "the only good spots in the show are the dirty ones," furnished as they were by a Jewish comedian in blackface. "If they'd only lower their voices a bit we could all take a nap and thus the evening wouldn't be entirely wasted," was Bert's comment along towards the middle

[290]

FLIGHT

of the last act. And Mimi was thinking that this was just the sort of show Jimmie would choose and enjoy.

Outside, the snow had ceased falling. Hurrying crowds flowed towards the subway and elevated, pouring in seemingly endless floods from countless theatres.

"What next?" Bert asked as he sought to shelter her from the rushing throng.

"I'll tell you—I want to see a Negro cabaret in Harlem. I've hinted to Jimmie but he had never offered to take me. Though he seems to know a lot about them himself——" she thought, leaving the last sentence unuttered.

Bert hailed a taxi and they were on their way. Mimi wondered just why she had suggested Harlem. It had been nearly ten years since she had been north of 125th Street—she wondered if she would meet any of the people she had known there years before. The vogue of Negro shows on Broadway, "Shuffle Along," "Runnin' Wild" and others, the popularity of Miller and Lyles and of Florence Mills, had not touched her directly. She suddenly realized that she had stayed away from them for fear she would meet some of her former friends or acquaintances and thereby suffer possibly embarrassing situations in explaining to Jimmie why she knew these people. She laughed at herself for a silly little goose as she leaned comfortably back in the warm cab—she had long since been forgotten in the ever-changing life of Harlem. She herself didn't even know who had taken over her Aunt Sophie's business when Mrs. Rogers had gone back to New Orleans to live.

It came to her suddenly why the impulse to go to Harlem had sprung to her mind. It was the statement Wu Hseh-Chuan had made—". . . only your Negroes have successfully resisted mechanization . . ." was the way he put it. Now that she was once again headed towards Harlem, she felt the old attraction which had come over her that first night in New

[291]

FLIGHT

York when her Aunt Sophie and she had come up in the subway and debarked at Lenox Avenue and 135th Street. Bert
Bellamy was singing the latest "Mammy" song in what he
fondly imagined to be Negro dialect but Mimi paid no attention to him—she felt an eager interest that contrasted vigorously with her gloom of the morning. . . .

Bert was apparently no stranger when they turned from
Seventh Avenue into a side street and alighted before a door
guarded by a huge uniformed Negro. Down a narrow stair
they went to a barred door which opened when the doorkeeper
above pressed a buzzer. Mimi was startled when a roar of
sound plunged from the opened door, sound which had been
wholly inaudible when the door was shut. Inside, bright
lights shone on the rectangle of dance floor but left the tables
along the sides in soft shadow. Crowded high upon a narrow
platform sat the orchestra, clad in dinner jackets and playing
as though they were paying for the privilege of playing. Scurrying waiters hurried and slid and expertly wove their way
in and out of the crowd of dancers and diners. A dinner-
jacketed, sleek-haired head waiter guided Mimi and Bert to a
table where they sat watching the dancers. Mimi eagerly
took it all in. She noticed that at the tables the parties were
either all white or all Negro, there being seldom any mixing
of the two groups.

At the table next to theirs sat a noisy group of younger people. With frequent regularity there appeared from underneath the table a large bottle from which glasses were surreptitiously filled. As the evening wore on, the boisterousness of
the party increased. Suddenly one of the girls, pretty in a
rather coarse way, slumped forward on the table. Two of the
men hurriedly carried her out.

"She's checked out," Bert coolly commented. "Too much
bad liquor." The orchestra played on. "Funny about these

coons," Bert went on. "They don't ever seem to pass out like white folks."

Mimi flushed at the word but Bert was watching the dancers and did not see it. Mimi suddenly hated him for using the detested word. She checked the remark which sprang to her lips—that the swinish guzzling was being done only at the tables at which white people sat. She was amazed at the sudden rekindling of the race-consciousness which had lain dormant for nearly ten years. I'm silly, she chided herself, for after all what difference does it make what a man is called? But immediately there came the answer that it apparently made a great deal of difference, whether one wanted it to or not. She watched the dancers. The floor was crowded mostly with white couples executing all sorts of fancy steps, swaying and bumping the others in their gyrations. Here and there a coloured couple moved with unconscious grace, a rhythmic sweep to their bodies that made the others seem awkward and graceless. She commented on the fact to Bert, whose answer was: "Yeah, all the showgirls down town come up here and get stuff for Broadway." And as she watched them Mimi began to see for the first time what Wu Hseh-Chuan had meant—it had taken an Oriental from half-way around the world to make her see things she had seen all her life and yet had never seen.

The floor was too crowded. Bert wanted her to dance but one attempt made her content to sit and watch. The music had a strange effect upon her. Analysed, it was all wrong when judged by conventional musical standards. Taken as a whole, it formed a weird and oddly exciting cacophony of chords and exotic rhythms. A muted cornet sent forth hair-disturbing peals like an eerie sound heard in a graveyard after midnight. The saxophone grunted and slid up and down a facile scale of gurgling harmonies. Drums and the piano pounded a steady beat that had in them all the power and mystery and inflaming beauty of the tomtom. Suddenly it became clear. Mimi knew that for her this wild music held its greatest charm in its freedom from rules, its complete disregard of set forms. It refused to be tied down, its creators wove harmonies out of thin air and transferred to their notes the ecstasy of a wild, unharnessed, free thing. She thought of nymphs gambolling in a virgin forest, on ground unsoiled by human foot. Dryads and hamadryads, wood- and water-nymphs every conceived creature of freedom came to her mind as she sat and listened and felt the ecstasy the music made her feel. . . .

The next night she slipped from the house after an early dinner and with the spirit of high adventure hurried through the melting snow towards the West Side subway station. She came to the surface again in Harlem and there she wandered through the streets. She wondered why in the days when restlessness had gripped her after a hard day at Francine's she had never come to Harlem as she had walked through the streets where French and Italian and Gipsy and Jewish people lived,—wondered even as she knew why she had not come to Negro Harlem.

It was a new Harlem she now saw, or rather, though she did not realize it, it was a new Mimi through whose eyes she saw it. Gone were the morose, the worried, the unhappy, the untranquil faces she had been seeing down town for years. Here there was light and spontaneous laughter, here there was real joyfulness in voices and eyes. Here was leisureliness, none of the hectic dashing after material things which brought little happiness when gained. She lingered near a crowd that chatted with frequent outbursts of spontaneous laughter. A wizened little Negro was being bantered by another as the first one sought to prove his non-existent prowess as a fighter.

"I hit him three or four times and he only hit me once," he boasted loudly.

FLIGHT

"Go on, Mushmouth, that's all David hit Goliath," his tormentor cheerfully answered. A third man who had seen the fight completed the boastful one's rout when he described pungently the expression on the face of the defeated one: "He made a face like a nigger tasting his first olive!" . . .

As Mimi sat in the roaring subway on her way home, she felt within her a renewing of her old eagerness towards life. Here was something real that the unknowing and unseeing had called "native humour" and "Negro comedy." But, somewhat vaguely, she felt the thing went deeper than that. She speculated as to the lasting value of machines and all that they brought—whether a radio over which came "Yes, We Have No Bananas" added measurably to the sum total of happiness. She was wondering yet when sleep overcame her. . . .

In the days that followed there came to her out of the tangled maze of her thoughts a clearer conception of the causes underlying her discontent. She loved the comforts of her home, from the shiny brass knocker on the snowy white front door to the full-length mirrors in which she loved to gaze at her rounded form after her morning bath in the big blue-and-white porcelain tub. But she wondered if the sombre, cynical companions she met in her home and in other places were worth the price she was paying for these luxuries. People who were playing at enjoying life but whose unhappiness shone through all they did or said. She wondered. . . .

CHAPTER XXIV

CARNEGIE HALL was surrounded by streams of people, white and black, that were swallowed up in the vast building. Their car finally edged its way towards the curb close enough for them to alight. Inside, Mimi noted that every seat seemed to be taken as she followed Jimmie down the aisle in the wake of the grey-clad usher. The tiers of seats on the platform too were rapidly filling. The rumble of voices hushed. Out of a door on one side of the platform came a short dark figure followed by a taller one whose skin was brown. A salvo of applause welled up and swept over the bowing figure as he faced the shifting panorama of up-turned faces.

Silence. The pianist leaned low over his instrument, and long brown fingers lightly touched ivory keys, prodding them gently in light, gentle touches. A chord. The immobile figure of the singer galvanized into tense attentiveness. Back went the head on which crisply curled hair hung close. Eyes shut, gleaming teeth were revealed as a thin pure note poured from parted lips. The harsh guttural tones of the German were transmuted into a finespun sound as pure and delicate as a silken thread. Out it poured.

If thou art near me, I will go with joy to death and rest;
Ah, how happy were my end, with the pressure of thy fair hands and
    the glance of thy true eyes.

Through songs by Bach and Schubert, by Brahms and Franck, by Quilter and Jensen, the singer made his way. And then he sang the songs of his own people. Not a sound disturbed the spell he had woven, the auditors dared hardly breathe. "Nobody Knows de Trouble I See," he sang, a strange, wistful sadness pervading the music.

As from a fountain of bronze, tiny jets of gold and silver sound were flung in a pellucid stream high above the heads of the silent throng. It broke against the ceiling, the iridescent bubbles bursting in radiant glory, dissolving into myriad little drops of sound, each perfect and complete in itself. Down they were wafted in gentle benediction upon the heads of the listeners. Soothing, comforting, they brought peace and rest and happiness. Before them fled all worries, all cares, all lines of sex and class and race melting the heterogeneous throng into a perfect unity.

Upon Mimi the music served as magic metal keys which opened before her eyes mystic rooms, some of them long closed, some of them never opened for her before, all of them musty through long dark days and longer nights of disuse.

"Nobody knows the trouble I see,
Nobody knows but Jesus. . . ."

Ghostly figures moved shadowily across the rooms—figures with eyes sad with the tragedies of a thousand years, eyes bright with the faith which is born of strength in trial. Figures which by some strange legerdemain began as she watched them to lose their unearthly diaphanousness and, like Galatea, to become flesh and blood. The transformation did not startle nor alarm her—instead, held fast in the spell woven by the black singer, the re-creation of life in the figures before her seemed the most natural thing in the world.

A vast impenetrable tangle of huge trees appeared, their pithy bulk rising in ebon beauty to prodigious heights. As she gazed, half afraid of the wild stillness, the trees became less and less blackly solid, shading off into ever lighter greys. Then the trees were white, then there were none at all.

[297]

FLIGHT

In their stead an immense circular clearing in which moved at first slowly, then with increasing speed, a ring of graceful, rounded, lithe women and stalwart, magnificently muscled men, all with skins of nidnight blackness. To music of barbaric sweetness and rhythm they danced with sinuous grace and abandon. Soft little gurgling cries punctuated the music, cries which came more sharply, like little darting arrows, as the ecstatic surrender of the figures to the dance increased.

A loud cry of alarm and of warning came from afar. The dance stopped, the dancers poised in wonder and indecision. Another cry, nearer, more intelligible. The black men seized their spears and short swords. The women were huddled in the middle of the living ring. From the murky darkness of the trees there burst weird creatures shouting. Weird, for their faces were not black as all men's faces were, but obviously covered with some white substance to make them more terrible, their hair not curly and black but straight and yellow. The fight was on. Gorily it went on and on. Back the ebon fighters were swept before the strange, diabolic weapons like black reeds which spurted lead and flame. Back they were swept treading on the bodies of their dead and dying comrades. Soon but a few were left. The invaders seized these, overpowering them through numbers. The women too were seized and hurried away to huge, stinking hulks of ships, vessels a hundred times as huge as the craft hewn from great trees of the black warriors. . . .

> "Sometimes I'm up,
> Sometimes I'm down,
> Oh, yes, Lord;
> Sometimes I'm almost to the ground. . . ."

Another door was opened for Mimi. This time she saw a ship wallowing in the trough of immense waves. Aboard there strode up and down unshaven, deep-eyed, fierce-looking sailors who sought with oath and blow and kick to still the clamorous outcries of their black passengers. These were close packed in ill-smelling, inadequate quarters where each day stalked the spectre whose visit meant one mouth less to feed. Black bodies were tossed carelessly overboard. No sooner did one of them touch the water than came sinister streaks of grey and white which seized the body long before the wails from the ship had died in the distance.

Under the spell of the music other doors opened one by one. This time it was an expansive field covered with white blossoms brilliant against the dusty green foliage of the cotton plants. Black figures bent low while near them stood with watchful eye and ready whip an overseer.

Another time it was at "the big house"; another, at muscle-wearying and spirit-crushing toil of another kind. But from them all there came these same weirdly sweet notes which now were being voiced by the slender dark figure on the platform yonder. A world of motion and of labour was caught up and held immobile in the tenuous, reluctant notes. Over them hovered that overtone of hope too great for extinction by whatever hardship or sorrow which might come to the singers. It was the personification of faith, a faith strong and immovable, a faith unshakable, a faith which made a people great. Against that faith, Mimi felt, contumely, brutality, oppression, scorn could do naught but dash and break like angry waves against huge granite cliffs.

To her sitting there in the semi-darkness came a vision of her own people which made her blood run fast. Whatever other faults they might possess, her own people had not been deadened and dehumanized by bitter hatred of their fellow men. The venom born of oppression practiced upon others weaker than themselves had not entered their souls. These songs were of peace and hope and faith, and in them she felt and knew the peace which so long she had been seeking and which so long had cluded her grasp.

FLIGHT

Tears crept unnoticed to Mimi's eyes and made little cascades down her cheeks. A line of verse sprang to her mind with poignant appropriateness: "The music yearning like a God in pain." She knew she had found the answer to the riddle which had puzzled her. She looked at Jimmie as he gruffly cleared his throat, ashamed of the emotion which too had seized him. He seemed alien, a total stranger. She marvelled that she had married this man, had lived with him, he whom she did not know. Silently they drove home through the quiet emptiness of lower Fifth Avenue. Mimi without speaking went to her room and closed the door. Calm peace filled her. She knew now why she had been ill at ease, restless, dissatisfied with the life which at first had seemed so happy a one.

She knew too that Jimmie would not, could not understand. Should she try to tell him? No, she decided. It were better to leave his dreams and illusions undisturbed—he had little enough real happiness as it was. And his convictions, his prejudices were too deeply rooted, she was sure, to enable him to comprehend without pain and suffering. He had done all he could—it was not wholly his fault. . . .

A brilliant but cold sun was creeping over the housetops out of the East as she softly closed the door behind her and stood upon the topmost step. Another book in her life was being closed with the shutting of the door. Mimi raised her eyes to the cross on the church across the Square. Her head went up and her shoulders straightened. She joyously drew into her lungs deep draughts of the cold air.

"Free! Free! Free!" she whispered exultantly as with firm tread she went down the steps. "*Petit* Jean—my own people—and happiness!" was the song in her heart as she happily strode through the dawn, the rays of the morning sun dancing lightly upon the more brilliant gold of her hair. . . .

$\mathcal{V}$ OICES OF THE $\mathcal{S}$ OUTH

Lee Smith, *The Last Day the Dogbushes Bloomed*
Elizabeth Spencer, *The Salt Line*
Elizabeth Spencer, *The Voice at the Back Door*
Max Steele, *Debby*
Allen Tate, *The Fathers*
Peter Taylor, *The Widows of Thornton*
Robert Penn Warren, *Band of Angels*
Robert Penn Warren, *Brother to Dragons*
Walter White, *Flight*
Joan Williams, *The Morning and the Evening*
Joan Williams, *The Wintering*